SHE WHO RIDES HORSES

A SAGA OF THE ANCIENT STEPPE
BOOK ONE

SARAH V. BARNES

Afterword by Linda Kohanov
Author of *The Tao of Equus*

LILITH HOUSE PRESS

Copyright © Sarah V. Barnes 2022

All the characters and events in this book are fictitious. Any resemblance to actual persons, living or dead, is entirely coincidental.

All rights reserved. No part of this book may be reproduced, scanned, or duplicated without written permission from the copyright holder. For more information, please contact the publisher through their website at www.lilithhousepress.com

ISBN 978-1-7369673-3-1 (softcover)
ISBN 978-1-7369673-4-8 (ebook)
Library of Congress Control Number: 2021923375

Cover and interior design: Jane Dixon-Smith / www.jdsmith-design.com
Editor: Page Lambert / www.pagelambert.com
Cover Artwork: Diana Lancaster / www.dianalancaster.com
Author photograph: David Barnes

DEDICATION

For Okotillo (Tio)
April 18, 2008 – September 6, 2021

Always and Forever
My Anam Cara

Contents

Characters	vii
PART ONE	**1**
Chapter One	3
Chapter Two	14
Chapter Three	27
Chapter Four	41
Chapter Five	54
Chapter Six	63
Chapter Seven	71
Chapter Eight	86
Chapter Nine	95
Chapter Ten	116
PART TWO	**135**
Chapter Eleven	137
Chapter Twelve	153
Chapter Thirteen	164
Chapter Fourteen	181
Chapter Fifteen	194
Chapter Sixteen	206
Chapter Seventeen	218
Chapter Eighteen	232
Author's Note	241
Glossary	248
References	249
Acknowledgements	250
Afterword	252
Coming Soon…	263
About the Author	268

Characters

Naya: A girl of fourteen summers.
Amu: Naya's dog and devoted companion.
Awija: Naya's paternal grandmother, medicine woman and wife of the old clan chief.
Sata: Naya's mother, originally from the southern mountains.
Potis: Naya's father, recently chosen to succeed his father as head of the Clan
Awos: Naya's grandfather, the old clan chief, in failing health.
Tausos: Potis' younger brother. Naya's uncle.
Oyuun: A trader from the far north, travelling through Clan territory.
Aytal: Oyuun's oldest son, a young man of sixteen summers, a gifted archer.
Dayan: Oyuun's younger son, Aytal's stepbrother, a boy of nine summers.
Bhermi: Potis's cousin and childhood best friend, killed by a bear.
Vedukha: Bhermi's widow, Sata's cousin.
Melit: Bhermi and Vedukha's daughter, Naya's friend & second cousin on both sides.
Skelos: Bhermi's brother, blames Potis and Naya for Bhermi's death.
Krnos: Skelos's son, a young man of fourteen summers, a skilled tracker.

THE WILD HORSES
Réhda: A two-year old filly with an unusual chestnut red coat.
MeHnd: The red filly's dam, lead mare of the herd.
BeHregs: The herd stallion.
Myräkkä: A young gray stallion who tries to join the herd.

PART ONE

Pontic-Caspian Steppe, c. 4000 BCE

Late Summer

Chapter One

Naya rose to her feet, blue eyes intent on the horizon. It didn't matter that she might be seen – the herd was too far away to take flight. She could just make out their individual shapes, moving slowly, partially obscured by the tall waving grasses. A small dun-colored stallion and four dun-colored mares foraged, making gradual progress in a westerly direction toward a low line of hills. Three of the mares were accompanied by foals, all of them born several moons earlier, just after the steppe winds changed to the south and the weather warmed. The fourth mare was shadowed by a two-year old filly. Looking into the setting sun, the horses were hard for the girl to distinguish against the pale gold of the drying grasses. All except the filly. Her red-gold coat, lit by the sun's last rays, stood out like a flame against the predominating brown and yellow tones of the surrounding landscape. Naya reached up to rub a lock of her own coarse hair between thumb and finger. It was almost exactly the same startling shade of copper as the filly. Turning to go back the way she had come, the girl cast one last glance at the disappearing herd. Tomorrow she would be back, with a rope.

To everyone else in Naya's world, wild horses represented a valuable resource, providing her people with meat, bones, hide, and sinew. More abundant than the bison, deer and saiga antelope who also roamed the vast grasslands, they were the hunters' preferred quarry, easier to herd into confined spaces where they made prime targets for the hunters' spears. But Naya had a different thought, a desire that came from deep within the center of her being. She wanted to touch the red filly. She wanted to run her hands through the unusual coat, so similar to her own head of flaming hair – and she wanted to do this thing with the consent of the warm and breathing animal, not just handle a lifeless pelt.

Absently she passed a palm down the front of her garment, a piece of tanned horse hide with the soft cream-colored belly hair left on. It was shorter than the typical dress worn by other girls her age, but still long enough to reach almost to her knees. Underneath, she wore boy's leather leggings, held up beneath her tunic with a thong at her waist, and with the bottoms tucked into tall lace-up hide boots. In this androgynous outfit she could run as swiftly as any of her cousins, boy or girl, but not offend anyone's sense of decency.

Now as Naya hurried along, mind absorbed with thoughts of the red filly, the clan's summer encampment came into view, tents outlined against a purple sky, cooking fires beginning to glow in the gathering dark. Cattle, sheep, and goats, not yet settled for the night, made plaintive noises. Dogs barked as women called to children to hurry with their evening chores. Picking up her pace, Naya fairly flew down the trail, sure-footed despite the gloom. Even so, she would be late, again.

Looking up from the coarse-haired flank of the goat she was milking and noticing the sun had slipped beyond the horizon, Naya's grandmother marked the girl's return to camp and wondered where she'd been all afternoon. If Awija had known what Naya had been up to, and of the plan beginning to take shape in the girl's mind, the old woman would likely have approved, just as she approved of most of her favorite granddaughter's unusual undertakings. Awija recognized that Naya was different from her cousins, not only because of her blue eyes and red hair. Bolder and more active than many of the other girls, she was prone to getting into physical scrapes, as if she were one of the boys. At the same time, she was exceedingly tender-hearted, especially when it came to the other creatures who shared the open grasslands where her people ventured during the summer season with their small herds of cattle, sheep, and goats. Although she could track as well as any of her cousins, and set snares for small game, she was more inclined to bring home an injured rabbit for Awija to nurse back to health than contribute it to the family's cooking pot. The boys especially often teased her for being more interested in spending time with animals than people. When she was younger, Naya's behavior had been tolerated, but she was no longer a child. Like her peers, she was expected to begin taking on more adult responsibilities, not wander off, doing whatever she pleased. After each of her transgressions, her father spoke sternly of duty, while her mother sighed and shook her head.

Awija, however, just smiled to herself. After all, her granddaughter's way with the wild creatures, although remarkable, was not inexplicable. Her son Potis, Naya's father, had the same gift for communing with animals. As for the independent streak that set her granddaughter apart, the old woman liked to think that her granddaughter got that from her, but she had to concede that some aspect of it came as well from the girl's mother. Awija and her daughter-in-law often clashed as a result, more often than not over Naya herself. Awija understood why Sata sought to curb Naya's wandering; she was concerned not only for the safety of her only child but for the reputation and status of her husband. Awija had different priorities. Knowing her granddaughter must spend time by herself out on the steppe if she were to develop her special gifts, she did what she could to channel the girl's resistance to being confined while still abetting her exploits. Yet even Awija had to admit such freedom could not last forever.

After squeezing a final spurt from the goat's teat into the wooden bowl she held between her knees, the old woman gave the animal an affectionate pat, then rose stiffly to her feet and surveyed the settlement's tents, still visible against the darkening evening sky. For her granddaughter, time was running out.

Long after noon the next day, Naya was at last able to slip away. This time she was better prepared. In a deer skin bag slung over one shoulder she carried flint tools and kindling for making fire, a flint knife and enough food to last a day, as well as a full water skin. Over the other shoulder was coiled a long length of braided rawhide, strong enough, she hoped, to restrain the filly. The rope had been fashioned by her mother. No one else could twist and weave the strands of sinew together with such expert skill. Naya herself lacked the patience. Glancing at the height of the sun, now well on its way toward the western horizon, she set off at a jog in the direction where she'd seen the herd the day before. Horses could cover a lot of territory in a day.

Still, Naya wasn't too concerned. As soon as the sun sank behind the western hills, she knew that the yellow disk of a full moon would appear on the eastern horizon behind her, giving her ample light to track, even after sunset. And because of the lunar phase, if she did not appear for the evening meal or to join her family to sleep, her mother and father would both assume she had retreated to the women's tent along with her other unmarried female cousins. Yet because this moon cycle would be only the second time for her to seclude herself with them, the other young women were unlikely to remark on her absence. If they did, she'd asked Melit, the only one of her cousins with whom she felt a close bond, to cover for her. Her mother would most likely wait until at least midday tomorrow to check on her, and even then, she would hesitate to raise an alarm over Naya's disappearance unless it became prolonged, for fear of attracting more attention to her daughter's unorthodox behavior. Neither large predators nor unknown hunting parties had been reported in the area for several weeks, meaning ranging alone on the steppe was relatively safe for the time being, and Naya fully intended to return by the following day. Adopting the relaxed, ground-covering lope she copied from her male cousins, she headed northwest.

She found the little band at dusk, when the sun's afterglow cast blackening shadows across the landscape. She had just gained the top of a small rise and could see for some distance, despite the gathering darkness. There they were – blurred shapes silhouetted against the next range of hills. Succeeding ridges gained in height, verdant meadows giving way to forested slopes, behind which the sun had disappeared. The horses had led her to the edge of the grasslands. Another day's journey and she would be surrounded by the thickly wooded hillsides bordering her clan's more open territory. These forest-steppes extended for a long way to the west and north. Had she turned instead to the east and travelled for an entire moon, she would have reached her clan's winter refuge along the banks of the great river, *Rā*. From there, heading south, she would eventually encounter actual mountains – the mountains bordering her mother's homeland. Naya didn't ever intend to go there again, at least not by herself.

She had been to these mountains almost exactly two years ago, when the clan spent the summer season at the southern-most reach of their territory along the great river and her father had not yet decreed she must try harder to behave more responsibly. Despite his bluster, Potis was partly responsible for his daughter's penchant for going off on her own and getting into trouble. He had actively encouraged Naya when she was younger to learn the skills necessary for tracking, hunting and otherwise surviving outside the protective circle of the settlement. More than once, he'd even allowed her to go along on longer foraging expeditions, including the trip into the mountains where one of their party had been savaged by a great bear whom they had surprised just outside a cave.

Naya shivered at the memory, then grasped the bear's tooth, tied with a thong at her neck. It was she who had first spotted the creature's hulking, shaggy shape, hidden within a grove of close-growing spruce, and given the warning. Without her sharp eyes, more of the men could have been lost. Instead, they had been able to kill the huge female before she could harm anyone else, despite her frenzied determination to protect the cubs waiting in the cave. Her father had given Naya the bear-tooth necklace in recognition of her bravery. Shortly afterward, however, he stopped allowing her to accompany him on trips away from the clan's summer encampment.

This year was no different, despite her pleading. Bitterly disappointed, she wandered as far as she dared by herself. Even had she wanted company, she did not have much choice but to go alone. The boys wouldn't include her in their explorations and the other girls seemed to have little interest in venturing beyond sight of their tent dwellings. No one shunned her outright – her family was too powerful for that – but more often than not, she found herself on her own. Most of the time she didn't mind, but even she was neither courageous nor foolhardy enough to travel too far from the safety of the encampment, especially not in the direction of the southern mountains. Still, she often thought with sadness and a little regret of the great mother bear who had died defending her cubs.

Shivering again in the rapidly cooling air, Naya brought her attention back to the horses. They appeared to have stopped for the evening. The mares' heads hung low, muzzles almost touching the ground in deep relaxation and she could make out several darker shapes that must be the foals, lying in the grass at their feet. Only the stallion stood alert, scenting the air for danger before dropping his head to grab a few mouthfuls of grass. Moments later, his head lifted again, keen eyes scanning the landscape.

Naya settled herself in the deep grass and rested her folded arms atop her knees. From her vantage on the rise downwind from the small band, she could sit and keep watch without arousing suspicion while she decided what to do. She wasn't sure she could see the red filly. Was she laying on the ground with the other foals? How could she get close enough to catch her? Should she use her rope to set a snare to trap a foreleg? Quickly Naya rejected this idea as likely to cripple the animal. Her best chance was to somehow get the rope around the filly's neck. To have any hope of doing this, she'd have to separate the two-year-old from the rest of the herd. The stallion and adult mares would never allow her to get close enough otherwise. Often hunters chased bands of horses into the ravines along the streams and smaller tributaries that flowed into one of the rivers bisecting the steppe, trapping them and making them easy targets for their flint spears. Naya was not after meat, but if she could get the filly into one of those ravines by herself, she might be able to throw the rope and capture the young horse. She'd have to be quick and accurate. She would likely have only one chance before the filly rushed past her to rejoin her family. Satisfied that she had at least the beginnings of a plan, Naya rested her cheek on her crossed forearms, closed her eyes and slept.

At some point later in the night, she thought she awoke. Her first instinct was to check the herd. Lifting her head from her folded arms, she saw them, as they'd been before, dozing in the lee of the hillside across from the rise where she sat. Even the stallion had relaxed his vigilance and stood with his head lowered. The full moon now rode high in the sky, bright enough to cast faint shadows. As Naya's eyes adjusted to the night, the moon's light seemed to grow even more luminous. Oddly, it appeared to shine particularly brightly along a faint track leading down the rise at an angle from where the horses rested. She hadn't noticed it before.

Rising, she moved as silently as she could, following the path in the moonlight. Soon, Naya found herself ascending another small rise, then descending, then rising again, until at last she stood at the edge of one of the ravines that cut into the earth along the tributary of the nearest river.

Below, she could see the stream itself, shining in the moonlight, gurgling quietly as it flowed over its rocky bed. Beneath her feet, the path was just visible, leading down the steep-sided ravine to what must be a smaller creek that drained into the stream.

Slipping and sliding, Naya made her way down, scratching her skin against sharp rocks and thorny underbrush. At last she reached the bottom and looked around her. The stream lay at her back, moving past the mouth of the ravine. Along the ravine's floor ran the creek, seeking to join the larger water course. Smooth white stones marked its way. Large boulders, interspersed with prickly bushes and gnarled birch thickets, covered both sides of the ravine. Looking back up the way she had come, Naya could not discern the trail that had brought her into the little gorge. Ahead of her, a few larger oaks, roots fed by the creek, hid its source. On the ravine floor, the moon's glow, reflected by the white stones of the water course, seemed to suggest a path. Drawn onward, Naya followed it into the grove of trees.

There, a wondrous sight met her eyes. The trees encircled a small pool of water, fed by an underground spring that served as the origin of the little creek. Reflected in the pool's clear, still surface was the round orb of the moon, casting its light from high above the rocky cliffs which formed the pool's backdrop. Beside the pool stood the red filly, burnished coat softly aglow. Naya froze, rooted as if she were one of the trees, and stared. The filly, startled by the girl's approach, stared back. Neither moved. Eventually, Naya remembered to breathe. In the next moment, she realized that she had left her rope, along with everything else she'd brought with her, back on the rise. Still, she and the filly stood motionless, looking at each other.

She must have come searching for water, thought Naya. *She must have gotten up in the night and wandered away from the others, looking for a drink.*

She continued to study the young horse, considering what to do next. Suddenly, time ceased its normal passage and in that moment, Naya's senses underwent an almost imperceptible shift; the moonlight became just a little brighter, the stream's murmur became just a little louder, the slight breeze rustling the leaves in the trees became just a little fresher against her skin. In the next moment, she seemed to feel the filly's thoughts.

I will grant your heart's desire, but only if you are able to grant mine. The musical voice resonated within the core of Naya's being, even though no sound other than the splash of flowing water and whisper of the wind in the trees disturbed the silence of the grove. *What is your heart's desire?*

Awestruck, Naya could only gaze back at the young horse, who now regarded her with luminous dark eyes in which fear had given way to curiosity. Finally, she found her own voice. "I wish to be with you," she said simply. "I wish to touch your coat." Then, from deep inside, another longing welled up, a yearning so audacious she almost couldn't bring herself to speak. Hesitatingly, she uttered the words. "I wish," she said, "to ride upon your back."

Ah, the red filly seemed to reply, *if this is indeed your deepest desire, then you must see with the eyes of your heart and create ties without the use of a rope. And when you have succeeded in granting my heart's desire, then shall yours be granted also.*

Before Naya could begin to ponder the meaning of the words, the filly brushed past her in a chestnut blur and was gone, disappearing through the trees toward the mouth of the ravine. Gazing after her, Naya shook her head, as if to clear her senses. With that blink of an eye, the light returned to its usual moonlit dimness. Water still flowed in the creek and a breeze still rustled among the leaves but the moment of utter clarity had vanished, just as suddenly as the young horse. Shaking herself again, as if awakening from a dream, Naya retraced her steps to where the creek joined the stream. There was no sign of the red filly.

The terrain became somewhat more open here, but the ground on either side of the tributary was marshy and impassable. She could only guess that the horse must have gone splashing through the shallow water itself, in which case there would be no tracks to follow. In any event, she needed to retrieve her rope and the bag with all her other tools, not to mention her food. Looking ruefully at the scratches covering her arms and legs and then back up at the steep sides of the brush-choked ravine, Naya decided that locating the path she had originally followed was both unlikely and unappealing. Instead, she would follow the filly's lead, wading downstream until she could find a place where the ground was dry enough for her to climb back up to the grassy hills of the steppe. From there, she'd have to hope that she could make her way to the featureless rise where she'd left her things.

By the time she was ready to give up, dawn still showed no sign of illuminating the eastern sky. The moon's pale glow served only to dim the vast field of stars, stretching in a dome above the steppe, without providing sufficient light to distinguish any landmarks. She'd found no evidence of the horses as she traversed up and down the shallow hills, all apparently identical. Fearing she had become completely disoriented and traveled in circles, Naya stopped at the top of a small rise. Better to wait until daylight and get her bearings. Besides, her hide boots were soaked from wading in the stream and needed time to dry. Her feet felt icy as she stripped the boots off and laid them beside her. Making a nest for herself in the tall grass and saying a brief prayer to her guardian spirits for protection, Naya curled herself into a ball and fell into an exhausted sleep.

She awoke to the sounds of strong teeth rhythmically cropping the grass on the hillside just below her resting place. With a start, she opened her eyes and sat up. In that instant, the small band of horses took flight, streaming down the slope and up the next shallow incline, where they wheeled abruptly and came to a halt, eyes intent on the creature who had materialized so unexpectedly out of the grass. Still close enough for her to distinguish quite clearly, next to one of the dun-colored mares stood the red filly.

Without thinking, Naya rose to her feet. Her precipitous movement sent the small herd fleeing once again and within moments, they had been swallowed by the vastness of the steppe. The wild excitement which had surged through Naya was immediately replaced with bitter disappointment, followed by concern as she remembered her predicament. Where were her things? Only then did she take stock of her surroundings. There, partially concealed by the grass at her feet, lay her deerskin bag and her rawhide rope. Somehow, miraculously, she'd found her way in the dark back to where she'd started.

Relieved, and suddenly famished, Naya seated herself again on the ground and opened her bag, taking out strips of preserved meat mixed with dried berries and roasted goosefoot seeds. Her people were primarily hunters, fishermen and herders, not farmers, but they did forage for greens and root vegetables and harvest wild grains and fruits. More recently they'd begun to supplement this diet with milk and cheese from the clan's goats, who were not native to the area but rather descended from the herd which had accompanied Naya's mother when she traveled from her homeland in the mountains of the south to marry Naya's father. She had also brought with her a flock of domesticated sheep of a type most useful for their wool. The fibers of their coats grew longer than the hair of wild sheep, so that the fleece could be beaten into felt or spun into yarn and then woven into various textiles. Naya had watched her mother teach these skills to the other women since she was a little girl, but although she'd managed to learn the basics, she lacked her mother's gift for inventing new techniques and uses for the raw wool. The clan's cattle, the most valuable of their livestock, were reserved for feasting and sacrifice on important ritual occasions or for exchange in order to secure the allegiance of allies. For daily survival, Naya's people still hunted and fished for most of their meat. Wild boar and aurochs inhabited the wooded river valleys, tributaries teamed with fish, and bison, deer and antelope roamed the open steppe – but the humans' favorite prey were the herds of wild horses.

After finishing her breakfast and taking a long drink from her water skin, Naya reached thoughtfully for her rope, intending to contemplate her next steps. Only then did her glance fall on her own arms and legs. Instead of being covered in scratches, her limbs were completely unblemished, except for the bruise on her right knee which she'd gotten two nights before when she tripped in the dark over a pile of hides carelessly left at the entrance of her family's dwelling. Something wasn't right.

Concentrating, she tried to remember exactly what had happened the day before, from the time she'd finally sighted the horses around dusk and stopped to rest and keep watch on the rise where she now sat. She remembered deciding on a plan to capture the filly and then she must have fallen asleep. After that, her memories were somewhat hazy, but not as elusive as a dream. She thought she recalled waking again later in the night and following a moonlit path down into a ravine where she found trees surrounding a mirrored pool… and the filly. They had made contact, her own incredulous eyes staring into fathomless dark brown depths. She saw again the curiosity and intelligence of the young horse's gaze. Something had passed between them. *What was it?* Naya made an effort to conjure the scene, but the details eluded her. Try as she might, she could remember nothing more, other than wandering the steppe in the dark, hoping to find her way back to where she'd left her belongings. Somehow, she thought with another wave of relief, she'd managed to stumble on the right place. Or had she? Maybe she'd never left her watching post on the rise and all the rest was a dream, or some kind of waking vision. Such experiences were known to occur. She'd have to ask her mother, or better yet her grandmother. Absently, still preoccupied by what may or may not have happened the night before, she reached to put on her boots which lay on the grass beside her, drying in the morning sun.

Chapter Two

When Naya returned to the clan's summer encampment, although the day's activities were well underway no one seemed to have taken note yet of her absence. Skirting the edge of the circle of tents to avoid being seen, she made her way stealthily to the large round shelter reserved for women and slipped through the flap at the entrance. The dim, muffled atmosphere inside the tent's heavy hide walls felt stuffy compared to the cool morning air outside. Searching the shadows, she discovered with relief that she was alone. No wisps of smoke curled from the hearth in the center toward the hole in the roof, signifying the tent most likely had been unoccupied overnight. This made things easier. There would be less explaining to do. Even if her flow had not started for this moon cycle, she could still claim to have spent the night by herself in the women's shelter, which girls her age sometimes did. Hopefully no one had seen her slip inside this morning. She would just remain a short time longer, then emerge as if nothing had happened and join in the camp's daily routine.

Unfortunately, her clandestine movements had not gone completely unobserved. Within moments of disappearing inside the tent, Naya heard a plaintive whine, followed by a sharp *yip* at the entrance. Crouching to lift the flap, she was almost bowled over by an ecstatic ball of gray fur. Her dog, Amu, wriggled into her lap, covering her face and neck with happy kisses. Evidently, he'd missed her. Laughing, she was trying to fend him off when someone outside spoke her name.

"Naya?"

She was silent. The dog must have given her presence away. "Yes?" she finally answered.

"What are you doing in there?"

"Resting?" It came out as a question, as if she were not at all sure her grandmother, whose voice she recognized, would find this an acceptable response.

"Aren't you feeling well?" came the reply.

"I'm fine."

"Amu missed you last night."

Dismayed, Naya realized her grandmother must know she'd been up to something. The dog was almost always with her. She had only left him behind yesterday because she wasn't planning to hunt and she hadn't wanted him to scare the horses. Her grandmother had noticed. Tentatively, Naya lifted the tent flap and looked up into the old woman's light brown eyes, shot through with flecks of green and almost hidden by wrinkles. Stooping, her grandmother followed the dog into the tent.

"Where have you been?"

Awija was nothing if not direct, a quality which Naya appreciated, except for when she became the target of her grandmother's scrutiny. Regardless of advancing age, the old woman's mind, like her eyes, remained clear and sharp. She missed little of what went on around her, even if she often kept her own counsel. Although as the wife of Naya's paternal grandfather, Awija was a revered elder of the clan, like Naya's mother, she was originally an outsider. Her people were farmers, living in large permanent villages to the west and south, where several rivers drained into the westernmost of the two great seas. Despite their settled existence, the farming folk interacted regularly with their neighbors, including the pastoralists of the steppes, trading livestock, hide products and the exquisite ceramics they were known for creating, as well as tools and jewelry made of copper. It was on such a trading expedition that Naya's grandfather Awos, then a young man, had convinced Awija's family to allow their daughter to become his wife. Such a thing was almost unheard of among the people of the farming villages, where women remained at the hearth of their mothers, grandmothers and great grandmothers. Yet somehow the handsome herder had managed to persuade not only Awija's family but Awija herself to agree to leave home for a very different life on the edges of the vast grasslands.

That had been nearly a lifetime ago. At the moment, Awija was curious as to what her granddaughter had been up to. Removing the leather-soled felt slippers she wore in camp and leaving them at the door, she picked her way across the circular tent, stepping carefully on the various hides carpeting the floor. Seating herself on a small pile of furs opposite the entrance, she pulled a nearby woolen robe up over her lap to ward off the morning chill, then gestured at her granddaughter to rekindle the hearth. One or two embers still glowed feebly and with the help of some kindling and the addition of a few lumps of dried dung, the girl soon had a small fire sending warmth and light into the close atmosphere of the tent.

Breaking the silence, Awija repeated her question: "Where have you been?"

"*Ud*," replied Naya, giving the word for 'away,' meaning beyond the immediate vicinity of the settlement.

Awija regarded the back of her granddaughter's head with a penetrating look, waiting for her to elaborate. The girl assiduously avoided meeting her gaze. When Naya failed either to turn around or to speak, Awija reached out a hand and placed it on her shoulder, turning her until she could see into her face. Her granddaughter continued to resist making eye contact. Extending a gnarled finger, Awija gently lifted the girl's chin until Naya could not escape her gaze, then raised one arched brow in silent inquiry.

Unable to withstand either the insistence or the sympathy in her grandmother's eyes, Naya related the whole story of the previous day's adventures, from the time she left the settlement in search of the band of horses until discovering herself alone on the small rise the next morning, watching the herd disappear into the distance and wondering what exactly had happened to her. Awija let her talk without interruption and without reproof. Rather than being concerned about her granddaughter staying out all night, the old woman was far more interested in the moonlit encounter with the red filly and Naya's apparent inability to remember the words she and the wild horse had seemed to exchange, even though she could vividly describe so many other details. Nor could she figure out why her legs and arms were not scratched, yet her boots had been damp.

"Was it a dream?" Naya asked when she'd finished.

Awija studied her granddaughter for a long moment before replying. "No, my child," she responded at last. "I believe you have been on an *etmn itājō* – a soul journey." The words she used signified a mystical passage, usually reserved for priests, who traveled to other dimensions in order to commune with spirits and seek knowledge and healing power for their people. Normally, such an undertaking was the product of years of training and preparation, not the spontaneous experience of a young girl. Of course, Naya had always been a little different, Awija reminded herself, continuing to regard her granddaughter. *That red hair and those blue eyes,* she mused, *a legacy from her mother's tribe, no doubt.* Certainly no one among her own people possessed such an appearance.

Awija recalled objecting when her husband had insisted on finding a wife for their son from among the mountain-dwellers to the south, particularly when the young woman selected had such unusually striking features and seemed so sure of herself, but then Awos had reminded her that he too had looked outside the circle of his tribe when he claimed her from among the farming folk. In that case, why not find Potis a bride from among her own people, she'd asked at the time, someone who shared her upbringing and beliefs? But her husband had reminded her that along with their son's southern bride, the clan would acquire both a hardier breed of goat and a new type of wool-bearing sheep, together with the knowledge of how to make use of the long-fibered fleece, and the subject had been closed.

Over the years, Awija had grown to respect her daughter-in-law. She made a fit wife for Potis in many respects. Unfortunately, in the one area that mattered most, at least in the estimation of the clan, the marriage had fallen short. Sata had never been able to produce a son, something viewed as a great tragedy, almost a curse among her husband's people. A boy had been born, Naya's twin, but he died within moments of taking his first breath and there had been no other living children, leaving Potis without a male heir. Only the couple's red-headed, blue-eyed daughter survived. Awija loved the girl fiercely.

At the moment, however, she could tell her granddaughter was becoming impatient.

"So it wasn't real?" Naya demanded, sounding both confused and disappointed.

"Oh no, it was real, more real than a dream, more real than you and I sitting here now," Awija declared. She allowed her gaze to follow smoke from the fire as it wafted upwards, seeking the hole at the top of the tent, before turning back to her granddaughter. "The other world exists always and forever, in all places all at once," she explained, "without any of the limits of this world. Sometimes a person can be in both worlds at once. I think this must be what happened to you. You have been given a precious gift."

Naya looked dubious.

"But what about the red filly?" she asked. "I know she's real – I mean real in this world. I saw her with the herd, not just by herself in the ravine."

"Yes, I'm sure she is real," Awija assured her. "The two of you are connected now. Your destinies are entwined."

And perhaps more than just your individual destinies, Awija added to herself. Again she paused, watching the smoke waft skyward, knowing she must consider carefully, as well as seek direction from her personal spirit guides, before saying too much more.

"Give me a moment to think about this," she said. "You and Amu stay where you are – I'm not finished with you yet," she added, forestalling Naya who looked as though she'd been about to attempt an escape. Amu must have sensed as much, for he'd sprung to his feet. Awija waited until both the girl and the dog had resettled themselves, then closed her eyes in order to concentrate. Although the sounds of camp life drifted in from outside the tent, inside the only noise was a faint hiss emanating from the hearth.

What had happened to Naya warranted careful attention, Awija recognized. This idea she had, of wanting to touch the young horse, essentially to tame her, was novel but not out of the realm of possibility. After all, dogs, cows, sheep, goats – all the animals with which they shared their pastoral existence – their ancestors had once been wild but had allowed themselves to be tamed. Now the humans and the animals who lived with them were so mutually dependent, it was hard to imagine how they could survive apart. Why not the wild horses? Had her granddaughter received a message from the spirit-herd, a request to enter a new type of relationship, something beyond predator and prey? It was hard to imagine how such a relationship would work. While perhaps not as wary and swift to flee as deer, the horses were cautious of people and could be dangerous when trapped, not like the docile cattle, sheep, and goats who willingly followed wherever the herders and their dogs guided them, trusting the humans would provide grass and water and protection from wolves.

Perhaps she should discuss the matter with her husband and their son, Awija reflected, opening her eyes for a moment to check on her granddaughter. She'd heard her move but was relieved to see that she'd only laid down, curling herself against Amu, who was stretched out full-length on the opposite side of the hearth. Naya was using the dog's flank as a pillow. Despite stiffened joints, Awija deliberated getting up to pull a blanket over the pair, but decided if they'd dozed off, she didn't want to disturb them.

Returning to the notion of revealing Naya's other-worldly experience to the girl's father and grandfather, Awija rejected the idea. With a matter of such import, they would immediately want to involve the rest of the clan, which she knew was not a good idea, not until Naya had an opportunity to fully understand what had happened to her. Certainly the priests would discount her granddaughter's story on every level and they held great authority in such matters. No, better for now to keep it to themselves.

Instead, she must find a way to help Naya to remember the message she had received from the filly's spirit-self, and then follow the path that had been revealed to her, wherever it might lead, without interference from those who might seek to turn the incident to their own purposes. Naya must be allowed to discover the meaning of her journey and to do that, she would have to spend more time with the wild horses. Yet sanctioning such an undertaking would not be an easy task, Awija reflected, still studying her granddaughter. Apparently exhausted from her escapade, Naya appeared to be sound asleep, snuggled against the comforting bulk of the big gray dog, who was also napping. Awija could see their chests rising and falling as they breathed in unison. Regardless of such moments of childhood innocence, Awija knew that her granddaughter was coming under increasing pressure to assume her adult role within the clan. Her solitary wanderings were frowned upon by everyone. An excuse would have to be found.

Turning the question over in her mind, Awija was struck by a sudden inspiration. As the wife of the old clan chief, as well as by virtue of her own status as the clan's medicine woman, she held a certain amount of authority, a situation she knew full well the priests resented. While Awos had recently been succeeded as clan chief by Potis, she herself had yet to choose someone to entrust with her knowledge and duties. Her daughter Swesor was not a candidate – she had neither the talent nor the desire – but Swesor's daughter Sora, who was close in age to Naya, did seem to have the right temperament and had already demonstrated a great affinity for working with plants. Still, not until after Sora's initiation would Awija be expected to name her as her designated successor. In the meantime, perhaps she could act as though both her granddaughters were being trained as her apprentices. Although unlike her cousin, Naya had not shown much interest in the herbal lore that underlay Awija's skill as a healer, she obviously possessed other gifts, especially when it came to animals. In this, she was like her father. The two of them seemed to have a sixth sense when it came to understanding the behavior and habits of every living creature inhabiting the steppe. It was part of what made Potis such a successful hunter.

Yet, because Naya, as the daughter of a chief, would be expected to marry outside the clan in order to secure alliances, she was unlikely to be allowed to truly follow in her father's footsteps, nor be encouraged fully to develop her particular gifts. Awija knew the girl had been confused and hurt when she was no longer permitted to accompany her father on expeditions beyond their summer encampment. Now, instead of willingly joining in the tasks of the other women, she escaped as often as possible to spend time alone out on the steppe, seemingly doing nothing useful. Perhaps by giving her granddaughter a reason to roam, under the guise of preparing to become a healer, Awija could provide a legitimate excuse for her to spend time in the company of the wild horses. If Naya were to acquire even the basics of her herbal skills, then plants would need to be identified and gathered, some of them rare and difficult to find. She could conceivably spend all day searching…

"*Ahem*," Awija cleared her throat. Although Amu raised an eyelid, her granddaughter gave no sign of having heard. "Naya!" she said. This time, the girl's eyes flew open and she sat up, looking for a moment as though she couldn't remember where she was, before scrubbing her hands over her face. As she did, Amu rolled onto his chest, yawned expansively, then rose and stretched. Awija regretted disturbing them but knew if her granddaughter did not get started with her share of the morning's tasks, there would be talk. Indeed, from the expression on Naya's face, now that she was fully awake, the girl must think she was in trouble after all.

"It's alright," Awija assured her. "I'm sorry to wake you but you had better go take care of your morning chores before someone else comes looking for you and finds that you've been catching up on the night's sleep you missed." She chuckled. "Come back with your mother when you've finished," she instructed. "I have a plan I want to discuss with both of you."

Counting on her granddaughter's relief at being dismissed without censure to forestall her curiosity, at least for the time being, Awija watched as the girl beckoned to the dog and together the two slipped out of the tent.

Alone, Awija uttered a quiet prayer to the Goddess, asking for further guidance regarding Naya's situation. While the priests might lead the clan in public worship of *Dyēus-Ptēr*, called Sky-Father, she herself still held to the practices of her own people, who above all revered *Dhéghōm-Méhtēr*, the Great Goddess. True, *Dyēus-Ptēr* ruled the heavens, literally raining bounty or catastrophe from on high. For the people of the steppes, he personified the most striking and powerful phenomenon of their world, the infinite, ever-changing dome of the sky. But in Awija's belief, the Goddess held still greater authority, for she embodied the creative forces of Earth-Mother: birth, death, and regeneration. Here, in the privacy of the women's tent, Awija shared this truth with those women of the clan who were inclined to listen, leading them in the ancient rites honoring the power and wisdom of the divine feminine. In addition, along with the wife of the senior priest, she oversaw the older girls' preparation for their initiation into womanhood. The priests themselves, while concerned that the clan's young women should understand their proper roles and responsibilities, viewed their spiritual training as a task best left to their female elders.

Awija sighed. Lately, time seemed to pass too quickly. Along with the other girls her age, Naya would most likely undergo her initiation as soon as next spring, marking an important stage in her life's passage. What did the future hold for her beloved granddaughter? What path was the Goddess calling her to follow?

Having offered up her prayer, Awija stood and reached for a small clay pot of dried herbs kept on a high shelf built into the frame of the tent and almost hidden in the shadows. The pot, one of the treasures brought with her years ago from home, was beautifully made, decorated over the entire surface with intricate spiral designs incised into the orange clay. Placing a few leaves into a similarly ornate clay dish, she added a burning coal from the fire. Inhaling deeply of the sweet-smelling smoke, she sat back upon the hide cushions and closed her eyes. Unlike the powerful herbs used by the priests on important ritual occasions, the smoke produced by burning the dried leaves of this particular plant was not intoxicating. It produced no visions, provided no special passage to the other world. It did, however, perfume the stuffy air within the tent and helped to calm her mind. Taking another slow, deep breath, she deliberately released her thoughts, focusing instead on the sensations within her body. Wherever she identified an area of tension, she sent her breath to encourage release. Then, still inhaling and exhaling, she simply listened.

By the time Naya and her mother returned, the sun had climbed to its zenith and the day was half over. Although the air outside had grown hot under the merciless rays of late summer, the interior of the women's tent remained relatively cool. One of Naya's female cousins, looking in on her grandmother at some point during the morning, had courteously rolled up the flaps around the lower perimeter of the circular structure, allowing a slight cross-breeze. Other than this, the old woman had not been disturbed. Having received the guidance she sought, she had spent the rest of the time while she waited in putting the finishing touches on her plan. Hopefully Sata would agree.

Holding back the flap, Naya allowed her mother to proceed her into the tent. Bending nearly double to enter, Sata had to take one or two stooped steps toward the center of the circular space before she could resume her full height. She was a tall woman, taller than some of the men of her husband's clan. She bore herself with an unconscious grace, moving through the settlement in a way that caused many eyes to follow her. She wore her long, auburn hair in a thick braid which swung between her shoulder blades as she walked. Although not as shockingly red as her daughter's flaming locks, the color was still highly unusual. Her blue eyes, which regarded her mother-in-law with frank appraisal, were identical to Naya's.

"What is this about?" Sata asked without ceremony. She could be just as direct as the old woman. "Naya has clearly been up to something but she wouldn't tell me anything without coming to see you first. What's going on?"

"Please sit," Awija responded, gesturing toward the cushions on either side of her and ignoring Sata's questions. Where she came from, manners were observed and she refused to allow her daughter-in-law to take control of the conversation.

Bowing her head slightly, Sata moved to seat herself at Awija's right. Naya remained standing near the door. Catching her granddaughter's eye, Awija looked pointedly to her left and then back. Hurrying to obey, Naya crossed the space and sat down. No sooner had she done so than Amu, not bothering to ask permission, entered the tent through the gap created by the rolled-up flaps, and curled himself at the girl's feet.

"Naya," said Awija, once everyone was settled, "tell your mother what happened last night."

Eyes carefully downcast to avoid her mother's gaze, Naya once again recounted her story. Listening attentively, Awija noted that none of the details changed. Her granddaughter's memories of her encounter seemed quite vivid, except for the crucial exchange by the pool, which remained frustratingly elusive. As she listened, Awija stole covert glances at Sata's face, seeking to assess her reaction. Although her daughter-in-law's expression revealed nothing, Awija thought she sensed growing apprehension. *Good*, she thought. *This is not something to be taken lightly.*

"What do you think it means, Mama?" Naya asked at last, lifting her eyes from her lap to meet her mother's. "Awija says I've been on an *etmn itājō*."

Shifting her attention from her daughter, Sata regarded her mother-in-law for a long moment in silence. Awija returned her daughter-in-law's gaze, also not speaking aloud. Naya looked between the two women, trying unsuccessfully to discern the meaning of their tacit exchange.

"My dear," Sata said at last, giving Naya a reassuring smile, "I believe you have indeed experienced such a journey. The question is, what are we going to do about it?"

Naya's face lost its anxious look and Awija breathed her own sigh of relief.

"Tell me again, what made you want to follow the horses in the first place?" Sata asked.

"I just wanted so badly to touch the red filly," Naya responded, "as if we're connected somehow and she pulled me to her." As though this might sound strange, she added, somewhat defensively, "her hair is just the same color as mine."

Again, Sata smiled, this time opening her arms in invitation. As she gave Naya a protective hug, Sata thought with nostalgia of a time when her little girl had fit much more comfortably in her lap. Now, Naya was almost a woman, and tall for her age. Already her moon flow had begun. Soon would come her initiation, followed by the likelihood of choosing a marriage partner, possibly as early as next summer's Gathering, when the tribe's various clans came together to celebrate the solstice, before dispersing once more to find fresh pastures for their herds.

Naya didn't seem ready for initiation, let alone marriage, Sata thought, cradling the girl's head against her shoulder and appreciating that her almost-grown daughter seemed content for the moment to be held as though still a child. She doubted Potis was in any more of a hurry than she was to find Naya a husband, especially if it meant that she would leave them. No, the pressure would come more from the other leaders of the clan, who expected young men and young women alike to follow the decisions of their elders about when to marry and the choice of a partner. Although personal preferences were considered, what mattered were the interests of the clan as a whole.

Yet to Sata, the burden had always seemed to fall unequally. Whereas young men generally stayed with their original families, often inheriting their fathers' duties, young women were often sent away, either to join another clan within the tribe, or to live among foreigners, thereby helping to solidify existing alliances or create new ties. In exchange for granting his daughter in marriage, a young woman's father would receive a bride price, most often in the form of livestock, thereby enhancing the family's personal wealth and status and by extension the wealth and status of the entire clan.

Sata knew that such arrangements were not always the custom. Among her mother-in-law's folk, daughters usually remained with their mothers, even after marriage – but they were farmers, not herders. Perhaps the practice had been different for her husband's ancestors as well, back in the time when they had depended solely on hunting, fishing and what could be gathered from the wild bounty of the earth. But then, according to the old tales, as a bequest from the gods the people had acquired cattle, followed by sheep and goats, and men who had once been hunters became herders. Because the animals could easily be stolen, men had also needed to become warriors. Since then, for as long as anyone could remember, livestock raids had been a way of life among the various tribes of the steppe, resulting in ongoing conflicts between neighboring groups. Alliances formed and then dissolved; grievances hardened into feuds. Even within the same tribe, factions formed, with rival leaders vying for influence. Those families who held the largest herds naturally commanded more authority and respect. Besides having the most to protect, they also had the most to bargain with and bestow and could thus secure others' allegiance. Under these circumstances, if a prosperous and powerful man had a son, he had the means to secure for the young man a desirable marriage. If he had a daughter, the young woman could be exchanged for even greater wealth in the form of additional cattle, sheep and goats, but only at the cost of leaving her family.

Unconsciously, Sata's arm tightened around Naya's shoulders. She couldn't imagine parting with her daughter, whatever custom might demand. Nor could she imagine her daughter meekly submitting to a marriage choice made for her by her father and the clan's other leaders, particularly if Naya didn't favor the young man. Yet while Sata wanted to believe that out of love for his daughter Potis would do his best to take into account Naya's wishes, she also had to acknowledge that the final decision would not be hers.

Meanwhile, despite admonitions to start acting more like a responsible young woman, Naya persisted in challenging the limits of acceptable behavior. This latest infraction was only the most recent that had occurred over the past summer, Sata reflected. While her female cousins preferred to spend their time working in or at least near the encampment, harvesting wild fruits, nuts and other useful natural materials or helping their mothers to look after children, milk the goats and watch over the sheep, Naya insisted on roaming freely. More often than not she was by herself, since she was not welcome among the boys her age, whose primary duty in any case was to keep track of the cattle. Warning her that now that she was almost grown, venturing too far beyond the safety of the encampment meant that she, like the livestock, might be vulnerable to being stolen had no effect. Sata knew her daughter, who she could feel even now growing restless within the protective circle of her arms. Naya resented any form of confinement, but what option did she have?

As if in answer to Sata's unspoken thoughts, Awija's voice broke the silence.

"Naya is not like the other girls," she said, stating the obvious. "They can discover who the Goddess intends for them to be within the walls of this tent, but she is different. We can't keep her here."

Sata started to reply but the old woman forestalled her with an upraised hand. "Before she becomes of marriageable age, she must be allowed to discover the meaning of this journey she has undertaken," she asserted. "She must be given a chance to tame that wild horse. You and I are going to help her."

Reluctant to release her daughter from her lap, Sata sat without answering. Other than the familiar sounds drifting in from outside, quiet filled the tent. Naya, ready a moment earlier to squirm free of her embrace, held still, waiting to hear what her mother would say. Awija also waited. Sata could feel the old woman's gaze upon her, studying her features in the dim light in order to gauge her thoughts. Rarely did Sata reveal much. Others had to pay close attention to what passed behind her eyes.

She wondered if her mother-in-law appreciated the conflict she felt between upholding propriety for the sake of her husband's position within the clan and honoring her daughter's unique spirit. In all her wisdom, did Awija know, perhaps better than Sata did herself, whether she would agree to support Naya in this quest to tame the red filly? Did Awija guess that once Sata, too, had possessed her own restless dreams, long since buried under responsibilities and others' expectations? Did the old woman realize that a wisp of memory of herself at Naya's age might be enough for Sata to decide to go along? Still, she said nothing, only tightened her arms around her precious child.

Chapter Three

Shivering slightly in the chill late-autumn air despite the midday sun, Naya pulled her hide cloak more closely around her shoulders but otherwise remained motionless where she sat with her back against a large boulder. Amu slept with his muzzle on his paws beside her. A short distance away, the herd, including the red filly, grazed peacefully. They had grown remarkably accepting of her presence in a relatively short period of time. Even more surprising, the small band of horses also tolerated the dog, but only if he stayed near the girl and didn't make any move that could be construed as threatening.

For almost two moon cycles now, Naya and Amu had spent some portion of nearly every day visiting the herd. At first, their approach had aroused alarm. Now, even the stallion only raised his head and snorted when he saw the girl coming but otherwise remained unconcerned. Naya was careful to avoid startling the horses, always advancing in full view and moving with casual deliberation. Even if she had wanted to sneak up on them, it was impossible. She discovered that the herd seemed to be surrounded by an invisible shield. Always, when she reached a point equal to the distance from which a spear could be launched or a predator charge, the horses sensed her proximity. At first, they had taken flight as soon as she breached this boundary. Now, they only swiveled their heads to look in her direction, but never did they fail to notice her approach.

Gradually, as they grew more accepting and allowed her to come closer, she discovered successive edges of awareness. She knew by watching the horses' movements when she passed through another layer. Often it was obvious; she would take one too many steps in the herd's direction and several of the horses would stop grazing and lift their heads to look at her. Sometimes, the clue was as subtle as the flick of an ear, just enough to let Naya know that her movements were observed. Whenever this happened, she learned to stop, shift her weight back so that she was no longer pressing on the invisible shield and wait for permission to proceed. If the horses showed no further signs of concern, she knew she could try to come closer. If not, she would stay where she was until the herd moved on in their quest for the next mouthful of grass.

By remaining patient and paying close attention, Naya hoped eventually to get near enough to capture the red filly. Unfortunately, she seemed to have reached an impasse. For the last several days, although willing to let her approach within a stone's throw, the horses had not allowed her to come any closer, especially if the rawhide rope was anywhere in sight. They tolerated her but did not entirely trust her. Today, the herd's wanderings had led them into a shallow valley, surrounded by rugged hills dotted with rocky outcroppings. It was against one of the boulders scattered along the valley floor that she sat, using it as a backrest while she considered what to do next.

Both her mother and her grandmother had cautioned her to take her time. Each evening, when she reported to them about what had happened with the herd that day, often lamenting that all she had been able to do was sit and watch, her grandmother would ask her, "What did you learn?"

Knowing this question was coming, Naya tried hard to remember all that she had observed about the herd's behavior, as well as the characteristics of each individual. Soon she recognized that every horse not only had somewhat different markings, but each also had a distinct personality and she gave them names to match. One of the mares she called *Mus*, both because of her mouse-colored coat and because of her timid nature. The foal at her side, who shared her dam's cautious approach to the world, she named *MiMus*, Little Mouse. Another mare, who was a golden dun, almost exactly the color of the late autumn steppe, became *Ghrasom*, Yellow Grass. Her foal, a little colt, she named *Bhrounos* for the four brown socks that stretched up over his knees and hocks. One mare was especially cranky and frequently warned off the other horses with ears flattened and teeth bared. She became *Rebhjo*, 'to be angry.' Her filly, the largest of the foals, often tried to bully her peers and Naya called her *Melos*, meaning strong.

The remaining mare, to whom the whole herd looked for guidance, she named *MeHnd*, the Wise One. Her daughter was the red filly and

Naya thought long and hard before settling on a name for her. Recalling the first time she'd laid eyes on the young horse, lit by the rays of the dying sun, she considered naming her *Bhokos*, Flame. More often than not, however, she thought of her as *Réhda*, the little red one, or simply 'Red'. The stallion, small but mighty, she called *BeHregs*, Brave Warrior.

Watching the herd graze, Naya tried to quell the impatience she felt. Her mother would advise her not to let frustration get the better of her and undo all that she had accomplished, but she was running out of time. Sometime in the next few days, perhaps as early as tomorrow, the clan would break camp for the season and move eastward for the winter. They were already late in getting started on the journey. It would be too much to hope that the horses might somehow follow them, which would mean it might be spring before she had another chance to capture Réhda, assuming she could even find the herd again and that nothing happened to the filly over the winter. Already, the encampment was busy with preparations for travel, making it harder to slip away, even with the collusion of her mother and grandmother. So far, they had been able to keep her secret. As far as they knew, no one had come upon the herd and no one had questioned her daily absences, assuming she was searching out medicinal herbs at her grandmother's behest. She did spend time gathering various plants as directed, always returning with something to show for her time alone on the steppe, but the excuse was wearing thin. If only she could let her father in on what was really going on. No doubt he would have ideas about how to proceed.

Just then, one of the mares closest to her, Ghrasom, raised her head, ears pricked attentively, as she focused on something over the girl's shoulder. In a moment, two of the other mares, Mus and MeHnd, had also come to attention. Naya turned, trying to see what had alerted them, certain it was nothing she had done.

There, at the edge of the valley, she spotted movement disappearing behind a pile of rocks. She held her breath. Seconds later, a dark gray shape came into full view – a lone wolf. Judging by his size and solitary status, Naya guessed it was a juvenile male. Slowly, she exhaled. Although never to be taken for granted, young wolves on their own were rarely dangerous. A pack on the hunt was another matter. Still, seeing one this close to the encampment was a clear sign of the change of seasons, signaling the necessity of returning to the clan's winter home near the banks of the great river, where high bluffs blocked the wind and marsh reeds provided winter forage for the herds. Beside her, Amu had come into a crouch, hackles raised and a low growl emanating from deep in his throat. Behind her, the horses had all stopped grazing to watch the predator make his way across the valley's edge.

Suddenly, the dog sprang forward, barking furiously and raced in the direction of the departing wolf. Startled, the wolf turned to look back and then broke into a lope, soon disappearing from sight. Dismayed, Naya came to her feet and called after the dog, commanding him to return to her. Amu, satisfied that he had routed the enemy, turned and trotted back to where the girl stood, seated himself on his haunches in front of her and looked up, the picture of obedient devotion.

"Bad dog!" she cried, concern for his safety making her voice harsh. Amu's only response was an inquiring tilt of his head. Hadn't he chased away the marauder?

"And you've probably scared off the horses too," she said with disgust as she turned to look behind her. She expected to see the meadow empty, with the herd long gone. Instead, the horses stood exactly where they had been moments before, only they were all now at full attention, even the youngsters. As she watched, MeHnd, the red filly's dam, made direct eye contact with her for one long moment. Then, calmly lowering her head, she returned to grazing. Soon all the others followed suit, except BeHregs, the stallion. He had to investigate for himself to be sure the danger had indeed passed and trotted off in the direction the wolf had departed. In doing so, he left the girl and dog in the company of the rest of the herd, something that had never happened before. Soon he was back, and the band began to meander slowly in the direction of a small stream. This time, however, instead of having to follow at a distance, Naya was permitted to move among them. Although still not allowing her to get close enough to touch any one individually, the horses had clearly decided to accept her presence within the sphere of the herd. Another boundary had been crossed. Naya couldn't wait to tell her mother and grandmother what had happened.

From a vantage point high at the edge of the valley, unseen by either the girl or the horses, a shape rose from behind a rocky outcropping. Not wanting to be detected, the figure took one last look at the scene below, then turned and disappeared down the other side of the slope.

That evening, as Naya sat with her mother and grandmother in their family's tent, companionably preparing the evening meal, she recounted the day's events.

"You've done well, my child," pronounced Awija when she'd finished. "The horses begin to welcome you among them."

"Yes, but now what?" asked Naya. "We'll be leaving in a few days. What will happen over the winter?"

"You might be surprised," observed Sata, looking up from the pot of aromatic stew simmering on the hearth at the center of the tent. "Remember the stories about how *Wakka*, grandmother Cow, first came to live with the people?"

Naya thought of the familiar tale, told around the big communal bonfire when the clan gathered in the evenings, of how the first cow had been tempted to join her cousins, Sheep and Goat, in living with humans, who offered to care for and protect them. "But Mama," she rejoined, "in that story *Ekwos*, cousin Horse, is much cleverer than *Wakka*. She doesn't need any help from the people to survive."

"Maybe not to find food beneath the snow," agreed her mother, sitting back on her heels and brushing back a lock of hair that had escaped to curl against her cheek, flushed from the steam rising from the stew. "But think. Is there something that you can offer the horses that would make them willing to follow you, to want to stay with you?"

Just then, the tent flap opened, allowing a gust of chill air to enter the dwelling.

Naya's grandfather Awos entered, followed by his son Potis. The family resemblance between the two men was striking. Both tall of stature, they were broad-shouldered and straight limbed, with brown skin made darker by the sun. They bore identical tattoos, a complex series of linked curving lines etched across high cheekbones, although whereas the markings on the old man's face were faded almost beyond recognition, the inked incisions on his son's face appeared fresh. Both shared hooked, almost beak-like noses and a strong, some would say stubborn set to their jaws. Dark brows levelled above deep-set eyes. Here, however, the resemblance had grown less strong over the years.

Whereas once Awos had regarded the world with the focused intent of a predator, of late his eyes had dimmed and his attention sometimes waivered. Potis, a man still in his prime, surveyed his surroundings with the fierce amber gaze of a bird of prey.

"*Ala!*" the two men said in unison as they entered.

"*Ala!*" returned the women, exchanging the usual greeting.

"Is the meal ready?" asked Potis, guiding his father to the seat of honor closest to the hearth. "I need to eat quickly and return to the central fire. The decision has been made. Tonight will be the last evening before we move and there's much to discuss."

Naya, who had been fetching the wooden trenchers her mother needed to serve the meal, looked up sharply at these words, her expression stricken. Awija and Sata exchanged glances but only Sata spoke.

"Yes, we just have to fill the bowls," she replied calmly. "Have a seat."

Once everyone was settled with food in front of them, conversation could resume. Concerned about everything that needed to happen the following day, Potis launched into a litany of instructions. Although much of the household had been packed up already, the tent would need to be disassembled and last-minute items stored for travel. He went on for some time before noticing that neither his wife, his daughter, nor his mother was contributing to the discussion. No one seemed inclined to join in the planning, let alone argue with him about the details as he would have expected. Potis looked inquiringly at each of them in turn.

"What is it?" he asked. No one replied but all eyes, including his, turned to Naya. "What now?" he continued, his tone indicating equal parts exasperation and resignation.

"Daughter," Sata spoke, her voice gentle but firm, "I think it's time you told your father what's been going on."

Potis saw Naya look at her mother, who nodded reassuringly, and then at her grandmother, whose green-flecked eyes smiled encouragingly back at her. Finally, swallowing and squaring her shoulders, his daughter turned to him.

"Well," she began, "I had this idea." With that, Naya described the day, now almost two moons ago, when she had first spotted the red filly and then gone back the following day with a rope, intending to capture the young horse.

"But after I finally located the herd, I fell asleep," she continued, "and when I woke up the next morning, even though the horses were close by, I ended up scaring them away. I've been going out almost every day since, trying to get close enough."

At this point Potis noticed his wife and his mother trade significant looks but they both remained silent.

"They've started to accept me," Naya went on, sounding proud. "I've learned so much from watching them, just like you used to tell me about when you were a boy learning to hunt the red deer."

Skeptical but knowing his daughter wanted his approval, Potis refrained from commenting and let her finish.

"Only I don't want to hunt the red filly," she concluded. "I want to climb on her back and be carried – I want to *ride* her."

As these last words escaped her mouth, Naya appeared as astonished as everyone else. Nonetheless, she recovered quickly and, lifting her chin, met the mounting displeasure in her father's hawk-like eyes with a defiant look of her own.

Potis, who had been just as impetuous when he was Naya's age and learned self-restraint the hard way, controlled his temper while considering which of several questions to ask his daughter first. Returning her silent look, he ran through them in his mind. *Did she know how reckless it was to spend so much time by herself away from the settlement? Didn't she have chores to do? Wasn't she supposed to be learning to be a medicine woman?* Potis shifted his attention to his wife and his mother, both of whom seemed suddenly occupied with cleaning up from the evening meal.

Turning back to Naya, he spoke at last. "Why," he asked, "would you want to sit on a horse's back?"

"Oh Papa!" she answered excitedly, "It would be like flying. Can you imagine, being able to race like the wind over the grass?"

"That would be impossible," Potis declared. "The horses would never let you get close enough. And besides, it wouldn't be safe. You'd never be able to stay on."

"But Papa, the horses *have* let me get close enough, or almost, and I bet I can figure out a way to hang on," Naya argued.

Belatedly recognizing that, given his daughter's intrepid nature, this was probably the wrong direction to steer the discussion, Potis shifted tactics.

"All this time spent alone with the horses!" he exclaimed sternly. "For one thing, it's dangerous. For another, you should have been making yourself useful. I thought you were supposed to be helping your grandmother."

He looked at Sata, then at Awija, then back to Sata. "What do you have to say about it?" he demanded.

"She just wants to tame a wild creature," Sata replied soothingly. "Don't you remember, when you were a boy, and you had the pet fox? You told me all about it. You loved that fox."

"This is totally different," Potis retorted, hiding his discomfiture. "It's dangerous and it's a waste of time," he declared, turning back to his daughter. "What would happen if hunters went after the herd and you got caught up in a stampede? Or if a wolf pack went after one of the foals and got you instead?"

"But Papa," Naya replied pleadingly, "the horses and Amu and I have been looking out for each other. We all know if anything is coming. Today, Amu and the stallion chased off a wolf together. I'm probably safer with the herd than anywhere else."

"How is it that no one has seen you or these horses?" Potis continued, as if his daughter hadn't spoken. "You've been going after this herd almost every day for two moons and no one else has spotted them, yet you've managed to keep track of them? That doesn't make sense."

"There's more to the story," Awija interrupted. Having finished cleaning up from supper, she had resumed her seat next to Awos, who had thus far remained silent. Facing Potis across the hearth, she spoke with quiet authority.

"Son," she commanded, "listen to the child."

"Naya," she then directed, "tell you father about the *etmn itājō*, about the journey."

With a freshly rebuilt fire crackling in the hearth and casting shadows against the tent walls, Potis and the others listened while Naya recounted what she could remember of her midnight encounter beside the moonlit pool. As before, the details were crystal clear, with the exception of the words exchanged.

"And I still don't understand why my legs and arms weren't scratched but my boots were wet," concluded Naya, looking perplexed.

Potis was speechless. The other-worldly aspect of Naya's experience with the red filly added a disturbing dimension to the situation, one that went beyond his usual realm of expertise. Should he consult the priests, he wondered? For a long moment, no one else in the dwelling spoke.

When a voice finally broke the silence, it belonged not to Potis but to his father, the first time since entering the tent that the old man had spoken. Indeed, other than nodding his thanks from his place by the hearth when Naya had refilled his bowl, he had been so quiet throughout the evening that the others had assumed the old clan chief had drifted into his own world, as he did more and more often. Yet obviously he'd been paying attention and moreover, had something he wanted to ask.

"When was it," he inquired, raspy voice hardly above a whisper, "that you decided you wanted to ride the horse?"

"I'm not sure," Naya responded. Her expression took on an interior quality. "I can't remember," she finally confessed. "Maybe as part of the vision?"

"Send Naya to stay with my sister's family tonight," Potis said abruptly, addressing his wife. "We need to talk about how to handle this."

Before Naya could protest, her mother silenced her with a look. Rising from her seat, Sata gathered a couple of hide blankets and handing them to Naya, began herding her out of the tent. Amu, who had been chewing on a discarded strip of rawhide, dropped it as he jumped up to follow.

"I'll give them some excuse," she said over her shoulder. "Don't talk about anything important until I get back."

"No, wait." Awija protested. "Naya is old enough to have a say in this discussion. She is the *etmn itājōr*, 'the one who journeys.' She must stay."

Pausing with her hand on the tent flap, Sata exchanged looks with Potis.

"The girl stays." Summoning his former tone of command, Awos clearly intended to put an end to the debate.

Raising an eyebrow, Sata again communicated silently with Potis. After a moment, he nodded and she allowed the tent flap to drop back into place. Giving both her grandparents a grateful smile, Naya handed the hides back to her mother and returned to her seat next to her grandmother. Amu, settling himself again in the corner, resumed gnawing his scrap.

"We should consult the priests," said Potis after a moment, addressing his father.

"Perhaps you're right," Awos agreed, but without conviction.

"Or perhaps not," interjected Awija. "What will they say?"

Turning to her son, she continued. "A *girl*," she emphasized, "who many already think is a little strange…"

At these words, Sata, who had resumed her seat next to Naya, put a protective arm around her daughter. In response, Awija held up a wrinkled hand, gesturing in a way to indicate that while she herself might dismiss such notions, they couldn't be ignored.

"This girl," she went on, "claims that she's had a mystical vision and wants to ride horses. How do you think they'll react? Even if she is your daughter. And your granddaughter," she added, turning back to Awos.

Potis watched as his father and mother spoke silently to one another, wondering if despite her wrinkles and the old man's fading vision, the former chief still saw in his wife's high cheek bones and green-flecked eyes the beauty she must have been when they married. He knew that in their many years together, his father had come to trust his mother's wisdom and rely upon her judgment.

"She's right," Awos said after a pause. "No one has ever imagined such a thing. Even if it is an intriguing idea." His clouded eyes turned thoughtfully toward his granddaughter.

"More important," Awija continued, "*Etmn itājō* is supposed to be the sole province of the priests. If they get wind of what Naya says happened to her, it will not go well for her. They will see her as a threat and seek to control her, in the name of protecting the clan, regardless of what anyone thinks about the horses."

"There is something about the horses," interjected Sata. "Potis," she continued, "what was it you said about no one else spotting the herd all this time? That *is* really strange. How do we know they even exist in this world? Perhaps they're a sacred herd, protected from anyone but Naya seeing them."

"But Amu knows they're there," Naya protested. "And I can practically touch them. They must be real!"

"No doubt they are," said Awija soothingly. "The steppe is a vast place. But your mother has a point. Up until now, you and that little herd have somehow managed to avoid being observed together, while you've gained their trust. Leaving tomorrow will change that."

"That's true." Potis confirmed. "If by some chance the herd decides to follow us, it will be only a matter of time before our hunters find them and want to go after them. If this filly is as unusual as you say, the priests will want to offer her as a sacrifice. And if the herd stays behind, they'll still be vulnerable. Winter is long. They could wander into another tribe's territory, be attacked by wolves, anything." He paused, looking across the circle to where his only child sat between his wife and his mother. "I'm sorry, Naya," he said sympathetically. "I'm afraid you've been wasting your time with these horses. Best to let it go."

"Nonsense," objected Awija. "She can't just let it go! She must honor the vision. She has to capture the filly."

"What would she do with the filly once she's caught her," asked Potis, "assuming she manages it?"

"Gentle her like we do with the calves," Naya replied promptly.

She'd had plenty of time to think about this while sitting and watching the herd. They were very social, even affectionate creatures, always staying close to one another, grooming each other's hard-to-reach places with their strong teeth and standing nose to tail so that they could swish flies away from their companions' faces. As with the offspring of the clan's small herd of cattle, Naya thought that if she could spend time one-on-one with the filly, handling her, scratching and petting her, bringing her handfuls of wild grass seeds or pine nuts, she would be able to make friends with the young horse, which would make it much easier to get a rope around her. Now, she'd add another step to her plan. Once the filly had grown up a bit, Naya would climb on her back, just like that, and they'd be able to fly together across the steppe.

"And what use would that be?" her father pressed, as if reading her thoughts. "Even Amu has a job to do. You can't just keep a creature of that size around for fun."

"It's not clear she would want to stay," added her mother. "As you've seen, the horses are very attached to one another. They remain together with their families. If you succeed in catching her and taking her away, she will always want to return. It's true of all wild things."

Naya knew her mother meant to remind her of the rest of the story she'd told her about her father and the pet fox he'd had as a boy. Her father had loved the fox, but the fox had not loved the boy enough to overcome her wild instincts. She had escaped from her cage one night and tried to return to her own kind but been caught instead by the boy's own dog. It was a tragic end.

"Are you sure you want to do this thing?" Sata asked, "Would you keep her tied up, a prisoner?"

Before Naya could answer, she heard her grandfather attempting once more to speak. "You must try to tame the whole herd," he declared in a voice so cracked that Naya wasn't sure she'd heard him correctly.

Apparently her father wasn't sure he'd heard correctly either. "Tame the whole herd?" Potis repeated, sounding incredulous.

"Tame the whole herd," reiterated Awija with a nod of approval. Naya saw her grandmother give her grandfather an acknowledging smile.

Awos coughed painfully, trying to take a deep breath. Evidently, what he had to say was important.

"When I was young," he began, palms spread open on his knees, "the herds were large, larger than they are now. We might want to believe the steppe will always be full of horses, deer, bison, antelope… but it's not true. In my father's day, the game was much more plentiful and in his father's day, still more abundant, and in his father's day, still more so. The winters were not so harsh, nor the summers so hot and dry and the people, especially the farming folk with their towns and fields cleared for crops, were not so numerous."

"This is why our cattle, sheep and goats are so important now," he went on, curling one hand into a fist and shaking it for emphasis. "We must continue to grow our own herds so that we will have enough to eat when the wild herds disappear, as well as being able to supply the priests with the necessary animals for sacrifice." Both palms upturned once more, he gestured toward Naya. "Our people have lived for as long as the oldest among us can remember by hunting the wild horses. Perhaps now it is time to tame them, so that they can be more like our cattle, our sheep, and our goats. Perhaps this is the meaning of my granddaughter's vision."

Naya shrank back, intimidated by her grandfather's words. Her grandmother, however, picked up the thread of Awos's thought.

"Before you came in tonight," she said to Potis, "Naya was recalling the old tale of how *Wakka* came to live with the people. Why couldn't it be the same with the horses? We could raise them for meat, instead of having to ambush them or round them up in traps. They can survive on poorer forage and fend for themselves much better during the winter than the cattle. Herding tame horses would be less work than hunting and more predictable, not to mention providing a steady source of hides, bones, and sinews – everything that we use already. And the priests would value having horses readily available to sacrifice for the rites and celebrations."

"But like I said before," Naya broke in. "*Ekwos* was much cleverer. She didn't need the people to survive."

"That's just your grandfather's point, my dear," returned her grandmother, "perhaps the horses need us more than they realize. There are no wild horses where I grew up and there were none in my mother's day or in her mother's day. They were all hunted down or disappeared into the grasslands. My people had their crops and their cows. We even had pigs. We didn't need the horses, and they didn't need us." Awija chuckled, prompting Naya to recall a particularly amusing story her grandmother had once told her about a certain querulous pig.

"It's different on the steppe," she continued. "There is nowhere else for the horses to go and even here, as your grandfather points out, they are beginning to diminish." Naya watched as her grandmother laid a gnarled hand on her grandfather's knee. "If he is right," she said, "and all the tribes continue hunting, someday there might be none left."

"But the horses don't know that!" protested Naya. "How could they?"

"Naya is right," agreed her father. "Why would any particular band of horses decide it was a good idea to let us tame them?"

"Well, perhaps this group of horses realizes they may need us," countered her mother. "Or at least they've been smart enough to recognize that Naya isn't a threat, and curious enough to allow her to join the herd. They may even have figured out that with her and Amu around they are less vulnerable to predators. Perhaps this is why they've stayed so close to the settlement."

For several long moments no one said anything. Then, as if her parents and grandparents had all arrived at some kind of mutual consensus, Naya felt their combined attention directed at her.

"What?" she responded defensively.

"You must find a way to tame the whole herd," declared Awos again, speaking directly to Naya but then widening his gaze to include the others in the tent. "This is my granddaughter's task. You must help her but you cannot do it for her."

"What about you, grandfather? You'll help me too, won't you?" Sensing something in the old man's tone, Naya felt suddenly anxious.

"As I can, my child," he replied, "but the task is yours. And none of the rest of the clan must know, at least not yet. There is no one with the heart for it but you."

Puzzled by these words, Naya would have asked her grandfather what he meant but his raised hand deterred her.

"I am weary," he rasped. "No more talk tonight."

"It is getting late," concurred Potis. "I have to return to the central fire to finalize preparations for leaving tomorrow. We'll finish discussing this later." He stood and made his way to the tent's entrance. Stooping, he pushed aside the flap and disappeared into the darkness outside.

"Best get to bed," said Sata, rising to begin the ritual of rearranging the dwelling for sleep. "Tomorrow will be a big day."

"But Mama," protested Naya, moving to help her mother pull out the bedrolls. "How am I going to make sure the horses follow us?"

"No more talk," repeated Awos from the darkened corner to which he had retreated for the night. "You can decide what to do tomorrow."

Receiving a look from her mother that said 'obey your grandfather,' Naya allowed herself to be kissed lightly on the forehead before retiring to her own sleeping mat. Curled under the softness of her sheepskin blanket and with Amu pressed against her back, she tried, without success, to fall asleep.

Chapter Four

The next morning dawned crisp, cold and fair, with a strong wind from the west. By the time the sun cleared the eastern horizon, the sky, an arc of brilliant blue, seemed as endless as the grassy plain stretching in all directions from the small cluster of tents. The settlement was soon alive with activity, young and old hurrying to accomplish final preparations for the clan's winter migration.

Rising at first light, along with everyone else, Naya attempted to be helpful to her parents and grandparents, as well as her aunt and uncle and their families, while also trying not to cross paths with other relatives whom she preferred to avoid. In particular, she steered clear of her great uncle Bhlaghmn, the clan's senior priest, and his wife Uksor, who always seemed disapproving toward her, even when she hadn't done anything wrong. Likewise, she stayed away from Bhlaghmn's nephew Korniks, the clan's younger priest, who evidently shared his uncle and aunt's poor opinion of her.

She also tried to stay away from her father's cousin, Skelos, who she could see directing the reloading of one of the sleds, apparently not packed to his satisfaction. Even from a distance, Naya could tell from his gestures that he was in a foul temper.

Skelos's older brother, Bhermi, had been her father's best friend since boyhood and Naya could remember asking her mother as a small child why Skelos seemed so unpleasant when Bhermi was always nice to her. Sata had explained that Skelos grew up resenting Potis for stealing his brother Bhermi's attention and affection. Unfortunately, the tragedy of Bhermi's untimely death two years previously, following the attack by the bear whose tooth Naya wore on a thong tied around her neck, rather than providing an opportunity for reconciliation, had only aggravated

Skelos's hostility toward Potis, as well as toward Naya herself. He made no secret of the fact that he blamed Potis for Bhermi's demise, contending the whole episode was Potis's fault. Skelos himself bore a vicious scar across his left cheek, where the beast's claws had a raked a deep furrow. As he declared afterward to anyone who would listen, if Potis had not permitted Naya to accompany them on the hunting expedition, they never would have encountered the She-Bear in the first place. *With that red hair and those blue eyes, the ill-favored girl is bad luck,* he insisted. Claiming Naya's cry of warning had only served to enrage the bear, he railed that if she'd held her tongue, his brother might have had a chance to escape.

Devastated by his best friend's savage end, Potis ignored Skelos's accusations as well as he could and advised Naya to do the same, while at the same time doing his best to help support Bhermi's widow, now responsible for raising four children without their father. As for Skelos, he had for many years been without a wife, having married the younger daughter of the chief of another tribe who had the misfortune to die in childbirth. The son she'd left behind, now a boy of fifteen summers, was named Krnos. Naya could see him, a younger version of his father, berating a smaller boy for incorrectly harnessing one of the dogs. He was the bane of Naya's existence and she did her best to avoid him as well.

Freed for the moment from undertaking any additional tasks, now that her family's tent had been taken down, Naya watched as the remainder of the encampment was similarly dismantled. Hide coverings, flapping vigorously in the wind, were removed and carefully folded into bundles as the long poles over which they'd been stretched were transformed into sleds, some to be pulled by the biggest and strongest of the clan's dogs and a few of the more cooperative goats, the rest by the people themselves. Belongings, including clothing, blankets, cooking utensils, and various other implements, were packed into baskets or tied into additional bundles and either loaded onto the sleds or strapped onto backs. Everyone except the very youngest of the children was expected to carry something. Even some of the more docile cattle were fitted with baskets held together by leather straps and carefully balanced on either side of the animal's back but this was a risky venture, as even the most good-natured among them were occasionally prone to running off without regard to their loads. Last year someone had tried hitching one of the younger bullocks to a sled but this had ended disastrously when the outraged creature's frenzied attempts to escape resulted in the destruction of two tent poles. Luckily the bullock emerged unscathed.

Migrating out to the steppe at the beginning of each summer season, in search of fresh pastures for the cattle, was a relatively new practice, begun by Awos and his brothers when they were young men. By the end of winter, fodder for their growing herds became scarce in the vicinity of the clan's settlement near the great river. At first they experimented with sending herders out on their own with the livestock for the summer, but this proved too risky. Without a full complement of warriors to defend the herds, the clan lost many cattle, and even some sheep and goats, to raiders from other tribes. Eventually, Awos convinced the others that the advantages of moving the entire clan to a summer encampment at some distance from the settlement outweighed the obvious inconveniences. Their traditional winter pastures would have an opportunity to regenerate and the men, women and children of the clan would remain together. Thus had begun the semi-annual trek.

Not everyone favored the practice, however, even after many seasons. One of Potis's tasks, now that he'd taken over from Awos as clan chief, was to placate the complainers. While he had done his best to keep the grumbling from getting out of hand, his efforts were being sabotaged by those hoping to undermine his newly bestowed authority. Naya understood enough from listening to her parents discuss the matter to know that her father would be glad when this year's migration was behind them.

At last, when everything had been packed and loaded, Naya heard her father give a call which brought everyone in the group to attention. Bhlaghmn, draped in his ceremonial raven-feather robe and matching conical headdress, stepped forward to address the milling confusion of people, dogs, and livestock. Korniks, also wearing a ceremonial robe, his made of owl feathers, stood by his uncle's side, holding a finely made pottery bowl in which burned a large bundle of fragrant dried herbs. Standing beside her grandmother, Naya watched as the senior priest, gesturing for silence, grasped the bundle in one hand and held it aloft like a torch. Then, waving it from side to side so that the strong breeze could carry the aromatic smoke over the heads of humans and animals alike, he recited the traditional journey blessing.

"*Dyēus-Ptēr,*" he intoned, "all powerful Sky-Father, thou who commands the heavens above as well as everything upon which the sun shines and the rain falls, grant us safe passage to our winter resting place." Circling the group, he stopped at four of the sacred directions, south, west, north and east, and repeated the words of supplication, flourishing the smoldering bundle each time for emphasis. Korniks shadowed the older priest, ready with the pottery bowl to catch any ash that might fall. At last, when they had completed the circuit, Bhlaghmn joined Potis, who bowed his head in acknowledgement of the older man's priestly authority. Then, lifting his gaze to encompass the entire assembly and squaring his shoulders, he opened his mouth to give the command that would set them on their way. Before he could speak the words, however, Awija standing to his left, interrupted.

"*Dukos*," Naya heard her grandmother murmur. The old woman had used her son's formal title. It meant leader and was accorded only to the clan chief. Awija's voice was pitched low enough that only Potis, with Naya standing next to him, could hear her. "*Dhéghōm*." Awija did not need to add more for her meaning to be abundantly clear. The priests might neglect to ask the blessing of the Great Goddess on the clan's journey but her son must not. Seeing her father's consternation, Naya wondered how her grandmother expected him to intercede in such matters without shaming his uncle, the priest. Just then her mother, who must have guessed the difficulty, stepped forward. Turning to face the entire group, Sata spoke in a voice at once loud enough for all to hear and at the same time deferential.

"*Dukos*," she said, echoing Awija's use of Potis's title. "*Sakrodhots*," she added, nodding respectfully to Bhlaghmn and using his official title as well. "On behalf of myself and the other women, may I ask for an additional blessing? Will you petition Earth-Mother for us?"

"Of course," Bhlaghmn replied, not quite succeeding in hiding his disdain. With a smile that did not reach his deep-set dark eyes, the senior priest turned to face east, the direction they would be traveling, and with his back to the group, spread his arms, palms upraised, in a gesture meant to encompass all they might encounter on the journey ahead. "May *Dhéghōm*, Earth Mother, welcome our feet as we travel her paths and grant us abundance along the way."

Naya saw her father glance at her grandmother, checking to see if Awija was satisfied. There was not much honor in such a blessing, Naya thought, but perhaps it was better than nothing. Indeed, her grandmother looked as though she would have liked to roll her eyes but she settled for an almost imperceptible lift of one brow and with that, the clan was at last ready to set out.

"*Leito!*" commanded Potis in a loud voice, giving the signal to go. In response, a ripple of coordinated movement began to spread through the group. Potis and his brother Tausos, with weapons slung at their sides, led the procession, followed by loosely organized family groups, each pulling or carrying their own possessions.

Further back, the clan's cattle, sheep and goats, who had been milling about in some confusion, began to bellow and bleat as they were prompted into some semblance of purposeful forward motion. Several of the older children, as well as the dogs not burdened by sleds, worked together to channel the animals in the desired direction. The secret was knowing which individual, generally an older female, the rest of the herd or flock would follow. By guiding the matriarch, the others could be persuaded to come along as well, as long as the total size of the group was not too large. Unfortunately, the herders always faced the danger of an unexpected stampede scattering the animals. To prevent this, Potis assigned four young men to act as scouts, traveling at a distance surrounding the main group to give advance warning of anything that might frighten the livestock so that all could be quickly tethered.

Earlier in the morning, when Naya, her parents and her grandparents had discussed in hushed voices how the horses might be induced to follow once the clan had gotten underway, Naya had suggested joining the scouts so that she would have an excuse to keep an eye on the herd, but her father had refused on the grounds that allowing such a thing would arouse too much notice. Despite using every argument she could muster, Naya eventually had to acquiesce to his insistence that she stay with the main body of the caravan. They couldn't risk drawing attention to the little band of horses. Awija's counsel to have faith and trust that the herd would follow at a safe distance had done little to reassure Naya. Now, as the clan finally set-off, she had no choice but to take up her assigned place beside her mother, trudging along in mutinous silence with Amu at her heels, pulling a sled.

In this fashion, the clan would spend the next moon cycle traveling along a course taking them eastward, across two tributaries of the *Dān*, before bringing them to the sheltering bluffs beside the great river *Rā*, where they and their animals could hope to more safely endure the harsh conditions of winter. Then, when the weather warmed and the land turned green again, they would venture back out into the more open grasslands of the steppe, completing once more the annual cycle of the seasons.

By mid-day when they stopped for water and food, the clan had covered a good distance, despite a pace dictated by the slowest among them. The sun-filled skies helped. With dry paths, the going was relatively easy. Although a cold wind still blew steadily, it came from the west, which meant it was at their backs, pushing them along. Naya and her mother had just set down their packs and begun to search for the dried meat and seed cakes that would provide the family's meal when Potis joined them, his expression tense. Setting down his heavy pack and then crouching so that his broad back shielded their conversation from view, he spoke in a low voice.

"They've been spotted," he said without preliminary.

"The horses?" Naya heard her mother ask quietly, worry creasing her forehead.

"Yes," came her father's terse reply.

"They're following us?!" Naya, barely able to contain her excitement, tried to whisper as Potis glared warningly at her.

"Yes," he replied again, obviously displeased.

"What should we do?" Sata sounded equally troubled by the news that the herd had been sighted by the scouts.

"Krnos is the one who saw them," Potis continued. "Following to our rear. He says they're not too far off. Five adults, three foals and a two-year-old of an unusual red color. There's no doubt it's them. There's talk of sending a small hunting party out for the filly. As I predicted, the priests want to offer her as a sacrifice to bless the journey. They're saying Krnos spotting her is a sign from the gods."

All the color drained from Naya's face as she heard her father's words, then rushed back, her flushed skin nearly as red as her hair.

"They can't!" she exclaimed angrily. "I won't let them." Rising to her feet, she would have taken off running, had her father not caught her wrist in a restraining grip and yanked her back down beside him.

"Just hold on," Potis growled. "No one is going after the filly without my permission." Naya stopped trying to pull out of her father's grasp and glared at him instead, eyes flashing a mixture of rage and panic. She felt like a trapped animal herself.

"What should we do?" asked Sata again, her voice still low but holding more than a hint of urgency.

"I'm going to argue against a hunt," replied Potis. "We're late getting started as it is and we need to cover ground while the weather holds. Surely the gods will understand."

"That might work for a few days," conceded Sata, "but sooner or later, you'll run out of excuses. Then what?"

"It would be better if the foolish animals weren't following us so closely," complained Potis.

"Perhaps after a day or two they'll move further off," responded Sata. "but still keep up."

"And they're not foolish," added Naya, resuming her unsuccessful attempt to liberate herself from her father's grip on her wrist.

"It's too much of coincidence," continued Potis, ignoring Naya's efforts to escape. "They've been around the settlement for two moons and now they've decided to head east, just when we set off?"

"Then you admit there is something special about this herd?" Sata lifted one eyebrow.

It was a look Naya recognized. Her father responded with the merest concessionary nod. Apparently, even after everything Naya had told them, and the support of her grandmother and grandfather, her father had never really expected the horses to come along when they set-out on their winter migration, and yet they had.

"Of course they're special," she interjected, at last wrenching her wrist free. "Papa, we have to find a way to protect them. Can't you convince the rest of the clan not to go after them?"

"Not without a lot of explaining," Potis replied. "What would I tell them? Until we have some sort of proof that the horses can be tamed, at best they are going to be seen as prey, just as always."

They were all silent for several moments. At last, Sata spoke. "You're going to have to let her join the scouts," she said, placing a hand on Potis's muscled forearm. "It's the only way for Naya to be able to keep an eye on the herd without the rest of the clan finding out about them. Post her in Krnos's place at the back and hope the other scouts are too busy elsewhere. Maybe she'll actually be able to capture the filly somewhere along the way and then we can make a more plausible argument for taming the whole herd."

Naya looked beseechingly at her father, hoping he would see the logic in her mother's argument. For a long moment Potis returned Sata's gaze, then gave a heavy sigh of resignation and rose to his feet.

"I'll arrange it," he said. "But we need to get underway again without delay. We've already gotten a late start and a lot could happen along the way – those horses are the least of my worries. Make sure they don't get you into trouble."

"Yes Papa," Naya replied, trying to sound obedient despite wanting to burst with excitement.

"Put one of the other dogs in Amu's place with the sled and take him with you," Potis went on, continuing to issue instructions. "Take up your position to the rear, keeping us in sight. Don't forget your main job is to watch for anything that might threaten the flocks." Naya nodded, barely listening. "Make sure you have your knife," her father concluded sternly. "And your rope," he added, almost as an afterthought.

"Yes, Papa." Naya said again, bowing her head to hide her triumphant grin. She would have set off immediately, had not her mother put out a hand to stop her.

"Don't forget to eat," said Sata, assembling a bundle containing dried meat, seed cakes and a couple of last season's apples in a small bag that Naya could sling over her shoulder. "And take this to your grandparents before you go," she added, handing her two bowls of roasted nuts and seeds, moistened with goat's milk. The dried meat was too tough for old teeth to chew. "And this for the horses." Sata filled another small skin sack, this one with a mixture of wild grains. The latter represented a precious commodity at this time of year. The stores they had now must last until the next harvest. Naya looked questioningly at her mother, not sure about taking such a valuable gift, but Sata smiled as she tucked the small pouch into her daughter's belt. "For the horses," she repeated.

Freeing Amu from the sled and harnessing another of the clan's dogs in his place, then shouldering her pack and the sack with her meal, Naya set off to find her grandparents. They were near the back of the group, having taken refuge in the scant shade of a lone wind-ravaged tree. Awos looked exhausted but Naya hardly noticed, in her excitement to find the horses. She told him and Awija what had happened, the words tumbling out so fast they had to ask her slow down and start again. As soon as she'd finished, she would have turned to go, but her grandmother stopped her.

"Say goodbye to your grandfather," she said, her voice serious. Suddenly ashamed of her lack of courtesy, Naya complied, putting down her pack and coming to kneel in front of where the old man sat. Bowing her head, she waited a moment before looking up into his face. His clouded eyes did not meet hers. Instead, as though no longer perceiving the world around him, he gazed into a great distance.

"Child," he said at last, his voice no more than a thin thread. "You must see with the eyes of your heart."

"Yes, grandfather," Naya replied uncertainly. She looked at her grandmother, not sure what to make of the words but strangely aware that she had heard them before. Reaching out a hand as gnarled as the limbs of the ancient tree in whose shelter he rested, Awos placed it gently on Naya's head in a gesture of blessing but uttered nothing further. After a moment, the old man withdrew his hand and seemed to forget her presence. Looking again to her grandmother for guidance, Naya received a brief nod, giving her permission to rise.

"On your way now," Awija said encouragingly. "We'll see you when we stop again for the night."

Reaching for her pack and calling to Amu, Naya moved off with purpose, first skirting the straggling flocks and then setting a course slightly to the north of the direction from which the whole group had just come. Several members of the clan noted her departure, most with surprise, a few with gratified satisfaction. No one tried to stop her and she did not look back.

Despite Krnos's report of their proximity, it took Naya half the afternoon to find the horses. While only two ridges of the rolling steppe separated the herd from the path taken by the clan, the valleys between were wide and took considerable time to traverse. She also had to ford more than one of the winding streams that flowed east and south through the grasslands. *Could Krnos really have sighted the herd this far away?* Naya wondered. It seemed unlikely. After topping a rise, she identified them in the distance and stopped to watch.

Moving slowly, they travelled in a loosely formed band, with MeHnd leading the way. The other mares spread out behind her, their increasingly confident foals often straying a good distance from their mothers' sides, while BeHregs, the stallion, brought up the rear. Naya increased her pace, hurrying now to close the distance and soon she and Amu reached the top of another small rise just to the south and a little distance ahead of where the herd grazed. Despite the horses' apparent nonchalance, they had spotted the girl and the dog as soon as they appeared over the hill's edge, as Naya knew they would. Heads lifted and nostrils flaring to scent the unrelenting wind, the horses identified the now familiar figures. Reassured, heads dropped again in search of more grass.

All except one. Standing a little distance from her mother and closest to where the girl and her dog had appeared, the red filly continued to gaze in Naya's direction, watching with interest as she and Amu began to descend toward her. When they had come as close as Naya thought the filly would permit, she stopped.

"Amu, sit," she commanded.

Naya allowed her heavy pack, along with the thick coil of rope she carried, to slide to the ground next to the dog. Tempted to return the filly's intent gaze, she instead took a deep breath, exhaled and deliberately looked away, hoping to signal her benign intentions. Cautiously, she moved just far enough to distance herself from Amu and her pack while closing the gap between herself and the filly. Eyes downcast, she waited.

After what seemed like a long time, she heard the sound of dry grass crunching beneath sturdy hooves as the filly began to take a few tentative steps towards her. Still not looking up, Naya tried to control her excitement by focusing on her own breathing. After a moment the rustling stopped and, unable to help herself, she lifted her gaze. The filly stood in front of her, almost close enough to touch. Dark, liquid brown eyes regarded her with a mixture of interest and caution. Naya blinked. Drawing air into her lungs, she began to reach shyly in the filly's direction. The young horse stood still, waiting, until the girl's outstretched hand was just in front of her long nose. Taking half a step closer, she lowered her head and sniffed.

Remaining motionless, Naya felt the long stiff hairs of the filly's muzzle tickle against her skin, followed by the soft sensation of the horse's exhaled breath. In response, Naya released a long sigh of her own. She'd dreamed of this moment. Smiling now, with the filly still sniffing one hand, she moved the other in slow motion until her palm rested against the filly's shoulder. Her red-gold coat, consisting of a coarse top layer and softer undercoat, felt warm and alive beneath her hand. Naya curled her fingers into the shape of a comb and began to move her hand in a circular motion, cautiously at first and then quicker. Amu loved it when she rubbed the thick fur around his neck this way. Sure enough, the filly was soon leaning into the pressure and shifting positions, offering Naya access to all the itchy places she couldn't reach herself. Giggling, Naya began using both hands, until eventually all ten fingers were buried in the thick hair of the filly's rump as she vigorously scratched on either side of the long red-brown tail.

At the sound of the girl's laughter, the young horse turned her head to look back over her shoulder, ears pricked, but otherwise did not move.

"That sound means I'm happy," Naya explained. "You seem pretty happy too," she noted, continuing to speak out loud. "You like this, don't you?" As if in response, the filly pressed her hind end against the girl's hands, asking for more.

"Okay, okay," Naya acceded, unable to suppress her laughter.

Eventually, the filly had enough and Naya was able to stop scratching. Stepping back and looking ruefully at her hands, filthy with dust and oil from the filly's coat, she wiped them against her own hide tunic before turning to check on the rest of the herd. Although MeHnd, initially somewhat concerned about the goings-on between her offspring and the girl, had moved closer, she was not truly alarmed and soon drifted further off, continuing to lead the other horses in a meandering easterly passage along the wide valley. Naya and Réhda joined them, moving side by side and stopping frequently as the filly cropped grass while Naya stood close by, occasionally reaching out to stroke Réhda's burnished coat. At one point she remembered the small bag of grain in her belt and spilling some of the seeds into the palm of her hand, she offered them to the young horse. The filly delicately sniffed the grains, then plucked them with gentle lips from Naya's outstretched hand. Chewing and tasting, she looked for more. Enchanted, Naya fed her until the pouch at her waist was empty. Disappointed, the filly returned to grazing.

"Greedy!" Naya proclaimed, laughing yet again.

The rest of the herd seemed accepting of Naya's presence. As they strolled, she considered what to do about retrieving her heavy pack, along with the rope. Although not making rapid progress, they were still moving steadily away from where she'd left her things on the ground, with Amu under strict instructions to guard them. As the distance between her and the dog increased, Naya knew he would grow agitated and she didn't want him to come running after her and scare the horses, not after the wonderful thing that had happened today. She was actually able to touch the filly! Not only that, she'd fed her from her own hand! Heart swelling in her chest, Naya turned again to stroke the young horse's firmly muscled back, imagining the day when she would climb on and ride.

Just then, the filly's head came up. Seeing all the horses' attention focused on the ridgeline opposite them to the northeast, Naya turned to look. She could clearly distinguish three shapes moving along the top of the rise, outlined against the horizon by the sun beginning to lower in the west. Strangers, she thought, before realizing they were moving in the same general direction as her clan, probably heading for the river crossing that marked the aim of the first leg of their journey. Able to travel more swiftly, they would soon catch up to the procession. She must give warning without being intercepted.

Crouching in the tall grass next to the filly, Naya tried to think what to do. Somehow, she must get back to where she'd left her pack, secure Amu to prevent him from chasing the strangers, and then circle away to the south without being spotted. Once back on the main path, she and the dog could run fast enough to outdistance the three travelers, arriving back in time to alert the clan of their approach. The horses showed signs of increased agitation and seemed inclined to reverse course, moving away from the figures on the ridge. If she stayed in amongst them, and with the sun shining in the strangers' eyes, she had some chance of remaining undetected while making her way to where she'd left Amu and her things. Her dun-colored clothing blended with the grasses and with the horses themselves. If she remained beside the filly, her red hair might not even give her away. Could she encourage the herd to head back in the direction they'd come? She'd have to be careful not to stampede them. She would also need to make sure Amu did not break cover before she could get back to him.

Naya felt a commotion coming from the opposite side of the herd and had to risk standing in order to see what was happening. Dismayed, she realized the dog had circled around the horses to the north and was now running past the herd toward the strangers. Amu began to bark furiously. Watching in increasing horror, Naya saw the smallest figure lift a spear, aiming directly at the swiftly approaching form. She stifled a cry. She must not draw their attention. Behind where she stood with the red filly, the other horses had gathered, all eyes and ears turned in the direction of the drama unfolding on the hillside beyond. Just then, another of the strangers, in one beautifully fluid motion, brought up his bow, arrow already nocked, and let fly.

Time ceased as the arrow traced a graceful arc through the air. Naya had an eon to admire the practiced skill of the bowman's movements. She had an epoch to scream, in a voice so piercing that it rent the valley air. She had an age to step in front of the red filly, before turning her back and urging the herd to flee. She did not have time to elude the arrow's path. With searing fire, its sharply napped obsidian point penetrated skin and muscle under her right shoulder blade, coming to rest between her ribs, its tip just breaching the delicate tissue of her lung. Any more force, and the arrow would have pierced her heart. As it was, the impact knocked her to the ground, where she lay, silent now, and motionless in the tall grass.

Startled by Naya's scream and sudden collapse, the horses turned to run, all except the red filly. With her soft muzzle, she tried to rouse the prostrate form at her feet. Only BeHreg's frenzied nipping at her hindquarters convinced the young horse to leave the girl's side. In a moment, the whole herd had disappeared.

Chapter Five

Oyuun, the oldest of the three strangers, watched the gray shape charging toward them. His youngest son Dayan had drawn back his right arm and was about to hurl his long-shafted spear.

"Stop," Oyuun commanded.

Startled but obedient, Dayan lowered his weapon and looked questioningly at his father.

"It's a dog, not a wolf. Wolves don't bark." The words were terse. "Stand your ground but don't try to harm him," he instructed. The animal came skidding to a halt in front of them. Hackles raised and teeth bared, he growled menacingly but did not attack.

"Sit," ordered Oyuun. There was no mistaking his meaning or his authority. The dog didn't sit, but he stopped growling and lowered his tail.

Keeping his attention on the dog, Oyuun addressed his other son. Aytal, a young man of sixteen summers, still held his empty bow loosely in his left hand.

"You hit something but I don't think it was one of the horses. Maybe a lion from the sound of that scream, but the horses weren't acting like there was a big cat in their midst. And it doesn't explain why the dog is here. Let's go investigate."

Dayan, a boy of only nine summers, continued to eye the wolf-like animal with considerable distrust.

"Don't act afraid of him. He will sense your fear and know he can intimidate you. Keep your spear handy and come along." Oyuun began to descend the grassy slope into the shallow valley. Both Dayan and Aytal followed. The dog stood watching for a moment, then following the path traced by the arrow's flight, he streaked past Oyuun and his sons.

Aytal, eager to see what his shot had brought down, caught up to the dog first. He stopped abruptly at the sight before him. A girl lay where she had fallen, face down in the grass, red hair spread like a pool of fire around her head and neck, his distinctive double-fletched arrow protruding rigidly from her back. The dog crouched at the girl's side, licking her pale face. At Aytal's approach, he turned protectively and growled.

"What is it?" asked Dayan excitedly as he gained his stepbrother's side. He too stared in stunned silence. Moments later their father joined them. Assessing the scene, Oyuun spoke rapidly as he knelt and began to rummage in his pack.

"Get this around the dog's neck and stake him far enough away that he can't interfere," he said, handing a rawhide lasso to Dayan. Swallowing hard, the boy moved to comply but hesitated when the dog, snarling, threatened to lunge at his approach.

"Give it to me." As if coming back to life, Aytal grabbed the rope from his stepbrother and in one smooth motion, tossed the noose over the dog's head and pulled back. Caught, the dog struggled, refusing to be dragged away from the girl's side.

"No," reprimanded Oyuun in a stern voice. "Go," he said, pointing to a spot a good distance away.

Reluctantly, the dog allowed himself to be dragged off. Taking another of his arrows from the quiver at his side and reinforcing its slender shaft with the short, thick handle of his hunting knife, Aytal drove both points through the matted grass into the hard earth of the steppe. He lashed his end of the rope to the makeshift stake, and satisfied the dog was secured, tried speaking words of reassurance. Whining and straining against the rope, the distraught animal ignored him. Aytal returned to his father's side.

"We dare not remove the arrow right away," Oyuun said without looking up. He sat on his haunches, studying the body before him. "It's gone in too deep. But we need to turn her over." Lifting his eyes, he addressed his younger son. "Get me the saw-blade knife so that I can cut down the shaft." Wanting to be useful, the boy obediently began to search through his father's pack. Turning to his first-born, Oyuun spoke in a somber tone too low for the younger boy to hear.

"You have done wrong, my son. Your skill is a gift from the gods but without honor it is a curse. You wield the power of death. Humility, not pride, must govern its use. You should have learned this lesson by now, yet again you have been reckless. Again, you have shot without being certain of your target, knowing your arrow would find its mark. And this time, it is this girl who has paid the price."

"Did I kill her?" Aytal's anguished voice was barely above a whisper.

"We won't know until we turn her over."

Returning with the knife, Dayan handed it to his father. Holding the arrow's slim shaft steady in one hand, Oyuun began to saw delicately, taking care not to risk driving the deadly tip deeper into the girl's vulnerable tissues. Within moments he was able to create a clean break, leaving a hand's breadth sticking up just above where the shaft pierced the tanned hide of the girl's garment.

"Aytal," he said. "You and I are going to turn her over but once we do, you must be behind her so that you can hold her in a sitting position. There must be no pressure on the arrow. Do you understand?"

Nodding, the young man moved next to his father and together, grasping the girl's body by shoulder and hip, they gently rolled her over into a semi-reclining position. Shifting awkwardly beneath the girl's weight, Aytal moved so that he could sit with her lower body laying across his lap and support her shoulders diagonally against his chest, leaving the stump of the arrow extending beneath his right arm. He gained an unobstructed view of the girl's face, now resting against his shoulder. Oyuun noted his son's stunned reaction.

"By all the gods," Aytal exclaimed, unable to help himself. "She's going to be beautiful!"

Eyes closed, cheeks streaked with dirt, lips bloodless except for a crimson trickle escaping from the corner of her mouth, the girl nonetheless took Aytal's breath away. She looked unlike anyone he'd ever seen. A riot of flaming hair framed an oval face with a high forehead, cheekbones starting to emerge from the undefined curve of childhood and the promise of a strong jaw. An aquiline nose beginning to acquire its adult shape sat above a wide mouth naturally upturned at the corners. Straight russet brows slanted over long, reddish lashes that lay against skin gone unnaturally pale. There was no sign of life.

"She's not going to be anything but dead if we don't do something to help her," replied Oyuun grimly. "Can you tell if she's still breathing?"

Aytal held his open hand near the girl's mouth and nose and paused, concentrating. He thought he could detect the merest whisper of breath stirring against his palm. Perhaps a pulse beat faintly beneath the exposed skin of her neck, just beside the bear's tooth nestled in the hollow of her throat.

"Breathe into her mouth," his father commanded.

"What?!" Aytal wasn't sure he'd heard correctly.

"Breathe into her mouth," Oyuun repeated. "She's not getting enough air on her own. Breathe for her."

Looking at his father with some skepticism, Aytal bent his head slightly, bringing his face close to the girl's. Filling his lungs, he began tentatively to lower his head the rest of the way when Oyuun stopped him.

"No, no! You have to open her mouth first. Like this." Grasping the girl's chin firmly in one hand, he gave a slight tug. "There," he said. "Now blow."

Aytal found it surprisingly difficult to force air into the girl's lungs, one of which had partially collapsed where his arrow had penetrated. If he blew too hard, his breath simply escaped through her nose without doing any good. If he blew too gently, nothing happened either.

"Pinch her nose," Oyuun instructed.

Aytal reached awkwardly around with his free hand to pinch off the girl's nostrils and was gratified to see her chest begin to rise and fall in rhythm with his efforts.

"Keep at it until you're sure she is breathing well on her own," his father ordered. "Dayan and I will take the dog and look for her people. She's most likely part of the clan of herders we spotted heading east on the trail earlier today and decided to avoid. If they continued in the direction they were headed, the river crossing will have slowed them, especially with all the livestock. They can't be too far away."

Pinned where he sat with the girl's full weight resting in his lap, Aytal watched as his father untied the dog and began tugging him toward a distant line of trees marking one of the many waterways that bisected the well-traveled route the girl's people were following. The dog fought to stay behind, but eventually had to acquiesce to Oyuun's obdurate determination to make him come along.

"Why are we bringing him?" Aytal heard Dayan ask as they set off.

"This dog is our assurance," Oyuun replied over his shoulder, "With him, the girl's family is more likely to believe our story of what happened. They might not risk coming to look for her on our word alone, but they will follow the dog when he leads them back to her. Now hurry, we haven't much time."

Aytal knew his stepbrother would have to jog to keep up with their father's long strides. In a moment the two were out of earshot, leaving Aytal with the unconscious girl in his arms, surrounded by the vastness of the seemingly empty steppe. He didn't see the lone sentinel, laying prone atop the ridge, observation post well-hidden by boulders. Neither Oyuun nor Dayan noticed either, even as the figure rose in a half-crouch and turning, slipped down the far side of the ridge, in a hurry to reach the river before they did.

Night had fallen by the time Oyuun spotted the cooking fires of the clan's makeshift camp along the river's west bank. No doubt the girl's people planned to wait until morning to make the crossing, he thought. They'd delay until after animals and humans alike had rested. In addition, the girl's absence must have aroused concern by now and they would wait to find out what had happened to her before fording the river.

The clan's dogs were the first to come out to meet Oyuun and his son, setting up a warning din until they recognized the dog Oyuun held on a tight tether. Confused to see one of their own in the company of people they didn't know, the pack ceased barking but held their ground. The alarm had been raised, however, and soon the young man on guard duty strode up, spear raised, to join the clan's dogs in confronting the new arrivals.

"Who are you?" he demanded. "What do you want?"

Maintaining his grip on the girl's dog with one hand, Oyuun held out the other to show he held no weapon and then indicated in the common sign language of the steppe that he intended no harm but had an urgent message for the clan's leader.

"Why do you have my cousin's dog," persisted the sentry, pointing.

Continuing with difficulty to restrain the increasingly agitated animal, Oyuun repeated his gestures with greater emphasis. He had an urgent message but he would only deliver it to the clan chief. "It's just the two of us," he added, indicating himself and Dayan. He hoped to reassure the guard but was also growing irritated at the delay. Every moment they wasted jeopardized the girl's life. Still suspicious, the young man swept his arm, palm uplifted, in the direction of the camp, indicating that the strangers should proceed ahead of him. He followed a pace behind, spear aimed pointedly at their backs.

The girl's dog, anxious to find help, nearly dragged Oyuun to one of the larger fires, around which several people were gathered, some standing at the periphery, the rest seated closer to its warmth. Those at the center appeared to be engaged in a heated discussion but at their approach a surprised silence fell, followed almost immediately by a clamor of excited voices. A word from the sentry and the circle parted. As Oyuun and the dog stepped into the light, the man who had last been speaking took one look at the frantic animal and rose to his feet, worry and anger emanating from him in palpable waves.

"Where is she?" he demanded without preliminary.

Oyuun turned to his escort, asking for confirmation that he was being addressed by the clan's leader. The young man nodded.

"Where is she?" repeated the chief, his tone becoming menacing. Not receiving an immediate response, he gestured emphatically. "Where is my daughter?"

The chief's meaning now clear, Oyuun realized the situation was even worse than he'd imagined. "Hurt," he signed, after releasing his hold on the girl's dog. "Alive," he added, trying to express reassurance. "You must come with me now."

"Who are you?" inquired another man who had also risen. By the look of him, Oyuun surmised he must be the clan chief's brother. "And who is this?" the man asked, gesturing toward the boy beside him.

"My son," Oyuun signed. "We are travelers from the north. We seek trade with the mountain dwellers who work the black stone."

"Where is my daughter?" The clan chief growled through clenched teeth, his voice communicating as clearly as his hands. The dog, who had gained his side, cringed at the tone but then, gathering courage, gave three staccato barks.

"We brought the dog so you would believe us," signed Oyuun. "Come now, she is badly hurt."

"How far?" queried the clan chief.

"Back the way you have come. Two valleys over," indicated Oyuun. "Where the wild horses graze."

A woman had stepped into the circle to join the clan chief and his brother. At Oyuun's words she inhaled sharply but said nothing.

"The dog knows," continued Oyuun, not failing to note the woman's reaction. *She must be the girl's mother*, he thought. *She looks just like her.* "The dog knows," he signed again. "Follow him."

"You left her alone?" The woman did not bother to sign, instead speaking haltingly in Oyuun's own tongue and then repeating herself more fluently in a language he recognized as belonging to the people of the southern mountains. Both surprised and relieved, he turned to address her.

"No," he said, wondering how this tall, strikingly beautiful woman came to speak both his language and the language of the stone-carvers. "My older son is with her. We must go now. Is there a healer among you who can come?"

Before the woman could reply, another man came forward into the circle cast by the fire's glow. From his raven-feathered cloak, Oyuun guessed he must be the clan's priest. Although the flickering light distorted his features, making them hard to read, to Oyuun, the man's expression appeared not merely distrustful but hostile.

"Why should we believe you?" the priest asked, drawing himself to his full height and gesturing dismissively. "You could easily be laying a trap."

Deliberately shifting his attention back to the girl's mother, Oyuun spoke earnestly. "I swear by the gods this is no trap," he said, no longer signing. He used the language of the southern mountains, in which the woman seemed most fluent. "But she is badly injured and we must return to her as soon as possible."

"How is she injured?" asked the woman, concern evident in her voice.

"I'd rather you see for yourself," Oyuun responded.

"What does he say?" demand the clan chief, frustrated at no longer being able to follow the exchange.

The woman gave Oyuun a penetrating look before turning to her husband. "He says that we must go with him – now," she answered.

The man whom Oyuun believed to be the clan chief's brother touched the chief on the arm to get his attention. Turning his head so that his mouth was close to his brother's ear, he spoke in a rapid whisper, too low for Oyuun to hear even if he'd been able to understand the words. Without taking his eyes off the stranger, the clan chief listened, then nodded and said something to his wife.

Searching for the right words, the woman communicated to Oyuun in a mixture of his tongue and her own that she and her husband would come with him, while his son was to be welcomed into the home of the clan chief's brother.

Once he understood the woman's meaning, Oyuun started to object, but one look at her husband's grim expression convinced him of the futility of arguing. He would have done the same thing in the clan chief's place. In any case, they had delayed too long already.

"What about a healer?" he replied.

"I will do what I can for my daughter," the woman answered him. "I am not as skilled as my mother-in-law." Here she gestured toward an elderly woman who was seated a little distance away, with an old man next to her. "But she is not able to travel quickly. And she cannot leave her husband."

Oyuun understood at a glance what the woman had left unsaid. Although the old woman was evidently following all that was happening with keen interest, the old man had the absent look of one who would linger but a short time longer in this world. If Oyuun understood correctly, they were the clan chief's parents, which meant the old man was most likely the clan's former leader. His passing would be a momentous event. And if there was any dissension regarding the current chief's leadership, it would surface after his father's death. Moreover, they had clearly just set out on their winter migration. Not a good time for a family crisis.

"Come then," was all he said.

"We'll just get a few things to take with us," the woman replied, indicating to her husband with a thrust of her chin the direction in which their packs lay, unopened, on the ground. "Everything we might need is still packed."

Striding over to the bundles, the clan chief handed the smaller one to his wife and then, shouldering his own, addressed Oyuun.

"Tell your son he's to stay with this man." The clan chief motioned toward his brother, who gave Oyuun a narrow look before indicating with a curt gesture that Dayan was to come with him.

Laying a palm on his son's thin shoulder, Oyuun spoke to him reassuringly in their own language. Meanwhile, a woman whom he surmised must be married to the clan chief's brother emerged from the circle of onlookers. Giving the boy a smile much more encouraging than her husband's grim expression, she took his hand and began gently to tug him in the direction of one of the other fires. Oyuun watched as his son, looking back at him doubtfully, allowed himself to be led away.

Relieved that the people seemed at last to have grasped the seriousness of the situation and were prepared to follow him, the girl's dog gave three sharp barks before trotting a short way in the direction from which he and Oyuun had just come. Stopping to be certain they were behind him, he barked once more and then set off with purpose. The clan chief and his wife looked at each other and then turned to Oyuun.

"The dog knows," he gestured for the third time. "Follow him." The three set off at a brisk pace and were soon swallowed by the blackness of the night.

Well away from the circle of light cast by the central fire, two figures stood side by side and watched them go. Alike in posture and profile, they differed only in height and bulk.

"Were they the ones?" asked the taller of the two.

"Yes father," came the reply. "I saw the whole thing happen. The arrow travelled as though guided by the gods. If not, then the archer is more skilled than any man alive."

"I doubt either is the case," said the other. *Still*, he added to himself, *never scorn a bit of divine assistance.* A malicious smile curved upward to meet the deep scar that deformed his otherwise handsome face.

Chapter Six

Above the shallow valley a hawk circled, keen eyes hunting for movement. Other than the drying grasses swaying in the late afternoon breeze and the bird's own shadow skimming the earth, nothing stirred, not even the two humans the hawk had observed some time ago. Deciding to look elsewhere for her evening meal, the bird flapped her broad wings until she found a current of air to carry her toward the river, where she might have better luck.

Aytal, who had been watching the hawk, regretted the bird's departure. Alone except for the unconscious girl he held on his lap, he wondered how much longer he would have to wait before help arrived. He wasn't sure the girl was still alive. Maybe he should try breathing for her again, he thought. He wished his father would hurry. With the late autumn sun beginning to descend toward the western horizon, not much remained of the day. Darkness would make him feel even more isolated in the vastness of the empty steppe. He was thankful for what remained of the light.

Naya's world was already as black as a moonless night when even the stars had been extinguished. The black seemed to affect not only her ability to see, but all her other senses as well. She felt as if she were wrapped in a suffocating blanket through which no sound or light could penetrate. The blanket made it hard for her to breathe. She thought about struggling, trying to throw off the heavy blackness, but couldn't summon the energy. Instead, she thought it might be nice to go to sleep. Perhaps she should surrender to the dark. It promised comfort, if she would only relax and let it cradle her. Just as she thought she would let go, a sound penetrated the silence. As if from a great distance, she heard the musical notes of a voice she recognized.

Not yet, said the voice. *It's not time yet.*

Who are you? Naya thought.

You must see with the eyes of your heart and create ties without the use of a rope, said the voice. *And when you have succeeded in granting my heart's desire, then shall yours be granted also.*

I know you, thought the girl.

There is much yet for us both to know before this life has run its course, replied the voice. *If you would not stay for yourself, stay for me.*

But I can't see and it's hard to breathe. Blackness threatened to overwhelm her. *I'm thirsty.*

See with the eyes of your heart, urged the voice. *Breathe from the place that lies deep within, drink from the source of all life.*

I don't know how. Naya felt a sob rise in her throat, choking her.

I will teach you. The voice spoke reassuringly. *We will learn together.*

But it's hard. She felt so tired, too tired to cry, too tired to breathe, too tired to keep trying.

There will be others to help, if you let them. Learn to trust them, just as I have learned to trust you. Open your heart.

But I'm afraid. Never would she have admitted such a thought before.

Good, said the voice. *I am often afraid. But I am also brave, as are you. We will be afraid and brave together.*

Who are you? Naya asked again.

You will know me by as many names as we share lives together, replied the voice. *I am the friend of your heart. You may call me whatever you wish.*

How will I recognize you?

You've decided not to go, then?

I want to stay with you.

You first gazed upon me while looking into the fire of the setting sun. You first spoke with me while bathed in moonlight. You have recognized yourself in me. You will know me when you see me. Rest now. Help comes.

You won't leave me?

I'll be close by. Rest now.

Naya became aware again of the darkness surrounding her but she no longer felt quite so suffocated. For what felt like a long time she let herself float in the blackness, trying to gather strength. At last she made a determined effort to rouse herself. In that moment, she became aware of another voice, this one very close and most definitely male. A voice she didn't recognize.

Although speaking in a language she could not understand, the meaning was clear. He was pleading with her not to die. He also seemed to be trying to kiss her but she didn't have the strength to make him stop. It was all she could manage just to open her eyes. With great effort, she lifted heavy lids and tried to focus on the face only inches from hers. Eyes as shockingly blue as her own gazed back at her. Surprise, quickly followed by relief, registered in their depths.

"Leave me alone," was all she could manage to utter, the words coming out in a croak before she closed her eyes again and the blackness returned.

Gathering his wits, Aytal stared down at the girl in his arms. She'd opened her eyes, if only for the briefest of moments, and even tried to talk. She was still alive then, and evidently able to breathe on her own. And her eyes were blue. He'd never seen blue eyes before, except for his own, reflected in the wavering glimmer of shallow water. His father had tried to describe them to him, just as he tried to tell him other things about the mother he had never known. *Her eyes were blue, like yours,* his father would say, *clear like the sky in summer when she was happy and hard like ice when angered.* It was all he had left of her. There were no memories that were his own.

Keeping his gaze fixed on the girl, Aytal considered trying to shift into a slightly less uncomfortable position but he was terrified of inflicting further injury. No, he would remain as he was, although one of his legs was starting to feel as if hordes of tiny ants might be stinging him. Hopefully his father and stepbrother would be back soon. Until then, he would continue to remain as still as possible and plead for the girl's life.

He resumed his entreaty, silently now, begging the gods not to punish her because of his own pride. His father had been right to admonish him. Knowing his arrow would always find its mark, he had been reckless to release the bowstring without clear intent. All life was precious. To shoot impulsively was to disregard the sacred act of killing, which must always be done with reverence for the life sacrificed. Hadn't he had cause already to learn this lesson? Worse yet, to kill another human, except in self-defense, was to commit an almost unforgivable offense, at least among his people. If the girl had been a member of his own community, even if she lived, he would owe her an obligation for the rest of her days. If she died, he would have been exiled for the remainder of his own life. If an outsider were to commit such an act, the punishment might well be death, whether or not the victim survived. Would he face a similar fate at the hands of the girl's family? He knew his father had no choice but to go looking for them. He hoped fervently, for the girl's sake and his own, that she would live and that her people would show him mercy.

Looking up, Aytal saw the last of the sun's rays turn the scattered clouds on the western horizon into a blaze of orange and gold, surrounded by the deepening indigo of the evening sky. It would be dark soon, and cold. He wished they had thought to build a fire, but there had been no time. Gazing down at the girl's dirt-smeared face, he was struck again by her features. The structure of her bones, the shape of her brows, the curve of her lips all tugged at his insides, as though somehow he recognized her. The highlights in her hair caught and reflected the colors of the setting sun. And those eyes. Something shifted near the center of his being.

If she survives, he thought, watching the sun's rays drain away between the low line of hills to the west, *my life will be hers.* The declaration held an acknowledgement of the justice that likely awaited him, but also a solemn vow, spoken from the heart.

Just then, on the crest of a rise, he thought he could discern several shapes. He strained against the gathering dusk, willing himself to see what they were. When his distance vision proved insufficient, he softened his gaze as his father had taught him, calling on his other senses, including intuition, to aid his perception.

"Wolves," he muttered. The hair lifted on the back of his neck.

By the time the pack began to move off the hilltop, most of the light had left the western sky, making it too dim for Aytal to follow their progress. All he knew was that they seemed to be coming toward where he sat, only partially concealed by tall grass, with the injured girl in his lap. Before departing to find help, his father had uprooted his arrow and flint knife and handed them back to him. They now lay within easy reach, along with his pack, but this was small comfort. Certain that if he moved the girl, she would die, Aytal felt trapped. Heart beginning to speed up, breath quickening, he had to fight back the visceral urge to escape. As if in response to his own mounting fear, a shiver course through the girl's body, followed by another and another. She had begun to shake uncontrollably.

Supporting her weight with his right arm and holding his breath so as not to disturb her, Aytal reached his left hand into his pack and drew out a thin blanket of felted wool, light but surprisingly warm. His father had brought it back from his last trading expedition. He managed to spread it over both of them. With his right arm still wrapped around the girl's shoulders, he held her against his chest as tightly as he dared, willing the shivering to stop. With his free hand he grasped his knife, their only defense against the oncoming pack. Staring into the deepening darkness, he trained all his senses in the direction from which the wolves would come. All he could do now was to wait.

Sometime later, Aytal heard the rustle of dry grass, followed immediately by footsteps approaching from behind. Unable to turn around, he could tell the sounds were too heavy and noisy to be made by wolves. Oddly, he felt no sense of threat. Thinking perhaps his father had returned, he exhaled for what felt like the first time since he had sighted the pack. About to call out, he heard a soft snuffling noise coming from somewhere over his left shoulder. Maybe the girl's dog? Relief turned instantly to panic. The wolves must have snuck up from behind after all. He opened his mouth to call out when a shape much too large to be either a wolf or a dog emerged from the night, resolving itself into two upright ears and two luminous dark eyes set on either side of a broad forehead from which extended an extremely long nose.

"A horse!" Aytal inhaled in astonishment. Startled, the creature took two steps backward, before lowering its head and once more sniffing inquisitively.

"She is my friend," said a voice. It took Aytal a moment to realize the girl had spoken again. Although she still shivered slightly, her eyes were open and lucid from what he could tell in the dark. Equally remarkable, her expression reflected no fear of the wild animal who now gazed back at them from just a few steps away, seemingly just as unconcerned.

"She is my friend," the girl repeated, her voice weak but insistent. "Don't hurt her."

Aytal's anxiety began to recede. Although he didn't understand the girl's words, she spoke with such determination that he couldn't help but believe her spirit remained strong. Perhaps she would not die after all. His relief was short-lived, however, as crunching grass heralded the approach of several additional large animals. The rest of the herd? Would they be trampled where they sat? But no, the newcomers kept their distance. Aytal could detect several shapes, blacker than the surrounding darkness, some larger, some smaller. He counted five adults and four youngsters, including the one who had initially approached and still stood almost near enough to touch. The rest of the herd, haphazardly taking turns at snatching mouthfuls of grass, encircled them.

Just then, one of the horses, the stallion, lifted his head sharply and the others all came to attention. They must scent the wolves, thought Aytal. A palpable wave of alarm ran through the group. The hair on the back of Aytal's neck lifted in response and again he fought the impulse to flee. He could tell from the horses' nervous snorting that they wanted to take flight as well. Instead, the herd closed in around him and the girl, forming a protective ring. The foals came closest, milling around where they sat but never actually stepping on them, while the five adults took up positions around the perimeter.

A menacing growl emanated from the darkness somewhere outside Aytal's range of vision. More growls echoed from all sides. The wolves had surrounded them. Fighting back panic, Aytal tightened his grip on the knife. The girl's body stiffened in his lap. Thank the gods, she didn't try to move. Aytal's senses were now on full alert. In front of him, the stallion, neck arched, stamped a front foot defiantly. The other adults, searching the dark with their keen night vision, wheeled to threaten whatever lurked in the darkness with their flint-hard hooves.

A lithe shadow darted forward, trying to break through the horses' defenses. One of the pack's younger males, the wolf was quick, but not quick enough. A glancing blow from one of the mare's powerful hindquarters sent him flying backwards, where he landed, whimpering, in a heap. Almost immediately, another shape repeated the maneuver and met the same fate.

Aytal wondered when one of the older wolves would give the signal for a more coordinated onslaught, with the aim of stampeding the herd. He'd seen wolf packs hunting often enough, although not with horses as their prey. He was astonished the band had chosen to stay and defend themselves rather than run, given their chances of outdistancing the pack. He heard an impatient *yip*, answered in kind, and braced himself but the anticipated attack never materialized. Instead, within moments, the pack had melted away, leaving nothing behind but a few paw prints in the vast darkness of the steppe.

Relieved by the wolves' sudden departure, Aytal had no time to wonder about the horses' role in driving them off. The girl began to struggle, trying to sit up on her own.

"*Ei!*" Tightening his arm around her shoulders to hold her still, he spoke urgently in his own tongue. "Don't move. You're badly hurt." Laying aside his knife and reaching with his free hand for the arrow on the ground beside them, he held it up and pointed it at the girl's chest, thinking he would show her that she had been struck. "Don't move," he repeated, hoping she would understand the gesture if not the words.

Wheezing, the girl tried to speak. Too late, Aytal realized the arrow he brandished above her might appear threatening and lowered his arm while continuing to restrain her with a strong hold around her shoulders. In response, the girl lifted her head enough to bring his forearm within reach of her teeth and bit down, hard.

"Owww!" Aytal exclaimed. Although the girl drew blood, she did not succeed in loosening his grip around her shoulders. Dropping the arrow, he used his free hand to pull her head back by the hair. With his fist buried in the thicket of her red curls, he twisted the girl's head, forcing her to look him in the face. Blue eyes met blue eyes, angry defiance confronting grim determination, although neither could see much in the dark. For one long moment, they glared blindly at each other, both refusing to yield.

Aytal's expression softened first. He couldn't help but admire the girl's spirit. Smiling tentatively, he tried again to explain.

"Please hold still," he said gently. "You're injured."

In response, the girl spat in his face. Aytal grimaced but otherwise refused to react. Afraid that if he loosened his hold on her hair, she would try again to bite him, he had no choice but to allow saliva to run down his cheek and into the corner of his own mouth. It tasted slightly salty. In that moment he realized that he'd been sweating, despite the chill of the late autumn night. Overhead, the stars glowed faintly in the infinite sky, their cold light barely reaching the earth. He could see the waxing moon, descending in the western sky. Soon it would be his turn to shiver.

In his arms, Aytal felt the tension leave the girl's body. Her efforts to escape having exhausted what little energy she possessed, her eyes began to roll back and her lids close. Head slumping back against his right shoulder, she lost consciousness again.

Aytal let out a long breath. For the moment, the girl no longer posed a threat either to him or herself. Cautiously withdrawing his fingers from the tangle of her hair, he wiped the back of his hand across his face. Only then did he think to look around to see what had become of the horses. Eyes and ears straining, he detected no darker shapes against the surrounding black, nor movement in the dry grass. The herd had left just as suddenly as they appeared. All around him, the steppe seemed empty but for the distant stars. Even the moon had disappeared behind the clouds, massing in the west.

Feeling oddly bereft, Aytal looked down again at the girl in his arms. As long as she continued breathing, he knew it was probably best that she remain insensible, yet he couldn't help wishing she'd stayed with him. Assuring himself that her chest still rose and fell, he wanted to reach again for her hair, this time to smooth the wild coppery strands away from her face, but he resisted the temptation. Best not to risk disturbing her. Back aching from sitting so long with no support, he shifted ever so carefully and resumed his wait, pondering the strange behavior of the horses, wondering if they would return.

Chapter Seven

As Sata covered the last few steps of the ascent, she could hear Potis ahead. "How much further?" he demanded. "Ask him how much further."

They had stopped for breath atop a ridge separating one undulating valley from the next. The landscape spread out below them appeared nearly featureless, any variation in the topography smothered by the darkness. Clouds had gathered in the west, shrouding the half-moon.

Potis turned impatiently as Sata joined him and the stranger beside a rocky outcrop.

"Ask him how much further," he repeated.

The stranger replied before Sata could translate. Pointing, he indicated a blurred shape, barely visible, moving rapidly down the hill in front of them.

Amu had long outpaced the humans, repeatedly doubling back to make sure they still followed and to urge them on with emphatic *woofs*. In this manner, the dog had covered more than twice the distance as the people and his energy was beginning to flag. Now he paused and turned back once more. Seeing that three upright shapes had gained the crest of the ridge, he stopped, giving them time to catch-up. Naya's pack lay on the grass in front of him. He barked loudly to let them know.

"There," said the stranger, still pointing. "The dog waits for us. We are close."

"He says we are close," said Sata, panting a little as she tried to see down into the valley spread out at her feet. "We must be almost there," she added. "Surely Naya wouldn't have gone much farther."

"She is already well beyond where she was instructed to scout. Either Krnos's report was wrong or she disobeyed orders." Potis didn't bother to disguise the anger in his voice but Sata knew it only hid the worry underneath. Her husband was as afraid as she was of what they might find.

"Come," interjected the stranger in his own tongue. "We should hurry."

Despite Oyuun's words, part of him wanted to hold back, delaying the inevitable moment when the girl's parents realized just exactly what had happened to their daughter. He counted on their rage being diverted, at least temporarily, by the necessity of dealing with her injury but he knew there would be a reckoning. At least the woman's ability to understand his words gave him some hope of being able to explain and ask forgiveness. But really, Aytal must be the one to speak. He would do his son a disservice if he tried to intervene on his behalf. He was no longer a child. He had endured his time of solitude, performed his initiation ritual, received his spirit name. He was a man and must take a man's responsibility for his actions. Once already he'd had to learn that lesson.

Still, Oyuun wished he could shield Aytal from the consequences of his latest transgression, whatever they would be. He was so like his mother, not just in appearance but in temperament as well. With her flashing eyes and her black hair, glossy as a raven's wing, his first wife had been passionate and determined, but also impulsive, especially when angered or if honor and pride were at stake. Her whole heart had gone into everything she did. She had loved with all her heart as well. How she would have cherished their son, the boy for whom she had given up her own life.

Sighing heavily, Oyuun moved to follow the girl's parents, who had already begun to make their way down the slope to where the dog awaited them. As they approached, the dog began to bark excitedly, running rapid circles around something on the ground. They'd found the girl's pack. Shouldering it, the clan chief gave an order to the dog, the meaning of which was clear. *Find her.* The dog set off like an arrow shot from a bow.

Aytal heard the dog barking, the sound carrying in the night air. The gods be blessed. He didn't know how much longer he could have continued to sit motionless, supporting the unconscious weight in his lap. His father would bring help, but at the thought, a wave of apprehension washed over him. Would the girl's people recognize his part in trying to keep her from dying, or would they only concern themselves with his role in jeopardizing her life in the first place? For a moment he considered whether he might rather confront the wolves again. Perhaps his father had been able to explain. But really, what could he say? It had been an accident. He hadn't meant to hit the girl but she must have been in amongst the horses and he hadn't seen her.

The horses. Sitting alone on the steppe after the wolf attack, waiting with the insensible girl in his arms, Aytal had plenty of time to wonder about her presence with the herd. How was it that she'd been surrounded by them, blending in to the extent that he'd been unable to distinguish her? Nothing in the animals' behavior had given any indication she was there. How odd, he'd thought. Almost as strange as what had happened with the wolves. And then he'd made the connection. It must have been the same herd – it had to have been.

Forcing himself to recall the day's events from start to finish, Aytal remembered coming over the rise with his father and stepbrother and first spotting the horses in the valley below. It was a small band, a stallion and three or four mares with their offspring. He'd just begun to consider selecting a target, not even necessarily intending to shoot, when the dog had surprised them, breaking cover and charging furiously up the hill toward them. Without thinking, he'd drawn and fired. Almost as if aimed of its own accord, his arrow had traced a path toward the closest of the horses, one of the youngsters who stood out because of its unusual red color, burnished by the rays of the westering sun. He could see his shot, arcing in his mind's eye. In that split second, the girl had materialized out of nowhere, placing herself in the arrow's path. He had no doubt she had saved the young horse's life.

Had she been there all along, hidden by the tall grass? But that seemed unlikely. The horses would never have tolerated her being so close. Yet later, after nightfall, one of the creatures had approached them of its own accord, coming almost near enough to touch. Although difficult to tell in the dark, it must have been the same copper-coated two-year-old, so distinctive in the daylight. And then the rest of the herd had surrounded and defended them against the wolves. Would anyone believe him if he told such a tale? A girl who appeared mysteriously out of thin air to save a horse's life and then a horse who appeared just as mysteriously to do the same for the girl?

Aytal looked down at the figure in his lap, more than a hint of awe mixed with the trepidation he felt. Who was this being, with wild hair the same red gold as the young horse's and eyes as blue as his own? He had no more opportunity to wonder, however, for just then the dog came bounding up, barking triumphantly and dashing in circles. Moments later, three figures emerged from the surrounding darkness. To his relief, Aytal recognized one as his father. The others he did not know. The taller and broader shouldered of the two came within a pace of where he sat cradling the girl's body, before halting abruptly and staring down at them. Looking up at the imposing form towering above, Aytal was struck by a surge of hostility. This could only be the girl's father, he thought, just before the man's fist crashed into his jaw and the stars went black.

Before Sata had time to react to what Potis had done, the stranger rushed forward, managing to brace the seated figure, evidently his son, before he slumped to the ground. Recovering herself, she saw that the young man held a body in his lap. Recognizing Naya's red hair, Sata hurried forward as well.

"Stop!" the stranger commanded, addressing Potis. "She has an arrow in her back. She mustn't be moved without extreme caution. If you don't control yourself, you'll kill her!" Crouching, his right arm wrapped around both his son and Naya, the stranger returned Potis's look of fury with a defiant glare of his own.

"Potis! Stop!" echoed Sata. "He says an arrow has gone into her back. If she's moved too suddenly, she could die."

"What is she doing sitting in this boy's lap?" Potis retorted. He continued to stand menacingly over the trio on the ground, unwilling to back down but making no further move to strike.

"It doesn't matter," responded Sata, sinking to her knees. "All that matters right now is Naya." She wanted to curse her husband's temper but held her tongue. Hand hovering over her daughter's mouth and nose, hoping to feel the warmth of her breath, Sata assured herself that the girl still lived before beginning to pull items out of her pack. Turning to the stranger, she spoke as calmly as she could. "Where exactly did the arrow enter?"

"Just below the right shoulder blade, half a hand's width from her spine," he replied. "I fear it has affected her ability to draw breath."

"I need light. Potis, torches?" Sata looked up at her husband, willing him to put away his anger and make himself useful. Shaking himself as if coming out of a trance, Potis nodded before setting down his own burdens on the ground beside Sata. Bending to rummage through his pack, he removed a small hand ax, straightened and without another word, moved off into the darkness in search of fuel.

"Is that your other son?" Sata spoke quietly as soon as Potis was out of earshot, her hands still busy searching for what she needed from her pack. Although she understood the stranger when he spoke in his own tongue, she found it easier to ask questions using her own.

"Yes, my oldest," he replied. Sata guessed that he too found it easier to respond in his native language, even though he understood the words she spoke. At least they could communicate.

"And she is your daughter, yes?" he asked. Sata nodded without looking up.

"He has stayed with her, guarding her life with his own," continued the stranger. "If she still breathes, it is because of him."

"Yet how is it that she comes to have an arrow lodged in her back?" Sata lifted her eyes to confront the man, knowing there must be more to the story and wanting the full truth before Potis returned and she had to decide how much to translate. Her voice betrayed neither anger nor accusation but she couldn't keep the ice from her gaze.

"My son must be the one to explain," the stranger demurred but without looking away. Indeed, he stared, almost as though he thought he recognized her, making Sata uncomfortable. Just then, the young man began to stir. Groaning, he opened his eyes and tried to put a hand to his jaw.

"Welcome back," said his father matter-of-factly. "Can you sit up on your own and help me support the girl?"

"What happened?" The young man's voice was groggy.

"That's what I'd like to know," replied Sata, allowing a hint of sarcasm to tinge her words. "Can you sit up on your own?" she continued, echoing the young man's father. "I must see my daughter's back so I can decide what to do."

"Be careful and take it slowly," cautioned the stranger. He and his son moved in concert, their entire focus on not jostling Naya. Sata found herself holding her breath for what seemed an eternity until they had shifted themselves so that they knelt on either side of her daughter, each supporting one of her shoulders to prevent her from falling forward from the waist. As conscientious as they had been, the girl moaned in pain.

"Naya?" said Sata, kneeling as well so that she could look into her daughter's face. Anxiety sharpened her voice. Naya's head hung forward, chin almost resting against her chest, hair creating a tangled curtain on either side of her face. Reaching out, Sata pushed aside the red-gold strands before laying one palm gently against her daughter's pale cheek, cupping her jaw. "I'm here," she continued more quietly. "Can you hear me? Try to open your eyes."

"Mama?" The voice came out in a hoarse whisper. Fluttering, Naya's eyelids lifted and her pupils tried to focus. For the first time since the stranger had caught up to where the clan had stopped for the night, Amu in tow, Sata felt a little of the dread lift from her heart. The dog, who remained close, whined anxiously when he heard the girl's voice.

Trying to smile reassuringly, Sata reached down to grasp one of Naya's hands in both of her own. Although her skin felt icy to the touch, the pulse of life still beat in her wrist, not as strongly as Sata would have liked, but it was there. Now it was up to her, with the help of the Goddess, to save her only child. Sending up a fervent prayer, she spoke as calmly as she could.

"You must not try to move. You have an arrow in your back. Can you breathe?"

"I'm ok," came the reply, followed by a strangled cough. Struggling to draw air, Naya managed to add a question of her own. "What happened to the filly?"

"What does she say?" asked the stranger. From where he knelt, he could look directly into Sata's face and she sensed him trying to read her expression for clues as to what Naya's words might have revealed.

"She asks about the horses," replied Sata, neither taking her eyes from her daughter nor reacting to the young man's sharply indrawn breath when she translated a version of Naya's question into the stranger's tongue.

"Be still now," was all she said, switching back to words Naya could understand. "When your father gets back with wood for a fire, I'll be able to see your wound."

Just then, Amu barked, announcing Potis's return. He had found a thicket of scrubby trees lining a small stream not far away and in his arms he carried a bundle of dead branches, collected from the ground beneath. As fuel they were unlikely to burn very hot, but when combined with dried grasses from the surrounding steppe and pitch from the store in his pack, they would provide light by which to see. Selecting several relatively straight, thick sticks, he set about fashioning torches. The remaining kindling he used to lay a small fire, lighting it expertly with sparks struck from his precious flint stone. From this in turn he lit two brands.

Motioning Sata out of the way, Potis knelt directly in front of Naya, offering his broad chest for her support. "I will take my daughter," he said roughly. "Leave her to me." He still grasped a burning branch in each outstretched hand. Needing no translation, the stranger and his son carefully draped first one and then the other of Naya's arms over her father's shoulders before each taking up a torch. Freed of the brands, Potis took Naya's full weight, wrapping one thickly muscled arm around her slim waist. Using his other hand, he gently cupped the back of her head, pressing it against his shoulder. To Sata, their daughter looked limp and insubstantial in her husband's embrace. It frightened her. Her eyes met Potis's.

"Save her," was all he said, the intensity of his amber gaze communicating more than words. She only nodded in reply before taking a deep breath and setting to work.

Carefully, using a knife fashioned of the black stone her people quarried from the slopes of her mountainous homeland, she cut away Naya's hide clothing, laying bare the girl's back to reveal the stump of the arrow's shaft protruding at an ugly angle. Although the surrounding skin was bruised, not much blood had leaked from the wound.

"Is it yours?" Sata asked the young man, looking up at where he stood holding the torch. Unable to escape the accusation in her eyes, he answered with a nod. Sata looked away first, returning her attention to the task at hand.

"I need to see one like it." She spoke in the stranger's tongue, knowing Potis would draw his own conclusions without benefit of translation and hoping his concern for their daughter would be enough to restrain his temper, at least for the moment.

After examining another of Aytal's arrows, she had a better idea of what she was dealing with. Handling the slim shaft, one end tipped with the same expertly knapped black stone as her blade, the other end double fletched with black raven feathers, she couldn't help but admire the workmanship. Luckily for Naya's sake, the point had an uncommon design, slimmer than usual, without barbs at the base that would have resulted in more damage coming out than going in. Still, causing further injury would be unavoidable. Although the arrowhead had not penetrated deeply into Naya's chest nor lodged in a bone, extracting it would necessitate enlarging the wound. Sata couldn't risk simply yanking on the shaft lest the arrowhead remain behind. Even if she succeeded in withdrawing the point without too much difficulty, she would need to apply pressure to stop the bleeding, and then pack the wound with a mixture of herbs and honey to help bind the tissues and prevent infection. Removing the arrow was far from guaranteeing that Naya would survive. Grimly, setting her teeth and shutting her ears against her daughter's cries, Sata set to work.

Sometime later, Sata rocked back on her heels, exhaling wearily. She had done all that she could. Now it would be up to the Goddess and her daughter's own guardian spirits whether she survived. Naya, insensible once again, still lay against her father's chest, head pillowed on his shoulder. Although Potis had shifted into a seated position, with Naya across his lap, he refused otherwise to allow her to be moved, and really it was best that she remain as still as possible. At least the need for extreme caution was passed. The arrow could inflict no further injury. Cutting free what remained of the shaft from the tip, Sata tucked the arrowhead itself inside a small pouch at her waist, saving it for Naya. Whether her daughter lived or died, the black stone now contained powerful medicine and was not to be discarded, nor returned to its original owner. Meanwhile, at some point, Potis would have to relinquish his hold on Naya but for now, if cradling her in his arms helped him to feel as if he were doing something constructive to keep her alive, so be it. It would prevent him from being able to go after the young man, at least physically. What he might have to say was another matter. Hoping to postpone the inevitable, Sata broke the silence herself.

"We need more wood for the fire," she declared, wiping her hands on a scrap of hide. She turned to the stranger, switching to her own tongue and then repeating herself in his for good measure. "Can your son go gather wood for the fire?"

The young man, only too willing to escape, had started to hand his torch to his father.

"No," interrupted Potis. His voice was pitched low, so as not to disturb Naya, but the tone was unmistakable. "You will tell us now what happened."

Potis's command arrested the young man. Looking to his father for direction, he received a single nod of the head, before the stranger moved to seat himself across the small fire. Another thrust of his chin indicated to his son that he should follow suit. Once they were settled, having each consigned their torches to feed the fire, the stranger began to speak.

"My name is Oyuun," he said simply, placing a hand on his chest. "This is my oldest son, Aytal," he continued, gesturing toward the young man at his side. "We come from the far north, where the reindeer live." Here, he looked questioning at Sata, not sure if she would have the word for the great antlered creatures that roamed his homeland, an area as vast and forbidding as the steppe.

"Never mind the introductions," cut in Potis when Sata hesitated in deciphering the stranger's words. "What are they doing here and how did this boy's arrow end up in Naya's back?" The barely contained fury in his voice needed no translation.

"My son is a man," replied Oyuun, guessing the meaning of Potis's words. "The story is his to tell."

He motioned for Aytal to speak. Swallowing hard, the young man turned to face Sata. She almost felt sorry for him. He looked at her as though hoping she would be able not only to translate his speech but help him to make sense of what had happened and explain in such a way as to deflect the worst of her husband's wrath. Taking a deep breath, he began.

"My father, step-brother and I have travelled for more than three moons from our homeland in the Taiga," he began. "We seek trade with the stone-knapping people of the southern mountains. Earlier today, we sighted a large caravan with many animals moving along the main trail leading east, toward the river crossing. Not wanting to interrupt their travel… we chose to continue our journey along this valley instead." Aytal had paused, glancing at his father before continuing. "Just as we arrived at the top of that ridge," pointing up the long slope behind him, "we came across a small herd of horses." He stopped, allowing Sata a chance to catch-up.

"How many horses?" she asked, as soon as she had repeated his words so that Potis could follow.

"A stallion and perhaps four mares and their young. I'm not exactly certain. Things happened very fast. I don't quite know how to explain." Aytal paused again, looking at the ground before lifting his eyes to meet Sata's silent gaze. She gave him no help, merely waited, expressionless, for him to continue. Potis, impatient, cleared his throat. Given no choice, Aytal resumed his story.

"We had been on the look-out for game," he continued, "so I had my bow to hand. Without really thinking, I must have sighted on one of the young horses, larger than the other foals, maybe a yearling or even a two-year old."

"What color?" interrupted Sata, not waiting to translate.

"A very distinctive color," replied Aytal. "Red. I had never seen such a color before on a horse, or…" his eyes slipping toward Naya. "…a person."

"What does he say?" demanded Potis.

"He aimed his arrow at the red filly." Sata looked at her husband, her expression unreadable in the darkness. "Let the boy finish and then I will translate."

Lowering his eyebrows to glare at Aytal, Potis produced a growl from the back of his throat, but otherwise held his tongue.

"Go on," said Sata, turning back to Aytal. "What happened next?"

"I'm not exactly sure," came the response. "It all happened at once." Gesturing at Amu, he continued. "The dog broke cover and charged us. I must have been startled and released my arrow. But then the strangest thing of all happened. Out of nowhere, this girl appeared." He pointed at Naya. "One instant it was just the herd – they had all turned to look when the dog started towards us – and then next she was there, just in front of the little red horse. I don't know where she came from. I don't understand how she could have been so close to the horses without them noticing." Aytal spread his hands in a gesture of supplication. "You must believe me. I did not intend to shoot her. I am sincerely sorry for the injury my arrow caused."

Before Sata could either translate or respond to the young man's words, his father broke in.

"Truly," Oyuun said, shifting his earnest gaze between Sata and Potis, "my son would never have intentionally aimed to shoot the girl. She simply appeared, out of nowhere."

Aytal nodded his head in agreement. "It was almost as if she was trying to shield the red horse," he added, puzzlement evident in his voice.

"Indeed," said Oyuun, turning to Sata with a questioning look, "how is it that the horses allowed her in their midst?"

"Enough," interrupted Potis impatiently. "What do they say?"

Sata paused a long moment before responding, her gaze passing between the stranger and his son, who both met her look with expressions reflecting a blend of sincere remorse and genuine perplexity, matching their words. Something within softened, ever so slightly. At last she spoke.

"It was an accident," she said simply, addressing Potis. "Naya was with the herd but they didn't see her until after the boy sent his arrow toward the red filly. She was trying to protect her." "They apologize," Sata continued, "but they also don't understand how Naya could have been with the herd without the horses noticing." Turning back to Oyuun, she asked a question of her own.

"What condition was she in when you found her?"

"Not conscious, barely breathing," came the reply. "We did all that we could to prevent further injury, cutting down the arrow, as you saw, and holding her upright so that she could get air. Aytal stayed with her to make sure she still breathed and my younger son and I came looking for you." Sata repeated all that the stranger said, then watched for her husband's reaction.

Closing his eyes, Potis absorbed Sata's words. Knowing him as she did, she could guess how badly he wanted to exact retribution for the harm done to his only child. Fear for Naya's life roiled within him, demanding to be expressed in a towering, violent rage. At the same time, he must see as well as she did that the strangers' explanation for what had happened was all too plausible. They would have had no reason to suspect a person would be among the horses when they came upon them, grazing peacefully in the little valley. It was just the sort of incident Potis had warned of when Naya had first proposed trying to tame the herd. Sata knew the internal effort required for her husband to throttle back his desire for revenge. He waited several breaths before opening his eyes again to speak.

"We are all to blame," he said to Sata, anger still simmering in his lowered voice. "You and I and Naya herself. I knew something like this would happen. But these strangers must also share responsibility." Turning to Oyuun and Aytal, he continued in a louder voice. "Tell them that on behalf of ourselves and the entire clan, we accept their apology but they must pay a price, determined by whether our daughter lives or dies."

Bowing her head in acknowledgement of this official pronouncement, Sata translated.

Expression carefully neutral, Oyuun responded, his eyes never leaving Potis's face. "Tell the clan chief," he said, enunciating each word, "that we accept his judgment, provided it is just." The two men held each other's gaze, equally unwavering.

After a beat, Potis continued. "They are travelling through our territory without our permission," he observed. "Do they wish to be acknowledged as guests, or remain strangers?" Again, Sata translated. This was a loaded question. As guests, Oyuun and both his sons would be entitled to hospitality and protection but would also be required to accept the clan's authority, as represented by Potis himself. As strangers, particularly strangers who had refused the invitation to become guests, their status would be only one degree removed from that of enemy. These customs were known and recognized by all who travelled across the steppe. Sata guessed that in steering clear of the clan earlier in the day, Oyuun had sought to avoid just this choice. Now, he had no option.

"Tell the chief," he said evenly, "that we gratefully accept his invitation to be guests of his clan." Once Sata had finished delivering his words, Oyuun continued to hold Potis's regard for several more heartbeats, both men still unwilling to be the first to look away. Finally, when Naya began to stir, moaning in her father's arms, Oyuun dropped his eyes. Turning to his son, he seemed about to suggest collecting more wood for the fire, when Aytal raised a hand to stop him.

"May I speak?" the young man asked politely, directing his query to Sata.

"The boy wishes to say something more," she said to Potis.

"I doubt there's anything he can say that I'll want to hear," he replied, "but let him speak if he must." Naya had shifted slightly but not opened her eyes.

Nodding assent, Sata listened and then translated as Aytal spoke.

"I don't understand how the girl appeared among the horses," he said, returning to his earlier question. "And other strange things happened after you left to get help," he added, turning to his father.

"Not long before it grew dark, wolves appeared on the far ridge." Aytal indicated the direction over Potis's shoulder. "A small pack, maybe six or eight. I could barely make them out as the sun was setting, but I could tell they were heading in our direction." Sata inhaled sharply before repeating what the young man had said. "I couldn't move because of the girl, and all I had for a weapon was my flint knife. I waited for what felt like a long time, expecting them to attack at any moment." Aytal by now held everyone's attention. "Suddenly, I heard a rustling, then heavy breathing. Whatever was making the noises seemed too big and loud to be the wolves but I couldn't imagine what else it could be. A moment later, out of the darkness appeared…" He paused, allowing Sata to catch up before continuing, "…a horse."

"A horse?" repeated Oyuun, incredulous.

"The red filly," said Sata in the same moment, her voice barely above a whisper. She and Potis exchanged looks.

"*Rêhda*," said another voice. Everyone's attention turned to Naya, still motionless in her father's lap, but eyes now open for the first time since her mother had drawn the arrow from her back.

"Red," repeated Sata, translating. She did not tell them it was Naya's name for the filly. Instead, switching to words her daughter would understand, she moved to kneel beside Potis and gently laid the back of her hand across Naya's forehead. "How are you feeling," she asked, her tone full of concern.

"Thirsty," came the reply. Before either Sata or Potis could respond, Aytal, guessing what she wanted, came to his feet. Locating his own water skin, he handed it to Sata, who held it up to Naya's lips, allowing her one small sip, which she managed to swallow without choking. Another sip followed, and a third, before Sata declined to offer her more.

"Let that settle," was all she said, handing the skin back to Aytal, who retreated back to his side of the fire.

"The horses saved us." More alert now, voice still raspy, Naya looked over her shoulder at the young man as she tried to turn in her father's arms and sit up. "You shot me, and the horses saved us from the wolves."

"What does she say?" asked Oyuun and Aytal simultaneously.

"She's delirious," said Potis to Sata. "It must be the wound talking. She doesn't feel hot, though. If anything, she's cold. Get a blanket out of my pack. And send that boy for more wood for the fire. Let's prop her up against the packs and get her covered."

Sata was about to comply when Naya spoke again.

"The horses saved us," she repeated, eyes still fixed on Aytal. "Tell them."

Potis and Sata exchanged glances. Oyuun looked first at Naya, then at her parents and then at his son.

"You had better finish your story," he said.

"She says the horses saved you," prompted Sata, desire to know what had happened overcoming caution about revealing too much about her daughter's unorthodox relationship with the herd.

"They did," replied Aytal. "Only the red one approached close enough to touch, but the others gathered around as if they were used to humans – wary, but not really afraid. It was the strangest thing. Almost immediately, the stallion sensed the wolves approaching but instead of running off, the herd formed a circle, with us and the foals at the center. The pack surrounded the horses but instead of panicking and trying to escape, they held their ground. Whenever the wolves tried to attack, the adults would fight them off. Before long the pack gave up and disappeared. The girl was awake during the attack, but then she lost consciousness again, and by the time I thought to look around, the horses were gone too."

Listening to Aytal's implausible tale, Sata felt the stranger watching them all closely, apparently trying to judge the effect of his son's words. He must think the story of the horses' behavior made no more sense than Naya's sudden appearance earlier in the day amidst the herd. He would wonder why they weren't more incredulous. Potis was scowling, Sata noted, but didn't look surprised. Despite her pallor, Naya appeared relieved. Sata tried to keep her own features impassive. Would the stranger demand an explanation? What could they possibly tell him, without revealing the otherworldly forces that seemed to be at work where Naya and the red filly were concerned?

"Your daughter needs rest," was all he said. "We all do. My son can fetch wood and perhaps we can make the girl more comfortable for what's left of the night. Time enough in the morning for more talk."

"What does he say?" interrupted Potis, before Sata could respond.

"Only that it's late and that we all need rest, especially Naya. He'll send the boy for more wood." With a nod from both Sata and Oyuun, Aytal got to his feet and in a moment had disappeared into the dark. Amu rose as if to follow, but Sata called him back. Speaking to Naya, she continued, "can you sit up against the packs? You mustn't move too much or you'll open the wound. Are you hungry? Thirsty? Cold?"

"Make a place for her," Potis interjected. In a moment, he and Sata had settled Naya on a sheep skin, propped against her own pack and draped with a felt blanket. Sata knew they both would have preferred the warmest bison fur the family owned, but the bulk of their belongings were back at the clan's camp. Pointedly ignoring Oyuun, Potis began to rummage in their packs for the remaining blankets they had with them. On the other side of the fire, Oyuun did the same. Sata found her own water skin and offered Naya several more sips of water, before cupping her palm against her daughter's cheek and looking into her eyes with a tender smile.

"Try to sleep now," she said gently.

"Mama," replied Naya, her voice a whisper that only her mother could hear. "The filly spoke to me again, and this time I remember more of what she said." Her voice, weak as it was, held an edge of excitement.

"Hush now. You can tell me the rest in the morning. Don't talk of it to anyone else."

"Yes mama." Looking more like a small, vulnerable child than the almost-grown young woman that she was, Naya closed her eyes while her mother smoothed strands of hair back from her face and pulled the blanket up around her shoulders. Amu got up from where he'd been laying out of the way and came to curl himself at the girl's feet. "Good dog," said Sata, patting him on the head. Then, sighing heavily, she accepted the blanket her husband held out for her, wrapping herself in it before seating herself again next to Naya and the dog. Potis took up a post slightly apart, where he could keep an eye on both his family and their two guests. Aytal returned shortly and together he and Oyuun built up the fire before retreating to their places.

With barely more than a nod, Potis let Oyuun know his intention to keep watch, which Oyuun acknowledged with a nod of his own, before laying down to try to sleep. It had been a long day and there was still much he did not understand about what had happened. His last thought before closing his eyes was for his younger son, alone among strangers.

Chapter Eight

"She's burning up." Sata looked up, concern in her expression. The sun had been over the horizon long enough to provide light but little warmth. Clouds had continued to gather overnight, promising an overcast day and the possibility of a storm. No one had slept much, but Oyuun and Aytal had kept the fire going and they'd all had something to eat from the traveling rations in their packs, all except Naya, who had been slipping in and out of consciousness and only managed a few additional sips of water. She was awake now, but staring glassy-eyed into the fire, seemingly unaware of her mother's hand on her forehead.

"We can't stay here for long," replied Potis. "The clan needs to keep moving and if we don't rejoin them, we'll be left behind."

No need to elaborate on the consequences of such a separation, thought Sata. Besides the dangers and hardships of being on their own on the steppe with winter descending, there were the tensions threatening to divide the clan. Without Potis's presence, feuds which had been developing over the summer and now simmered just below the surface might turn violent. At the very least, his own authority would be significantly diminished by a prolonged absence. In addition, his father would surely be making his passage soon to the other world, a sacred transition which Potis should not miss, not least because it was bound to further destabilize the clan. He could not risk staying away.

"But we can't move her in this condition," protested Sata. "It will kill her."

Potis was silent, considering their options. Oyuun, who had been trying to guess the meaning of their words from their expressions and tone of voice, spoke up.

"What will you do?" he asked Sata solicitously. "The girl is surely too injured to travel far."

"My husband must return to the rest of the clan as soon as possible," she replied. "And yes, it's true that my daughter cannot be moved yet without further risk to her life."

"How much further has your clan to travel?" Oyuun asked, furrowing his brow.

"Our winter settlement is one moon to the east, along the great river *Rā*. There is better shelter there, and fodder for the animals. The storms are not so fierce. The clan cannot wait. We've already gotten a late start and once the weather turns, travel will be difficult." Sata would say nothing of clan politics to this outsider, but still she looked worried. "My daughter is in no condition to make the journey, at least not right away."

"Father?" Aytal spoke hesitantly. "What if we remained with the girl and her mother until she recovers?"

The stranger did not reply immediately. Sata watched him regard his son, apparently weighing the young man's suggestion. While the wisest thing for them would be to resume their journey as soon as possible, the young man seemed to find the prospect unacceptable. Did he truly want to stay, regardless of the risk, especially to himself?

"What does the boy say?" demanded Potis.

Sata considered the young stranger's offer. Naya could not be moved. Potis had to return to the clan. Those were the two implacable facts with which they must deal. She could stay, but by herself, exposed on the steppe and with her daughter to care for, she would be too vulnerable. Could they trust the stranger and his son to protect them? So far, they had behaved honorably. They could easily have left Naya to die alone and hidden by the tall grass, with the arrow in her back, but instead they had done all they could to save her life. They might be more worthy of trust than some members of the clan, thought Sata ruefully. But would they actually be willing to stay? It could be weeks before Naya was strong enough to continue the migration east, and winter would likely make further travel impossible by then. There was a good chance they would have to remain where they were until the spring thaw. Would the strangers be willing to wait that long before resuming their own journey?

Oyuun pondered the same question himself. He had planned to reach the lower reaches of the southern mountains by mid-winter at the latest, remaining there through the rest of the season to trade with the local inhabitants as well as travelers from further south, before returning north to his own people. This was an arduous trip he'd made only once before. Already, he and his sons had been on the trail since early summer. If they kept to their intended schedule, they would be away for more than a full year. If they delayed too long, they would miss the short season of mild weather when they could complete the return journey to their homeland.

Yet, as he thought about going back, he felt no sense of urgency. His current partner, Dayan's mother, would probably prefer that he stay away. She had been the wife of his brother, who had been killed while defending their reindeer, leaving his mate heavily pregnant. With his own beloved wife years gone, Oyuun had done the expected thing and taken his sister-in-law into his tent, claiming her child as his own. For the most part, no one remembered that the boy was actually his nephew, not his son. He wasn't sure Aytal had any recollection that Dayan was not truly his stepbrother. And really, at this point, what did it matter? He loved the boy as his own.

Dayan's mother was another matter. While they tolerated one another well enough, there was no true bond between them, more a sense of mutual obligation. Sometimes, Oyuun thought his insistence all those years ago on doing what he believed to be both generous and right had robbed them both of finding happiness with someone else. The rules around such things were strictly observed by his tribe. As long as his brother's widow lived in his tent, no other man would dare claim her and it would cause the utmost loss of reputation for himself were she to leave. But if he were to stay away for an extended period, perhaps never come back, she certainly wouldn't miss him and it probably wouldn't be long before someone stepped in to take his place. Indeed, there had been no shortage of offers to look out for her while he was gone and if much more than a full year passed, she would be considered not only available, but obligated to accept another partner. She was, after all, a healthy, strong, good-looking woman and still young enough to have more children, something he had not given her. She would miss Dayan, if he didn't bring the boy back to her as expected, but perhaps that couldn't be helped.

As for himself, since the death of his first wife, no woman had drawn him, until... Ruthlessly strangling the thought before it could even form in his mind, Oyuun turned to Aytal.

"Would you want to stay?" was all he said.

"I would," Aytal replied, declining to elaborate.

For a long moment, Oyuun and his son regarded one another without speaking, as though trying to read one another's thoughts. Oyuun could well guess what the young man was feeling, perhaps better than Aytal himself. His son did not want to leave the girl, at least not yet, not until he knew that she was going to be okay. He must know that she lived, both for her sake and his own. Had not the girl's father explicitly tied his fate to hers when he declared that the price owed for his actions would depend on whether she survived or not? If Aytal left without paying his debt, he would be forever dishonored, which Oyuun knew his son could never abide. He also suspected that if Aytal left without being assured that the girl lived, his heart might not forgive him.

"What are they saying?" Potis asked again, obviously irritated at not being able to follow the dialogue, let alone the silent exchange taking place between the stranger and his son.

Switching to the clan's tongue, Sata spoke slowly, still considering the idea. "They are proposing to stay with Naya and me while you go back to the rest of the clan." Seeing her husband's expression cloud, she continued more quickly. "It may be the only way. You know you can't stay here and you know Naya can't be moved. It's too dangerous for me to stay with her by myself and there's no one from the clan who could take your place. You need your brother by your side and he and the others have their own families to look out for. Besides, the boy can't pay his debt until we know whether Naya pulls through. You yourself decreed it."

"But will you both be safe left with these strangers?" Potis looked dubious.

"They have every incentive to be sure Naya lives and it's unlikely that I'll be in any danger from either of them. Plus you'll still have the other boy," Sata pointed out. "In any case, I don't see that we have a choice, if Naya is to have a chance of surviving. We'll rejoin you as soon as we can."

Reluctantly, Potis had to agree. "Are they willing to stay?"

Sata turned once again to Oyuun. "Do you join your son in his offer to stay with my daughter and me?" she asked, trying to assess his countenance. There was a depth behind the stranger's dark eyes, set in a lean and weathered face, that she couldn't quite penetrate. Could the man indeed be trusted?

Oyuun paused before responding, holding Sata's gaze with his own, wishing to reassure her, aware that long years of practice in guarding his thoughts made his expression difficult to read. Turning to Potis, he addressed the clan chief formally, using the gestures of the common sign language to reinforce his words.

"My son and I will care for your wife and daughter," he signed. "We will keep them safe." Sata translated and Potis nodded his assent.

"Thank you for your willingness to stay with them," he replied with equal formality, pausing for Sata to repeat his words. "For as long as my family is in your care," he added, "your younger son will continue to enjoy the protection of my clan." The implication of his words escaped no one. Dayan would remain a hostage. It was Oyuun's turn to bow his head in agreement.

Shifting to practical matters, they discussed where would be the best place to establish a temporary camp, situated so as to provide sufficient protection from the increasingly cold weather, not to mention the other dangers of the steppe in winter. Aytal offered to scout nearby locations while the others took inventory of their supplies. Potis, who knew every feature of the land over which his clan wandered, gave him directions to a site he thought might be suitable for their needs.

Aytal returned shortly, confirming that, just as Potis had indicated, the thicket where they had found firewood the night before actually represented the edge of a larger area of dense undergrowth which in turn hid a sizable clearing. Bordered on three sides by thick vegetation, the open space was bisected by a small stream along whose banks grew a stand of taller trees, mainly birch and larch, with a scattering of scrub oak and hemlock. After flowing into the clearing from the southwest, curving north and east and then cutting its way out again beneath the surrounding undergrowth, the little waterway eventually joined the larger tributary to the east along whose banks the clan was currently encamped. A single game trail provided the only means of access to the clearing.

Otherwise, the thickness of the surrounding brush effectively screened it from sight, while gaps in the trees along the southern edge still allowed the sun's warmth and light to penetrate. On the northern side, the clearing's boundary was defined by a rough wall of dirt and rock, rising to a height taller than three men. As if the steppe had been sliced open to reveal the earth beneath, the cliff formed one face of a small hill, the other sides of which sloped gently away. Although nearly vertical, the edifice could easily be climbed using natural handholds. From its top, the outcropping afforded a vista of the surrounding landscape, while at the same time blocking the north wind and disguising the little grove from view from all but one direction. Only someone approaching from the southwest would have noticed the trees and underbrush growing along the creek. From every other angle, the hillside and the clearing it sheltered looked like just another undulation in an ocean of grass.

"It will do," was all Oyuun said when Aytal had finished describing to him what he had discovered. Sata translated for Potis, who nodded confirmation that Aytal had found the location he'd had in mind. He then began issuing instructions.

"Stay with Naya while we move the packs and set-up as much of a camp as we can," he said to Sata. "I'll come back and move her when we have a place ready."

Turning to Oyuun, Potis addressed him directly, signing as he spoke. "After we move my daughter to the clearing, your son and my wife will stay with her while you and the dog come with me to meet up with the clan. You can bring back additional provisions." Pausing to allow Sata to repeat his words for Oyuun, he then added, "And you can tell your younger son yourself of the change in your plans."

Although no variation in tone or expression accompanied this last directive, Oyuun thought he detected a hint of compassion behind the apparent afterthought. How much easier it would be for Dayan if he could explain to him in person what was happening and reassure him that everything would be alright. Oyuun wanted to express his gratitude for this indication of the other man's good will but before he could, Potis had turned away to gather up his pack, leaving Oyuun to stare thoughtfully at his back. His eyes finding Sata's, he tried smiling at her instead.

"Thank you," he mouthed silently in his own tongue. She looked back at him, weariness and worry etched upon her face, and only acknowledged his words with a brief nod before turning her attention back to Naya. Shouldering his own pack, Oyuun prepared to follow Aytal as he led the way to the little clearing that would serve as home for the foreseeable future.

By late afternoon of the same day, the space between the creek and rock face had been transformed. Once Naya had been resettled on a pile of furs in a sunny patch out of reach of the wind, Potis and Oyuun, accompanied by Amu, left to catch-up with the rest of the clan. Sata and Aytal stayed behind and did what they could to prepare the site. Scattered rocks had been gathered into a circle to serve as a fire pit, with stray brush piled to the side for kindling. They said almost nothing to each other as they worked, beyond what was necessary to cooperate in moving the larger stones. Sata struggled silently to control the anger she felt toward the young man for harming her child, while he in return did not know how to express his shame and regret, beyond what he had already said. Both were relieved when Oyuun and Amu returned, each dragging a pole sled piled high with hides, furs, tools, cooking utensils, food stuffs and spare clothing. Before long, two snug shelters had been erected side by side in the lee of the cliff wall, well-protected from the wind. In addition, Oyuun had brought back one of the clan's hardiest and most productive goats, also pulling a laden sled, along with her twin kids and these had been corralled into a hastily constructed pen. Able to survive on rough forage, the she-goat would provide milk while the youngsters might serve as an emergency source of meat in the event game became scarce. Although the clan never slaughtered animals under a year of age if avoidable, circumstances such as these might require such a sacrifice.

Negotiating to include the goats with the other provisions had taken some doing. Without understanding the details of the interchange, Oyuun had watched with interest as Potis first tried reason and diplomacy to convince the other family heads that the she-goat and her offspring should be sent along to his wife and daughter. For most, the clan chief's assertion of his family's need of the goats in question seemed sufficient to justify separating them from the rest of the flock, but Oyuun noted a faction, including the clan's priest, as well as three or four others, who apparently required further persuasion before they would agree. Oyuun recognized the leader of this group, a tall, broad-shouldered individual with a scarred face, as the man who had been lurking in the shadows when he'd first arrived to get help for the girl. He could sense a hum of hostility emanating from him, directed not so much at himself, which he might have expected, as at Potis. In the end, despite the undercurrent of enmity, the clan chief succeeded in achieving consensus that the goats should be sent along. Oyuun could tell the scar-faced man and the priest acquiesced reluctantly but were unwilling to mount too direct a challenge to Potis's request. Nonetheless, he could see why the chief felt the necessity of remaining with the clan, despite his daughter's grave condition.

Oyuun's reunion with his younger son was brief and somewhat anticlimactic. Far from being troubled by his situation, the boy appeared to be thoroughly at home with his new best friends, the two younger sons of the clan chief's brother. While glad to see his stepfather, Dayan seemed far from dismayed at the prospect of a prolonged separation and barely said goodbye before scampering off to rejoin the other boys, who were busy trying to keep the goats and sheep from straying too far from the trail. Having traversed the river without incident earlier in the day, the clan had stopped for a mid-day break when Oyuun and Potis caught up to them, but they did not linger long. As soon as explanations had been given and the negotiation over the goats settled, provisions had been quickly gathered and loaded on three sleds, after which the main body of the clan prepared to move off again.

Before resuming his place at the head of the column of people, dogs and livestock, Potis called Oyuun over to him and fixing him with his hawk-like gaze, silently raised his hands to sign. "Take care of my family," he gestured, expression fierce. Yet Oyuun could sense the vulnerability hidden behind the amber eyes. Gravely, he nodded, placing his right hand over his heart in silent confirmation of his oath to do as the clan chief commanded. He then stepped aside to allow the crowd of people and animals to pass. Just as the last stragglers went by, an older woman whom he recognized as Potis's mother broke away and made her way toward him. She struggled under the weight of a large deerskin sack which she pressed into his arms. "For my granddaughter," she signed. "And the horses." Placing both hands over her heart, she closed her eyes and bowed her head in what could only be a blessing, then turned and resumed her place beside an old man, who Oyuun saw was her husband, the clan chief's father. He looked somewhat stronger than when he'd seen him the day before. Maybe he would survive the journey to the clan's winter settlement after all. Still, Oyuun stood wondering, watching as the clan moved away from him down the well-trodden path. Before long, people and animals had all disappeared from sight around a bend in the trail. Just as they did, a sudden chill passed over him, as though the sun had also disappeared, and he knew that misfortune stalked the clan, bringing with it loss and death, but for whom he could not say.

Stowing the heavy sack the old woman had given him among several nearly identical deerskin bags and settling his pack on his shoulders, Oyuun turned to the west, anxious now to return to where his oldest son, the girl and her mother awaited. Taking up the poles of his sled, he called to Amu. The dog, harnessed to a second sled, had been remarkably willing to stay behind with him when the clan departed but the she-goat was considerably less cooperative. Protesting at being separated from her flock, she had to be tethered behind Oyuun's sled, which was going to make travel over rough terrain a bit tricky, but it couldn't be helped. Luckily the kids could be trusted to stay with their mother. Calling again to the dog, who seemed as eager as was he to return to the girl and the others, he set off.

Chapter Nine

"Will you answer a question, something I've wondered about since we first met?"

They were gathered around the fire, Naya bundled in hides and propped against a small boulder which Aytal had shifted into place for her, the others seated on their heavy cloaks. The evening was surprisingly mild, as it had been for the last few days, with barely a breath of wind. Clouds had been gathering to the west and north but were still too distant to do more than provide a spectacular back drop for the sun's last rays as it slipped beneath the horizon. No one had remarked on the sunset however, and their evening meal had been eaten with barely a word spoken. Still, with a blazing fire, it was warm enough to remain outside the shelters, at least for a while longer, and witness the early evening shadows and emerging stars. No one had yet moved, and little by little, the unseasonably warm night air seemed to be dissolving at least some of the tension that had permeated the clearing since they had first settled in five days earlier. Even Naya, who had spent much of the afternoon drifting in and out of a restless sleep, appeared marginally brighter after her mother was able to convince her to sip some of the broth from the stew the others had shared for their evening meal.

Still, Sata wished there had been more improvement in the girl's condition. Although Naya did not seem to be growing any worse, neither did she appear significantly better. There had been a crisis the first night in the clearing, when her skin burned with heat, sweat poured from her body and her heart beat wildly as she thrashed and called out in a voice choked with terror. There followed brief periods of alarming stillness, when the thin thread of her exhausted breathing seemed too weak to continue to tether her to life, and then her temperature would spike again, bringing on a fresh bout of violent struggle. All Sata could do was to bathe Naya with cold water from the creek and coax a few sips of her precious supply of willow bark tea between her cracked lips during her moments of semi-consciousness. Otherwise, she could only keep watch and pray. The fever lasted into the second night, until sometime close to dawn, when Naya gave a heart-wrenching sob, followed by a single inhale. Sata feared it might be her last and held her own breath, waiting. At last, the exhale came, and in that moment, the crisis passed. Yet the lethargy that took its place was almost worse. Although her temperature returned to normal and the wound in her back looked and smelled as though it had begun to heal cleanly, the work of her lungs remained shallow and labored.

Of even greater concern to Sata was her daughter's uncharacteristic dispiritedness. Naya spent most of the daylight hours in an apparent trance, uninterested in her surroundings and unresponsive to her mother's voice. Even Amu could not elicit a reaction, despite his best efforts to wiggle into her lap and lick her face. When she did doze off, she gathered no strength from her fitful sleep. The nights, if anything, were worse. As Sata lay awake in their shelter, Naya tossed beside her, no longer fevered but still calling out in a strangled voice, as if confronting enemies in the shadows. For three nights it had gone on this way, with no dramatic change for the worse, but no obvious progress either, beyond the slight improvement she seemed to exhibit this evening. Throughout the entire time, other than the few sentences she'd spoken that first night out on the steppe and her incoherent cries in the dark, Naya had not uttered a word.

Nearly sick herself with worry, Sata had done everything she could to help her daughter, steeping herbs in boiling water so that she could breathe in their healing vapors and brewing medicinal teas which the girl had to be persuaded to drink. She continued to pray constantly, silently pleading with the Goddess to spare her child, and brought daily offerings to the altar she had set up in a corner of their shelter. Nothing seemed to make any difference, one way or the other. Sata wished Awija, with all her herbal lore, were here. Her mother-in-law might know of something beyond Sata's own store of remedies that could help. Yet even if there were some plant whose properties Sata herself did not know, she feared that what afflicted Naya went beyond the reach of even Awija's healing skill. Her spirit was gone, fled somewhere beyond this world, and unless it returned, her body would never recover. Sata did not know how to bring her daughter back, and the possibility that she might never return filled her with despair.

Lost in thought, staring into the flames of the campfire, Sata started in surprise at the sound of Oyuun's voice. It was he who had broken the silence. Setting down his stew bowl, he gazed at Sata in a way she found unsettling, his dark eyes compassionate but otherwise impossible to fathom.

Will you answer a question, he'd asked, *something I've wondered about since we first met?*

Sata let his request hang between them, floating in the night air. She did not really know this man and his son and they still had much to answer for in her view. Yet they were bound together for the time being. To be fair, the two of them had gone out of their way to be solicitous, anticipating her needs and doing whatever they could to help her care for her daughter. Still, she could not quite bring herself to fully relax in their presence. Her anxiety over Naya didn't help. Conscious of not wanting to reveal too much, yet too tired to go on maintaining her guard, Sata responded with a question of her own.

"What is it you want to know?" she asked, speaking in the stranger's tongue.

"How is it that you come to understand both our language and the language of the black-stone knappers?"

Relieved that this was all he wanted to know, Sata for the first time in days allowed the hint of a smile to cross her lips. Oyuun returned it encouragingly, waiting for her reply. Aytal, who had been sitting with head bowed on the far side of the fire, looked up, interested as well.

"The language of the black-stone knappers, as you call them, is the language of my homeland," she answered, straightening a little with pride. "My people are known for their skill with the stone we call obsidian, found in abundance in the valley where I was born. The quality of what we quarry is better than any available anywhere else, and our knappers are the most skilled at finding the sharpest edge within each stone. Our blades are much in demand." "As for your tongue," she continued, her expression softening at the memory, "my grandfather taught me. In his younger days he was a great traveler, a trader. He and his brother, his father, and his uncle visited all the lands in the four directions from our home in the mountains, traveling with obsidian blades of all shapes and sizes for trade."

After so many days of near silence, sharing more than a few words came as a relief and Sata allowed herself to elaborate, switching back and forth between the stranger's tongue and her own as the words flowed. "North, they travelled, to the grasslands and forests beyond, south through our own mountains to the lands on the other side, and east and west along the shores of the two great seas, returning with goods we could not produce ourselves and tales of distant places, strange sights and tribes with languages and customs very different from our own."

Here she paused, inquiring to see if she'd made herself understood. Again, Oyuun nodded encouragingly. "He learned other tongues easily," Sata went on, "and found it the best way to gain the trust of those with whom he traded, not to mention dissuading others from taking advantage of him. By the time I came along, he was an old man and no longer ventured far from my family's fire, but he remembered the words he'd learned and passed them on to me, along with stories of his travels. They made me want to see the world beyond our mountains." Her voice had become a bit wistful. Recalling her manners, she turned to the stranger. "But your tongue, if my grandfather is to be believed, comes from beyond the forests, far to the north. How is it that you are able to understand the language of my homeland?"

"Ah," replied Oyuun with a deprecating smile, eyes not meeting hers, "that is perhaps a tale for another time. I'd like to know more about you," he said, deflecting the conversation back to her. "Did you get your wish, your desire to see more of the world?"

"Yes, I suppose," Sata answered, her tone noncommittal. "As a girl, not much older than my daughter, I left my own people to join my husband's clan. He and I became *sneubhō* – joined for life – at the plain where the two great rivers, the *Rā* and the *Dān*, run closest to one another before each flowing to their own great sea. Do you know the place?" It was a popular crossroads. No doubt the stranger intended to stop there himself on his way south. He nodded.

"Since then," she continued, "I have traveled with my husband and his people, mostly through the grasslands that lie between the two great rivers, as far north as the edges of the forest lands. We venture out on the steppe during the summer, looking for good grazing for our animals and following the herds for the hunt, but then return to more sheltered areas closer to the *Rā* for the winter. It's the same every year. We had just begun this season's journey to our winter settlement when…"

Sata's voice trailed off and her gaze shifted back to Naya, worry returning to the lines of her face. The girl stared unseeing into the fire's dying flames, the brief improvement in her demeanor from earlier in the evening replaced once again by disquieting lassitude. Amu looked up from his place beside her, whined softly, then lay his head back on his outstretched paws. Aytal, who had risen to retrieve more wood from the nearby stack, returned to his seat and began stirring the embers. A shower of sparks briefly pierced the surrounding darkness. The air smelled of smoke.

"Will you tell me more about your family?" Oyuun asked. "Do you have other children?"

If he'd thought to further distract Sata, he'd chosen the wrong question. The slight smile he had succeeded in coaxing from her as she talked of her homeland and her childhood vanished, replaced by a flash of pain so raw she could not turn away quickly enough to hide it from him. Reaching out a hand to feel Naya's forehead, she answered in a low voice, scarcely loud enough to be heard.

"No," she said, without looking at him. "She is my only living child."

Naya shifted her head slightly as if to evade her mother's touch, but otherwise remained unresponsive and Sata withdrew her hand without making contact. Instead, she sat motionless for a long moment, eyes closed, fingers entwined tightly in her lap, calling on reserves run nearly dry. At last, exhaling, she opened her eyes and was about to stand when Oyuun stopped her with another question.

"Will you tell me her name?" he asked gently.

This time when Sata lifted her gaze to the stranger's, the mask was back in place. She had forgotten herself, allowing his kindness to lead her into sharing more than she should. Her gestures, like her voice, were now carefully neutral. "Naya," she replied briefly. "Her full name is Satanaya, as is mine, but just as I am called Sata for short, she is called Naya."

"What does it mean?" Aytal spoke from his place on the far side of the fire. Sata looked at him across the freshly rekindled blaze. For days she had pointedly ignored his existence, directing whatever communication was necessary toward his father. For the first time since exchanging words with him over Naya's nearly lifeless body out on the steppe, she deigned to fully acknowledge the young man whose arrow she had extracted from her daughter's back.

"In the language of my people," she replied, "it means something like 'mother of heroes.' The exact translation is 'mother of a hundred sons.'" Sata did not bother to sign. She did not care whether Aytal understood her, nor whether he or his father grasped the irony of her words in light of what she'd just disclosed about Naya's status as an only child. Neither did she drop her gaze. Having regained control over her own features and decided to give the young stranger her full attention, she was unwilling to grant him the reprieve of being the first to look away.

Discomfited, Aytal shifted his own gaze back to Naya, where it lingered. Her hair caught the glint of the fire, reflecting back the glow of the flames with deceptive vitality. Her lids were closed now, as though resting, lashes delicately outlined against pale cheeks, but marks of strain were etched between her brows and her breathing remained labored. Taking a deep breath himself, Aytal returned to Sata, who had still not released him from her scrutiny. The expression she read on his face, illuminated by the fire's light, contained both sorrow and regret.

"It's a beautiful name," he replied haltingly, as though wanting to say more.

Silence followed. Aytal seemed to be gathering courage to continue, but before he could, Oyuun broke in, obviously hoping to forestall another awkward moment.

"I'm sorry there is not more that can be done for her," he said, directing the conversation back to Naya's condition. "She appeared a little better earlier, but now her breathing seems worse."

Freeing Aytal at last, Sata turned back to Oyuun. "I've done all that I know how to do," she answered, trying not to sound as desperate as she felt. "Her body and spirit must take their own path to healing."

"Indeed," agreed Oyuun. "Yet, it is as though her spirit is the more grievously injured. She is not with us."

"Is there nothing we can do to bring her back?" Aytal turned earnest eyes toward his father, before returning his gaze to Naya. "Is there no way to retrieve her spirit?"

They were all silent for several long moments, the only sounds in the clearing the crackle of the fire, the murmur of the icy stream and Naya's difficult breathing. Finally, Sata shifted as though once more intending to rise but again she was interrupted.

"Father?" Aytal's voice was serious. Oyuun did not immediately respond, but he seemed to know the unspoken question his son was asking. Sata looked at each in turn, recognizing that something passed between them.

"What is it?" she demanded, hope sharpening her voice. "Do you know of a cure that can help my daughter?"

Still, Oyuun hesitated, as though debating with himself. At last, sighing deeply, he replied.

"There is one thing we could try, but it is dangerous and it does not always work. If the sufferer does not possess sufficient strength, they can end up in a worse state. In addition, there must be a healthy person willing to risk themselves for the sake of the cure."

"It is dangerous," he repeated, looking at his son.

"I am willing to take the risk," Aytal replied.

"What are you talking about?" cut in Sata, looking from father to son in turn. "I will not allow my daughter to be further harmed. Especially not by you," she finished, addressing Aytal.

"We agree that your daughter is afflicted as much by a malady of the spirit as a wound to her body." With a nod, Sata acknowledged the truth of what they had all observed. Oyuun continued, "the cure my son proposes seeks to heal the spirit so that the body may follow."

"What is the nature of this cure?" Sata asked warily. "What is it that you propose to do to help Naya?"

"Among my people, there are those who are able to travel between the worlds. Do you know what I mean by this? Those who visit the place where spirits dwell?"

"Yes, I think so," replied Sata cautiously. "We have a name for such people. *Etmn itājōrs* – 'the ones who journey.'"

Oyuun saw her glance at Naya. "In our tongue, they are known as *shamans*," he said. "They are not the same as priests, whose responsibility is to conduct the ceremonies and intercede with the gods, nor do they heal with ointments and herbs, although in rare cases the same person might possess skill in more than one area and thus serve in multiple capacities. Yet to be at once *shaman*, priest and healer is unusual. More typically, the *shaman* is someone who at some point has crossed the divide between life and death, between this world and the other, and chosen to return."

Again, Sata's gaze shifted to Naya, the girl's form visible in the soft glow of the fire. Beyond the circle cast by the flames, the surrounding night felt like a black void. Light and dark, thought Sata, this world and the other. Did her daughter's spirit languish in some twilight in between? She could see the stranger studying Naya as well, as though pondering the same question. After a moment, he continued.

"When *shamans* come back," he explained, "they bring with them the knowledge of how to travel at will between the worlds and the ability to commune with spirits in either place. But the knowledge and ability come with a cost. In the worst cases, those who have undergone such a death-in-life experience become so consumed by their visions of the other world as to be unable to continue to exist among us. For those who become true *shamans*, they are able to use what they learned for the benefit of their people, returning again and again to the spirit world to seek wisdom and healing. Yet even they are never again entirely at home among the living."

After a pause to be sure she had understood everything Oyuun had said, Sata spoke. "I have heard of such individuals," she said slowly. "Our priests warn us that those who experience anything like you are describing must be brought under their protection and oversight, for their own well-being as well as that of the clan. They believe there can be great danger associated with the power to journey between the worlds, if not carefully controlled by the priests themselves." She hesitated a moment, her eyes dropping to her hands still clasped in her lap, before continuing without looking up. "Do you know, does the skill run in families?" she asked.

"Yes, among my people we often see the gift passed in the family line. Sometimes it skips a generation." Sata could feel the stranger watching her, waiting to see if she would elaborate.

"Why do you ask?" he inquired at last. "Is there such a one who dwells among you now?"

"No," she answered, more quickly than she intended. "But my mother-in-law believes in such powers, and she herself is able to communicate readily with those she calls her guides. The priests are very suspicious of her. Only the respect commanded by my father-in-law, the old clan chief, as well as my mother-in-law's own standing as a healer, keep them from denouncing her to the rest of the clan. And more and more lately, I wonder about my father-in-law as well. As he approaches his time of transition, he seems frequently to gaze into a world beyond this one, as though the mist between them grows thin."

"Yes," agreed Oyuun. "It is often thus when the spirit is allowed to take its time in its final crossing, but rarely does one such as your father-in-law – a warrior and a chief – survive long enough to face death as the natural consequence of age, and not as the violent end of a life cut short in its prime."

"But what does this talk of journeying between worlds have to do with my daughter?" asked Sata, returning to what concerned her. "Are you a *shaman*, capable of restoring her spirit?"

"No, not I," returned Oyuun. "Nor my son," he added, seeing her glance at Aytal, who had moved once again to stoke the fire. "No," he repeated, "but I believe your daughter may be, how did you say, 'one who journeys.'"

"*Etmn itājōr*," murmured Sata, hearing her mother-in-law's voice as she'd pronounced the words for the first time almost three moons ago and then again, the evening before they'd left on their winter migration. It seemed an age ago but it had only been seven nights. She and Potis had wanted to send Naya away so that the adults could discuss what to do about the horses, but both the girl's grandparents had insisted that she stay. *Etmn itājōr*, Awija had called her, and Awos had concurred. If only she had not agreed to honor her daughter's vision, thought Sata, allowing her to spend time with the horses and try to tame them. Nothing but disaster had ensued. Now Naya seemed to be in this frightening in-between place and the knowledge filled her with fear. She recalled the words Naya had spoken out on the steppe, before she fell into this awful stupor. The filly had spoken to her again, and this time she remembered. What had been the little horse's message, and would it bring Naya back to this world, or somehow draw her deeper into the other, beyond where any of them could reach her?

"What is this cure you propose then?" she finally asked. "Can she be healed from this state she is in?"

"If her destiny is to be a *shaman*, nothing we can do will change that," Oyuun replied. "But if her spirit is to return from the other world, whole and strong so that she might serve her people, I believe someone must go to help guide her back."

"How is this thing done?" Sata asked. "How can someone bring her back?"

"That person must also journey," replied Oyuun.

"But if we have no *shaman* among us, who can do this thing?" Sata sounded doubtful.

"One of us must make the attempt," Oyuun answered. "You cannot go, for if anything were to happen to you, your husband would be justifiably angered. I cannot go, because someone with knowledge of the ceremony must be in charge of the drum. The drumbeat is what guides those who journey and most importantly summons them back. That leaves Aytal."

Oyuun looked at his son. From across the fire the young man returned his father's gaze, unwavering.

"Alright then," Oyuun said after a moment. "If this is truly your choice, it is perhaps fitting." Turning to Sata, he continued. "He owes your daughter a debt. He is willing to risk his spirit for hers. Are you willing that he should make the journey to find her and ask her to return?"

Sata did not answer right away. She feared what she did not completely understand and she still did not fully trust the stranger and his son, but she also knew that something must be done for Naya.

"If we have no other choice," she replied at last. "But she may yet come back on her own. Let us give her more time."

"As you wish," said Oyuun. "However, keep in mind that the longer her spirit wanders the other world, the harder it may be to bring her back. How long would you wait? Tomorrow will mark seven days since she first received her injury."

"You mean since your son shot her in the back?" Sata's blue eyes flared icily in the firelight. Oyuun stared back, holding her gaze, his own eyes dark. Again, as on that first night out on the steppe, Sata had the uncomfortable sense of the stranger looking at her as though he recognized her.

"My son has apologized for his mistake and has already risked his life once since then to save your daughter," he said after a moment. "He is willing now to risk his spirit. What would you have us do?"

It was Sata who lowered her gaze first. She was too tired and worried to sustain her anger against these two. It had been an accident, after all, and not entirely their fault. "There will be a sign," she replied at last. "If we are meant to undertake this thing, there will be a sign." To her relief, Oyuun appeared to agree and let the matter drop.

Life in the little clearing quickly fell into a rhythm of sorts, with Oyuun and Aytal spending their time hunting and gathering firewood while Sata tended to the goats and took care of Naya. The day following Aytal's offer to journey on Naya's behalf was no different. When Sata checked on her daughter just after sunrise, she found her condition unchanged. She'd stayed with her within the larger of the two shelters for most of the day, leaving only to milk the she-goat and move the picket line to a new location within the clearing. Otherwise, she'd remained inside, taking care of small chores while Naya stared unseeing into the fire burning in the hearth, Amu at her side. Sata worried that the smoky atmosphere within the hide walls of the tent did nothing to help her daughter's breathing, but she had not liked the look of the clouds she'd seen massing along the horizon throughout the day, nor the chill breeze that had replaced last night's mild air. She did not want to risk moving Naya outdoors. Now, with daylight almost gone, she stood just outside the shelter's entrance, looking west through the break in the trees. She considered the deteriorating weather with a worried frown.

"Winter is coming," observed Oyuun, coming to stand beside her.

"Yes," Sata concurred, pulling her cloak more tightly around her shoulders, "carried on the back of the North Wind." She knew from long experience that the first storm of the season could easily bring with it enough snow to leave them trapped for days or more.

Oyuun studied the sky as well. "We've spent the day preparing," he said, as though sharing her thoughts. "Aytal and I stacked extra firewood in both shelters and we've moved the antelope carcass from yesterday's hunt inside as well." They had been fortunate to surprise a herd grazing not far from the clearing and Aytal's quick reflexes and expert technique with his bow had brought down a large buck. "We should make sure that we all have enough stored water to last through the storm. What about the goats?" he asked.

"Make a place for them in your shelter and bring your hides and other things next door. You and your son can join us until after the storm passes."

"Are you sure?" Oyuun queried.

"Yes," returned Sata. "It will be better if we're only burning wood for one fire." She didn't need to point out that without a well-tended blaze, and the shared warmth of multiple bodies within the larger shelter, they would all be in greater danger of freezing. Survival meant more than observing the propriety of separate accommodations. Using the last moments of daylight, they hurried to complete their preparations and then gathered in the larger shelter, now crowded, to await the storm's arrival.

The wind came first, beginning sometime in the middle of the night. Heralded by a keening that grew rapidly in intensity, a ferocious gale soon clawed at the walls of the tent, threatening to strip the heavy leather hides from their frame. Sata, woken from a light sleep by the increasing roar, could just make out the nervous bleating of the goats coming from the tent next door. She hoped Oyuun had driven their stakes firmly into the ground. Not long after, pellets of ice began pinging dully against the larger shelter's walls, the crescendo so loud and rapid that Sata would have had to shout to be heard. No one tried to speak, however, although by now they were all awake, even Naya. Oyuun moved to add wood to the fire, which was beginning to smoke from the moisture coming through the hole in the shelter's roof. As he did, he caught Sata's eye and gestured with a glance toward the girl. She sat bolt upright, staring at the wall of the shelter as though she could see through it and listening intently. Beside her, Amu rose to his feet growling, hair bristling on the back of his neck.

Knowing it was futile to try to make herself heard over the force of the storm, Sata moved next to Naya and took her by the shoulders to turn her back toward the fire. Naya shook her off, refusing to look away from the unseen presence she perceived beyond the walls of the tent. Whatever it was, Amu knew something was there as well. Hackles raised, he stood motionless, nose and ears on full alert. After a moment, he gave a sharp bark. At almost the same instant, Naya lunged toward the entrance to the tent, moving so suddenly that it took the rest of them by surprise. Fumbling with the thongs holding the tent flap closed, she'd almost succeeded in untying them before anyone could react. Aytal responded first, thrusting himself between Naya and the opening before she could rush out into the elements.

"*Në!*" he shouted in her own tongue, one of several words he'd picked up over the last few days. It was not enough to stop her. She continued to struggle, even after he'd wrapped his arms around her and pulled her away from the entrance.

"*Nē!*" he repeated, tightening his hold.

"Naya, what is it?" demanded Sata, raising her voice over the storm. Naya shook her head wildly, making one last futile effort to wrench free of Aytal's grasp before going suddenly still. Amu remained beside the entrance, whining.

Sata, Oyuun and Aytal looked at one another, the same mute question on each of their faces. What could have roused Naya from her lethargy? Clearly something was out there in the storm. The dog sensed it, even if they could not. Whatever it was, thought Sata, better that it remain where it was while they all stayed safe inside. She wondered briefly if Potis or one of the other men from the clan might have returned but no one attempted to enter the shelter. Wolves or other large predators were unlikely to be out in such weather. No sound could be heard, beyond the noise of the wind and sleet battering the tent walls.

After a moment, Amu left his place beside the entrance and went to sit in front of Aytal, who still held Naya in his arms. Cocking his head to the side, he looked up into her face expectantly and lifting a paw, laid it on her knee. Naya did not acknowledge the dog, nor any of the others. Instead, she held herself rigid in Aytal's arms, avoiding his touch, entirely focused on whatever was outside. Looking wordlessly over Naya's head at his father, Aytal waited until Oyuun had shifted positions to block the way out before relinquishing his hold. As he did, Sata reached out, taking her daughter firmly by the shoulders and guiding her back to a place on the opposite side of the fire. The girl did not resist. Seating herself next to Naya, Sata wrapped her arms around her, smiling gratefully as Aytal bundled them both into a fur-lined hide.

Inside the tent, the temperature was dropping rapidly. Sata could feel Naya beginning to shiver and wished she could hold her even closer. Although Naya did not struggle against her embrace, neither did she relax at first, remaining erect and turning her head several times as if still trying to see into the storm raging beyond the shelter's walls. Eventually, Sata felt her surrender. Apparently exhausted after the sudden rush of energy that had nearly propelled her out into the storm, she leaned into the support of her mother's arms, resting her head against Sata's shoulder. Concluding that they weren't going out to investigate after all, Amu resumed his place by the fire, circling twice before laying down at the girl's side. He lowered his head to his paws with a sigh, resigned to wait out the storm.

Outside, a short distance from the shelter, several large shapes bunched together in a tight circle. Although still lashed by ice and wind, they at least gained some protection where they stood in the lee of the cliff face, curtained by the surrounding underbrush. They too settled themselves to wait for the storm to end.

Sometime later, Oyuun stirred from his post just inside the shelter's entrance. The worst of the wind had subsided, leaving in its wake an eerie calm. Snow, he thought, recognizing the muffled silence that enveloped the tent. Glancing across central hearth, he could tell from the still shape of the girl and her mother beneath their shared hide blanket that both were likely dosing, if not actually asleep. The dog lay beside them, curled in a tight ball, nose tucked under his tail for warmth. Not much heat radiated from the fire. Despite Oyuun's efforts to feed the blaze, he could see his breath in the frigid air. They would need to retrieve more wood soon from the other shelter, he thought, eyeing critically what was left of the stack. It also wouldn't hurt to check on the goats. Moving stiffly, Oyuun reached over to shake Aytal by the shoulder, rousing him. Gesturing so as not to disturb the other sleepers, he indicated that the two of them should venture next door. Nodding his understanding, Aytal pulled up the hood of his cloak and crawling on hands and knees, followed his father outside.

Snow fell thickly, already accumulating in deep drifts throughout the clearing. Luckily although the entrance of the larger shelter faced into the prevailing wind, the smaller tent blocked some of its force, leaving a relatively open path for the fur-clad figures to make their way the short distance between the two structures. Inside, they were met by the pungent aroma of the goats, who bleated an unhappy greeting. Until the storm abated, there was not much that could be done to make the animals more comfortable.

"Be glad you're not out in it," Oyuun rebuked them mildly. Assured that all was well, he loaded Aytal's outstretched arms with additional wood before lifting as much as he could carry himself. Gesturing for the young man to go first, he followed, backing out of the tent. Pausing to attempt the awkward task of re-securing the tent flap without setting down his burden, Oyuun nearly lost his balance when Aytal nudged him from behind. Irritated, he turned. Pointing with an elbow, Aytal directed his father's gaze to a spot on the far side of the larger shelter. Swirling snow and lack of moonlight made visibility difficult but Oyuun thought he could just make out something that looked like an unusually large drift a little distance away. Squinting against the stinging flakes, Oyuun realized the mound of snow had what looked like a long black tail. As he looked more closely, he could actually see several tails, each attached to a snow-covered rump.

"Horses!" he thought. A small herd stood knee-deep in the accumulating snow, hind ends facing the icy wind, heads lowered against the worst of the onslaught. He couldn't tell how many there were but it was a small band, no more than four or five full-grown individuals. If there were youngsters, they were hidden from sight by the sheltering bulk of the adults. Surrounded by blowing flakes, the animals seemed oblivious to the humans' presence.

Signaling to Aytal to stay silent, Oyuun finished tying shut the smaller tent and then the two crept as unobtrusively as they could back to the larger shelter. Once inside, they each deposited their burdens as carefully as possible on the wood pile and without needing to consult one another, began searching for their weapons in the dark recesses formed by the shelter's walls.

"What are you doing?" asked Sata. She had awoken when they'd left to get the wood. Relief at their return with more fuel quickly turned to concern as Aytal located his bow and quiver and Oyuun pulled his spear out of the shadows.

"Shhh," returned Oyuun, gesturing for her to keep her voice low. "There's a herd of horses outside. With any luck, we'll survive this storm with fresh meat."

"No!" Sata whispered urgently.

"*Nē!*" cried Naya, stopping the hunters in their tracks. "Don't hurt them!" She lunged for the shelter's entrance, not to escape this time but to block the others from leaving. Crouching in front of the opening, hair in wild disarray, she glared about defiantly, eyes unfocused, as though in the grip of some kind of trance. Taken aback, Oyuun and Aytal looked first at each other, then at Sata for an explanation.

"Naya knows the horses are there," said Aytal, stating what seemed obvious, but his voice held a question as well. "She knew they were out in the storm even before we did. How does she know?"

"More importantly," cut-in Oyuun, "why should we not try to kill one?"

The question was aimed at Sata but it was Aytal who replied. "Because," he said, comprehension dawning on his face, "it's the same herd, the herd who saved us from the wolves, the herd she saved from us."

Sata hesitated a moment, then nodded. "It must be."

Naya, unable to understand what the others were saying, appeared not even to hear them. She maintained her posture barring the entrance to the shelter, eyes darting about in agitation. Oyuun exchanged looks with his son. Both set down their weapons. Only then did Naya relax her defensive stance. Almost immediately, she crumpled into a heap. As before, the sudden movement seemed to have drained her reserves. Both Sata and Oyuun moved to help the girl, but Aytal reached her first, lifting her in his arms and transferring her back to the nest of hides closer to the fire. Amu whined in concern, licking first Naya's face and then Aytal's. Pushing the dog away, the young man pulled one of the hides up over the girl's shoulders, tucking it gently around her before returning to his own place by the hearth. Hunched under the blanket and staring blankly into space, Naya seemed to retreat once more into another world.

"Enough," said Oyuun. He waited a moment for Sata to resettle herself beside Naya before confronting her. "Either you explain about these horses or we hunt them."

With a sigh, Sata acceded to the inevitable. "It's a long story," she said.

"Good," returned Oyuun, reaching over to stoke the fire. "Apparently we don't have anything better to do than listen."

Sata told them everything. When she had finished, Oyuun and Aytal sat in silence. Sata didn't know whether to regret her candor or feel relieved. Had she done the right thing in being so open? At least everything would make more sense to them now, Naya's presence among the horses, the herd's baffling behavior, but especially the state her daughter had been in for the last seven days. They would understand her own ambivalence about Aytal's offer to undertake a journey on Naya's behalf. How could she not be troubled when her daughter already walked between the worlds? Clearly a deep connection existed between Naya and the red filly. Had the girl's willingness to sacrifice her life to protect the young horse triggered an existential struggle that went beyond her physical wound? Was some unseen battle taking place in the spirit world, with Naya's very survival at stake? And now the herd was here, just outside the shelter.

"This is the sign," said Oyuun, holding Sata's gaze with his own.

"I know," was all she replied but she did not look away, nor try to disguise the fear in her eyes.

"There is something else," he said. "This night is the year's longest. In my home at this season, the sun struggles to rise beyond the horizon and its rays no longer warm the earth. On this night, we acknowledge the power of the darkness, but we also celebrate the rebirth of the light."

"We too mark the longest night and the sun's rebirth," said Sata. "I'd lost track of the days."

"It is an auspicious time," Oyuun observed. "If we undertake the ceremony while this night lasts, the dawn may bring healing, along with the sun's return."

Sata nodded her assent. "What must we do?"

"Naya and Aytal should lay near one another, eyes covered. If you have the proper herbs, we can burn them to purify the air and help draw the helping spirits close. I will drum to open the passage between the worlds and if you have a rattle or any other means with which to call the spirits, you should use them as well. Aytal will undertake the journey on Naya's behalf, but we must have her consent before he sets out. He will call on the help of his guide, and together they will search the other world for your daughter's missing spirit."

"You have a guide?" Sata asked, turning to the young man in surprise.

"Yes," Aytal replied. "My guide came to me when I went on my vision quest."

"Among our people," explained Oyuun, "boys of fourteen winters are sent away from the settlement to spend one moon during the darkest time of the year in total isolation, with little to eat or drink. Although they have the shelter of a small tent, they must endure hunger, thirst, cold and solitude. In truth, they must confront death. Not all survive. During this time, those who are fortunate may be visited by a spirit who reveals to them their life's purpose and becomes their helper and guide.

The identity of one's spirit guide, as well as the messages brought from the spirit world during one's vision quest, are considered sacred knowledge, only to be shared with others under very special circumstances."

"Our boys undergo a similar trial," responded Sata. "The priests guard the details, but when the boys return, they are considered men. During a special ceremony that follows, they are all given the same mark, a tattoo of braided lines encircling the right wrist, signifying their new status as adult members of the clan, sworn to live and die for one another. At the same time, in private, with only the priests as witness, each boy claims his totem – his special guardian spirit. The priests then tattoo the totem's symbol in a hidden place."

Sata thought of the design signifying a hawk in flight etched in black ink in the small of her husband's back. Even he could not see the image, although by reaching behind he could feel the raised scar. Once he had delighted in having her trace the lines with a seductive fingertip but many seasons had passed since they had shared such intimacy.

"Speaking openly of one's totem is discouraged," she continued, pulling her thoughts back to the present. "Among my husband's people, only the priests are empowered to communicate directly with the spirits."

"So it is for us," concurred Oyuun, "in that a man's relationship with his guide is sacred and not to be spoken of lightly. But we do not have priests, only *shamans* and healers, so no other person stands between a man and his guardian spirit." Oyuun paused a moment, as though deciding whether to say more. "Do your priests journey on behalf of the people?" he finally asked.

"They intercede with the spirits and our gods, yes," answered Sata, "but they are also very suspicious and fearful of the other world. I do not think they venture there willingly, nor do they look with favor on anyone who does." Having decided to trust Oyuun and his son with her daughter's life, she no longer felt compelled to hold back any information that might be helpful. "Naya's grandmother, who was originally an *alteros*, an outsider like me, communes often with her guides, but she must do so in private. The spirits give her knowledge of plant medicine and taught her long ago how to talk with the plants themselves. It is why she is such a powerful medicine woman. Our priests are a little afraid of her."

"And your daughter," asked Oyuun, looking over at Naya, who was still huddled under her blanket, apparently oblivious to their conversation. "What do the priests think about her?"

"If they knew, they would be outraged. It's why we've been so secretive about the horses."

The last thing the priests would condone, thought Sata, is for Naya to have the kind of power with animals that her grandmother had with plants. Yet from the time she was small, she had demonstrated an uncanny connection with them, even greater than her father's. The sheep, goats and cattle followed her everywhere, and the small wild creatures – rabbits, foxes and birds – held no fear of her. Because of her gifts, she could be a better hunter than any of the boys her age and even some of the men.

"My husband had to stop taking her along on hunting trips," she said out loud. "The others complained she brought bad luck, with her hair, but really it's because she has skills they cannot fathom. If she were a boy, with the proper training, she could learn to call the wild herds for the hunt. This thing with the horses, though, it goes beyond anything anyone has ever imagined. Always, my husband's people have hunted horses. Who would ever think to try to tame them, to try to ride on them?"

"My people have tamed the reindeer," put in Aytal.

"Or rather, they have tamed us," corrected Oyuun.

"Are they not like our cattle?" protested Sata.

"In some respects, they are," replied Oyuun. "But unlike your cattle, our reindeer would probably be just fine without us. We follow them, not the other way around. Yes, we protect them from predators and give them salt, and in exchange they allow us to milk them and provide us with meat, but really they have much less need of us than we do of them."

"Then your reindeer are indeed more like the horses," conceded Sata. "The horses have no need of us at all. To them we are just like any other predator, nothing more."

"Yet still, a herd waits outside," observed Oyuun. "Do they seek nothing more than shelter from the storm?"

"I don't know, it's what I don't understand." The apprehension and concern were back in Sata's eyes.

"The spirits will have an answer." Oyuun laid a comforting hand on her shoulder. "Come, we must prepare for the ceremony before the night ends."

Uncertainly, Sata turned to Aytal. "Are you sure about this?"

She searched the young man's face, her own expression no longer so unyielding.

"Yes," he replied. "My guide will be with me. I want to do whatever I can to help your daughter."

"Thank you." She wanted to offer more than gratitude, maybe even forgiveness, but couldn't find the words.

"Naya," she said, addressing her daughter in her own tongue. "Can you hear me?" The girl gave no indication of heeding her mother's voice.

"Naya," Sata persisted. "The stranger's son is going to undertake an *etmn itājō* – a journey – on your behalf." Still no response.

"He goes in search of your spirit, to bring you back to us." Was that a flicker in Naya's eyes? "He seeks to help you." Yes, definitely awareness. Anger, she would guess, perhaps defiance. Maybe her daughter was still in there somewhere after all. Hope kindled in Sata's heart.

"They know about the horses," she continued, speaking soothingly. "They've promised not to harm them. We just want you to find your way back to us." As she spoke, she gently guided Naya into a reclining position. The girl did not resist.

"Do you consent to the journey?" she asked, reaching out to take Naya's hand in her own. "Squeeze my hand if you do." Nothing. They all waited. Naya's cooperation in the healing was essential.

"For the horses?" Sata asked at last. Still nothing. Then, ever so faintly, Sata felt Naya's fingers tighten on her own. Relieved, she nodded at Oyuun and Aytal, letting them know they could proceed. Withdrawing her hand, she reached toward the altar where she kept her sacred objects, lifting a small clay bowl which she set down beside the fire before turning back to the altar to retrieve a pouch containing dried herbs, along with a rattle, made from a withered gourd, that had rested beside bowl. Murmuring a prayer, she placed a lighted stick from the fire in the bowl among the herbs, causing a curl of smoke to waft gently upwards. The smoke didn't get far before being met by a draft of cold air and Sata had to blow repeatedly on the glowing tip of the stick to keep the herbs alight but eventually the air immediately surrounding the hearth was scented with their sweet aroma.

Meanwhile, Aytal settled himself in a prone position beside Naya. Together, Sata and Oyuun drew hide blankets over both figures, leaving only their heads uncovered. Searching about for something to place over their eyes without smothering them, Sata finally unwound from around her own neck a long, woven scarf of soft wool. This she carefully draped over each face.

"Is there anything else I should do?" she asked, looking to Oyuun for further instructions.

"Take up your rattle. Try to stay in time with the drum. The rhythm is very important." Seating himself once again on the other side of the hearth, he carefully unwrapped a small hide-covered drum, its surface painted with colorful geometric designs. At the center had been rendered the outline of an animal which could only have been a reindeer. Compared to the large ceremonial drums used by the clan's priests, thought Sata, it was a diminutive object, barely bigger than the double span of a man's hand. It had to be so of necessity, she presumed, to have fit so unobtrusively in Oyuun's pack, yet he handled it with great reverence. She hoped the sound it produced would serve its purpose as well as the great booming drums of the priests.

"You say you are not a *shaman*, yet you travel with a drum?" Sata let the question in her statement hang in the air. Her eyes searched the stranger's enigmatic face. Who was this man?

"No," he reiterated. "I do not call myself a *shaman*."

It was the extent of his reply. Motioning her to silence, he sat for a moment in total stillness. Then, taking up a small beater, he began to drum, softly at first and then with gathering intensity. Closing her eyes, Sata waited a moment to find the rhythm, then began shaking her rattle in rapid accompaniment. Soon, the staccato percussive beat filled the entire shelter. As if in response, the blizzard renewed its onslaught. The wind, which had settled for a time, began to rise again, buffeting the shelter with blast after icy blast, smothering any sound that might have escaped.

Outside, oblivious to all but the storm's fury, the clearing's other refugees continued to wait patiently for it to be over.

Chapter Ten

To Naya, the night seemed never-ending. Even when she struggled from time to time to become momentarily aware of the world around her – her mother's anxious face, her voice, her touch – still the darkness seemed more real and staying present required strength she could not muster. The night kept pulling her back. Even when she sat in the pale winter sunshine with eyes open, staring blankly into the clearing around her, a gray mist shrouded her sight. Exhausted, she would have liked to give up the struggle – and still, the nightmares came.

At first, they had terrified her. She felt herself running, limbs pumping, heart pounding, lungs gasping for air. She was surrounded by other beings like herself, their fear magnifying her own until it felt like a tangible force, pushing them all irresistibly onward, fleeing in desperation from some unknown horror. "No!" she wanted to call out. "Stop! We must stand and fight." But the rush of panic was too great and if she tried alone to turn and confront whatever it was that drove them, she would be trampled.

Then the scene would shift. She and the others were no longer running. Instead, they toiled in the darkness, endlessly pulling heavy loads in a world devoid of sky or grass or water, staggering under the weight of burdens impossible to bear. Flight no longer existed as an option. Despair replaced the fear. Still, she sought to resist and by resisting, somehow manage to dispel the nightmare.

But no matter how hard she struggled against both fear and despair, a third scene always came, worse than the first two. She found herself surrounded by the others like her. Again, they ran together, almost as one being, but this time urged on by a force more insistent even than panic. Instead of fleeing, they streamed headlong into the danger, driven by a fierce exhilaration more terrifying because it seemed to annihilate even the instinct to survive. This was the worst nightmare of all. All around her, cries of pain and death threatened to drown her senses and the darkness turned crimson. This was when she screamed.

As suddenly as they appeared, the nightmares would retreat back into the darkness, leaving her drained. When they came a second time and then a third, she knew a little better what to expect. Still, she could not prevent herself from experiencing the visceral sensations they aroused in her, until exhaustion finally numbed her and at last, after what seemed an eternity, the visions receded. They never left her entirely, however, either when she slept or in the semi-conscious world she inhabited throughout much of the day. She could not muster the strength to pull herself out of their grip and back to full awareness. She felt as though she wandered in an indistinct, featureless landscape infused with the nightmarish echoes of fear and despair.

And then had come the storm and with it, the arrival of her kindred spirits in the clearing. She knew they were there, felt them, recognized them. They had been with her in the nightmares, along with countless more like them. She wanted to go to them, feel surrounded and safe in their midst. She'd tried, but one of the strangers prevented her.

Afterwards, she was too weak to move. And it was so cold. It had taken all of her remaining resources, driven by instinct, to try to stop the two men when they'd reached for their weapons. She didn't understand who they were or why they always seemed to be present now. She didn't understand why her mother deigned to speak with them any more than she understood the words they exchanged or why they were still with them. It seemed a betrayal. One of them had nearly killed her. But then he had protected her too, calling on her not to leave. She didn't understand. And she was so tired.

Now, hearing the drum, Naya felt at first afraid. Its rhythm was rapid, insistent, like rushing hoof beats, drowning out the quieter rattle. Panic rose in her chest. But there was no increasing intensity, no crescendo, just the steady driving beat. At last, rather than resist, she surrendered to its force, allowing herself to be carried by the sound. As soon as she did, she felt her awareness released from her body. Relief flooded through her, as she realized how hard she had been struggling to remain even partially present in the world she knew.

Gone were both the shelter and the storm. Instead she found herself in a landscape at once new and strangely familiar. A grassy valley stretched around her, surrounded on all sides by rocky slopes, some in sunshine, the rest in shadow. Above her, the sky formed a backdrop of brilliant cloudless blue. Looking down at her feet, she recognized her own hide boots and the sight gave her comfort. A trail stretched before her, its dirt track clearly outlined against the surrounding grass. This led up out of the valley and into the hills, where it seemed to disappear among the boulder-strewn heights. She thought she could just make out the dark shape of a cave opening. Drawn onward by the sound of the drum, she began to climb.

Feeling neither fatigue nor difficulty breathing, Naya reveled in being able to move freely across the valley and up into the hills. Scrambling over rocks, she reached the cave's opening. It was larger than it had appeared from the valley floor and she entered easily. A worn path descended deeper into the cave. She followed it and soon found herself swallowed by darkness. Pausing, she looked upward from where she had come and could see a mere sliver of sky. All around her was black. For the first time, she thought to be afraid. The drum, however, continued its by-now familiar beat and this darkness did not hold the same terror as her nightmares.

Taking a deep breath, she reached out to find the solid walls of the cave, feeling them rough and damp to her touch. How much further should she go? The drum urged her onward. Keeping one hand on the wall to her left and the other outstretched before her, she resumed her descent. Within a few steps, she found her way blocked by a solid barrier of dirt and rock, down which flowed a trickle of water that gathered in an ankle-deep puddle at her feet. With seemingly no option other than to turn back the way she had come, she considered what to do next. Her boots were rapidly become soaked and her feet would soon be as icy as the water. Blind in the darkness of the cave, Naya closed her eyes and placed her bare palms against the earthen wall in front of her, wondering how to proceed.

When she opened her eyes again, she found herself still up to her ankles in water, but the cave was gone. Instead, she now stood in the midst of a shallow pool, surrounded on three sides by a clearing ringed by trees. On the fourth, a small waterfall trickled down a high cliff. Beneath her hands, the rocks felt pleasantly cool and wet. The flow hardly disturbed the pool's surface, leaving it smooth enough to reflect the soft glow of a full moon riding high in the night sky.

Even in the dim light, Naya recognized this place. She hadn't noticed the waterfall the first time but she knew she had been here before. Hope lifting her heart, she looked around, searching the shadows beneath the trees for any sign of the red filly. Nothing but stillness greeted her. Apparently, she was alone. Elation gave way to disappointment. She splashed her way out of the pool, scattering shards of moonlight in her wake. Seating herself on a fallen log a little way from the water's mossy edge, she pulled off her sodden boots and looked around once again, taking further stock of her surroundings. The drum beat continued unabated, surrounding the quiet little grove with its pulsing rhythm.

"Welcome," said a voice.

Startled, Naya turned her head, trying to locate the origin of the sound. She looked for movement among the trees.

"Who are you?" she said nervously. Although she recognized the voice, she was no longer sure it belonged to the red filly. "I can't see you." Nor could she tell from which direction the sound came.

"You must see with your heart," said the voice. "Close your eyes. *Feel* for me instead. Maybe then you will see."

Naya closed her eyes. Immediately, she became more conscious of the subtle sensations in her own body and then of the vibrations in her surroundings – the murmur of water gently flowing down the rock face, a mild current of air brushing across her skin, and the reverberations of the drum. Everything else remained still. Against her palms she could feel the crumbling bark of the fallen tree where she sat. Beneath the soles of her bare feet she sensed layers of thick, spongy leaf mold. *This is an ancient place*, she thought.

"Now can you see me?" the voice asked.

"Yes!" Naya responded, eyes still closed. She was afraid that if she opened them, the new awareness would disappear.

"What is your heart's desire?" asked the voice.

"To be with you." She answered without hesitation or even conscious thought. The words seemed to speak themselves.

At the same moment, a vision came to her, of herself and the red filly together in a vast field of sunlit grass, the greenest she could imagine. Blossoming flowers of red, orange and yellow dotted the meadow. The sky was an intense blue. Toward the horizon, she could see the indigo of the night sky, pierced by countless glowing stars. Where dark met light, the orange crescent of a new moon embraced the blazing orb of a fiery sun and neither the brilliance of the day nor the mystery of the night was diminished. She was seated on the filly's back, could feel her warm coat, at once soft and scratchy against her skin. The young horse began to move, first one tentative step, then another. Surprised, Naya clutched the filly's mane, sure she was about to slide off but within moments, the two were moving as one, trotting, cantering and finally galloping across the verdant plain, racing toward where day joined night. Laughing, red hair streaming behind her, Naya abandoned her hold on the filly's mane and rode, head thrown back, arms outstretched. Pure joy suffused her entire being and she knew, somehow, that in that moment, the young horse's happiness matched her own.

As quickly as it had come, the vision faded and Naya, eyes still closed, sensed herself back in the stillness of the moonlit grove.

"This," she said simply. "This is my heart's desire."

"And when you have granted my heart's desire, then shall yours be granted also," returned the voice.

"What is your heart's desire?" Naya asked. For days, ever since she'd heard the voice in the suffocating blackness, she'd wanted to ask this question.

"That is your task to discover." The voice was kind but firm.

"But I'm so afraid," said Naya, surprising herself.

"Of what are you afraid?" asked the voice.

"Of what I see in the dark," she responded, thinking of the nightmares that tormented her. "Of what I see when I open my eyes." Fear and despair seemed always to obscure her sight, even when she tried to awaken.

"Those are the shadows of what is to come," said the voice. "They are indeed terrifying, but they are not all that haunts you. Of what are you truly afraid?"

"Of being hurt. I am afraid of the pain." Embarrassed, Naya said no more. Again, the words seemed to have come by themselves.

"Ah," said the voice. "Now we are getting somewhere. What is this pain that you fear?"

Naya thought of the arrow that had pierced her back as she tried to protect the red filly. She was about to answer but the voice interrupted.

"No," it said, "you know you do not fear physical pain, especially if you are protecting someone you love. What is the pain you fear?"

Pressed by the voice, Naya's heart constricted within her chest and she found it hard to breathe.

"I don't know," she said, fighting back tears that welled up out of nowhere. Anger overwhelmed her. All her life she had rejected fear. She was nothing if not brave. "I don't know," she repeated belligerently.

This outburst was met by silence. Stubbornly, eyes shut tight, Naya waited for the voice to speak again, ready this time to refuse to answer its questions. Finally, when she could no longer endure the silence, she opened her eyes and looked around defiantly. She found herself alone in the grove. The tears burst forth, great sobs that began in frustration and ended in desolation.

"I'm sorry," she said at last, closing her eyes once more. Head bowed and elbows resting on her knees, she buried her wet face in her hands. "*I'm sorry*," she repeated, the words no more than an anguished whisper.

"Do not apologize," said the voice.

Relief flooded her. She was not alone after all. She remained as she was, eyes closed, forehead resting in her hands.

"Never apologize for your tears or mistake them for lack of courage," the voice continued. "Nor should you believe that in order to be brave you must feel nothing, especially fear. Bravery and fear walk together, always. Sometimes, however, fear masquerades as anger. Discovering what you fear is the first step in understanding the difference and learning to trust. Trust is the most powerful weapon against fear that you can possess. But in order to trust, you must first be brave enough to feel. Do you think you can do that?"

"I don't know," said Naya.

"Everything begins with a choice," said the voice. "Do you understand?"

Lifting her head, eyes still closed, Naya nodded. "Yes," she said, then changed the nod to a shake. "No. I don't think I understand at all."

"Do you love the red filly?" asked the voice.

"Yes," cried Naya passionately. "But who…"

The voice cut her off. "Then your heart understands more than you know."

After a pause, the voice continued. "You must return, you realize. If your choice is to claim your heart's desire, then you must find the strength to become fully present again in your own world. That is where your task awaits you."

Going back seemed unappealing, especially if it meant contending with the darkness. She would rather gallop with the red filly across the endless plain. "I can't stay here?"

"You must go back," said the voice. "Your task lies in the ordinary world."

"Then I must go back," echoed Naya, doing her best to sound resolute. Somewhere in the back of her consciousness, she became aware again of the drum. The rhythm had changed, becoming more rapid and insistent.

"There is one more thing." The voice seemed to be coming from farther away.

"Yes?" said Naya, straining to hear, the drum threatening both to distract her and drown out the words.

"Forgiveness," spoke the voice, now faint. "Yourself and others. Don't forget. Forgiveness and trust. See with the eyes of your heart. Create ties without the use of a rope. Can you remember?"

"I'll try," said Naya.

"Good," said the voice, as if from a great distance. "Follow your heart to where the green grass grows and the wild wind blows."

Opening her eyes, Naya found herself still alone in the grove, but moonlight had been replaced by daylight and hushed stillness by a pleasant breeze. Sunshine filtered among the trees, casting dappled leaf shadows throughout the cool interior. Unlike the first time she had visited this place, she saw no pathways leading in or out. The creek that once flowed from the pool had disappeared. Unsure about how to do as she'd been instructed, she decided to try departing as she had come. The drum's returning call urged her to hurry.

Rising from the log where she sat, Naya put on her still-sodden boots and stepped out into the water. Sparkles danced on the pool's rippled surface, intensifying as she waded deeper. Dazzled, she laid bare palms against the cool stone of the rock face and closed her eyes again. When she opened them, she was surrounded by impenetrable darkness. She might have panicked, were it not for the reassuring feel of earth beneath her fingertips. She must be back underground where she started. Turning toward the way out, she took a few tentative steps forward. Almost immediately the ground began to slope upwards. Right hand following the wall, she made her way up the incline, gaining confidence as she went. Moments later she emerged once more at the mouth of the cave, her boots completely dry. The valley spread before her, surrounded on all sides by rocky hills. A relentless wind bent the tall grass. Far below, she could see the red filly, copper coat flaming in the sun. Even at this distance, Naya could see the young horse lift her head to look in her direction and in a moment she heard, carried on the sharp breeze, the sound of a joyous neigh. Impelled by the drum's insistent beat, she began to run.

Laying prone beneath heavy fur robes, cold air burning in his nostrils, Aytal felt the drum's steady rhythm, calling him to surrender. His mind wanted to resist, but if he was to help Naya, he must let go. He had no experience to guide him. All he could rely on was his intent to somehow find her spirit-self and persuade her to return with him. Would he be able to navigate his way? And even if he located her, would she return with him willingly? How would he even communicate with her?

For the first time since impetuously suggesting this journey, Aytal felt uncertain and afraid. Heart speeding up, he wanted to fight the power of the drum's driving beat. *No*, he thought, *I must try to help her*. Taking a deep breath, he sought to slow the throbbing within his own chest and thereby calm his mind. Gradually, with each breath, he began to abandon his consciousness to the drum. At some imperceptible threshold, vision replaced thought. Although a small part of him remained aware and watchful, the rest yielded to what felt like a waking dream.

Looking around, Aytal at first could see little. He was surrounded by mist. His feet, clad in his reindeer hide boots, stood on stony ground. The air felt chill and damp, muffling sound, even the rapid but now distant thud of the drum. The rattle could not be heard at all. He could discern a faint path, which he began to follow. Climbing steeply, the trail led him upward until it reached a ledge of granite high up on a rocky hillside. Beyond the ledge, accessible through a narrow crevice, lay what appeared to be a shallow cave.

Squeezing through the opening, Aytal found himself in an alcove carved into solid rock. Opposite the entrance, a rough-hewn tunnel descended into blackness. Pulled onward by the drum, he began to move down into the earth. Surprisingly, the space was large enough for him to stand comfortably upright, with no need to crawl or even stoop. Sightless in the dark, keeping one hand on the irregular surface of the tunnel wall, he felt himself spiraling downward with each step. After a short distance, the tunnel leveled off and he sensed that he'd entered some kind of cavern. The air felt less close against his skin. Still, he was in total darkness. Groping for the rock wall, he maneuvered until his hand encountered another void. Reaching forward with one foot, he could feel the ground once more sloping away and he began again to descend.

This time, the tunnel dropped steeply for what seemed like a great distance. Struggling to retain his footing on the slippery gravel, he half-slid the final stretch, coming to a stop at the base of a sheer granite wall. Panic threatened to overwhelm him. The barrier in front of him seemed impenetrable. There was no way to ascend the steep incline down which he had just come. Had he somehow taken a wrong turn? Was he trapped, deep beneath the earth? Aware once more of the frenetic beat of the drum matching the frantic pounding of his heart, Aytal made a conscious effort to recall his purpose. Surely, if this were the entrance to the spirit world, there must be a way in. Willing himself to be calm and ignore the drum, he placed both hands, palms outstretched, against the cold surface of the rock wall and closed his eyes. When he opened them again, the solid granite had melted away at his touch, revealing what lay beyond.

He stood with his back to a cliff face, much like the one in the clearing, but instead of being surrounded by a dense thicket of trees and underbrush, this rocky outcropping lay at the base of a steep hill and was more exposed. Aytal guessed he must somehow have passed through the stone itself. Ahead of him, clear sunlight illuminated an endless meadow, more limitless even than the steppes through which he and his father and stepbrother had been traveling. Overhead, a sky stretched, vast and impossibly blue. The grass, greener than any he'd ever seen, harbored innumerable small blossoms of brilliant yellow, orange and red, their vibrancy dazzling him. The scent of the flowers was intoxicating. He wanted nothing so much as to stand and absorb all that surrounded him, allowing the landscape to engulf his senses.

Lifting his gaze, delight turned to awe as he viewed the distant horizon. There, in a sight that confirmed he no longer occupied the familiar ground of a world he knew, he beheld sun and moon conjoined, their shared radiance illuminating both the day-lit world in which he stood and the night-dark terrain that lay just along the edge of his range of vision. Strangely, perhaps because the moon's gentler glow moderated the sun's brilliance, he did not have to look away. Instead of being blinded, he stared, breath held in wonder.

Movement caught his attention. Shifting his gaze back to the plain stretching away before him, he witnessed a sight nearly as astonishing as the sun-moon hovering above the horizon. Close enough for him to see clearly, but not so close that he could call out and expect to be heard, he saw Naya and the red filly. The two were unmistakable. The girl rode astride the horse, slim figure erect, arms outstretched, chestnut hair streaming behind her as they galloped as one toward where day ended and night began. He thought he might have heard the sound of her laughter, carried back to him on the wind. As he watched, the pair disappeared from view, swallowed by a waving sea of grass.

Should he try to follow the girl and the horse on foot? Except for the persistent beat of the drum, he was alone in this strange yet familiar world. How would he ever catch up to them? Just then, he spotted a distant winged silhouette against the dome of the sky. Circling overhead, the shape spiraled downward, closer and closer, eventually resolving into a creature Aytal recognized – his spirit guide – a gyrfalcon who had first come to him during his vision quest. He held out his forearm. The bird, not quite so large as an eagle but still the swiftest and most intrepid of the winged predators of his homeland, came to rest, clamping onto his wrist with strong claws. Wincing at the bird's grip, Aytal braced his arm against its weight. Blinking far-seeing onyx eyes, the gyrfalcon regarded him intently for a moment or two before once again taking flight. Sensing he was to follow, Aytal set-off across the meadow, aiming in the direction traced by Naya and the filly. Amazingly, he seemed able to keep up with the bird, traveling at a greater speed than the fastest runner, yet unaware of any effort. With a start of delighted surprise, he realized that he too was flying.

"Where are we going?" he asked his guide.

"To find the girl and her horse. That is why you came, is it not?"

Below, the landscape sped by, affording Aytal a perspective he'd only imagined. Grasslands gave way to forests and forests to mountains, their snowy peaks jagged beneath him. Carried by an updraft, he could see the mountains ringed a hidden valley. At the center lay an alpine lake, its still surface mirroring blue sky and a scattering of passing clouds.

Descending, Aytal regained his footing a little distance from the edge of the water. The gyrfalcon, wings beating vigorously to slow its own descent, landed gracefully on his outstretched forearm, then climbed to his shoulder. Together, they gazed into the clear depths of the lake. At the center, Aytal thought he could see an image shimmering. Sunlight seemed to glint off something red. He wondered if it was the girl and the horse, but the vision, refracted through the water, wavered and would not come into focus, no matter how hard he stared.

"What do you see?" asked the bird.

"I can't be sure," answered Aytal.

"See with the eyes of your heart," the bird suggested.

"I think maybe it's them." Uncertain, he closed his eyes, opened them again, looked harder.

"Who?" asked the bird.

"Naya and the red filly." Aytal continued to gaze into the deep water, willing himself to be able to see clearly what lay beneath its surface. Frustrated, he abruptly turned away, nearly dislodging the gyrfalcon. Stretching its spotted wings for balance, the bird tightened its hold on Aytal's shoulder. He felt the bite of sharp talons through the heavy leather of his cloak. Again, he winced.

"How will I find them? How will I bring them back?" he asked, sounding a little desperate. "Must I capture her? Capture the horse? What am I to do?" He realized he had ventured into the spirit world with no weapons, no tools, nothing but his intention to help the girl and thereby atone for what he had done. The drum beat insistently.

Ignoring Aytal's questions, the bird posed one of its own.

"What is it that you most desire?"

"To fulfill my life's purpose." The answer came promptly. This was a discussion they'd had when the bird first appeared to Aytal during his vision quest.

"And what is your life's purpose?" continued his spirit guide.

Aytal spoke quietly, trying not to sound petulant. "You told me I would only discover it after I set out to find it." Back still turned to the lake, he starred, unseeing, at the surrounding peaks. He'd been so embarrassed, when all the other boys had come back from their vigils, smug with the knowledge they'd gained from their spirit guides about their designated path in life. Of course no one dared share the details – such discussion was forbidden – yet every one of the others seemed certain of the message they'd received. Only Aytal returned from his quest more confused than enlightened. His father had tried to console him. *In my experience*, he'd said, *those whose way remains hidden have the most to discover*. It was in part why Aytal had been so eager to accompany his father on his trade expedition, hoping to learn something about his own destiny. His other reasons for wanting to leave home he preferred not to think about.

And now, after traveling for months, he felt more uncertain than ever. Unless his future had something to do with Naya. Closing his eyes, then opening them again, he turned back to face the lake, more slowly this time so as not to upset his guide's perch on his shoulder. After a moment the bird spoke.

"And so you shall discover your life's purpose, having set out to find it," the gyrfalcon confirmed. "But in the meantime, what else is it that you desire?"

This time Aytal hesitated before answering. The gyrfalcon bent its head, preening the snowy feathers on its chest as though possessed of all the time in the world. In his mind's eye, Aytal saw Naya's face as he had when she'd lain in arms, unconscious, fragile and bewilderingly beautiful, before her lids had opened to reveal eyes of an unexpected crystalline blue. Although weak in body, those eyes had been fierce. She seemed at once vulnerable and unconquerable, a powerful combination.

"I want to see her smile," he said at last, surprising himself, yet he knew it to be true. At that moment, beyond anything else, he wanted to see Naya happy, laughing, alive. More than that, he wanted her to smile at him.

"Then you must remain as true as a well-aimed arrow," replied the bird. "And when you have succeeded in granting her heart's desire, then shall yours be granted also."

"But how do I do that?" Aytal asked, dismayed. "I don't understand. I'm just here to rescue her."

"Do you believe that to be your task?" The guide's tone was mild.

"Yes," Aytal replied. "It's why I've come on this journey."

"So that you can save her?" Head swiveling, the gyrfalcon regarded Aytal with its fathomless black-eyed stare.

Glancing sideways at his guide, then back out at the lake, Aytal repeated his resolve. "I'm here to find her and bring her back," he declared earnestly, "so that I can atone for what I did." He still couldn't fully understand how or why he had shot that arrow without conscious intent, except that it was not the first time such a thing had happened. As before, he knew that he must accept the consequences, only in this instance they were far more serious.

"Is that what you truly believe?" persisted his guide, "that you can save her?"

"Her body heals from the wound but her spirit does not. Some part of her is lost. I've come to find her and bring her back, and I will."

Despite attempting to sound determined, Aytal's voice betrayed his doubts. Naya was not getting better. He didn't know that she would live, and if she did not… Burdened by shame, Aytal's shoulders wanted to sag. He squared them instead, requiring the bird once more to adjust its balance. "I've come to find her and bring her back," he reiterated.

"How do you propose to do that?" asked the guide, refolding its wings.

"I don't know." Aytal replied, almost angrily. He felt completely unequipped. Without his bow in hand and quiver at his back, he was powerless. Taking a deep breath, he tried to continue more calmly. "What should I do?" he asked.

The bird only cocked his head and looked at him.

"I suppose I must sacrifice something," Aytal said at last. In all the stories his people told of journeying to the spirit world, especially the tales of rescue and atonement, some sort of ransom was required.

"What do you value most?" asked his guide.

Aytal thought for a moment. He owned little. His clothing, his knife. Then he knew – his most prized possession – his bow. Fashioned of yew, it had taken him months to craft. Lovingly shaped and smoothed, balanced perfectly for his hand, strong yet flexible and able to send an arrow flying both straight and far, it was not only a work of art, but an embodiment of his most unique gifts. Already, he had won respect and admiration among his peers for his skill as an archer, along with the disapprobation of his tribe's elders for the recklessness with which he'd shown off his prowess. To Aytal, his bow symbolized the essence of his manhood. He couldn't imagine giving it up.

"What do you value?" repeated the bird. A long silence ensued, broken only by the incessant staccato of the drum. Aytal stared out over the lake, not seeing the water in front of him. Waves, pushed by a freshening breeze, lapped against the stony shore.

"Honor," he said at last. "To save Naya, and save my honor, I will sacrifice my bow."

As Aytal spoke, the weapon appeared on the ground at his feet. Reaching down, he lifted it reverently. Wrapping his left hand around the familiar grip, fingers of his right hand drawing back the taut, finely twisted sinew of the bowstring, with one effortless motion he brought the weapon into firing position. The movement displaced the gyrfalcon, who rose, wings flapping, until Aytal lowered the bow and the bird could come to rest once more on his shoulder.

"Must I leave it behind?" he asked quietly. The bird did not answer.

Still facing the lake, Aytal once again gazed out over its surface, now stirred by the wind. No longer could he glimpse anything in the depths. The lake offered no more answers than his guide about where or how to locate Naya. Suddenly, in a violent motion that sent the gyrfalcon awkwardly into the air, he flung the bow as far as he could out over the water. It rotated, end over end, before dropping with a sickening splash. Landing broadside, the bow floated for a moment, then disappeared. Empty-handed, Aytal watched as the ripples left behind made their way to the shore where he stood. The surge of grief he felt nearly overwhelmed him.

"It's all I can do," he said at last. "Will it be enough?"

"It's all you can do for now," replied the bird, who opted this time to land on the rock-strewn ground at Aytal's feet. "But your task has only begun."

"I must do more?" Incredulous, Aytal looked down at his guide. He couldn't imagine being required to perform a yet-greater sacrifice.

"You've been given your task," repeated the bird. "Start with finding the girl." With that, the gyrfalcon unfurled its wings, took several short hops along the stony shore and then pushed off. Lifted by powerful strokes from its wings, the bird circled upward into the blue sky.

"How do I do that?" Aytal called after the receding form. He watched, necked craned, until the small speck disappeared overhead. "Now what?" he said out loud, realizing there was no one but himself to hear.

No longer able to fly without his guide, Aytal set off running across the valley away from the lake. He must have been mistaken in thinking he'd glimpsed something in the water. If he could find his way through the mountains and back to the great plain where he'd first seen Naya and the filly, perhaps he'd come across them again there. He moved easily and swiftly through the landscape but missed the exhilaration of soaring through the air. How much time did he have, he wondered, aware of the drum's steady beat, and what would he do once he found the girl and the horse? Surely, having surrendered his bow, he would succeed in saving Naya. Any other outcome was unthinkable.

At last, having followed a clear path up through a high mountain pass and down again on the other side, Aytal paused atop a ridge that afforded a panoramic view of his surroundings. Behind him, the forested slopes through which he had just travelled descended from the mountains' snowcapped peaks. Ahead of him, as far as he could see, vast grasslands stretched away to the horizon, above which hung the mysterious sun-moon. There was no sign of either Naya or the red filly. What next?

Barely had he begun to consider his options, when suddenly, and to his horror, Aytal heard the sound of the drum quicken, calling for him to return. How could he go back now? Yet the drum's rapid beat demanded obedience. He knew that if he didn't immediately retrace his way, he risked being left behind, his spirit trapped forever in this other dimension. He'd seen what happened to those who journeyed to the spirit world and did not follow its rules. As a small boy, he'd been terrified of an old man who haunted the outskirts of his settlement. Vacant eyed, incoherent, the pathetic figure was rumored to have once been a great *shaman* who unfortunately believed himself more powerful than the drum and did not heed its call when the time came to return. Yes, Aytal knew the danger of ignoring the drum's command. What he did not know was how much time it would give him to get back. He scanned the sea of grass, searching for a landmark. Spotting a small rise in the distance marked by a familiar rocky outcropping, he began to run.

Sata moved to drape another hide around Aytal's shoulders before resettling herself once more beside her daughter. The young man stared unseeing into the fire, shivering beneath the fur robe.

"I failed." Aytal said, teeth chattering so hard Sata could scarcely understand the words. Oyuun had added more wood to the fire earlier and the flames blazed high, crackling and sending sparks through the smoke hole, but their warmth didn't seem to reach him. Naya lay curled on her side beneath her own pile of hides, only the tip of her nose exposed. She had opened her eyes for a brief moment just as the drum fell silent, acknowledged Sata's anxious look with a half-smile, then rolling sideways and drawing up her knees, she'd closed her eyes again and fallen into a sound sleep, despite the storm continuing to rage outside. Sata and Oyuun, agreeing with a glance between them that this was probably a good sign, had together tucked the robes around her and let her be. It was the first true rest the girl had had since the accident.

"I failed," Aytal said again, loud enough this time to be heard over the wind.

"Not now," his father said in answer. "Time enough to talk when the storm ends and the sun returns."

Silenced, Aytal continued to stare into the fire.

Three days later, the unthinkable happened. Able at last to break a path out of the clearing with their snowshoes, Oyuun and Aytal had set-off early in search of fresh meat. Almost immediately they picked up signs of a herd of red deer and soon located the animals near another small creek flanked by bushes offering cover. Nocking an arrow, Aytal waited patiently for a shot and was rewarded when a large buck, thick neck supporting a massive rack of antlers, stepped directly into his line of sight. In a move so practiced as to be without conscious thought, he released the arrow, only to see it bury itself harmlessly in the snow between the stag's front legs. The whole herd vanished in an instant, leaving the hunters stunned and empty-handed.

At first Oyuun said nothing, reminding himself that even the most accomplished bowman often missed the mark when hunting deer, but when later in the morning Aytal failed to hit the broadside of a slow-moving auroch, he grew concerned. Fortunately, this time he had his spear to hand and was able to bring down the cow, who was weakened from age and unable to keep up with her herd. Still, Oyuun waited to speak until they'd finished field dressing the carcass, setting aside the less palatable organs and carving off as much of the choicer meat as they could carry. They would need to cache the rest, burying it deep enough to remain preserved by the cold earth and out of reach of scavengers. It would be a long day, but well worth the effort.

"Your arrow chose not to fly as you intended," he said mildly, eyeing the shaft embedded in a snow-covered mound of earth well beyond where the auroch's dismembered body lay on the frozen ground. Despite his matter-of-fact tone, the statement held a question.

Aytal, busy using his hand ax to separate one of the auroch's curved horns from the animal's massive head, at first did not respond. Watching his son struggle, Oyuun belatedly offered up a prayer of gratitude to the auroch, thanking her for sacrificing her life and for sparing them. Not as large and impressive as a male would have been, the female still represented a respectable kill. These were dangerous animals, fearless and aggressive when cornered. Aroused, even an unhealthy auroch could inflict significant damage and one in its prime could easily kill a man. The cow's advanced age and weakened state, as well as Oyuun's readiness with his spear, had worked in their favor. Aytal's missed shot might otherwise have had lethal consequences. At last, the young man sat back on his knees in the snow with the bloody prize in his lap, looking down at the severed horn as if he didn't know how it got there. When he lifted his eyes to meet his father's, they were anguished.

"I failed," was all he said.

"Everyone misses a shot, or two." Oyuun tried to sound reassuring.

"No." Aytal's voice was vehement. "I failed. On the journey. I failed to save Naya."

For the three days that had passed since the storm, the young man had not spoken of what transpired in the spirit world, brooding instead in silence. Oyuun, who regretted discouraging his son from telling his story in the journey's immediate aftermath, was relieved that he finally seemed willing to talk about what had happened.

"But she improves," he pointed out, laying a hand on Aytal's shoulder. "Her spirit seems whole again. She rests well. She will grow stronger. Whatever you did must have helped."

"But I did nothing to save her. All I did was make a foolish sacrifice that gained nothing and lost everything." The despair in Aytal's voice brought his father up short.

"What do you mean, you made a sacrifice? At whose behest? What did you give up?" Oyuun spoke sharply. He knew enough about what could happen on a journey to be concerned at his son's words.

"My bow," said the young man, his voice hollow. With that, he told his father as much as he could remember of the night of the drum, of finding the entrance to the spirit world and the wondrous landscape beyond, of seeing Naya astride the red filly, riding with the speed of the wind toward the merging of day and night and then the appearance of his guide and the exhilaration of flying high above forests and mountains until coming to rest along the shores of the hidden lake.

"That's where I threw it in," he said, hanging his head.

"Your bow?" asked Oyuun, confused. "I don't understand. Why would you throw your bow into the lake? Who would ask it of you? Not your guide?" In his experience, such a thing was unheard of. The spirit guide's role was to pose questions, and much more rarely to answer them, but not to make demands.

"That's just it," replied Aytal, "I realize now that it was my own stupid idea. I had some notion of making a grand gesture in order to redeem my honor and atone for what I did to Naya. I thought that if I sacrificed my bow, it would mean I would be able to save her. Not only did I do nothing to rescue her, I threw away my most precious possession."

"But..." Oyuun started to protest before realizing the possible truth of his son's words. He thought of the two missed shots, so uncharacteristic. He began again. "Naya is getting better," he reminded Aytal. "Perhaps whatever you did was not in vain. Tell me what else happened."

"Other than glimpsing her and the horse at the beginning, I never laid eyes on them. If Naya's spirit was saved, I don't see how I could have had anything to do with it." Bitterness nearly choked him.

"Did your guide say anything else?" Oyuun pressed his son to recall.

"There was one other thing." Closing his eyes, Aytal recited the lines he'd spent the last three days committing to memory: *You must see with the eyes of your heart and remain as true as a well-aimed arrow. Find the girl, and when you have succeeded in granting her heart's desire, then shall yours be granted also.* Opening his eyes again, he glanced at his father, then down at his lap. Dark brows drawn together, the normally smooth planes of his face creased with frustration, he spoke as if to the mutilated horn still held in his hands.

"I can't even shoot!"

Compassion softening his own expression, Oyuun considered a long moment before replying. Squatting next to Aytal and taking up the horn, he carefully cleaned away blood and bits of flesh using a piece of soft hide, all the while turning over in his mind what his son had said. The irony of the spirit guide's words did not escape him.

"Patience," he said at last. "We have a long winter ahead of us. It will be three moons at least before we can bring Naya and her mother back to their people. She will live, I think, for which we can all be grateful. Whether your journey to the spirit world had anything to do with her survival, we cannot know. Whether you have truly sacrificed your greatest gift, or merely had a couple of unlucky shots, we also cannot know. All I can say is whatever you believe to be true is likely to be so." Oyuun paused to wipe his hands on the hide cloth before tucking it back in his belt. "As for the rest, no doubt you'll have plenty of opportunity to discover the answers to your questions while we wait for spring to come. In the meantime, turn that into something useful."

Oyuun handed the trophy back to his son and turned to the task of wrapping up the meat for transport. Aytal sat for a moment more, gazing wordlessly down at the auroch horn, shoulders slumped in defeat. Then, as though resigned, he shoved the prize into his belt, stood, and retrieving his arrow, jammed it back into his quiver. Taking up his bow, without a word, he unstrung it and strapped it to his pack. Noting his son's actions, Oyuun also without a word handed Aytal one of his own spears, along with the young man's share of the kill to carry. Traveling with fresh meat, they would be vulnerable to other predators all the way back to the clearing. It wouldn't do for either of them to be without a weapon.

PART TWO

Pontic-Caspian Steppe, c. 4000 BCE

Late Winter

Chapter Eleven

A blanket of fresh snow sparkled in the sunlight that beamed down into the clearing. The surrounding trees, bare branches encased in ice, stood like frozen sentinels. Nothing stirred in the crisp early morning air, with the exception of a thin trail of smoke escaping from the larger of the two shelters, and the small clouds of steam exhaled from the frost-rimmed nostrils of the small herd of horses. The animals stood in a loose circle with muzzles lowered, still resting from the onslaught of the previous night's storm. Only when the shelter's entrance flap twitched did the horses react, and even then only a single head lifted, ears alert, to assess what might emerge from within. When a tousled red head appeared, the equine sentry nickered a soft greeting but otherwise the herd remained undisturbed.

By now the horses had grown accustomed to seeing the girl and the others come and go. Since that longest night of the year, when the herd had initially sought protection in the little clearing from the fury of the season's first blizzard, the moon had waxed, growing full, then slowly waned into darkness, before reappearing and growing full again, marking the passage of a winter that was the worst in memory. One storm followed another with little respite, forcing all of the steppe's inhabitants to seek whatever sanctuary they could in order to survive. In the immediate aftermath of each snowfall, huge drifts made any movement in the open both difficult and dangerous, and although within a day or two a cold north wind would have scoured the landscape clean, inevitably each frigid blast brought in its wake another storm and more snow. During the brief interludes of calm, prey and predator alike emerged to find food, then retreated again to whatever refuge served as their winter home.

So it was for the residents of the little clearing. The morning after the first storm, the drifts had been too deep for the horses to scatter quickly when the humans first emerged from their nearly buried shelter. Instead, they waited tensely to see how the people behaved, prepared to flee through the chest-deep snow if they must. But the three figures who had come outside remained at a respectful distance, giving the herd a wide berth while struggling to break a trail down to the little creek. Although disappointed that the red-hair girl was not among those who had left the shelter, the horses knew she was inside and this gave them confidence. They also recognized one of the other three from the night of the wolves. He had been with the girl, so perhaps could be trusted.

Thus the herd had stood their ground, watching and waiting, more curious than afraid. Once the humans disappeared again inside their hide tent, the adult horses, moving in single file, pushed their way laboriously through the deep snow in the direction of the path that had been created by the people and their snowshoes. Once they reached it, the going became easier and they were able to widen the passage as they too made their way to the creek for a drink. By the time the stallion and four mares had each gained the water's edge, a wide trail had been packed down, making it easier for the youngsters to follow.

Thereafter, in the wake of each storm, the humans would clear a path to the creek and once they had disappeared again inside their shelter, the horses would take advantage of ready access to the water. In addition, the people cleared away larger patches of snow throughout the clearing for the goats, making it easier for the horses to find something to eat as well. Gradually, the herd seemed to grow accustomed to sharing the clearing with the humans. Although they left when conditions allowed to forage further afield, sometimes staying away for several days, always when the next storm approached, they returned and each time they lingered a bit longer.

Then came the morning, one moon past the solstice, when the horses saw the girl herself emerge for the first time from the shelter. The most recent storm had occurred a few days previously and most of the snow had melted, leaving behind bare ground beginning to thaw into mud. Mild air and sunshine had tempted small birds to abandon their hiding places and they flitted busily amongst the trees of the clearing, chattering to one another as they went. Supported by her mother, the girl moved slowly, with an air of weakness that concerned the horses. Such vulnerability attracted danger. Looking on from a safe distance, the herd watched as the older woman helped the girl to a seat propped against a boulder a short distance from the shelter. Here she rested, face turned upward to welcome the sun's warmth and after a while, once the two men had left with their weapons and the girl's mother had disappeared again inside the shelter, the herd relaxed and returned to grazing idly nearby.

All except the red filly. As if drawn by an invisible thread, she approached the girl with tentative steps. Smiling in response, the girl held out her hand, inviting the little horse to sniff. Coming as close as she dared, the filly stretched out her head and neck until the delicate tip of her muzzle was just a breath away from the girl's fingertips.

"You remember me, don't you?" The girl spoke softly so as not to frighten the animal. "I've been very sick," she continued. "But knowing you've been here waiting for me has helped me get better. I think now I'm going to be alright." The red filly blew gently on the girl's outstretched hand, making her smile again.

Since that day, Naya had grown steadily stronger, until eventually she was able to help her mother with simple chores around the camp. When not thus engaged, weather permitting, she spent most of her time sitting quietly in a patch of sun, observing the horses whenever they were in the clearing. Although not willing to allow her to mingle in their midst as freely as they had on the open steppe, still the herd did not seem to mind her presence, nor even that of the young stranger who often attempted to join them. He and his father were typically absent for a good portion of each day, for which Naya was grateful, but on fine afternoons, he often found something with which to occupy himself in the clearing so that he could sit watching Naya as she in turn watched the horses.

Initially she had been considerably less willing than the animals to welcome his company, retreating back inside the shelter whenever he appeared. Nevertheless, much as Naya herself had done when first introducing herself to the herd, the young man persisted, as though determined to accustom her, as well as the horses, to his presence. Stationing himself at a distance, he would work quietly at some handcraft or another, neither saying nor doing anything to disturb the others. Realizing that going back inside the tent only robbed herself of the opportunity to be with the horses, Naya resorted instead to shooting hostile glances in the young man's direction, hoping thus to drive him away.

Unfortunately, this had not at all the effect she intended. Infuriatingly, instead of being put off by her best attempts at silent intimidation, he returned her glares with shy smiles or else kept his dark head bent to his work. The horses, in contrast, reacted to her undisguised animosity with evident concern, growing restless and sometimes abandoning the clearing altogether. This only further aggravated Naya.

Eventually, she decided just to ignore the young stranger, much as she succeeded in doing in the closer quarters of their shared shelter. Although her mother interacted comfortably with him and his father in the cramped space, conversing with them in their incomprehensible tongue as if they were all friends, Naya refused. Having neither forgotten nor forgiven what the young man had done to her, she insisted on confining herself to one small corner of the tent, where she either sat or lay with her back pointedly turned. Only the need to warm herself by the fire when the weather kept them all indoors brought her into the communal circle, and there she kept her eyes resentfully downcast, responding to no one other than her mother. Nothing Sata said to her about the strangers' kindness or their role in saving her life altered Naya's stubborn determination to remain aloof. "You're simply being rude," her mother eventually told her and gave up trying to make excuses for her.

Naya, holding tightly to her antagonism and mistrust and counting her self-imposed isolation as the price of her dignity, consoled herself with daydreams about plans for the red filly. As soon as she was strong enough, she vowed, she would resume her quest to tame the young horse. Before long, she told herself, she would try again to get close enough to touch her, to bury her bare hands in that thick, warm coat, to scratch her withers and the base of her tail. She recalled the joy she'd experienced on the steppe that day when the filly had first allowed herself to be stroked, the connection she'd felt with the young horse just before…

In her mind's eye, Naya would see again and again the perfect arc of an arrow outlined against blue sky. Loath to follow its flight, she would deliberately bring her attention back to the miracle of the herd grazing peacefully in the clearing. No one could explain why the horses had chosen to stay after that first storm, but the two strangers seemed convinced that something unique was happening and they had agreed not to hunt or otherwise harass the animals.

Watching the herd, Naya decided that as soon as she felt more herself, she would try to approach the rest of the horses as well, starting with the filly's mother, MeHnd. The mare was visibly pregnant, her flanks swelling with new life, even as she struggled, along with the others, to survive the harsh winter. Either despite or because of her more vulnerable state, the mare watched the girl with almost as much interest as did the filly, often drifting closer to where she sat as the remainder of the herd grazed nearby. Lifting her head to chew a mouthful of the dried straw-like grass that was all the forage available, she would study Naya with thoughtful brown eyes.

Returning MeHnd's gaze, Naya felt almost as drawn to the mare as she did to the filly. *As soon as I am strong enough*, she told herself, *I will tame them both, and the others in the herd as well.* But for now, it was enough to sit quietly nearby, sharing the meager warmth of the winter sun.

As she rested, Naya turned over in her mind all that she could remember of her time in the darkness following her injury and especially of her journey with the drum on the night of the winter solstice. The night marked some kind of sacred passage or turning point, she realized, but full comprehension eluded her. At first, in the days immediately following the storm, as the darkness lifted and her mind began to clear, images and feelings remained jumbled, troubling and confusing her. Her mother, seeing that Naya still seemed inordinately preoccupied, even as she gained day-by-day in vitality and awareness, sought to draw her out. Yielding to her gentle urging, Naya eventually agreed to share what unsettled her. As she spoke, her words became like the beads of a necklace, strung together to form the truth of her experience. Contemplating the story's details as she might finger beads on a string, Naya tried to discern their meaning.

"After I was shot," she told her mother, "I can remember a smothering blackness." A familiar voice had urged her to hold on. She vaguely recalled slipping in and out of consciousness in the young stranger's arms, the incident with the wolves and the horses, and, briefly, her father's presence. Then a different kind of darkness had come, and along with it the terrifying nightmares, the details of which she could no longer summon. "All I remember is feeling hopeless and afraid," she told her mother, shuddering. Yet, even in that dark place, Naya realized she had never been alone.

"I think I was with the horses," she said. "It felt like I was one of them."

"Perhaps you were," her mother replied.

More vividly, Naya recalled journeying with the drum to a place familiar yet not of this world. To her mother she tried to describe the exhilaration of riding the red filly, galloping as a single being through the endless sea of grass beneath the wondrous sight of the sun and moon joined together as if they too were one, but she had trouble finding words sufficient to capture the experience.

"It was glorious," was all she could say. "But what does it all mean, Mama?" Lifting her gaze, Naya sought her mother's face, looking for an explanation. "I recognized the voice that spoke to me, but I can't seem to recall what it said."

"Are you sure you can't remember anything more?" her mother asked.

Furrowing her brow in determination, Naya hesitated before speaking. "Something about my heart's desire," she said at last. "And about forgiveness." Her mother had raised an eyebrow but otherwise did not interrupt as Naya sought to recapture more of what the voice had told her. "That's it," she sighed at last. "That's all I can remember. But I'm sure it was something about the horses. I wish I knew what I'm supposed to do!" She wanted to wail in frustration.

"What does your heart tell you?" Her mother spoke soothingly. "I'm sure if you listen, you will know."

So, day by day, weather permitting, Naya sat watching the horses and pondering.

Today, however, when Naya first lifted the tent flap, she was met by the morning sun sparkling on fresh snow. One of the mares nickered a greeting, which she acknowledged with a smile, before withdrawing back inside.

"It snowed again last night," Naya said to her mother. "The horses are back."

"How deep is the snow?" This from Oyuun, who by now had learned the basics of the clan's language. He had not been outside yet to check the snowfall for himself. As usual, Naya declined to answer, acting as if she did not understand him and looking to her mother instead.

"He wants to know how deep is the snow. Honestly, Naya!" exclaimed Sata, exasperated. "You know perfectly well what he said. Answer him."

"Not too deep," she responded, still addressing her mother.

"We'll hunt then." Oyuun turned to Aytal. The young man was folding his sleeping hides in a corner of the shelter and had his back to the others. "Let's get an early start," he said, once Aytal had turned around.

Oyuun refrained from suggesting to his son which weapons to bring, watching instead as Aytal placed his flint knife and hand axe in the leather belt at his waist and gathered up the two long-handled spears he'd fashioned for himself. His bow and quiver lay in the furthest recess of the shelter where they'd remained untouched for two moons. Still, Oyuun couldn't help the deep sigh that escaped as he took up his own spears.

He himself had never learned to shoot with a bow and arrows. It was not a common practice among his people. But for some reason as a boy Aytal had been drawn to the challenge of bow-hunting, learning its secrets from one of his great uncles who had been a trader like Oyuun and gleaned the knowledge somewhere along the way during his travels. Aytal had quickly mastered the techniques needed not only to shoot with unerring accuracy, but to craft both the bow and the arrows so that one would make the other fly straight and true. Although not himself a bowman, Oyuun recognized that his son possessed something more than acquired skill – an innate grace that could not be taught, only perfected – but sometimes he wondered if perhaps success with the weapon had come too easily for the young man. At first, Aytal had not seemed to fully appreciate that his natural ability represented both a sacred gift, not to be taken for granted, as well as an awesome responsibility, not to be misused or exploited. Now, after a couple of hard lessons, the young man's response was apparently to give up. *Such a waste,* thought Oyuun, even if more than once his son had been unconscionably reckless.

As he held the entrance flap for Aytal to proceed him out of the shelter, Oyuun's eyes met Sata's. She glanced at the bow, forsaken in its corner, then back at him, her own eyes troubled.

Today, as every day when the strangers left to hunt, Naya could tell that Amu found his devotion to her sorely tested. The dog desperately wanted to go along to lead the hunters to the game they sought, but loyalty dictated that he remain behind by her side. Whining softly, he looked longingly at the shelter's entrance through which the two men had just departed but made no move to follow them.

"He wants to go," observed her mother. She'd noticed as well.

Naya said nothing, busying herself with folding away her sleeping mat and hide blankets. As she did, she found herself speculatively eyeing Aytal's bow and changed the subject.

"Do you think I could learn to shoot?" she asked.

"Why would you want to do that?" countered her mother.

"To hunt, of course." Naya sat back on her haunches, intrigued with the idea that had just come to her. "If I could learn to use a bow and arrow, not just a spear, maybe Papa would let me go again with him and the other hunters."

Naya expected her mother to tell her not to get her hopes up. Hadn't her father made clear that after what had happened to Bhermi, the men of the clan, especially Skelos, would never accept her as a hunter? Sata's response surprised her.

"Why don't you ask Aytal to teach you," she suggested, voice carefully neutral.

Rather than object automatically, Naya caught herself and reconsidered. For another long moment she continued to look thoughtfully at the bow. Standing at last, she addressed the dog, who still gazed wistfully after the departed hunters.

"When I can go, then you can go," she said to him, ruffling the fur on the top of his head. "Meanwhile, you and I are both stuck inside until the snow melts."

Taking up a fresh antelope hide, Naya seated herself close to the fire and began the laborious process of scraping the skin free of all remaining particles of flesh in preparation for tanning. The task was arduous and she could only do a little at a time without stopping to rest but she wanted something to occupy her hands and hopefully her thoughts as well.

For what seemed like a long time following her injury, she'd been too sick to even notice much of what went on around her. Lately, however, she had begun to feel restless, chafing at her confinement. It wasn't just the winter weather, which kept them all trapped inside much of the time. It was irritation at not being able to execute even the most basic physical tasks. Naya calculated that nearly two moons had passed since her injury and still she felt short of breath whenever she tried to walk as far as the creek, never mind trying to carry water back. How would she ever be able to run again, let alone be strong enough to ride the red filly? At the same time, she was growing both lonely from her self-imposed isolation and tired of her own thoughts. She never seemed to gain any new insights. She needed a project, something to distract her until she'd recovered enough to pursue taming the herd. Meanwhile, she continued to chew on her grievances, even as she scraped away at the antelope hide.

Although Naya knew she was not being entirely fair, she couldn't help directing her frustration toward the young stranger, Aytal her mother called him. He was responsible for what had happened to her, she told herself, ignoring the fact that he had no way of knowing that she was there among the horses that day on the steppe. She hadn't told her mother all that she remembered, about waking up in the young stranger's arms, seeing a tangle of jet-black hair and dark, expressive brows framing those startling blue eyes, eyes that gazed down at her with such evident relief. Despite all he had done to save her, she disliked him anyway. *I can't stand the sight of him*, she told herself indignantly, *and I resent the way he looks at me.* Naya didn't appreciate the way Aytal's father looked at her mother either, although her mother didn't seem to notice, or if she noticed, she didn't seem to mind.

"When will Papa come for us?" she asked for the hundredth time, looking up from the antelope hide. Sata sat on the opposite side of the fire, head bowed, fingers busy with the sinews she was twisting into cord.

"I told you, not for another moon or more," she answered without looking up. "Travel is too dangerous this winter. As soon as there is a sign of spring, he will come."

Sata hoped the assurances she gave her daughter were true. In the meantime, their stores were growing thin. Oyuun and Aytal had been relatively successful in bringing in game, despite the abandonment of Aytal's bow, but the creek in the clearing was too small to provide fish and there were only two bags of grain left, not including the one her mother-in-law had sent along.

Not for the first time, Sata wondered why Awija had given the sack to the stranger, on top of what had already been sent along, knowing it contained more food than could reasonably be spared. Meanwhile, the she-goat's milk production had nearly dried up and the kids were not yet old enough to be slaughtered for food. Sata had explained to Oyuun the clan's prohibition against killing young animals who had not yet had the opportunity to reproduce, adding that even if she herself might be willing to look the other way, Naya would never stand for it. At least they still had an abundance of apples and nuts, as well as a few packets of preserved meat mixed with dried berries. Perhaps if there was a thaw, she and Oyuun might take a day to try to reach the closest river. In past winters, she had usually been able to find edible roots growing along the banks of larger tributaries, where the ground was less frozen. They might even catch some fish. She would propose the idea when the men returned from today's hunt.

A few days later, Sata and Oyuun set-off for the tributary, leaving Naya, Aytal, and Amu behind. When her mother had first suggested the idea, Naya had objected vociferously, she and Sata exchanging fierce whispers, but eventually she had to concede the necessity of the trip. Only Sata knew exactly where the best roots could be located along the banks of the river, as well as the most likely fishing spots at this time of year.

"Why can't the young one go with you instead?" Naya had asked petulantly. She still refused to use Aytal's name, which she knew annoyed her mother.

"Because," replied Sata wearily, "Oyuun has made the trip back and forth to the river twice already and knows the way. You will be fine here with Aytal and Amu." Naya suspected her mother hoped that some time alone with the young man would change her attitude. *No chance of that*, she told herself.

The day chosen for the trek to the river was the mildest they'd had so far. Sun and wind had eliminated all traces of the most recent storm and by mid-day, the temperature had climbed enough in the clearing to make being outside much preferable to remaining in the stuffy confines of the shelter. Sata and Oyuun, who had departed as soon as it was light, had left behind a host of small projects to be completed in their absence and as the morning progressed, Naya and Aytal found themselves seated on logs a little apart from one another, each working assiduously on their own tasks.

Naya's involved pounding the tendons from a deer's legbones between two stones until she could separate the fibers into strands which her mother could then twist and braid into strong yet pliable cordage. It was a good day to prepare the sinews, when the weather was warm enough to work bare-handed. As she did, her thoughts drifted, as they always did, to the horses.

A rope would have been so handy, she mused, handling the rough tendon fibers. Immediately she discarded the idea. Unlike when she'd first set out to capture the filly, Naya had lately become aware of a sensation just below her ribs that made her think that relying on a rope was the wrong approach. The feeling was reinforced by the very practical realization, garnered after all the time she'd spent observing the filly and the other horses, that trying to restrain the creatures against their will would be futile in any case. They were too strong. Moreover, such a betrayal would destroy the very relationship she hoped to establish and she wasn't willing to sacrifice what she herself most desired. But without a rope, Naya still had to ask herself, what could she do that would cause the filly to choose, on her own, to be with her? *How can I create such ties?* she wondered as she worked the sinews. She didn't have an answer.

Aytal, meanwhile, was toiling over the auroch's horn he'd brought back with him from the hunt nearly two moons ago. Watching him covertly from under her lashes, Naya admired his patience. He'd already spent days sanding the great horn until the exterior was smooth and shining. Once the inner material had dried and separated from the external horn, Aytal had been able to extract the core, creating a hollow chamber. The final step, which he was working on today, was to cut off the tip and then, using a bow drill equipped with a tiny piece of hard, sharp quartz, bore through the solid horn into the hollow chamber. Glancing up, he caught Naya looking at him and smiled.

"Do you want to test it?" he asked, coming to stand in front of her and offering the newly finished horn.

Although she did not understand his words, Naya had no trouble deciphering his gesture. She hesitated momentarily, but her curiosity overcame her reticence and she reached out to take the horn from the young man's hands. Placing the narrow end in her mouth, she blew as hard as she could. No sound emerged. Disappointed, she was about to hand the horn back when she noticed what looked to her like a smirk on Aytal's face. Angry now, Naya shoved the horn back into his hands and made a show of returning to her own work. He continued to stand in front of her, however, and finally, after he'd tapped her lightly on the shoulder, she had to look up. All sign of amusement wiped from his expression, Aytal met her scowl with a contrite smile. Reluctantly, Naya allowed her own countenance to soften.

Aytal proceeded to demonstrate for her, placing the horn's mouthpiece against his pursed lips and blowing firmly. The note that sounded was pure and loud, reverberating throughout the clearing. Fleetingly, Naya thought to be grateful the horses had departed at first light, along with Sata and Oyuun, or they would have been greatly startled. As it was Amu and the goats set up a raucous clamor in response to the noise.

"Now you try it," said Aytal, passing the horn back to Naya.

This time, rather than putting the whole mouthpiece inside her own mouth, she used only her lips, as she had seen Aytal do. Although not able to produce the same big clear note, she still made the horn speak. In spite of herself she smiled, delighted by the sound. Aytal grinned back, equally pleased. Naya tried again, keeping her lips pursed but this time blowing as hard as her damaged lungs would allow. The horn rang out again, still not as loudly as when Aytal had sounded it, but a respectable effort nonetheless. Still smiling, Naya tried to hand the instrument back but Aytal refused to take it.

"I made it for you," he said, gesturing. "If you need help, you can blow it." Looking as though he might have said more if he'd had the words, he indicated again that she should keep the horn.

In that moment, some of Naya's hardness toward Aytal began to melt. Without saying anything more herself, she resumed working the deer sinews, the horn placed carefully on the ground at her feet. She couldn't remember anyone ever giving her such a gift, with the exception of the bear tooth she wore around her neck. She didn't know quite how to respond. After a moment, she stood and went back to the shelter, disappearing inside only to reappear with Aytal's bow and quiver.

Seeing what Naya held in her hands, a look of dismay came over Aytal's face and he began to shake his head adamantly, arms outstretched as if to ward off her advance.

"*Nē*," he declared. "I will not shoot. Put them back."

Naya stopped a few feet away. Seeing Aytal's reaction, she tried to indicate that she wasn't asking him to use the weapon himself but that she wanted to learn how.

"Will you teach me?" she asked. Aytal had turned his back and she had to walk around to face him.

"Teach me?" she asked again. Aytal shook his head.

"Fine," replied Naya. "I'll figure it out myself." Her father had instructed her in how to hurl a spear, but he'd always resisted allowing her to handle his bow, which was too big for her, and he'd never fulfilled his promise to show her how to fashion one for herself. She tried now to repeat the steps she'd observed her father use to string his weapon but Aytal's bow was likewise too tall and stiff for her to bend. When Aytal saw her struggling, he reached out and grabbed the bow from her. He would have returned with it to the shelter had Naya not stopped him by waving her arms. Placing her hand on her own chest, she first patted herself, then mimicked holding the weapon in her left hand and drawing back an imaginary bowstring with her right. She then patted her own chest again.

Comprehension dawning, Aytal looked down at the bow in his hand, obviously conflicted. After a moment, having apparently made up his mind, he placed one end of the bow on the ground at his feet. Grasping the attached bowstring, in a single deft motion he flexed the long shaft against his knee while dropping the loop at the string's other end over the bow's notched tip. He handed it back to Naya.

Impressed and a little envious, Naya accepted the proffered weapon. Using her left hand to grasp the bow around its leather grip, she held it up at arm's length and with the fingers of her right hand wrapped around the taunt string, tried to draw. Left arm shaking with the effort of holding the shaft steady, she was able to pull the string back only a little way before she had to release the tension. Determined, she was about to try again when Aytal put out a hand to stop her.

"It's too big for you," he observed. "If you really want to learn, we'll have to make you one of your own." Gesturing, he described with his hands a smaller weapon, specially fitted for Naya's height and strength.

"You'll need your own arrows as well," he added, gesturing again.

Nodding that she understood, Naya reached into the pouch at her belt and withdrew a small black object, holding it out to show Aytal. Nestled in the palm of her hand was the obsidian arrowhead – Aytal's arrowhead – that her mother had extracted from her back. Sata had saved it, giving it to Naya on the day when she recounted for her mother what she remembered from her solstice journey. 'A talisman,' Sata had declared solemnly, handing the arrowhead to Naya. 'Let it be a reminder of your ordeal and the gifts it will bring to you throughout your life.'

Not fully understanding, Naya had tucked the arrowhead away in the pouch where she kept other small objects for safekeeping. She intended at some point to ask her mother to make it into a necklace for her, to be worn along with the bear's tooth.

Seeing what she held, Aytal searched Naya's face. She could see his own concerned expression held a question. *Did she still blame him for what he had done?* In response, Naya raised one delicately arched eyebrow and held the young man's gaze. With that one look, at once a challenge and an invitation, she managed to convey that the first step in gaining her forgiveness would be teaching her how to shoot.

By the time Sata and Oyuun returned from their foraging expedition at the end of the day, weary but successful, the new project was well underway. After considerable searching, Aytal had located an ash tree in the grove surrounding the clearing with limbs strong yet flexible enough to serve his purpose. Climbing into the slender tree's upper reaches and selecting a branch of the right length and diameter, he lopped it off with his hand ax, nearly losing his balance in the process and eliciting a gasp of genuine concern from Naya, watching from below. Safely back on the ground, he quickly stripped the branch of smaller twigs and bark, leaving a relatively straight, round pole that measured to the height of Naya's shoulder. Seated again on their logs in the clearing, with his wood-working tools spread on the ground, Aytal showed Naya first how to remove chunks of wood with the adze and then how to plane the pole's surface into the correct shape for a bow. The task was meticulous, requiring patience and a precise eye. If the bow did not taper evenly from each end to the thicker grip in the middle, it would not withstand the stress of repeated flexing.

Over the following days, as long as the fine weather held, the two worked together in the clearing, Aytal watching critically as Naya carefully removed curl after curl of shaved wood, using the sharp edge of a specially knapped stone, stopping her often to test the bow's balance. Once shaped, the green wood was dried over a banked fire. Later, notches were carved at each end and a temporary string attached in order to further assess the weapon's draw, with minute adjustments being made so that the amount of flex was consistent from top to bottom and the force required to bend the bow matched its owner's strength. Then, once the proper form had been attained, the surface was polished along its entire length, using a hunk of sandstone, until it felt smooth to the touch. The final step was to wrap the grip, specially carved to fit Naya's hand, with softened hide and attach a permanent bow string, fashioned by Sata from the sinews that Naya had earlier prepared.

While Naya worked on the bow, Aytal began making arrows. First, he cut the straightest, stiffest branches he could find to the right length to match the bow. Next, in order to control each arrow's flight, he fletched the end with raven feathers. The painstaking task involved splitting the vanes from the rachis, and then anchoring them into tiny grooves etched in the arrow shaft with pitch that had been heated and mixed with charcoal. Thin fibrous threads of reindeer sinew were then wound through the individual barbs of each feather and wrapped around the arrow shaft, further securing the fletching in place. Finally, each shaft was fitted with a sleek black arrowhead, identical to the ones Aytal himself used. When finished, Naya would have a dozen black-feathered, black-tipped arrows, able to fly straight and true, to go with her new bow.

Neither Aytal nor Oyuun could take credit for fashioning the arrowheads. These came from the collection of points and blades stored in their packs, alongside the feathers, pitch, and reindeer sinew intended to be exchanged for other trade goods as they journeyed south. Although like all hunters, they had skill enough to work with common chert and keep basic tools reasonably serviceable, they did not possess the talent to give the coveted obsidian its characteristic finished form, sharp enough to slice with ease through hide, meat, and sinew. Such knowledge belonged only to those who spent years practicing the necessary techniques. True artisans required the gift as well of seeing within the stone and understanding its structure. Just as Aytal had an innate feel for how the living form of a tree limb could be whittled away to reveal a bow, a gifted knapper knew how to work with the spirit of the stone to elicit a finely crafted edge, beautiful but deadly. It was tedious and sometimes dangerous work. One ill-aimed blow could turn hours of painstaking effort into a pile of worthless debris, while flying shards could easily cut skin or even put out an eye. Obsidian was particularly tricky and those with the skill to work the precious black stone were greatly revered.

Observing one afternoon as Aytal crafted Naya's arrows, Oyuun thought of the expert knapper whom he had once known, widely recognized as among the greatest artisans ever to have worked with stone. It was to this person that he and Aytal travelled now, not only to replenish their supply of obsidian for trade but also to fulfill a long-standing promise. Oyuun only hoped he was not too late. Yet the present delay could not be helped nor, apparently, could the sacrifice of valuable materials in service to the task at hand. Considering the mutual regard Oyuun noticed developing between his son and the girl over the course of the days they'd spent working together, he declined to count the cost in lost trade.

Chapter Twelve

Next came learning to shoot. Standing at a safe distance on the first day, Sata and Oyuun observed as Aytal adjusted the positioning of Naya's fingers against the line of her jaw and then showed her how to lift her elbow ever so slightly to change the integrity of her stance. They were gathered in an open spot in the woods a little way from the clearing, where Aytal had set-up a target.

"I've never seen my daughter so willing to be told what to do," Sata remarked in a low voice to Oyuun, who stood by her side.

This didn't mean that Naya did not become frustrated, frowning fiercely in concentration and stamping a foot from time to time, only that the girl's determination to succeed outweighed her irritation at repeatedly failing. As Sata watched, she drew, aimed, released, and drew again, repeating the motions Aytal had shown her until Sata was sure her daughter's arms and scarred back must have ached. She could see that the skin of her left forearm was scraped raw.

Finally, after everyone had lost count of the number of times the arrows had been launched and retrieved and launched again, one at last found the target, a hide bag stuffed with grass. Aytal had drawn the profile of an auroch on it with charcoal and although Naya's shot only managed to hit the outline, not the bull's eye at the center, the grin she gave Aytal was triumphant.

"I did it!" she shouted, her voice jubilant. Aytal answered her with a wide smile of his own.

Sata likewise smiled at her daughter's enthusiasm. Turning to Oyuun, she spoke in a whisper so that the girl couldn't hear. "Before, I would have expected her to give up by now," she confessed.

"In my language," he replied, "we would say she has *sisu*. It means a combination of courage, tenacity and toughness. It's the quality of a great hunter, or a warrior."

"If only she were not a girl," he added.

"If only she were not almost a woman," murmured Sata in return.

Aytal proved to be a patient and meticulous teacher, demonstrating all the nuances of technique required to produce a successful effort. Posture, grip and draw could all be shown without actually allowing the bow to gift the arrow with flight. This he could not bring himself to do. While using his own weapon several times to show Naya how to handle hers, encouraging her to mimic the motions of nocking an arrow, bringing the bow into firing position and drawing back the string, each time in the split second before he might have let fly, he felt his arms begin to shake and his gut clench such that he thought he would be sick. Certain that if he released the arrow, it would miss its mark, each time he lowered the bow before his worst fears could be confirmed.

If Naya noticed, she had the good grace not to say anything. Instead, she continued to practice diligently until she could reliably hit the edges of the target. The bull's eye at the center, however, still eluded her. One day, after several attempts when the arrows still landed wide of the mark, she turned to Aytal, baffled.

"What am I doing wrong?" she asked.

With neither Sata nor his father on hand today to help with translating, Aytal attempted to explain. He'd learned enough of the clan's language by now to communicate on at least a basic level.

"You're trying too hard," he said. "Don't stare so long at the target. Close your eyes." "Breathe," he added, demonstrating with an exaggerated exhale. "Believe."

Skeptical, Naya attempted to do as directed. Bringing the bow into firing position, she closed her eyes, picturing the target in her mind. When she released the arrow, it wobbled, landing well short.

"Try again," encouraged Aytal. "Be strong."

Naya's next effort flew with more authority but still went astray, completely missing the hide bag. Lowering ruddy brows in irritation, she nocked a third arrow and bringing the bow up into firing position, drew back until she felt the taut string bite into the delicate skin of her cheek. Closing her eyes, she hesitated, then opened them again before releasing the tension and lowering the weapon without firing.

"I can't do it," she said, trying not to sound defeated. "I don't know how to see with my eyes closed."

"Let me help you," said Aytal, his voice gentle. Blue eyes silently asked permission before he encircled her in his arms. With his left hand over hers, they gripped the bow together, the fingers of his right hand hooked on either side around the string. They stood so close that she was tempted to lean her back into the support offered by his broad chest. The top of her head fit just beneath his chin. Together, they brought the bow up into position. With his added strength, drawing seemed effortless. She could feel the knuckles of his right hand brushing against the line of her jaw.

"Now close your eyes," he murmured. She complied.

"Breathe," he said and she could feel his words tickling the strands of hair at her temple. She took a deep breath, exhaling slowly.

"Now see not the target but the arrow. See it finding its mark. Believe." As he spoke, Aytal took half a step back, releasing his hold on the bow. Bereft of his embrace, Naya almost lost her balance but she kept her eyes shut and steadied her stance. Instead of envisioning just the target, she pictured the arrow's flight, seeing its black tip slice into the hide bag at its very center.

Believe, she repeated to herself. Without conscious intent, the fingers of her left hand opened smoothly, as if of their own accord, and in that split second, with a twang of the bow string, the arrow was gone. The briefest moment of silence ensued, punctuated by a satisfying *thwap*, followed by an animated whoop from Aytal. Naya's eyes flew open.

"You did it!" he exclaimed, catching her up in his arms and spinning her in a delighted circle.

"You did it," he repeated, setting her back on her feet.

He gazed down at her, a huge grin on his face, waiting expectantly for her to turn and look at where the arrow protruded from the exact center of the auroch's eye. Naya stared up at him, too dazed to move. Grin fading slightly, Aytal stared back. Then, as though suddenly realizing that he still held his hands around her waist, he dropped his arms and took an awkward step back, breaking the connection.

"You did it," he said for a third time, almost shyly now. "Look."

Feeling not quite awake, Naya turned to see where her arrow had landed. "I did it," she echoed wonderingly, looking at the target and shaking her head as if coming out of a trance. "I did it," she said again, louder this time. Turning back to Aytal, she gave him a radiant smile. "I hit the bull's eye!" She too whooped in jubilation.

"Now you know the secret," he said, grinning once again. "The rest is just repetition. Of course, eventually you'll have to learn to hit the target when it's not standing still."

Naya groaned in response. She knew he was teasing – she still had much to learn before she could think of trying to hunt – but she wanted to savor her success. She was also still trying to process what had happened in the moments immediately before and after she released that last shot. Regarding Aytal from behind, quiver slung easily over his back as he went to retrieve her arrows, she grew thoughtful. Why had she felt so giddy when he'd twirled her in his arms? Was it just because the arrow had finally gone where she'd aimed? And what about before, when he'd cradled both her and the bow? He'd made her feel powerful and protected, all at once. And something else, something that still vibrated in the pit of her stomach. It was a good thing he'd told her to breathe. Confused, she shook her head again. She'd think about it later. Meanwhile, she wanted to go and tell her mother what had happened. Hurrying, she went to help Aytal find the rest of her errant shots.

A little while later, arrows all safely tucked away, hide bag hefted onto Aytal's shoulder and bow slung over Naya's back, the two turned to walk together from the makeshift archery range back to the clearing. They'd set-up out on the grasslands well away from the clearing, where they wouldn't risk accidentally shooting Amu or one of the horses. Stopping on a slight rise to take in the vista of the steppe in winter, they stood side by side, their figures silhouetted against the forbidding landscape. When Aytal reached out, offering his free hand to Naya, it seemed the most natural thing in the world for her to take it.

Those same days of late winter were also spent with the horses. Gradually, as cold and snow began to loosen their hold, sunshine and gentler winds tempted the creatures of the steppe, human and animal alike, to venture farther afield. Naya grew stronger, finding herself able to walk greater distances without fatigue. Accompanied by Aytal, she began to range beyond the confines of the clearing, either to practice with the bow, or in search of the herd. Fewer storms meant the horses came less often seeking shelter, yet they never seemed to stray too far and could usually be found with only a little effort.

Once they were all out in the open again, and Naya could move with increasing naturalness and ease, she found she could establish a physical connection with the horses that had eluded her in the clearing, first with the red filly and then eventually with her dam, followed by the other mares and their offspring. Aytal, after a brief period of probation, was likewise welcomed into the herd's midst and allowed to make contact, so long as he followed Naya's lead in paying close attention to the horses' body language and approached with the required degree of gentleness and respect. Just as he had shown her the nuances of the bow, Naya taught him what she had learned from the horses about communicating through gesture, expression and above all, the breath. Only the stallion remained apart, unwilling to let either of them come near him. The rest of the herd could soon be counted on to greet Naya and Aytal with a friendly nicker whenever they appeared over the rise of the nearest hill. Often the youngsters, led by the red filly, would come trotting up in search of apple cores or a much-appreciated scratch on the withers. Naya supposed the horses must feel safer, knowing the surrounding grasslands offered the boundless possibility of escape. As a result, they were more willing to make themselves available to the humans' overtures of friendship.

One day, as Naya and Aytal sat side by side on the crest of a low hillock, idly watching the herd graze nearby, their attention was caught by a sudden movement. BeHregs, the stallion, lifted his head and stood on full alert. A split second later, every other head lifted as well and the two humans could feel a shiver of energy pass through the herd.

"What is it?" Naya asked, sitting taller in order to scan the surrounding steppe for whatever might have caused the change in the horses' demeanor. Amu, who lay on the ground beside them, also sat up, ears pricked.

"Look," replied Aytal, gesturing with his chin in the direction toward which the dog and the horses were all looking. On the opposite hilltop stood a lone horse, dark shape outlined against a slate-colored sky.

The first thought to cross Aytal's mind was that the creature must be starving. He looked to be a juvenile, no more than three or four, and painfully thin. Likely a bachelor, Aytal surmised, expelled from his original herd and trying to survive on his own. Without the company and protection of his own kind, the unfortunate animal had probably spent too much of the winter without shelter, searching for forage and fleeing from predators, and was now desperate for the companionship of other horses. Clearly the young stallion was in no shape to challenge BeHregs for possession of the mares, nor were they likely to accept him if he tried. No, if he was truly by himself, thought Aytal, he probably only wanted permission to join the herd. A horse alone was one of the most vulnerable creatures on the steppe, with the possible exception of a solitary human. The question was, would BeHregs and the rest of the horses allow it?

Aytal's next thought was that he and Naya should probably not stick around to find out. So involved had he been in watching her watch the horses that he hadn't noticed the change in the weather. The mild overcast with which the day had started had been replaced by lowering clouds almost the same dull gray as the horse on the hilltop. There would be snow by evening. He should get Naya back to the clearing.

"Let's go," he said, rising to his feet. "We shouldn't be out here any longer."

Naya, taking in the scene, including the change in weather, nodded her assent.

"I wonder what will happen to him," Aytal mused as he and Naya made their way back to the clearing, Amu trotting ahead through the dead brown landscape. "I hope they let him stay."

"Me too," Naya agreed, "especially given the weather. He doesn't look like he'd survive another blizzard. Maybe he'll follow the others to the clearing."

The next morning, they had their answer. As heralded by the previous afternoon's darkening skies, a late-winter storm had struck overnight, dumping a heavy layer of moisture-laden snow that caused tree branches to droop nearly to the ground and the hides covering the shelters to sag dangerously under the weight. With temperatures warming in advance of the arrival of spring, the snow would melt within a day, leaving behind a quagmire of mud and slush. In the meantime, everything groaned beneath the burden.

This included the band of horses. Cold and wet, they huddled together in a knot at the edge of the clearing, broad backs covered in an accumulation of snow despite the screen offered by the surrounding trees. When Aytal and Naya emerged from the shelter not long after the sun cleared the horizon, the animals had begun to stir, shaking themselves in an effort to dislodge the unwanted blanket of white and fluff-up the insulating underlayer of soft fur at the base of their coats. Before long they would make their way back out to the open steppe, where movement and exposure to sun and wind would complete the task of drying off.

"Look," exclaimed Naya in an excited whisper. "There he is."

She pointed to a dark shape standing a bit apart from the circle of adults and youngsters. Hide so soaked as to be almost black, the newcomer gazed at the other horses, his expression a mixture of misery and hope. As Aytal and Naya watched, the young stallion took a tentative step toward the nearest mare, who happened to be the ill-tempered Rebhjō, only to be warned away by an angry swing of her head in his direction. Retreating in the face of the mare's flattened ears and bared teeth, he looked around as if searching for an alternative means of approach, and suddenly caught sight of the two humans.

Startled, he tried to bound away through the deep snow but stopped after only a few steps when he realized none of the other horses were showing any signs of alarm. Turning, still poised to escape, he looked back at Aytal and Naya. Standing immobile, head lifted, ears pointed in their direction, white-rimmed eyes riveted on the apparent danger, tension was evident in every line of his emaciated body. Fear fought against exhaustion, instinct telling him to flee even though he no longer had the physical resources. Yet, the other horses didn't seemed to share his concern. Indeed, although several of them looked expectantly toward the two figures standing just outside the shelter, their attitude communicated anticipation rather than unease. After remaining frozen for a moment longer, the young stallion felt some of his overwhelming panic subside and he lowered his head slightly, expelling air from his nostrils in a loud snort, his breath producing a small cloud of steam in the cold morning air. He remained wary, but now also felt curious. The other horses continued to ignore him, focused instead on the humans.

"They're waiting for us to clear a path to the creek," said Aytal. "We've spoiled them."

"I wonder if we could show him that the other horses aren't worried about us," speculated Naya, studying the young stallion with concern. "Then maybe he wouldn't be so scared. Poor thing."

"He's already figured out the others are more impatient than afraid," replied Aytal, watching as BeHregs and a couple of the mares pawed dramatically at the surrounding snow. Just then the red filly whinnied in their direction, clearly demanding that they hurry up and make themselves useful.

Naya laughed in response. "You'd better get busy breaking a trail then. Maybe once they've all made it to the creek for a drink, Réhda and MeHnd will let us help them dry off and we can show him we're not so bad. I'll ask Mama for a couple of wool scraps we can use."

"…and maybe a few handfuls of grain, if there's any to spare," Aytal called after her as she disappeared back inside the tent. "The new one could use a hand-out."

A short while later, with Oyuun and Sata's assistance, a path had been cleared leading from the shelter down to the creek, with a spur heading in the direction of where the herd waited under the protective overhang of the trees. Standing just outside the tent, all four humans watched as the horses made their way one after the other to the water's edge. The normally quiet stream had become swollen with snow melt and rushed by in an icy torrent. Hanging back, the young stallion had to wait until all the others, even the yearlings, had drunk their fill. Only after the herd had retreated a little way from the water's edge did he dare approach to slake his thirst.

After the horses had finished drinking, Aytal and Naya made their way toward them through the knee-deep snow, felted wool cloths held loosely by their sides in plain sight.

"Would you like help drying off?" asked Naya, approaching the red filly first.

Stopping several paces away, she held out the cloth, then took a few steps closer until the young horse could stretch out her nose to sniff what the girl offered. Finding that it didn't smell edible, she at first looked away, communicating her disappointment but then turned back, still inquisitive. Naya continued to come closer until she stood at the filly's shoulder. Although quivering slightly, the little red horse turned a trusting eye to the girl at her side, waiting to see what she would do.

Gently, Naya began to slide the absorbent cloth along Réhda's rough topcoat, slicking off the worst of the moisture. Before long, she was rubbing vigorously all along the young horse's back, rump, shoulders, and neck until the wool fabric in her hand was thoroughly saturated and the coppery coat nearly dry. Stepping back to admire her handy work, Naya giggled when the filly shook herself vigorously from nose to tail, as if to finish the job, then nearly lost her footing in the snow when Réhda turned and head-butted her in the chest.

"Take it easy!" she laughed, taking a step backward while fending off the filly's advances. "You're welcome. Don't knock me over."

"We don't have enough spare rags to dry them all off," called Sata from her vantage point outside the shelter where she and Oyuun watched the scene unfolding by the creek.

"Let me at least try to help the newcomer," called Aytal over his shoulder. He, along with the horses, had stopped to observe Naya working on the red filly, but now he resumed his slow progress toward where the young stallion stood, a little apart from the rest of the herd.

"Take it easy big guy," he said in a steady voice, neither too loud nor too soft. "I'm not going to hurt you."

The dark horse turned a wild eye on the young man. Fear rolled off his taunt body in waves, but he managed to hold his ground. "That's a brave fellow," said Aytal, pausing to give the gray stallion a chance to calm himself. "Settle down. Take a breath." As if he understood, the horse exhaled, less explosively this time, followed by a deep inhale. Drawing in an array of scents, the horse detected not only the normally frightening man-smell, but also something that spoke intriguingly of food. A little of the panic retreated from his expression, replaced by wary interest.

"Are you hungry?" Cupped in his outstretch palm, Aytal offered the stallion a scant handful of grain, taken from their dwindling stores. "It's not much," he apologized, "but you can have it."

Sniffing, the stallion stretched his muzzle tentatively in the direction of the young man's hand. *Nourishment*, his senses told him. *Danger*, his instincts warned. Yet the other horses did not seem bothered by the humans. Hunger at last prevailing, the dark horse took one step closer until, neck fully extended, his strong, mobile lips could just reach the young man's hand. Within seconds, the grain had all disappeared. Ears pricked, fear now rapidly giving way to hunger-fueled greed, the stallion clearly wanted more.

"Only a handful," replied Aytal, reaching into the small pouch at his side. "That's all we can spare. But you're welcome to it." This time, while offering the grain with one hand, he reached out with the other to lay an open palm against the stallion's dark hide. Trembling at the unfamiliar touch, the starving horse still did not shy away, too drawn by the offering of food.

"That's a good man," said Aytal, leaving his hand where he'd placed it against the horse's shoulder. He felt skin, sinew and bone but almost no meat. "We'll look after you now. You're safe with us." Again, as if he'd understood the young man's words, the dark horse responded in kind, lowering his head, and letting out a deep sigh.

Over the next several days, the gray stallion remained in the clearing, even after the other horses departed to forage on the open steppe. Whereas the herd had persisted in warning the newcomer off with threatening gestures, the lonely horse discovered that the humans, particularly the tall, dark-haired one, actively welcomed his hesitant advances. Before long, he and Aytal established a routine that involved exchanges of small handfuls of grain in return for the ravenous horse's willingness to allow the young man to run his hands wherever he might choose along the rough gray-black coat. Although at first too focused on eating to register concern about the unfamiliar sensation of being stroked, soon the young stallion sought out the friendly, reassuring human as much for the comfort of his touch as for the offering of food.

Meanwhile, Aytal and the others wondered at the new horse's unusual coloring, perhaps not as novel as the red filly's, but still a departure from the more typical shades of yellow dun that provided better concealment against the backdrop of the steppes' seasonal hues of glistening gold or lifeless brown. Even more, they continued to worry about the young stallion's gaunt appearance. Although the air of abject misery had left him, still, even after several days, he did not seem capable of fending for himself. Either too weak to venture out after the rest of the horses to seek food on his own, or too intimidated by the herd's unwillingness to accept him, he stayed where he was, using what little energy he had to paw fitfully at the ground in a nearly fruitless search for something to eat, all the while casting hopeful looks toward the humans' shelter.

Most of the once-abundant forage in the clearing had been consumed over the course of the winter and Aytal could see that what little remained held not enough nourishment to stave off the young stallion's hunger, nor could they spare sufficient grain from their diminished supply to meet his needs. Instead, in order to feed the starving horse, he and Naya came up with the idea of gathering sheaves of tall straw-like grass from the surrounding steppe to bring back for him. Using a scythe normally employed to harvest wild grains in season, they cut armloads of dry, brittle hay and brought them back for the grateful horse. Thereafter, he made rapid progress and before long, an attitude of alert interest replaced the look of desperation in the horse's dark eye.

Behind that eye, Aytal in turn began to sense a keen intelligence, as well as curiosity. Intrigued, he wanted to get to know the young stallion better. Thus when nearly half a moon after the new horse's arrival, Oyuun speculated that perhaps the gods had sent him to the clearing as an answer to their own increasingly critical need for food, Aytal reacted with indignation.

"You can't mean to slaughter him for meat!" he exclaimed.

They were out gathering the last of the readily available firewood from the undergrowth surrounding the clearing. Aytal was glad Naya wasn't along to hear what his father seemed to be proposing. She would have been outraged. He'd come to share her feelings. Just as Naya had convinced them all that the red filly was special, along with the rest of the herd who had spent the winter in the clearing, Aytal had grown to think of the young stallion as much more than potential prey.

"How can you even suggest such a thing?" he demanded, straightening from picking up a dead branch that had lain partially concealed by leaves. They had to search hard these days to find anything left on the ground that would burn. He stared at his father, incensed, before adding the stick to the woefully small pile of kindling stacked in Oyuun's outstretched arms.

Oyuun, about to give Aytal all the reasons, took in the look on his son's face and thought better of it. Having watched the rapport forming between the darked-haired young man and the slate-colored horse, even he had to admit that once again, something mysterious appeared to be at work. Just as Naya seemed linked by an intangible bond to the red filly, Oyuun could see that his son and the gray stallion shared a connection that defied easy explanation. He sighed.

"Never mind. You're right," he replied. "Forget I said anything," and he let the matter drop.

Chapter Thirteen

Oyuun's concern about their food supply was real, nonetheless. The time of the starving moon was upon them, a desperate season for all creatures of the steppe. Last season's sources of sustenance had been nearly depleted and spring's promise of returning abundance was not yet fulfilled. Predators, emboldened by their own hunger and the winter-weakened state of their prey, ranged beyond their usual territories, taking greater risks in their quest for food. In turn, the herds of antelope, deer, bison and horses that roamed the grasslands grew increasingly wary. They travelled even more widely, becoming nearly impossible for human hunters, less mobile, to track down successfully. Smaller game, too, had grown scarce in the vicinity of the clearing, forcing Oyuun and Aytal to wander farther afield in search of food and return home more often empty-handed. Hence the disagreement between father and son regarding the young stallion.

Sata, likewise, had exhausted all the plant resources within easy range of their winter home and it was impractical for her and Oyuun to keep making day-long trips back and forth to the river. Discussing the matter with Oyuun one afternoon when they were alone in the clearing, she wondered if he shared the worry that had been gnawing at her for days. They stood side by side in the smaller shelter, surveying what remained of their stores. Aytal and Naya had gone out on the steppe to hone Naya's archery skills.

"It's been more than half a moon since we've brought in any game," Oyuun observed in response to Sata's question about how much longer they could hold out. He sounded remarkably unperturbed, she thought, given the gravity of the situation. "The herds are all too far away for us to track, unless we plan to be gone for several days," he continued, "and then we'd have trouble bringing enough meat back to make it worth the effort. With what's left here, we'll be lucky to make it through."

Sata, who had been contemplating the once-bulging skin sacks, now nearly empty, turned to search Oyuun's face. The seriousness she read there, belying the matter-of-fact tone of his words, brought her up short. In the time they'd spent together, she had grown to trust and even like this man, appreciating his competence and common sense. He also made her laugh, with his understated, subtly irreverent sense of humor. Unlike her husband, whose burden of responsibility to the clan made him so stern and pre-occupied much of the time, Oyuun seemed to have no greater concern than to entertain her and find ways to serve her small needs. His outlook on life appeared to be one of amused, slightly cynical detachment. Although reticent about himself, he was never unkind, never uncaring, always even-tempered, practical, and efficient.

Above all, he was not one to over-react. On the contrary, more often than not, he was inclined to point out the absurdity of a difficult or uncomfortable situation, thereby making it seem less of a crisis. Thus when no quip about their current predicament followed this last statement regarding the state of their provisions, Sata's own concerns were not only confirmed but magnified.

"Do you really think we'll run out before Potis can return for us?" she asked, biting her lip.

"Or before we can head east," he returned. "Naya is so much stronger now. Perhaps the time has come to pack up and go." The look he gave her begged the question.

"But the weather – what if we got caught in a storm?" Sata had lived long enough on the steppe to know the dangers of a spring blizzard.

"We may have to risk it. I don't think we can stay here much longer."

Holding the tent flap aside so that Sata could stoop and precede him, Oyuun followed her outside the shelter. Standing side by side again, they surveyed the clearing that had been their shared home for more than three moons. The grass, once abundant before being cropped short by the horses and then eaten to the roots by the goats, had disappeared, replaced by a swamp of mud. All the underbrush and downed trees available for firewood had been cleared, with the result that they now had to go much further in search of not only food but fuel. The shelters, battered by the winter's repeated storms, looked tattered and forlorn.

"We can't stay," Oyuun, repeated, stating the obvious. He looked at Sata, seeking a sign of agreement. Not for the first time, he found himself appreciating the elegant planes of her face, dark auburn brows and high cheekbones framing those strikingly familiar blue eyes. Although the trials of her life were evident in their depths, as well as in the furrows along her high forehead, smile lines also appeared at the corners of her eyes and around her generous mouth whenever he succeeded in amusing her. Whether from laughter or sorrow, the traces of life left on her face only added to her beauty in his view.

"The time of balance is almost here," he continued, turning away to assess the angle of the sun overhead. Tomorrow, he knew, the length of daylight would match the darkness, signaling the departure of winter and the return of spring, at least in terms of the sun's journey through the heavens."

Sata followed the direction of Oyuun's gaze, finding herself relieved when his dark eyes were no longer on hers. He sometimes made her uncomfortable when he gave her that searching look, at once inquiring and enigmatic, as if he sought to discover something she wasn't even aware she hid from him, while revealing nothing of himself. Was it any surprise that she couldn't help but respond with covertly speculative glances of her own? Who was he, exactly? He and his son did not seem to be misleading in anything they'd disclosed about themselves, but nonetheless there were unanswered questions, many of them. She was intrigued, and she had to admit, more than a little attracted, by the mysterious stranger, so different from her husband. The realization registered as an uncomfortable tightening in the region just below her ribs. Danger or excitement? Perhaps both? She couldn't tell, she only knew the sensation frightened her a little, and this in turn made her impatient with herself. She was the wife of a chief, not in a position to be having such feelings. Time to go indeed.

"Then we should return," she said abruptly, irritated that she sounded flustered. When Oyuun turned back to her, she quickly looked away, hoping he would assume anxiety about their dire circumstances had upset her. "We can discuss it with Naya and Aytal tonight when they get back," she said without meeting his eye, unwilling to risk allowing him to see whatever unacknowledged feelings her face might betray. "I'll start packing."

Not waiting for a reply, Sata made her way across the short distance to the larger shelter and disappeared inside, leaving Oyuun to ponder her hasty retreat. The air filling the space where they had stood together still vibrated, making him wonder if she was becoming aware, as he had been for some time, of something powerful that had the potential to take shape between them. For him, the possibility had been there from the beginning, for reasons he fully understood but was reluctant to explore, even with himself, let alone share with her. He had tried to suppress the pull he felt toward her, taken care not to let it show, but now had to admit that he'd failed. The days they'd spent together, and the woman herself, were more than he could resist. What had started as an almost reflexive attraction, rooted in memory, had evolved into something all its own. Something hazardous for both of them, judging by what he'd sensed from her today, despite her evident determination to hide it. Time to go indeed, he said to himself, his thoughts an unconscious echo of hers. *Time to go indeed.*

In their shared concerns over the perils, spoken and unspoken, of the situation in which they found themselves, neither Sata nor Oyuun voiced one of the more obvious complications. If they left now, what would happen with the horses? For the moment Oyuun remained persuaded, albeit reluctantly, not to consider the animals as a solution to the problem of their mounting hunger. Still, what was to become of the herd once they set out from the clearing?

That evening in the tent, Naya was quick to raise the issue. "We can't leave them behind," she declared when the decision to head for the clan's winter settlement was announced. "I won't go without them."

They were gathered around the fire, preparing to consume a meager meal.

"No one is asking you to," returned Oyuun. "If you don't think they'll come of their own accord, couldn't you find a way to lead them? Certainly the red filly and even the gray stallion shouldn't be too hard to catch. And the mare, the one who is soon to foal, even she might let you put a rope on her. The others would probably follow her, including the stallion, although he might not be too pleased about it." He paused a moment as they all considered the likelihood of this scenario. "Even better," he continued, "would be if one of them would let you harness them to a sled. That would make the trip much easier on us."

Naya looked dubious. "I've never been able to get close to any of them, even Réhda, with a rope in my hand." Although still unable to fully recall the words of the voice in her visions, she'd grown increasingly certain that coercion was not the answer to interacting with the horses.

"Mama," she said slowly, brows knitted in thought, "do you think the herd has come to trust me?"

"Not only you, but Aytal as well," replied Sata. "They're not as sure of us yet," she added, indicating herself and Oyuun, "but they seem entirely comfortable with the two of you."

"So you might say we're friends, we've made a connection?" Naya pressed her point.

"Yes." Sata agreed. "I'd say you've created a bond."

"Then," Naya said, turning to the others, "hopefully we don't *need* a rope." The voice from her visions seemed to whisper to her, urging her to believe what the core of her being knew to be true. *Trust what you and the red filly have created. Trust the ties that connect you.* There didn't seem to be any other choice. They had to go. She had to have faith that the horses would follow.

"We'd never be able to use a rope anyway," she continued. "It would be too much restraint and they're too strong. They'd panic and break away and never let us near them again."

"It's all in the intent and what they are used to," countered Oyuun. "Our reindeer herds are free to go where they please, but when they are young we get them accustomed to being with people and allowing themselves to be harnessed when we need their help. Most of the time, though, we don't try to control them. In fact, it's more the other way around. We follow them. But perhaps it's not the same with your cattle?"

"Well, they definitely don't like to be tethered like the goats and they are not very good at carrying burdens," observed Sata, recalling to herself the incident of the young bullock run amok. "And we do tell them where to go, not the other way around. We drive all the animals, sheep, goats and cattle, back and forth each season between our winter settlement and the open steppe."

"Mama," interrupted Naya excitedly, caught by a sudden inspiration, "imagine how much easier it would be if we could ride horses to drive the herds!" While she thought constantly of the arrival of the day when she could finally ride the red filly, she'd never truly considered of what use tame horses might be, despite her father's skeptical query. Now she had an answer for him. "And think how it would be to hunt with them!" Turning to Aytal, she sought to enlist him in her enthusiasm. "We could keep up so easily with a herd of deer or bison," she exclaimed. "And if we had bows and arrows..."

"...we would be the greatest hunters of the steppes." He finished the sentence for her, smiling from his seat beside her at the fire.

"No, I'm serious!" she retorted, shoving his shoulder. "If you and I could learn to shoot from the back of a galloping horse, we *would* be the greatest hunters of the steppes."

"Be that as it may," put in Oyuun, "no one has even sat on one of those animals and we have not been the most successful hunters of anything lately, however good you may be getting at hitting that stuffed target. We really should get moving and if the horses are going to come, we need to figure out how to keep them with us and keep them safe."

Naya was as aware as everyone else of the paucity of their supplies and the scarcity of game. Only the extra sack of grain sent by her grandmother had enabled her and Aytal to share as much as they had already with the horses. Naya wondered, again, what had prompted Awija to make such a sacrifice. The sack represented half her grandparents' winter supply. She was flooded by a sudden wave of longing to see them again, accompanied by a sharp stab of worry.

"We must go, I see that," she said, her voice now sober. "The horses will come." Trying to sound more certain than she felt, Naya's eyes sought Aytal's, looking for reassurance. In response, he smiled at her again, no longer teasing this time, and winked instead. They had been working on a project that might help.

Noting the exchange, Sata laid an arm around Naya's shoulders. "They will come," she echoed, giving them a squeeze. For her daughter's sake, Sata hoped it was true, whatever the two young people were up to. The look she gave Oyuun over the top of Naya's head could not entirely disguise her doubts.

"It's settled then," said Oyuun, returning Sata's gaze, his own expression relieved. "We leave in the morning."

The process of packing what they could that evening did not take long. With little food remaining, only the extra hides, along with various tools and cooking implements, needed to be stowed away. The shelters would be taken down in the morning and the long tent poles turned into sleds for Amu and the she-goat to pull. Oyuun and Aytal would take turns with a third sled, which would mean the packs Sata and Naya carried would not have to be quite so heavy.

Searching for room to store the auroch horn Aytal had given her, Naya thought again of the plan they'd come up with only a few days earlier. Knowing they might need a way to encourage the horses to come when called, they had decided to try to teach them to respond to the sound of the horn. At first, the horses had all been too startled to notice that a particular two-note call was followed by the offer of a tempting apple core and a good scratch on the withers, but gradually they began to make the connection. At this point only the filly and the young stallion could be counted on to show up whenever either Naya or Aytal blew the horn, but perhaps once they were on the move the others would answer reliably as well.

Naya was considering the possibilities when Oyuun, who had been outside checking on the goats, pushed aside the tent flap and stuck his head in.

"Come," he said quietly but with an undercurrent of urgency. "Something is going on with the horses."

The others left what they were doing and followed him out. The clearing was shrouded with evening shadows, but it was not so dark that the four humans could not distinguish the shapes of horses on the far side of the grove.

"Where are the rest of them?" whispered Aytal. Only the red filly, the gray stallion, and the pregnant mare were present. Never had the entire herd not been seen together. MeHnd, head drooping almost to the ground, looked exhausted. The other two stood sentinel on either side of her.

"Her time must be near," answered Naya, also keeping her voice low. She could feel the mare's weariness from across the space that separated them. "Something isn't right." Worry gripped her. "Why isn't she with the others?"

"Normally mares give birth out on the steppe, with the rest of the herd around them for protection," confirmed Sata. "Perhaps the foal won't come."

Naya thought of the many times she'd watched her mother reach within one of the clan's ewes or she-goats, attempting to rearrange a small body struggling to enter the world backwards. With the cattle, only her father or one of the other men had the strength to battle the force of the cow's contractions, one arm extended up to the shoulder in order to turn a recalcitrant calf. Often they were successful, but not always. Sometimes the newborn did not survive the process and sometimes, despite their best efforts, the mother died as well. For the people of the clan, who valued every one of their animals as family members, such an outcome represented a tragic loss. Naya could only imagine what it would be like for the mare if her foal lay wrong.

"We have to try to help her," she said, voice urgent.

"Careful," cautioned Oyuun, "if you're too upset, you'll only frighten her more."

"What can we do then?" With difficulty, Naya restrained herself from rushing over to the mare.

"Start by taking a deep breath," advised Oyuun. "Nothing can happen until she decides to lie down. Until then, you and Aytal stay out here and keep watch. Be calm, and only approach as close as she'll let you without getting upset."

Sata, who had slipped inside the shelter, returned with two heavy robes. Although the worst of winter's bitter temperatures were behind them, nights were still cold.

"Wrap up in these," she said. "We can pack them tomorrow."

"Come get us if anything changes," said Oyuun over his shoulder as he held open the shelter's entrance flap for Sata to go back in. He made Amu follow as well, much against the dog's wishes.

Aytal moved several paces away from the tent to where a large log with space for two flanked the cold fire pit. Keeping his movements contained so as not to disturb the horses, he pulled the larger of the two fur-lined robes around his own shoulders and then, seating himself on the log, extended an arm to Naya, inviting her under the cloak's sheltering folds. Anxiety for the mare crowding out any hesitation about accepting

Aytal's offer, Naya sat down next to him, pulling the additional blanket up over both their laps. She felt one of Aytal's arms settle around her shoulders. The other encircled her from the front, ostensibly to hold the end of the robe in place. She discovered she didn't mind. Encased in a warm cocoon, she settled in to wait.

Stillness returned to the clearing, broken only by an occasional rustle as one of the horses shifted a hoof or a muffled grunt escaped from MeHnd. Otherwise, nothing in the clearing moved or made a sound. Above, the stars one by one began to appear in the darkening night sky. The waning moon provided just enough light to distinguish the silhouetted horses from the surrounding shadows.

Inside the tent, Oyuun and Sata busied themselves with the remaining preparations for tomorrow's departure until finally they were left with nothing else to do.

"One of us should get some sleep," said Oyuun. "I'll wake you if anything happens with the mare."

"I don't think I can sleep," Sata replied. "Can we build up the fire instead? No point in conserving any more fuel at this point. We'll only have to leave it behind."

"True enough," Oyuun acknowledged, reaching over to do as she asked.

Before long, the last of the sticks blazed brightly, chasing shadows into the empty corners of the shelter. Everything was packed for their departure and already what had served as home for the past three moons felt deserted, except for the fire burning in the hearth. Oyuun watched Sata, wrapped in her cloak, stare into the flames as if she might read the future there, or perhaps the past. Tomorrow this interlude would end and they would begin the journey back to her old life. He wished he could guess how she felt about it.

At last, after a long silence, Sata spoke. "Who is she?" she asked quietly, still gazing into the fire.

"Who?" returned Oyuun, distracted by the vision before him. Light from the flames caught the highlights in Sata's auburn hair, flickering amidst the rich tendrils that framed her face.

"The woman you think of when you look at me."

"I don't know what you mean," denied Oyuun.

"You do," countered Sata, lifting her eyes to meet his. "Tell me about her."

Now it was his turn to stare into the fire. Kindling crackled. At last, having made up his mind, he cleared his throat and spoke. "Her name," he said, "was Zerashsha and she was my wife."

"Was?" Sata asked.

"She died giving birth to our only child."

"Aytal?"

Oyuun nodded.

"You loved her?"

"With all my heart."

"Why do I remind you of her?" Sata asked. "Do I look like her?"

"The resemblance is subtle but unmistakable," Oyuun acknowledged, lifting his eyes from the flames to meet her gaze. "Your hair and features are a little different, and you are taller, but there is the color and shape of your eyes, which are identical, as well as the way you move and carry yourself and of course the way you sound. She spoke your tongue."

"She spoke the language of my people?" Sata sounded astonished. "How is that possible?"

"She came from your homeland," Oyuun answered. "I met her the first time I travelled there, to trade with the stone knappers. She was the daughter of Waig, the-one-eyed…"

"…most skilled of all my people." Sata finished the sentence for him, a note of awe in her voice.

Oyuun was not surprised that Sata knew of the famed artisan, who was widely revered. Of those who worked the black stone, Waig possessed a talent that came along only once in several generations. Oyuun remembered watching the carver's gnarled hands, scarred from years of handling the sharp, potentially lethal shards of obsidian, caressing each one as if it represented something infinitely precious, a gift from the gods. Yet those same gods had been as cruel as they were generous, demanding a great sacrifice in return not only for the stones themselves but the skill to shape them. A leather patch hid the scarred and empty socket of the carver's right eye. The other eye, which had come to survey the world with a degree of cynicism, was blue.

"But then I knew her," continued Sata, "Your wife. She and I played together as children, whenever my family travelled to Waig's village. As a girl she went by the name Zera, just as my full name is Satanaya but I'm known as Sata. People often said we could be sisters, or at least cousins, we were so similar, even though we weren't related. But then I left to marry Potis and never learned what happened to her."

"Like you, she left her home in the mountains for another life." Oyuun lapsed into silence.

Sata wondered if the silence held regret. "And now you return?" she asked eventually, not wanting to probe too deeply into Oyuun's feelings for his lost mate, but still curious.

"Yes," he said, staring once more into the fire. "I promised Zerashsha before she died, just after she gave birth to Aytal, that one day I would return to her family, tell them what happened to her, and bring them word of our son." "Of course," he added, looking up and giving Sata a wry smile, "I also want to replenish my supply of blades and arrowheads."

This last was said lightly, and with a hint of self-mockery, as if a practical reason were required to justify such a sentimental journey. Certainly, Sata thought to herself, a trading expedition was the explanation Oyuun had provided for traveling through the clan's territory. She wondered if his trip had lost any of its urgency. How did he feel about getting underway tomorrow? Did the man seated across the hearth, enigmatic eyes meeting hers, have any qualms about their sojourn in the clearing coming to an end?

"Do you ever think of returning to your family for a visit?" Oyuun asked, breaking in on Sata's thoughts. His voice sounded innocent.

"I have never been back," she replied. "Although there has been word from time to time as traders have passed through." She had to stop to swallow the lump that had suddenly appeared in her throat. "I miss them," she continued after a moment, then paused even longer before speaking again. "And I miss the mountains."

Sata heard the yearning in her own voice and wondered if Oyuun noticed. She'd shared with him her worries for her daughter, concerns about the ongoing challenges of their winter exile, but never this soul-deep ache of longing. The sudden stab of homesickness she felt took her by surprise. Immediately she regretted having acknowledged, let alone uttered, what she had believed buried long ago.

She missed her home, missed the land as well as the people. No matter how long she spent with her husband's clan, the limitless grasslands of the steppe still felt foreign to her, boundaryless, with nothing to which she could anchor her spirit like the majestic, snow-clad peaks where she was raised. And as much as she felt accepted and honored by Potis and his immediate family, there were others in the clan who never allowed her to forget that she would always be an *alteros* – an outsider among them. Most of the time, she succeeded in ignoring the innuendos and her sense of alienation remained a subterranean undercurrent, barely troubling her day-to-day life. Somehow talking with Oyuun, being reminded of her childhood friend, brought everything to the surface, where a dam threatened to burst.

For several heartbeats, only the hiss and snap of burning wood disturbed the silence inside the shelter, but finally Oyuun could no longer prevent himself from speaking. "You could see them again," said he quietly. He had hesitated long enough to recognize that the idea he was about to propose was both unlikely and imprudent, before giving voice to it anyway.

"Come with me," he said, not allowing himself time to reconsider. "I could take you along for a visit to your people, and then return with you. Aytal may well have to stay behind with your husband's clan to fulfill the terms of his debt and thus could not make the rest of the journey with me to your homeland if I am to arrive within the year, and I dare not postpone any longer. Indeed, I may be too late already. So I would need to come back by the same route in any case to retrieve him, once his obligation is paid…"

Oyuun's words trailed off, the fleeting eagerness he'd begun to feel extinguished by the distress he read in Sata's face.

"I cannot," was all she said. Oyuun raised a questioning brow, waiting for her to give all the obvious excuses for why she would not want to undertake even a brief visit home. She had ties, responsibilities. After what they had been through and still had yet to face, even assuming they made it safely back to the clan, leaving her daughter and being separated again from her husband would be unthinkable. The answer she gave instead astonished him.

"I can't go," she repeated. 'I might never come back."

Just then, the tent flap opened, revealing Aytal's concerned face.

"Come," he said urgently. "Something is happening.

Moments earlier, Naya, who had been dozing with her head against Aytal's shoulder, started suddenly.

"What is it?" she asked in confusion, still not fully awake.

"Nothing," replied Aytal. "Nothing has changed."

"Something *has* changed," contradicted Naya. "I can feel it." Indeed, just as she spoke, movement from where the horses stood signaled a shift. The mare had started to pace in a small circle. After only one or two revolutions, she lay down with a grunt.

"Get my mother," whispered Naya, throwing off the robes as she stood up. Although stiff from sitting, she hardly noticed, all of her attention trained across the clearing. "I'll try to get closer."

Reminding herself to breathe, Naya walked carefully in the dark toward the edge of the grove where the horses were gathered. Although she wanted to move slowly enough not to startle them, she also didn't want to give the impression that she was trying to sneak up on them.

"It's only me," she said, her voice as reassuring as she could manage. "Let me see if we can help." As if comprehending the girl's intent, the red filly and young stallion made space for her to approach. The mare lay prone on the cold earth, head outstretched, belly impossibly distended. Naya watched as a powerful contraction rippled beneath the winter-thick dun coat. The mare lifted her head, then lay back again, groaning.

This was not her first foal. She understood what was happening, but this time seemed much more difficult than before. And she was already so tired. She wasn't sure she had the strength to see this new life into the world. Wearily, the mare closed her eyes, waiting for the next powerful wave to seize her.

"What's wrong?" Naya turned anxiously to her mother, who had joined her in crouching beside the horse. A short distance away, the red filly whinnied and pawed the ground fretfully, echoing the girl's concern.

"The foal may be laying wrong, as we suspected," answered Sata. "And MeHnd doesn't have much strength. The winter has been hard on her." She stroked the mare's flank. "Naya," she continued, "you and Aytal stand with the filly and stallion and keep them quiet. If MeHnd will let me, I'll check on the foal but if it's backwards or twisted, I won't be strong enough to turn it. Oyuun, you'll have to do it."

Sata glanced back over her shoulder to where Oyuun waited. Nodding, he came forward to kneel next to her. Ceding her place at the mare's side, Naya rose and moved to put a comforting arm around the filly's withers, while Aytal did the same for the gray stallion. Together, the four watched as Sata and Oyuun worked over the mare, who seemed either grateful for the humans' help, or simply too tired to resist. Stripped down to the sleeveless tunic she wore beneath her warm outer garments, Sata coated one bare arm with nearly the last of her supply of purified sheep grease and then reached as far as she could into the mare's birth canal, eliciting hardly any reaction from the exhausted horse. Feeling her way past delicate front legs, already extended into the canal, she sought in vain for the foal's muzzle, which should have rested along the outstretched forelimbs. Instead, reaching as far in as space would allow, she could just barely make out a narrow chest. There was no sign of the foal's head. Just then another contraction started, a powerful wave that clenched down on Sata's forearm, causing her to gasp in pain until the mare's muscles relaxed and the contraction passed. Trying again, this time Sata identified the curve of the little creature's neck. Withdrawing before the next contraction could trap her arm, she turned to Oyuun.

"Its head is twisted back against its right flank," she said, wiping away blood and mucus with the wool rags she'd brought out with her. "Can you see if you can find the nose and guide it into position?" They both knew that if he failed, neither mare nor foal were likely to survive.

"I'll do my best," was all he said. Following Sata's example, Oyuun removed layers until his arms were bare. Taking Sata's place and coating his right forearm up to the shoulder with grease, he reached inside the unprotesting horse.

Watching, unable to do anything to help, Naya wanted to hold her breath. Instead, she focused on the technique her father had taught her to use when hunting, inhaling and exhaling slowly and silently in order not to alert the animals they were stalking. Maybe, Naya thought, she'd be able to calm the filly, who vibrated anxiously beside her. Still unable to draw air deeply into her lungs without an uncomfortable tug at the back of her ribs, she did her best. "It will be alright," she whispered into the young horse's ear. "Mama and Oyuun will save them." It was the first time Naya had uttered the stranger's name.

The struggle lasted for what seemed an eternity but was in reality only a matter of minutes. Arm extended as far as he could reach inside the mare, Oyuun endured several powerful but unproductive contractions. When the mare's muscles momentarily relaxed, he felt for the foal's nose so that he could guide it into position, but each contraction jammed the little creature's chest against the mare's pelvis, leaving scarcely any room to maneuver. At last, with both of them beginning to sweat despite the cold night air, he withdrew his arm from the mare and sat back, panting.

"The neck is fully extended backwards. There's not enough space and my arm isn't long enough."

Naya could tell Oyuun was trying not to sound defeated. She also knew that MeHnd had to be almost out of strength. Most likely the foal's heartbeat was weakening as well. With the birth sac already ruptured, if they didn't free the little creature soon, it would suffocate, while the mare, unable to give birth to her lifeless offspring, would die as well.

"What if we try to get her up and moving," suggested Aytal from where he stood with the gray stallion. "Maybe the foal will reposition itself."

"That's not a bad idea," answered Oyuun. "Naya, you come by the mare's head and encourage her. The rest of us will push from behind."

Yet, even with all four of them, they could not convince the mare to rise. She was too spent. Naya stood with the others in a circle around the prone body, a large dark shape against the darker ground. For a moment no one spoke. Only the red filly made a sound, nickering nervously for her mother. The mare, barely able to lift her head, tried to answer, then lay back again. Naya stifled a sob.

"Let me try again," said Sata. "Oyuun, during the next break between contractions, you and Aytal push the foal away from the mare's hind end from the outside, so that it's not so jammed. Then see if you can get its head started back in the right direction. Maybe with more room, I'll be able to reach the muzzle from the inside and guide it the rest of the way. Naya, do whatever you can to keep MeHnd from struggling against us."

Acting as Sata directed, the two men, palms braced against the mare's side where the outline of the unborn foal could be felt through its mother's dense coat, waited for the last contraction to subside and then pushed in the opposite direction. For a moment, nothing happened, but then Naya thought she could see a slight yielding. "It's working," Oyuun confirmed. With steady pressure he and Aytal were able to move the foal's body just enough to allow the little creature's head to drop forward. From there, Sata took over and within seconds, she had the foal's nose lined up along its forelegs. Recognizing that something had shifted, the mare gathered what little energy remained for one final heroic effort. With a grunt, she expelled the foal into Sata's waiting arms.

"It's a colt," she proclaimed.

"Is he alive?" asked Naya anxiously.

"Give me a rag to clear his nostrils," Sata replied.

Rushing to comply, Naya knelt at her mother's side, gazing in wonder at the small, wet creature who seemed to be all long, spindly legs, with tiny hooves and a head too big for his narrow body.

"Is he going to be okay?" she asked again.

Just then, the mare lifted her head and looked around at them, as if she too wondered if her efforts had been worth the travail. Seeing Sata working over the foal, still and apparently lifeless, the mare lay back again, as though in utter defeat. Naya felt the hope drain out of her own body. Were they going to lose them both? Moving next to the mare's head, stretched out against the cold earth, she began to stroke the long neck while speaking urgently into one fur-lined ear. "Don't give up," she kept murmuring. "Don't give up! Your baby needs you."

For a long moment, nothing happened. Naya felt her mother's hand on her shoulder, about to urge her to turn away, but she didn't want to move from the mare's side. A shudder passed through MeHnd's body and Naya leaned back slightly to give her space. With evident effort, the exhausted horse lifted her head once more to look around at her foal but this time she found the energy to call to him, producing a rumbling whinny from somewhere deep in her chest. Another followed, louder this time. Miraculously, the colt answered with a tiny burble of his own.

Naya looked up at her mother, beaming triumphantly. Sata reached out to check for the rise and fall of the foal's rib cage, just to be sure. "He's breathing," she verified. "Here Naya," she said, handing over the rag. "Start drying him off while I see to the mare."

Sometime later, Naya and the others regrouped inside the larger shelter, nearly empty except for bundles waiting to be strapped to sleds in the morning. Amu, unsettled by the clear signs of imminent departure, not to mention the night's events from which he'd been so unceremoniously excluded, greeted them eagerly when they stepped into the tent's dim interior, lit now only by the feeble remains of the dying fire. They were weary but exhilarated at the same time.

Together, they'd watched in relief as a second plaintive call from the foal galvanized the exhausted mare. Despite her fatigue, she had heaved herself to her feet and made her way to where he lay, propped on his sternum, long legs folded underneath him. Recognizing that the experienced mother was ready to take over the task of gently rubbing warmth and life into her offspring's fragile body, Naya had retreated to join the others a short distance away. She looked on, awed and amused, as the colt made his first clumsy attempts to rise. Within moments of finding his feet, the hungry newborn had successfully located the source of his first meal and Sata signaled to the others that it was time to leave the pair in peace. The red filly and young stallion had also moved off to a respectful distance, allowing the mare and foal to bond while still remaining close enough to keep watch.

Now, settled in their places around the fire but too overwhelmed by what they'd witnessed to go immediately to sleep, Naya and the others marveled at the experience. Never before, as far as any of them knew, had humans been privileged not only to observe but to assist in the birth of a horse. To all of them, even Oyuun, the consummately practical reindeer herder, and Sata, experienced midwife who had been present at many a difficult delivery, the event felt sacred. Aytal couldn't stop grinning and Naya was nearly beside herself with child-like wonder. Already, she'd fallen in love with the little creature.

"Can we...?" she started to ask.

Oyuun cut her off. "We're still planning to start first thing in the morning," he said, firmly but not unkindly. "We don't have a choice."

"The foal will be fine," added Sata. "You'll see. He'll have no trouble keeping up. Now try to get some sleep." Hand on Naya's back, she guided her to lay back among the furs, tucking them warmly around her. "The fire is nearly out, we have no more wood and the sun will be up before you know it."

"Mama?" said Naya before Sata could turn away.

"Yes?"

"Thank you." Tired but happy, Naya held her mother's gaze in the flickering shadows. Sata smiled in response.

"You're welcome. Now sleep." Sata began to shift toward her own bed, but Naya, voice no more than a whisper, called her back.

"Mama?"

"Yes?

"I love you."

"I love you too."

Chapter Fourteen

Early the next morning, they set off, leaving the clearing behind and heading due east across the open steppe. Even though the main path lay further to the south and offered easier places to ford the two large tributaries of the *Dān* that lay between them and their ultimate destination, they'd decided to attempt a shortcut instead. By heading directly east and counting on both rivers remaining at least partially frozen and thus easier to cross, they hoped to reduce the overall distance by several days' travel. The main path, after traversing the second of the two tributaries, turned slightly north, so they should eventually be able to rejoin it and from there continue on to the clan's winter settlement on the banks of the *Rā*.

Oyuun went first, choosing their route and setting as energetic a pace as the terrain and their burdens would allow. In addition to the pack strapped to his back, he dragged behind him one of the three heavily laden sleds, while Amu, who came next, pulled another. The dog would have preferred to be scouting ahead but submitted patiently to his task. The she-goat, hitched to the third sled, was less cooperative and Sata, who retained hold of her tether, had to stay by her side, encouraging her to keep up. At the same time, Sata kept an eye on the two kids, now all grown up. Although she knew that the time was approaching when at least one of the young goats might be called upon to sacrifice its life in order for the humans to survive the journey ahead, Sata was grateful that for now they could still cavort by their mother's side, occasionally snatching a mouthful of withered grass. She knew that she should be grateful as well for the lack of snow on the ground and the firm, dry earth beneath their feet, which made walking relatively easy. The next storm, whenever it came, would render travel considerably more treacherous.

Until then, Sata reminded herself each time she adjusted the leather straps of her pack to keep them from biting into her shoulders, they must strive to cover as much ground in a day as they could. The problem was that every step brought them closer to rejoining the clan, a reality about which she found herself feeling increasingly ambivalent.

Naya and Aytal ranged further afield, keeping the small caravan in sight but also maintaining contact with the horses. Much to Naya's relief, when they set out from the clearing not long after sun-up, MeHnd and her foal, along with the red filly and gray stallion, had all seemed inclined to follow along. The little band stayed fairly close, travelling a parallel route and easily keeping up, even the newborn, who quickly learned to take advantage of each time his mother paused to graze in order to help himself to a drink. Naya marveled at how quickly he'd mastered the art of managing his long limbs. While there was still no sign of the rest of the herd, which was worrisome, Aytal pointed out that BeHregs, the stallion, was not likely to have abandoned one of his mares and no doubt would show up soon with the others. Each morning they blew the auroch horn before setting out, which reliably brought the red filly and gray stallion trotting over the closest rise from wherever the little band had passed the night. Not long after, the mare would join them, her foal trailing a little way behind. Eventually, Aytal predicted, the morning would come when the rest of the herd appeared as well.

The first portion of the journey thus passed uneventfully. They made good time, arriving at the second large tributary of the *Dān* at the end of the seventh day of travel. Stopping only briefly to replenish their meager supplies with fish from the river's icy waters, they crossed safely the next morning, along with the horses. Another half day brought them back to the main path, now heading slightly north as well as east. Estimating that their shortcut across the steppe had saved them at least three days, Sata tried to calculate when they might expect to reach the clan's winter settlement, located just below where the *Rā* carved a sharp bend to the east around high limestone cliffs before continuing southward toward the great sea. Here, along the river's west bank, stretched a broad alluvial plain, flanked on one side by the river and on the other by high flat-topped bluffs. While the latter afforded shelter from the fierce winds blowing off the open steppe, the waters of the river and the marshy eastern shoreline harbored more abundant resources to feed humans and livestock alike throughout the winter months.

Sitting around their campfire on the evening after they'd rejoined the main route, Sata described the location to Oyuun in detail. "If the weather holds," she told him, "and we don't have trouble crossing any of the other smaller rivers, we should make it before the fullness of the next moon."

She ladled into his outstretched bowl the remaining scraps of the fish stew she'd prepared for their evening meal. The last of the lingering light had begun to drain from the sky and the current moon, no more than a new sliver, would set soon as well. Naya, apparently exhausted from walking all day, had already eaten her share of the fish, then fallen asleep beside her mother. Aytal sat across the fire, intent on re-sharpening the fishing spear they'd used to catch their dinner. They'd been lucky; the fish knew how to hibernate out of sight and were hard to find in the depths of the mostly frozen river.

"The weather should hold for at least a few more days," confirmed Oyuun. Clouds on the western horizon had produced a vivid sunset but posed no immediate threat. "We need to keep pushing while we can, especially now that we're back on the main trail." He glanced down at Naya, wrapped in furs, and back at Sata, concern on his face.

She guessed that he too had noticed that Naya was acting increasingly subdued and seemed more tired than could be accounted for by the journey alone.

"Do you think she's managing with the pace we're setting?" Oyuun asked.

"She'll be alright," Sata replied, wanting to reassure herself as much as him. "Perhaps we can take a break in a day or two and rest a little."

Hopefully that would be enough to revive her daughter's flagging energy. Sata knew Naya was still not as strong as before the accident but didn't want to say anything that would bring up the event itself. Once Naya's life was no longer in imminent danger, they'd mostly succeeded in avoiding the topic of how she'd been injured in the first place. Now, however, they were traveling toward an inevitable day of reckoning. Sata dreaded the confrontation that awaited Oyuun and especially Aytal when they rejoined the clan, knowing the hostility they would face, regardless of what she and Naya might say about all the two strangers had done to care for them over the winter. By harming the clan chief's daughter, Aytal had earned the enmity of the entire clan and punishment would be expected. Even if Potis might have been persuaded to be lenient, he could not risk appearing weak in front of the others. The priests, especially, would insist on an appropriate penalty, claiming it in the name *Dyēus-Ptēr*, who was a vengeful god. And then there were those within the clan who, if they knew of the friendship that had developed between the two young people, would seek all the more determinedly to exact retribution against Aytal, if only out of a malicious desire to cause Naya distress. Sata reminded herself to caution both of them to be on guard once they'd returned. She should warn Oyuun to take care too, she thought, remembering what had passed between them before they'd left the clearing. She'd need to watch herself as well.

"What is it?" Oyuun asked, pulling Sata back to the present. Despite the uncertain light of the fire, as well as her determination to hide her thoughts, she realized he must have seen a shadow cross her features. The man was entirely too perceptive.

"It's nothing," she replied, drawing her robe more securely around her shoulders. "I'm tired too, that's all." She forced a weary smile, meant to discourage further inquiry. Time enough when they got closer to their destination to have such conversations. For now, she wanted to keep things as uncomplicated as possible.

"Aytal?" she queried, changing the subject, "when are you and Naya going to try riding those horses?"

"I'm not sure," the young man responded, laying aside the spear he'd been sharpening. He kept his voice pitched low so as not to risk waking Naya. "The filly is still not fully grown. Naya's often talked of wanting to be sure she is strong enough to carry her." Aytal hesitated a moment, then continued. "Something else seems to be holding her back as well. If I didn't think she'd bite my head off, I'd say she is afraid." Still shy around Sata, he met her eyes across the fire as he spoke, then dropped his gaze. "I've tried bringing it up, but she either ignores me or gets irritated, so lately I've just let her be."

"You are wise to avoid pushing her too hard, any more than she would push the filly," commented Oyuun, also keeping his voice low. "All the same, she may need some encouragement. It's no small thing, the feat she is proposing."

"*Hän, joka ratsastaa hevosilla,*" intoned Aytal solemnly, eyes resting on Naya's sleeping form. He uttered the words in his own tongue with an air of reverence, as though bestowing a title. Sata followed the direction of his gaze, then looked back at him inquiringly before turning to Oyuun for an explanation.

"It means 'She Who Rides Horses,'" he translated. "Among our people, when someone distinguishes themselves in some way, they are given a new name, one that reflects their special gifts. It's often considered a final stage of their initiation, their passage into adulthood and the full possession of their unique power." Oyuun paused, turning his attention to the task of adding fresh kindling to the fire from the stack close at hand. "My son has received his," he added without looking up, "but only conditionally." Sata turned back to Aytal in time to see him shoot his father a look of genuine embarrassment.

"Please Father," he beseeched. "Please don't speak of it."

Noting the young man's evident distress, Sata thought of what Oyuun had told her more than a moon ago, when they'd made their foray together to the river. Normally reticent about himself and his son, on that day, as they'd walked side by side along the path and later as he'd helped her gather roots, he'd disclosed enough to indicate that Aytal's past was troubled. Without going into details, Oyuun told her that his son's talent with the bow had tempted the young man to commit a sacrilegious act which, while gaining him considerable notoriety among his peers, had brought down the condemnation of the community's elders. Unfortunately, Aytal's reaction when confronted with his transgression had not been viewed as sufficiently contrite, further compounding the gravity of the original offense and resulting in the suspension of his newly bestowed honorific title. The young man's steadfast refusal to implicate any of the others who had also been involved, while no doubt enhancing his status among his fellows, only added further to his difficulties with the elders.

When they'd left on their trading expedition, Oyuun confessed to Sata, Aytal had still been in disgrace. The trip was intended in part to give him a fresh start. Without excusing his son's conduct, Oyuun had been at pains to make clear to Sata his belief that Aytal's actions stemmed from an overzealous desire to prove himself to his peers rather than any serious character flaw and that the young man's apparent lack of remorse actually masked a deep sense of shame, while his unwillingness to name the others who were involved reflected a highly developed, if sometimes misplaced, sense of honor.

That said, Oyuun had admitted to Sata, the first stage of the journey with his two sons had been far from pleasant. For the most part sullen and withdrawn, on the occasions when Aytal did have something to say for himself, he'd either been rude towards his father, or else unkind to his stepbrother, who sulked in return. It had not been a happy time. Then had come the terrible accident with Naya. Oyuun had explained to Sata that he'd wanted her to know something of his oldest son's earlier troubles, not to excuse what he had done but to ask once again for her understanding and forgiveness. Aytal had been devastated by the harm he'd caused Naya, Oyuun had assured her that day by the river, and wanted nothing so much as to make amends.

For Sata, Oyuun's revelations about Aytal's past had helped her to comprehend why, on the night of the winter solstice, despite the danger and risk, the young man had voluntarily gone to the other world in search of her daughter's lost spirit. She guessed that something profound must have happened to him on the journey, causing him afterwards to renounce entirely his skill as a bowman. Of this, Oyuun had not spoken to her, either on the occasion of their talk beside the river or in the days that followed, except to say that Aytal alone must discover how to regain his gift – and apparently with it, the power of his true name. Now, observing across the fire the young man's reaction to his father's mention of the matter, Sata wondered at the lapse in Oyuun's usual circumspection, but concluded that, as with their earlier conversation, it was meant to help her to understand his son.

"Naya has not gone through her initiation yet," she said mildly, intending to divert attention from Aytal's obvious discomfort. "Most likely she will begin preparations as soon as we return, in order for her to be ready to undertake the rites just prior to the tribe's annual Gathering."

The Gathering. Sata wished on second thought that she'd found another topic of discussion altogether. As soon as she'd brought it up, she realized she was dreading this year's summer solstice observances, when all the separate clans that made up her husband's tribe came together to celebrate before scattering again to find summer pasture for their herds. Beginning at dawn on the longest day of the year, just as the sun breached the horizon, priests from each of the clans would preside over an impressive ceremony honoring *Dyēus-Ptēr*. The solemn ritual of supplication, sacrifice, and thanksgiving would be followed by a raucous feast. Games, contests, and feats of skill and daring accompanied the celebration, which would last for days. In addition to providing an opportunity to see friends and relatives from other clans and swap stories of the hardships and triumphs of the previous year, the Gathering was a time to trade livestock and other valuable goods, settle disputes and make plans for the coming season. Marriages were often arranged, along with the negotiation of all sorts of other alliances.

This was the aspect that most troubled Sata. She'd hoped that Naya would be able to postpone the necessity of having to take a husband for another year or two at least, but circumstances were not in her favor. In a world where marriage constituted one of the primary means of securing allegiances, the daughter of a clan chief represented a valuable commodity.

"Will she be married this year?" asked Aytal, as though having followed Sata's thoughts. Behind the young man's carefully neutral tone, she detected a note of more-than-casual interest.

"My wish is that she be allowed to wait," Sata replied honestly. "But that may not be possible. We shall see what the situation is when we return. Who knows what has happened while we've been away?"

She thought of Potis's father. Had he survived the winter? What else might have happened while they were gone? Last year during the starving time, between the end of winter and the beginning of spring, the clan had struggled, barely managing to fight off raiders from a tribe from further west who had intended to steal their herds. This year's weather had been so much more severe, putting even greater pressure on resources and increasing the likelihood of such threats. Which meant even more pressure on her husband, Sata thought. Although Potis had resisted arguments in favor of a retaliatory raid, preferring instead to rely on raising their own animals rather than stealing and thereby creating enemies, others in the clan were of a more warlike persuasion. As long as the old clan chief lived and supported his son's judgment, there would be no hostile actions, Sata knew, but once Awos was gone, other clan members would redouble their efforts to assert influence. Even if nothing had happened so far while they'd been away, the Gathering was still bound to be fraught with power struggles, as factions within their own clan sought allies from among those who made up the other clans of the tribe.

Glancing down at Naya, asleep beside her, Sata wondered what impact the horses would have on this dynamic. What would happen when their little caravan showed up with the herd accompanying them? Would Naya be able to persuade her father, and by extension the rest of the clan, of the horses' potential to be tamed, and of the value of taking the trouble? A lot depended on demonstrating that not only could they be bred and raised for meat but that they could be ridden. This was the truly revolutionary aspect of Naya's vision. Once proven possible, the superior ability of a mounted herder to control not only horses, but other livestock as well, would be obvious to everyone. And what of the Gathering itself? Certainly Potis would be guaranteed to improve his standing and influence if his daughter arrived at the ceremonies on horseback. Reaching over, Sata pulled the fur-lined robe more closely around the girl's sleeping form. One way or another, she concluded with a sigh, a lot would be riding on those slim young shoulders once they'd returned.

"Aytal," Sata said, returning to their earlier discussion. "I think it might be important that Naya is able to show the clan right away that the horses can be ridden. Otherwise it will be hard to argue against slaughtering them for food or prevent the priests from wanting to sacrifice them as part of the solstice ritual. Can you encourage her to try, even if she doesn't believe she or the filly is ready?"

"That could be risky," Aytal responded, looking up from stirring the fire's embers with a stick. "If Naya thinks she is being pushed into something she's not ready to do, she'll resist." He met Sata's eyes across the flames.

"You know my daughter well," she acknowledged, returning his gaze, "but time is running out."

"Perhaps we should just explain the urgency to her," put in Oyuun. "Surely she will have considered the implications of what she's doing, luring the herd closer and closer to the clan and its hunters. She must understand the importance of demonstrating the bond she's established with the red filly is more than sentimental. If the gray stallion can also be ridden, it will go a long way toward proving that horses can be useful in ways far beyond what the clan gains from its other animals."

As though having understood at least the last part of what Oyuun had just said and needing to remind everyone of his own indispensability, Amu left his place at Naya's side and tried to climb into Oyuun's lap in order to lick the man's face.

"Present company excepted," Oyuun clarified, laughing as he pushed the dog away. He rubbed him behind the ears instead, eliciting groans of canine pleasure. "What would we do without you?"

"I have something that might help," said Sata, once Amu had resettled himself beside Oyuun. "I've been working on it for a while but I didn't want to show it to Naya until the time seemed right." Reaching behind to rummage in her pack, she pulled out a length of intricately braided rawhide, about twice the length of a man's outstretched arm. The center span was stiff and had been shaped to form a semi-circle, while the two ends were soft and pliable.

"What is it?" asked Aytal, looking on with interest. The rawhide seemed too short to be useful as a means to catch or restrain a horse.

"It's not a rope, if that's what you're wondering," replied Sata. "It's just something to provide some guidance, a way of communicating. It can be made to go around the neck, like this." She demonstrated, tying the two ends of the rawhide together to make a circle, which could easily be slipped on or off over a horse's head. "The stiff part goes at the base of the neck, and you can sit on the horse's back and hold on to the ends where they're joined together. When you pull up, the stiff part will put pressure on the horse's chest. When you move your arm to one side or the other, the horse will feel the soft part against the side of the neck. I thought it might help with stopping and steering. I got the idea from the harnesses we use for the dogs and the goats."

Rising, Aytal took the length of rawhide from Sata's hands and examined it carefully. "That's brilliant," he exclaimed after a moment. "And beautiful as well," he added, admiring the handiwork.

"I made one for you too," Sata said, pleased by the young man's reaction. From her pack she withdrew an identical length of rawhide and handed it to Aytal.

"Excellent," observed Oyuun. "We'll show them to Naya in the morning. Now let's get some sleep. We have another long day ahead of us, and it may be the last of the good weather. We'll need to make an early start."

The next morning they were all up with the sun. Sata could tell Aytal was eager to show-off the new invention, but prudently waited, allowing Sata herself to be the one to introduce Naya to the idea of putting something around the horses' necks.

"It's not a rope," she said quickly, in response to the girl's expression when first shown one of the collars. Naya's ruddy eyebrows had drawn together in a straight, hard line while the corners of her mouth turned down in a disapproving frown.

"What is it then?" she asked suspiciously.

"A way to stop and steer," explained Sata. Demonstrating how the collar worked, she continued, "there will have to be some way to guide the horses, if they're going to be useful."

"And eventually a means of attaching a harness, so they can pull a sled or carry burdens," added Oyuun. Naya shot him a look and he decided he'd be wise to keep quiet and leave Sata to persuade her.

"Naya," Sata said quietly, coming up behind her daughter and laying her hands on her shoulders, "I realize you don't want to rush the filly but think about what's going to happen when we get back to the clan." She felt the girl stiffen.

"I know!" Naya snapped, sounding at once irritated and a little desperate. And then Sata felt her shoulders sag, as all the resistance seemed to drain out of her. "I had a dream last night," she said, turning blue eyes to her mother. Sata realized that what she saw there was not the defiance of a moment before but uncertainty and even fear, just as Aytal had suspected.

"What kind of dream?" she asked.

"A nightmare, like the ones I had after the accident." Naya squeezed her lids shut and turned her head away, as if trying to block out the images. "I've had them almost every night since we left the clearing. They're keeping me from sleeping." Opening her eyes again, she looked once more at her mother. For the first time Sata noticed the dark circles bruising the delicate skin beneath the girl's lashes.

"Why didn't you say something sooner?" Sata reached out, drawing Naya into her arms. "No wonder you're so exhausted."

"Is this why you haven't wanted to try riding the filly since we started the journey?" Aytal's question was gentle, his voice filled with sympathy. Naya, head buried in her mother's shoulder, nodded miserably.

For days she'd been hiding what she'd been going through, alone in the dark as the others slept. In the depths of the night the desperate scenes would unfold, just as they had before, filled with inchoate terror and despair, with no way to stop them. She would wake, shaking, then lie under the cold stars, afraid to fall asleep again. Towards dawn she might slip into a fitful slumber, then awake with the others, feeling groggy, as though she hadn't slept at all. And all the while, she thought about what would happen if she failed, or perhaps worse, if she succeeded.

"We will go no further today," said Oyuun after a moment.

Naya, head still cradled against her mother's shoulder, did not look up. "We've made good time so far," she heard him go on, his tone deliberately practical. "I know I said we needed to keep pushing, but this is a good time to take a break. We'll find a place where we can shelter and give ourselves a few days to rest and try our luck hunting. If we're not successful, we can slaughter one of the goats."

"What about the horses?" Naya heard her mother ask.

"The mare and foal could use the rest as well, plus BeHregs and the remainder of the herd might be more likely to catch-up with us," Oyuun replied. "And it will give Naya a chance to try riding the filly."

Her head came up then, mutinous expression back in place.

"I can't," she declared stubbornly, her cheeks tear stained. "I won't," she corrected. "We're not ready. It's not the right time yet." Remaining within the circle of her mother's embrace, Naya glared at Oyuun over Sata's shoulder. Standing nearby, Aytal watched the exchange in prudent silence.

Unfazed by Naya's outburst, Oyuun fixed her with an impenetrable look. A formidable stillness seemed to emanate from him, frightening Naya a little. Guardedly, she continued to return Oyuun's regard. No one else moved.

"What is your heart's desire?" he asked, voice quiet yet compelling.

"Why do you want to know?" Wary, Naya wondered if he was playing some sort of trick but found herself unable to turn away.

"Because if what you want is to ride the red filly," Oyuun answered, "you must not allow fear of what comes in the dark to stand in your way."

His dark eyes held hers. It took the length of another heartbeat before Naya found the will to look away. Yet in the space of that moment, when the authority of his presence and the strange power of his gaze eclipsed everything else, the words he spoke dispelled the miasma of self-doubt that had descended over Naya in the wake of her nightmares. As though bidden by his admonition, she remembered other words, uttered by the voice in her visions, charging her with a task and urging her to be brave. Pulling herself out of her mother's arms, she looked once more at this man she still did not entirely trust. How had he known just what to say to restore her courage? Oyuun merely lifted one brow, as if daring Naya to argue with him. Too mystified to challenge him further, she instead took a deep breath and squaring her shoulders, stepped back and reached for one of the collars that Sata held.

"Will you help me?" she asked, turning to Aytal. She still felt weary, but considerably more determined.

"Of course," he responded, giving her an encouraging smile. Shyly, Naya smiled back.

"First you both need to help erect the shelter," Oyuun interjected, sounding once more like his ordinary self. "Then you can go be with the horses. Let's see if we can find a place out of the wind, maybe in the lee of one of the hills."

By mid-morning, they'd establish a temporary camp a short distance from the trail, tucked against the eastern-facing slope of a small rise. The location gave some protection from the prevailing wind that blew more or less constantly across the open steppe. The wind's direction was beginning to shift to the southwest as the air warmed, a sign of the changing season. As long as this milder weather held, Oyuun assured himself, they'd be comfortable enough, and if it did snow, they would just have to hope that the storm would not be as severe as those they'd already endured. The ensuing mud would surely further delay travel, but it couldn't be helped. They'd be exposed no matter where they were along their route. And Naya needed to rest, that was clear.

The goats had been picketed in a patch of tough, fibrous grass that looked completely dead after the ravages of winter but they seemed happy enough, especially the she-goat who appreciated the break from her sled-pulling duties. Amu was not quite so lucky. Before being allowed out of his harness, he had to submit to helping Oyuun and Aytal to haul wood from the thickets lining the banks of a smaller tributary running parallel and just to the north of their route. Sata and Naya meanwhile cleared a patch of bare earth in front of the make-shift shelter to serve as a fire pit and unpacked their personal bundles which held all they might need for the next few days, leaving the bulk of their belongings strapped to the sleds.

These tasks completed, Sata proposed returning to the larger tributary they'd crossed earlier to search along the shoreline for edible roots. Oyuun, equipped with both the hunting and fishing spears, offered to join her.

"Go check on the horses," Sata said to Naya, giving the girl permission to set off in search of the herd. Oyuun nodded at Aytal, releasing him to accompany her.

"Take your weapons," he instructed them. Although Naya usually insisted on going unarmed to meet the horses, in order not to frighten them, the circumstances now were different. If she and Aytal should happen to come upon a deer or even a hare, the opportunity could not be wasted, but danger lurked as well. Oyuun didn't need to remind his son of the lion tracks they'd spotted while gathering firewood, imprinted in the dried mud at the stream's edge. The marks weren't fresh, otherwise they might have thought twice about setting up camp, but still they'd need to be cautious. "Leave Amu here to guard the goats," he added.

Oyuun watched as Naya, fatigue apparently lessened somewhat by the prospect of being with the horses, readily gathered up her bow and arrows, while Aytal more absently took up one of the other hunting spears. Seeing his son's choice of weapons, Oyuun sighed but otherwise held his tongue. Amu, waiting for permission to accompany the young people, looked up at him inquiringly. "No," he said to the dog, perhaps more impatiently than was warranted. "You stay."

"Sorry, Amu," Naya called back over her shoulder as she and Aytal set off to climb the rise behind the tent. "We'll tell you all about it when we get back." Moments later, the pair disappeared over the hilltop.

Chapter Fifteen

Pausing to catch her breath and feel the breeze against her cheeks, Naya took in the vastness of the land stretching away in front of her. Low, rolling hills, covered in yellowed grasses, reached to the south and east as far as she could see. To the north and west, the view was bisected by stands of trees marking the nearby water courses. Beyond stretched more open grasslands, bounded at the distant horizon by a darker line of densely forested hills. Ominous clouds were massing in that direction. Depending on how strongly the wind blew, the storm might get to them as early as tonight. It was probably a good idea they'd interrupted their journey. Naya knew Oyuun had proposed the idea mainly out of concern for her, even if she couldn't quite bring herself to thank him for it. But the storm was not upon them yet. The breeze, though chilly, still felt relatively benign, while the sky above remained mostly blue, dotted here and there with puffy white clouds that only occasionally obscured the sun.

Indeed, with each day of travel, the sun had climbed ever higher in the sky, where its rays promising to reawaken the frozen ground. Today for the first time Naya could detect a welcome freshness in the air, and with it, carried on the breeze, a smell that predicted the emergence of green and growing things. Before long, her senses told her, spring would return in earnest to the steppe. She inhaled as deeply as she could, despite the twinge at the back of her ribs.

"Let's call the horses," she said, lifting the auroch horn to her lips and filling her lungs again before sounding the two notes. Although still not as powerful as when Aytal blew the horn, her call nevertheless carried easily to where the little band waited, grazing just on the other side of another nearby rise. Within moments, they appeared, led by the red filly, who neighed a greeting as soon as she caught sight of the girl. There was still no sign of BeHregs and the other mares. Naya sighed in disappointment.

Aytal stood next to her, gaze turned, like hers, in the direction of the approaching horses. "Will you try today?" he asked.

"Yes," was all she answered, not looking away from horses who were now almost upon them. Setting down her bow and quiver on the ground, Naya reached into the pouch slung over her shoulder, drawing out the length of rawhide her mother had given her. *It's not a rope,* she reminded herself, remembering another day that felt like long ago, when she had set out to capture the young horse who now came so willingly to her side. The filly had taught her much since that first encounter. She possessed a wholly different level of awareness, both of herself and of this creature whose eyes held an intelligence every bit as alive as her own. Grasping the collar loosely by the two ends, Naya offered it to Réhda, stopped within arm's distance, to explore.

"Today," she said, speaking matter-of-factly while allowing the filly to thoroughly investigate the unfamiliar object, "today, we are going to try something new." The gray stallion and the mare, along with the foal, gathered around, curious as well. The horses first sniffed along the entire length of the rawhide, then began to sample delicately with lips and teeth. Before Naya knew it, the filly and the stallion were engaged in a playful tug of war.

"Hey, hey," she laughed, pulling the collar out of their grasp. "Don't chew on it." Moving a little away, Naya beckoned to Réhda, who stepped trustingly in her direction. "It's for you," she said, passing the collar underneath the filly's neck before reaching over her withers to grab the free end. For a moment, horse and human stood motionless, the length of rawhide and the girl's two arms encircling the filly.

"I'm going to tie the ends, okay?" Naya said, once she was sure Réhda showed no sign of objection to the unfamiliar feel of the collar. The filly continued to stand still while Naya knotted the rawhide. "What do you think?" she asked, stepping back.

In answer, the filly arched her neck and pulled her muzzle in toward her chest to try once again to sniff the strange object the girl had placed around her, then looked back at her expectantly, as if to say *alright, what next?*

Aytal, with the mare and the gray stallion on either side, watched the whole procedure with interest, while the foal took advantage of his mother's preoccupation to help himself to a drink. Naya, her first objective accomplished, let out a breath she hadn't been conscious she was holding.

"Okay," she said, turning to Aytal, "help me up."

They'd talked often about this moment, debating about how best to manage the feat of getting astride the filly when the time finally came to ride. Rejecting the idea of simply grasping Réhda's thick mane and scrambling aboard as likely to frighten the young horse, they'd come up with various ways for Aytal to boost Naya into position to ease herself onto the filly's back – lifting her by the waist or getting down on his hands and knees to provide a platform. Finally they'd decided the best method would be for him to stoop beside the filly with fingers laced to form a makeshift step, so that Naya could place one foot in his cupped hands, raise herself up, and from there, lean her body across Réhda's back until the filly grew accustomed to the feel of her weight, before eventually swinging a leg over.

Accordingly, Aytal left his vantage point next to the other horses and joined Naya at Réhda's side, giving the filly a reassuring rub on the shoulder as he came up next to her. His hand came away covered in fine, clinging hair.

"She's shedding!" he exclaimed, trying to wipe the hair away on his own clothing. "You're going to be covered – everywhere – if you sit on Réhda without something between you and her," he observed to Naya.

This was a complication they hadn't considered. Naya's leggings extended well up past her knees, providing not only warmth but protection for most activities, and normally she would not have worn anything else under her tunic, leaving the more delicate parts of her backside unprotected. As it happened, however, Naya was in the midst of her moon flow and wore a cloth lined with cattail fibers wrapped snuggly around her waist and loins. The cattail fluff was soft and absorbent and could be replaced as needed. The undergarment would serve well not only to cushion her seat on the back of the young horse but also to protect her bare skin.

Turning to Réhda and positioning herself by the filly's left side, Naya looked at Aytal over her shoulder, lips quirked as if in possession of a secret. "I'll be fine," was all she said. "Help me up."

Despite Naya's best intentions to stay calm, she felt a buzz of nervous excitement, mixed with the fears and doubts that still lingered. *This is it*, she thought to herself. Acutely conscious of the effect her movements might have on the young horse, she tried to ignore the jitters, reminding herself to breathe. Left foot supported in Aytal's cupped hands and her two arms braced along Réhda's spine, she pushed herself up, leaning her body against the filly's. Bending at the waist, she slowly draped herself over the horse's narrow back, head turned to the side so that she could watch for a reaction. Réhda looked around at her, seeming more curious than afraid, as if to ask *what new game are we playing?* but otherwise held still. Aytal, too, remained immobile, uncomplaining despite his awkward posture, continuing to support Naya's left foot and a good portion of her weight.

After a moment, Naya stepped back to the ground and Aytal straightened. They looked at one another but neither spoke. Aytal raised one dark eyebrow. *Want to try again?* he inquired silently. When she nodded, he stooped once more and laced his fingers together. Again, Naya boosted herself up, laying her torso over the young horse's back. This time, she let the filly take more of her weight. As before, Réhda stood without moving, not even turning her head to look, which Naya took as a sign of the young horse's confidence. Her own anticipation mounting, she failed to notice that the outer rim of the filly's eye had begun to show just a touch of white. Twice more they repeated the maneuver until Naya, inattentive to the increasingly anxious expression in Réhda's eye, assumed the filly's willingness to remain standing still must mean she was not worried. Aytal, his concentration focused entirely on Naya, also missed the signs of the young horse's growing concern.

On the next try, Naya boosted herself high enough that she could manage to swing her right leg over Réhda's haunches. Simultaneously she lifted and rotated her upper body until she sat upright. She was astride! Aytal released his hold on her foot, straightened and took a step back, leaving her legs to dangle on either side of the filly's ribcage. He and Naya looked at one another, still not uttering a sound, matching grins spreading across both their faces.

The filly, now wide-eyed, remained frozen in place.

At last, Aytal broke the silence. "Now what?"

In that instant, as though released from a spell, Réhda came to life. Spinning in a half-circle, she gave a tremendous buck. Unseated, Naya felt herself launched into the air. She landed flat on her back with a thud. Réhda bolted as if shot from a bow, taking off at a dead run. The other horses, startled by the filly's sudden explosion, joined her, the foal running at his mother's side. All four raced to the top of the small rise a short distance away. There they stopped, turned and looked back at the two humans. Aytal, dumbfounded, gazed after them. Naya remained where she had landed, outstretched in the dry grass near his feet.

When she came to moments later, Aytal was leaning over her, looking panicked.

"Are you alright?" she heard him ask anxiously. Confused about what had happened, Naya could tell that he feared she'd been seriously hurt. She tried to answer that she was fine but realized she couldn't draw breath. Gasping, she in turn started to panic. Only after Aytal had helped her to sit up was she able to take several shallow gulps of air.

"Do you feel like anything's broken?" asked Aytal, obviously still concerned. As yet too breathless to speak, Naya shook her head. She just needed a chance to gather her wits.

"You must have gotten the wind knocked out of you," Aytal observed, squatting beside her. Still unable to speak, Naya nodded. After a moment, feeling calmer, she reached out two hands for Aytal to help her to stand. Scrambling to his feet, he grasped her by her outstretched forearms, steadying her as she rose. Once upright, Naya continued to lean on him for support. Her whole body reverberated from the shock of hitting the ground. Head bowed, she took several slow, careful breaths, inhaling and exhaling to test the functioning of her lungs. At last, lifting her eyes to Aytal's, she found her voice.

"Well," she said, letting go of his arms and taking a step back, "that didn't go quite as planned." She gave him a rueful smile.

Aytal smiled back, relieved. "Now what?" he asked.

Rather than answer right away, Naya bent over to dust herself off, giving herself time to think. Straightening, she caught Aytal looking as though he wanted to reach forward to pull some of the bits of dried grass out of her hair.

"It was my fault," she answered, turning slightly away. She ran her fingers impatiently through her tangled mane in an effort to dislodge the grass stems herself. "I was in too much of a hurry," she admitted, angry with herself. "I sat on her too soon. I should have lain over her back a few more times and let her carry me so that I could have slid off if she panicked. I wasn't paying enough attention to her reactions." She turned back to face Aytal.

"Do you want to quit?" he asked, tone neutral. She couldn't tell if he thought she should give up or questioned if she had the courage to try again. Perhaps he simply wanted to know how she felt.

"No," she responded, adamant. "I want to tell her I'm sorry, and then I want to start over. I just hope she'll forgive me."

"Look," said Aytal, gesturing over Naya's shoulder toward the small rise. The horses, with the red filly in the lead, were making their way back down the hillside and across a stretch of open turf toward them. "Maybe Réhda wants to apologize as well."

Indeed, the filly's gaze was fixed on Naya as she picked her way purposefully down the slope in her direction, the other horses trailing in her wake. Naya waited, uncertain. The rawhide collar still hung around Réhda's neck but didn't seem to be bothering her. Slowing her pace as she approached closer, the filly stopped just beyond arm's reach. From this distance she stood, head lifted, regarding Naya with anxious eyes. Realizing from the slight heaving of the horse's chestnut flanks that she was still breathing hard from her wild gallop, Naya could sense the rapid beat of the filly's heart. Wanting to reassure her, she took a deep, somewhat ragged breath herself, letting it out gradually while willing her body to relax, despite still feeling shaken from her fall. As she did, the filly extended her muzzle hesitantly towards her, offering to make amends.

"I'm sorry," Naya said, reaching out with the back of her hand. Delicately, Réhda touched her whiskers to Naya's bare skin and inhaled. The exhale that followed was both a sigh and a release. With the outrush of air, tension drained from the young horse's body. Her head lowered and her eye softened. For a long moment, horse and girl stood without moving, Réhda's breath lightly caressing Naya's still-outstretched hand. At last, Naya took a step closer to Réhda's side. The filly turned her head in the girl's direction, continuing to regard her gravely but now without fear. Slowly, watching carefully for any sign of anxiety or alarm, Naya moved to enfold Réhda in a gentle embrace, the crook of her elbow cradling the filly's soft muzzle, open palm resting lightly against the curve of her jaw. Thus entwined, Naya let out a deep sigh of her own. Together, the two stood motionless, breathing quietly together. After a moment, Naya rested her forehead against the wide spot between the Réhda's two dark eyes and closed her own. "I'm sorry," she whispered again, and knew the red filly was sorry too.

Aytal, standing a short distance away, watched the exchange. The other two horses, behaving as though nothing untoward had happened, took turns dropping their heads to crop the course, winter-ravaged grass, while the foal, worn out by the sprint up the hill, folded his long legs awkwardly beneath himself and lowered his body to the ground. Soon he was stretched out flat on his side, napping in the mild sunshine.

After a moment, Naya stepped back but her eyes remained focused on the filly. "Let's try again," she said to Aytal.

"Are you sure?" he asked.

"Yes." She turned to him and gave him a brave smile. "I'm okay and Réhda's okay. We just need to take it even more slowly and I need to pay better attention to what she's telling me. She has to want this as much as I do. I won't try to sit astride right away. Let's see what she does if you lead her a few steps by the collar while I'm laying over her back."

And so they tried again. And again. And again. Now that she was better attuned, each time Naya started to stretch herself over Réhda's back she could sense the filly beginning to tremble, and so she slid back to the ground and waited for as long as it took until she settled. Only after multiple attempts was the young horse at last able support the girl's full weight without concern. Naya looked back over her shoulder at Aytal and grinned.

"Should I try leading her?" Aytal asked.

"Not yet," Naya replied, slipping off Réhda's back and motioning Aytal to help her up once more. "I want to be sure she's genuinely comfortable." Finally, having repeated the sequence twice more, with long pauses in between and no adverse reaction from the filly, Naya was satisfied.

"Ok," she said, "that's enough for now."

"You're not going to try to sit on her again, or at least have me lead her with you laying over her back?" asked Aytal, surprised.

"No," she replied, "We've accomplished enough for now. I'm tired and Réhda's tired. Let's go back."

Naya untied the collar from around the filly's neck and gave her a friendly scratch along her crest before releasing her to rejoin the other horses. Retrieving her bow and arrows from where she'd left them, she and Aytal turned back in the direction of their camp.

Sata and Oyuun appeared not long after they returned, downcast and empty-handed except for the spears. Their foray had not been successful. Even Sata's gathering sack, slung over her shoulder, hung empty.

"We did see more lion tracks," Oyuun remarked. "Fresh ones, further upstream. They're hungry too. We'd better bring the goats into the tent with us tonight."

He didn't mention what they all knew to be inevitable. With no game anywhere to be found and fish difficult to locate in the depths of the still half-frozen river, one of the young goats would have to be sacrificed. It would be the male, who was probably destined to be slaughtered at some point in any case. The two females, mother and daughter, were more valuable because they could be bred to one of the clan's rams upon their return but they too might have to give their lives if the hunting did not improve. Later in the day, out of sight of the others, Oyuun would speak words of gratitude to the young goat's spirit and do what had to be done.

"How did it go with the horses?" asked Sata, putting down her empty sack and drawing Naya into her arms for a quick hug.

"We made a good start," said Naya innocently, trying not to wince as she returned her mother's embrace. Over her shoulder, she gave Aytal a quelling look. She'd made him promise not to tell about getting bucked off. "It might take longer than I thought, though," she continued, stepping out of her mother's arms. "The main thing I learned was to go *really* slowly and be sure to notice if Réhda seems in the least bit nervous."

"Did you try getting on the stallion?" Oyuun asked Aytal.

"Not yet," he responded. "Naya and the filly are showing us what to do." He winked at Naya. "One or two more days should be all it takes."

"Luckily, that won't be a problem," returned Oyuun. Indeed, the signs that a storm was headed their way were increasingly evident, as marked by a steadily rising wind throughout the morning, accompanied by a thickening in the cloud cover. The decision to interrupt their journey seemed prudent indeed. "We'd be wise not to plan to travel again until the weather improves," he concluded.

"Should we try to bring the herd closer, where we can keep an eye on them?" asked Sata.

"What about the lions?" added Naya. "Will the horses be safe?"

"Safer than we are," replied Oyuun. "As long as they're in the open and can escape if they need to. But I doubt they'll stray too far in any case."

Following his gaze, the others looked up toward the top of the hill beyond the shelter. A chestnut head had appeared, joined moments later by a dun and a gray. The foal could just be seen, nudging his way between his mother and big sister. Even though the sun still shone overhead, the sky behind them had taken on the same dark shade as the stallion's coat.

Myräkkä. Aytal mouthed the word silently. *Storm.* He'd been waiting for the stallion's name to come to him.

The horses stood for a moment, returning the humans' regard, then began heading down the slope.

The storm arrived during the night – not as fierce as the blizzards they'd endured over the winter, with neither the howling gales nor the bone-penetrating cold, but leaving behind a thick blanket of wet snow too deep to walk through without a struggle, let alone pull a sled. Given their burdens, snowshoes would be of no use. They would have to wait for dry ground before continuing their journey. For the next several days, they would have to remain close to camp except for trips to the nearby stream to replenish their fuel, fill their water skins and, with luck, catch a few fish.

As Oyuun had predicted, the horses stuck close as well, clearing a broad swath encircling the camp as they pawed through the heavy snow to find what was left of last season's grass. Clearly the little band had come to feel more secure in the vicinity of the friendly humans and their dog, seeming to know that predators would be less likely to stalk them.

While all waited for conditions to improve, Naya and Aytal spent time each morning with the herd, accustoming all three adults to the practice of being guided from the ground by one of the rawhide collars around their necks, as well as the sensation of weight resting across their backs. The foal, who had never experienced a snowfall, nor the slick mud that followed, gamboled about, taking frequent tumbles as he learned to manage his long legs in the slippery footing. Whenever he became bored with his own explorations, he would come in search of the other horses, curious about what they were doing and showing no shyness about butting in. Naya and Aytal laughed at the little colt's intrusions but his mother and sister were not always so tolerant. They did not hesitate to give the youngster a lesson in manners if he grew too rude. Myräkkä, still somewhat unsure of his status, stayed out of the disciplinary fray.

Sata took advantage of the delay by introducing MeHnd to the concept of being milked. While under normal circumstances, the idea might not have occurred to her – after all, the clan did not rely on their livestock for dairy production, with the exception of some of the goats – their situation at the moment was dire. If she could convince the mare to share some of the rich, nutritious fluid she produced for her foal, the humans' need for sustenance might be somewhat eased. On the first morning following the storm, just after the youngster had finished a meal and with Naya standing by the mare's head to soothe her, Sata crouched by the horse's side and pulled gently but firmly at her teats, directing the resulting stream into a wooden bowl gripped between her knees. At first MeHnd expressed some concern at the unfamiliar handling, shifting away and attempting to kick out, but Sata stayed with her, singing softly under her breath the tune her own mother had taught her long ago to help calm the family's milking goats. Within a day or two, the mare had accepted the procedure and began to look forward to this new bond shared with the kind and reassuring woman who had saved both her life and her foal.

At first, the raw mare's milk upset everyone's stomachs – not surprising since usually only children could drink unprocessed cow or goat's milk – but they were hungry enough to try anyway. Familiar with various fermentation methods, Sata quickly discovered that by funneling whatever she was able to collect into a skin sack and shaking it periodically over the course of a day, the beverage became much more palatable. Aytal declared he actually preferred the fermented mare's milk, which was less fatty than the reindeer milk he'd grown up on. However, everyone doubted it would produce very good cheese. More experimentation would be required.

"Even so," Naya pronounced on the fifth evening following the storm as they sat around the hearth in the shelter, appreciatively sipping the latest batch of mare's milk, "this is better than anything we have to drink at home."

"True," Sata agreed. "But you know that's not enough. To truly convince everyone to go to the bother of taming horses, you still have to prove they can be ridden."

Naya wanted to be irritated with her mother for pressuring her, but she also recognized that, with the ground nearly dry, their journey must be resumed as soon as possible. If she was going to make another attempt to ride before they got underway again, now was the time.

"I know we can't put it off any longer," she said, lifting her eyes to meet her mother's. "I want to ride the filly," she went on, hearing the ambivalence in her own voice. "I just want to be sure we're really ready. I want to be sure Réhda wants this as much as I do."

Naya was aware that her reluctance required more explanation, but she didn't fully understand it herself. She should have been impatient to try again to get on the filly's back. After her exchange with Oyuun, the nightmares had stopped, so that wasn't it, not exactly. Nor was it the physical fear of falling off that held her back, so much as the sense of standing at the edge of a precipice and needing to gather courage before stepping off the edge. Ever since her first encounter with the young horse, and even more so since the accident that nearly cost her life, the vision of riding the red filly had sustained her. It was what had brought her back from the other world and given her a reason to regain her strength.

But the moment had come, and she hesitated. She'd been bucked off the first time she tried. What would happen if she tried again and utterly failed? If the filly absolutely refused to allow herself to be ridden? Could she bear the disappointment? And what would her failure mean for Réhda and the others? Habituated to humans, they would be easy prey. Just as her mother pointed out, she had to demonstrate that horses could become as tame as their other livestock and, if they could be ridden, vastly more useful. Even more troubling, what if she succeeded? Her nightmares may have ceased for the moment to disturb her sleep, but what if they portended a terrifying future, brought about because she managed to do what no one before her had dreamed of doing? Would she forever bear responsibility for the consequences? Naya dropped her mother's gaze, instead seeking out Aytal where he sat on the opposite side of the fire, looking to him for reassurance.

Sata watched as the young man returned her daughter's regard, his expression full of encouragement, and, to a mother's eye, something more. She wondered if either one was aware of what so obviously had taken root between them. She glanced over at Oyuun. *Had he noticed?* As usual, she could read little of his thoughts.

When Naya spoke once more, her voice was resolute.

"And we are ready," she declared, picking up the discussion where she'd left off. "If we could just wait another half a day before starting out?" She directed the request to Oyuun as well as her mother. "That should be long enough. We're much better prepared now than we were the other day before the storm. This time, nothing will go wrong."

"Oh?" asked Sata, her maternal instincts alerted. "Did something go wrong the other day that you haven't told us about?"

"Not really," replied Naya hastily. Sata saw her glance again at Aytal, who had adopted an expression of feigned innocence. "It's just that…"

Before Sata could pursue the subject, Oyuun interjected. "The mud has almost fully dried up," he observed. "Even if we wait until mid-day to start, we should still be able to travel a good distance before nightfall without difficulty."

"There will be time for me to ride?" Naya looked first to her mother, then to Oyuun for confirmation.

Sata, still suspicious, merely lifted an eyebrow, leaving Oyuun to answer.

"Yes," he concurred, "before we leave, you can ride."

Chapter Sixteen

The next morning dawned fresh and clear. No clouds obscured the brilliance of the day. From the hilltop above the camp where Naya, Aytal and Amu stood, the sky's dome curved toward the horizon, endless cerulean blue arching over an equally boundless expanse of rolling grasslands just beginning to show the first delicate green of spring. Thanks to all the moisture from the recent storm, combined with the warming rays of the sun, the steppe had at last begun to burst into new life.

Naya breathed in the soft air, noting the smell of damp, fertile soil. Unlike before, today she felt sure of herself, and sure of the filly. Yesterday's bout of self-doubt had given way to a calm and certain confidence. Perhaps it was simply that she'd slept well, untroubled by dreams, awakening feeling refreshed, strong, powerful. Spreading her arms wide, as if to embrace the world, she spun in a circle for the sheer pleasure of being alive on a spring day. Aytal smiled at her delight.

Below them, the little band of horses lifted their heads, startled by the girl's gyrations. Curious, rather than go back to grazing, they began to move up the hillside toward the humans. The girl's exuberance must have been infectious, for the filly broke into a canter as she climbed, coming to a stop a short distance from where Naya and Aytal waited. Tossing her head, the young horse pawed the earth, releasing more of the pungent scent of rich, dark soil. Naya laughed but Amu barked disapprovingly.

"It's okay, silly," Naya reassured the dog. "Réhda's just feeling good too."

"Ready to try again, sweet girl?" she asked. The filly tossed her head once more, as if nodding in the affirmative, then lunged playfully at the dog, who leapt out of the young horse's way, looking offended. Amused by the filly's antics, Naya drew the rawhide collar from the pouch at her waist. "Hold still now," she said, laying a quieting hand on the horse's shoulder.

Over the last several days, while they waited for the snow to melt and the mud to dry, she'd used a brush made from a bundle of split willow twigs to curry all the loose hair and dirt from the filly's coat, burnishing it afterwards with a soft leather cloth until it glowed now like copper beneath her hand. Deftly, Naya tied the collar around the young horse's neck, then stepped back. Réhda stood without moving, as she'd learned to do. Nodding to Aytal, Naya waited while he got into position and then, with his assistance, laid her weight across the young horse's back.

The filly stood quietly, unconcerned. She knew now what to expect, how it felt to have the girl draped over her back. She'd discovered that, even while supporting all of her weight, she could still move her feet and that there was no reason to panic. She understood better what was required of her. Above all, she liked the feeling of pleasure she sensed from the girl.

Naya slid down. Aytal, who remained crouched next to Réhda, looked up at her and once more smiled his encouragement. Afterwards, when Naya tried to relive what happened next, the last thing she could recall noticing was that the blue of his eyes matched the sky overhead. After that, time ceased and she became lost in the flow of the moment. She couldn't remember stepping up again or swinging her leg over the filly's back but somehow, with Aytal's help, she was astride. For a moment she and the red filly remained as they were, horse and human, gazing together across the wide expanse of the grasslands. Then, as if of one mind, they began to move.

At first, the steps were tentative. Naya, feeling the filly's body shift beneath her seat, thought she might slide off, but soon realized that with each push of Réhda's hind legs, she was lifted back into a secure position. The filly, in turn, was unsure about the pressure against her ribs but soon understood that sometimes the girl squeezed, just a little, in order to stay upright. Step by step, they began to learn how to move together, responding to changes in each other's position. Naya discovered that if she tried to balance by bracing against the thrust generated each time Réhda pushed off the ground, the filly would hesitate or stop moving altogether. Instead, she had to loosen her thighs, relax rather than resist, and absorb the energy of the horse's momentum into her own body, allowing her hips to follow the rhythm of the filly's walk. When she succeeded in not tensing up, Réhda could more easily carry her. With each step they gained confidence in one another, moving in synchrony. The more Naya trusted in herself and the filly, surrendering to the sensation of being carried, the more willing Réhda seemed to go forward under her weight.

To Naya, the feeling was magical. Gradually, as she discovered how to follow Réhda's motion and grew more secure in her balance, she began to try influencing her steps. Taking hold of the rawhide collar, she directed the filly first to the right, then to the left. Réhda answered as Naya had taught her from the ground, turning away from the gentle pressure against either side of her neck. A slight backward tug, accompanied by an audible exhale, signaled a halt. Pressure from Naya's calves along Réhda's ribcage, associated with the clucking sound she had earlier taught her meant 'go forward,' became the cue to move off. Eventually, no more than a thought would be required for Naya to communicate her wishes to the filly and for the filly to understand and respond.

As Aytal, Amu and the other horses watched, the two walked circles around them, stopping, turning, weaving in and out among them. At first, MeHnd and Myräkkä seemed concerned about this new development, unsure of what to make of a human in the position of a predator on the filly's back, but they quickly took their cue from Réhda, who now seemed entirely at ease. Indeed, the young horse appeared increasingly pleased with herself, arching her neck and lifting each foreleg high at the knee.

Naya laughed, a joyous sound that made Aytal's heart swell. She and the red filly were a magnificent pair, the slim figure astride the young horse, matching chestnut heads held proudly. For a moment he almost couldn't breathe, so awed was he by the sight of the two, surrounded by an aura of sunlight reflecting off the highlights in the filly's fiery coat and the girl's red-gold hair. '*Hän, joka ratsastaa hevosilla,*' he whispered reverently to himself. *She Who Rides Horses.*

"Come on," cried Naya, interrupting the moment, "try getting on Myräkkä!"

Roused by her enthusiasm, Aytal reached for the second collar which hung crossways around his shoulders. Pulling it over his head, he moved in the direction of the gray stallion, who had wandered a short distance away to graze. The horse's head came up at the young man's approach but otherwise he stood quietly for the now-familiar rawhide collar to be tied around his neck. He then responded obediently when Aytal asked him to come alongside a convenient tussock. Although naturally less secure than Réhda, Myräkkä was nonetheless game to follow her example and remained next to the makeshift step as Aytal climbed atop the raised mound of earth, from where he could ease himself into a sitting position astride the stallion's narrow back.

Like the filly when Naya had first mounted, the stallion stood for moment as though frozen in place. For a heart-stopping instant, Aytal braced himself for a similarly explosive reaction. Indeed, Myräkkä's initial instinct was identical to Réhda's. He wanted desperately to rid himself of the frightening sensation caused by the human sitting astride his back. Yet he restrained himself. Although filled with nervous tension, he trusted Aytal enough to override his fear and instead of bucking, he continued to stand stock still. Aytal, once he realized with relief that the stallion was most likely not going to toss him to the ground, became conscious of an equally desperate desire not to embarrass himself by falling off. Fighting back his trepidation, he reminded himself of how he had trained himself to shoot. *Quiet the mind. Let go of expectation. Stay with what happens in the moment. Breathe.* As Aytal's intent shifted, Myräkkä's energy changed subtly as well. Both let out a long, careful exhale. Cautiously, together, they began to move. At Aytal's gentle prompting, the stallion took a few steps forward, stopped, then stepped forward once more, this time more boldly.

And so, just as moments earlier Naya and Réhda had set out on a journey of mutual discovery, Aytal and Myräkkä began to explore a new sort of partnership. The horses suppressed the urge to unload their riders, adjusting instead to the novel sensation of moving while carrying weight. The riders' task became learning how to integrate into their own bodies the powerful motion of their mounts. Uncertainty came first, followed by increasing confidence. Little by little, between the young man and the stallion as between the girl and the filly, a shared language began to develop. Delicately, respectfully, each pair probed one another's thoughts, questioning, answering, asking and responding, continuously seeking to move together in harmony.

On that first day, they did little more than walk, stop and steer. Still, Naya couldn't resist the urge to ride the horses back to camp.

"I want to show my mother," she told Aytal. "And I want your father to see."

Aytal looked back toward the rather steep slope they would have to navigate in order to return to their campsite and seemed about to object when he pointed instead.

"We won't have too far to go," he said, relieved. "Here they come."

In the distance, Sata and Oyuun had appeared over the edge of the rise and were headed toward them.

"Come on," said Naya, grinning triumphantly at Aytal, "let's go meet them." The riders turned their mounts to face the approaching figures, and with Amu trotting ahead, started walking in their direction. The mare and the foal ambled behind. When they got as close as Naya thought the horses would be comfortable, she asked Réhda to halt, slid from the filly's back to the ground and pulled the collar over her head. Following Naya's example, Aytal dismounted and turned the gray stallion loose. Free of the unaccustomed sensation of being ridden, the two horses shook themselves vigorously from head to tail. Apparently not satisfied, they both got down and rolled, first to one side, then the other. Rising, they shook once more, then wandered away to join the mare, who had moved a little way off to graze, all of them acting as though nothing momentous had just happened.

"Did you see?" Naya asked excitedly as her mother closed the distance between them. In answer, Sata stopped and smiling, opened her arms wide. Naya threw herself into her embrace with enthusiasm, then pulled away, unable to contain herself. "It was amazing!" she stammered, lacking sufficient words to describe what had happened. "We did it!"

"You did it!" Sata echoed, laughing.

Naya allowed herself to be encircled once more in her mother's arms. This time, she stayed long enough to savor the feeling of Sata's shared pride in what she'd accomplished. Her mother had believed in her, and Naya had not let her down.

Pulling away for a second time, Naya turned to Oyuun. He stood with an arm around Aytal's shoulders, as though having just congratulated him. Aytal wore an expression of sheepish pleasure. Returning Naya's gaze, Oyuun gave her a nod.

"You did well," was all he said, but then he winked, letting Naya know that he, too, was proud of her. She grinned back.

In the days that followed, as the little band of horses and humans continued their journey east, Naya and Aytal found time along the way to practice their new accomplishments. They did not ride every day, and they never rode for very long, wanting neither to over-burden the horses, who were unused to carrying loads, nor sour them on the experience. Nonetheless, as humans and horses alike became accustomed to riding and being ridden, their skills progressed and their trust in one another grew.

Once Naya and Aytal both felt they had mastered their balance at the walk, they ventured a slow jog, each grabbing hold of their horses' manes in order to steady themselves. Although challenging for both, Naya proved more adept than Aytal at managing the faster gait because she didn't try as hard to fight the force of her horse's movement. Soon, her body learned how to absorb Réhda's regular two-beat rhythm and the trot felt less jarring. Aytal, in contrast, tried initially to grip and brace against Myräkkä's motion and ended up shutting down the stallion entirely, to the point where he refused to move forward at all, much to Aytal's chagrin. Only when he returned once again to the lessons of the bow – relaxation, awareness, surrender of the need to control – was he able to find the poise necessary to sit the gray horse's movement.

Thus they journeyed on, following the well-worn path that would eventually lead them to the great river. Spring greeted them as they travelled further east, everywhere evident in the greening vegetation. Wildflowers began to appear, dotting the steppe with splashes of brilliant red, orange, yellow and purple. Birdsong filled the air in the mornings and small animals, especially rabbits, which had long been hidden in underground burrows, reappeared in profusion, seeming to proliferate overnight. No longer did the travelers worry about finding enough food before rejoining the clan. As they made their way ever closer to their destination, they even began occasionally to encounter large herds of antelope and bison, calves running at their mothers' sides. There was no sign of other horses, however, not even BeHregs and the rest of his mares, which worried Naya, who still held out hope that the band might catch up to them. At least Réhda, Myräkkä and MeHnd, along with her colt, could increasingly be counted on to stay close at hand, even when not being ridden, milked or otherwise handled. During the day, they remained in sight, meandering along a track slightly south of the main path, while at night, their dark forms lingered just outside the ring of light cast by the campfire's glow.

With every passing day, Naya and Aytal became more proficient riders, learning to grab a fist full of mane and leap onto their horses' backs from the ground and keep their balance over rough terrain. Each morning, while Sata, Oyuun, Amu and the two remaining goats headed down the trail, trading off pulling the sleds, Naya and Aytal would mount up and wander a bit farther afield. With the mare and her colt tagging along, they would explore the surrounding landscape, sometimes scouting ahead for hunting opportunities, before returning to the little caravan and taking their turn at the sleds. By late afternoon the entire group would stop for the day, giving Oyuun and Aytal time before nightfall to catch something small for dinner while Sata and Naya stayed behind to set-up camp, milk MeHnd and gather the edible greens now growing in abundance. As often as she could be excused from helping her mother, Naya would accompany the hunters, hoping to gain practice with her bow.

Finally, after more than a moon had passed since their first successful ride, the morning came when Naya felt ready to attempt what she had been yearning to try almost since she first conceived the idea of sitting astride a horse – galloping with the red filly across the open steppe. Riding next to Aytal, flanked by the wide-open grasslands, she shared with him the image from her winter solstice journey, of herself and Réhda racing the wind over a verdant plain, so similar to the one that stretched away before them now. Naya had not spoken of the vision, except to her mother. That she was now willing to talk of it with Aytal testified to the friendship that had developed between them, not unlike the trust that had grown between herself and the red filly, or between Aytal and the gray stallion, crafted over time of small gestures of kindness, understanding and mutual respect.

"I want to feel that way again," she concluded with longing, looking out at the expanse of spring grass dotted with wildflowers. "I want it to be real, real in *this* world, even if I fall off trying. But I don't think I will.

I think we're ready." Naya turned to Aytal, her expression at once earnest and determined.

Looking back at her as their horses walked side by side, Aytal felt his heart stir as it had on the morning when Naya had first mounted the filly. Just as on that occasion, she sat proudly erect but also at ease, as if riding a horse were entirely natural. A playful wind had pulled tendrils of chestnut hair free from the braid that hung down her back and she put up an impatient hand to push the errant strands out of her eyes. *How brave you are*, Aytal thought, *and beautiful, and altogether breathtaking.* In his mind's eye, he saw again his own vision, when he had journeyed to the other world to rescue her and ended up giving up so much. He'd seen the magnificent sight as well, exactly as Naya had just described for him, of her and the filly racing as one across the flowing grasslands. But just as Naya had long kept her own vision close to her heart, neither had he spoken of what he'd witnessed, nor of what else had transpired on his own visit to the other world, except to tell his father. It had all been worth it, he thought now, and for this reason, despite what Naya had shared with him of her own journey, he still chose not to reveal the sacrifice he'd made. *She must never know*, he swore, for if she learned the truth, it might negate whatever he might have done to save her life.

Naya waited for a response to her confession, but Aytal said nothing, merely smiled. The look in his eyes could not be disguised, however, and gave Naya the encouragement she needed. The smile she returned to him brimmed with confidence and anticipation.

"Here goes then," she said, taking a deep breath and setting her sights straight ahead.

Threading her fingers through the filly's mane and taking a firm grip, Naya leaned slightly forward and whispered to the little horse. Listening, Réhda twitched one ear back, then pricked both ears forward. Together, the pair took several steps at a walk before shifting into a slow jog. Gradually, at Naya's urging, they began to build speed. The faster the filly went, however, the bouncier became her movement. Just when Naya thought she might no longer be able to maintain her balance, she felt Réhda shift beneath her. Gone was the jarring trot, replaced by a smooth, rolling gait which proved infinitely easier to sit. Loosening her grip slightly on the filly's mane, Naya wrapped her legs more securely around her ribs, leaned forward and once more urged her on. Beneath them, the grassy earth began to fall away, faster and faster as the filly accelerated until Naya felt they must be flying. Wind stung her cheeks, making her eyes water, and she could hardly breathe. Never before had she experienced such speed. At once terrified and exhilarated, she did not want the feeling ever to end.

The red filly's tail streamed behind them like a banner. She too loved the sensation of running, feeling her muscles bunch and release, tendons and ligaments storing energy with each rhythmic strike of her hooves and then unleashing it with each powerful thrust from her limbs. A creature of earth and air, she skimmed the ground, moving for the sheer joy of movement. She could sense the girl's elation matched her own, and it fueled her desire to keep going, far out into the endless grasslands. Eventually, instinct telling her not to risk exhaustion, she slowed, first to a trot, then to walk, and finally halt. Flanks heaving and nostrils flaring, she tried to draw breath. *That was fun!*

Struggling to catch her own breath, Naya looked back, searching for Aytal, and realized with a shock that in what felt like no more than an instant, she and Réhda had travelled far beyond the distance she could ever have sprinted on her own. And yet here she sat, winded yes, but not in the least tired, while Aytal and the other horses were no more than barely discernable specks against the skyline. In that moment, Naya's perception shifted. To her, the vastness of the steppe had always represented freedom but a freedom constrained by traveling on her own two feet. How often had she envied the swift flight of hawks and eagles, or imagined herself to possess the fleetness of the deer or antelope? Of course she had envisioned exactly this, galloping effortlessly across the landscape on the back of the red filly. Yet the reality of what she'd just experienced was more awesome than anything she could have imagined. The limitless steppe became truly without limits and a whole new perspective opened before her.

Leaning forward, Naya encircled the filly's neck with her arms, burying her face in the little horse's mane.

"Thank you," she whispered against her red-gold coat, now dark with sweat. "Thank you for showing me your world."

Sitting up, she waved emphatically, signaling to Aytal that he and Myräkkä should join them. But of course, he was much too far away to see her trying to get his attention. She was about to suggest to the filly that they start back when she noticed, away to the south, a small band of horses. Meandering along an easterly course, they were far enough in the distance that Naya could only guess at their number – six or perhaps seven. But something about the way they moved together as a group seemed familiar. Naya's breath caught in her throat. She couldn't be sure, but just possibly it was BeHregs and the other mares and their offspring. If so, the herd must have been following a parallel track ever since they left the clearing, just far enough away that she hadn't been able to spot them until her wild gallop with the filly.

She didn't dare go any further in the herd's direction today. Last year, before all that had happened, she might have, disregarding her responsibilities in order to follow her first impetuous impulse, but she was not the same willful young girl she'd been then. Today, the sun was nearing its zenith. Naya knew that she and Aytal needed to get back to take their turns with the sleds. She couldn't risk delaying their travel by taking off on her own. After what had happened last winter, she understood her actions could have serious consequences. No one had ever blamed her in so many words, but Naya knew it was ultimately her fault that she and her mother had been forced to spend the winter in the clearing, away from the safety of the clan, and away from her father. Aytal may have shot the arrow that almost killed her, but she should never have been concealed among the herd in the first place. She'd ignored her father's cautions and disobeyed his orders. Aytal could not be held responsible. When they returned, she planned to say as much to her father, hoping it would be enough to spare him from punishment.

Meanwhile, Naya thought excitedly, in addition to describing to Aytal and the others her thrilling ride out into the steppe, she would tell them that she may have located BeHregs and the other mares. Perhaps tomorrow, if she could persuade Aytal to try a gallop on Myräkkä, they might be able to find the herd again and this time get close enough to use the auroch horn to encourage them to come closer. For now, she must get back.

Just as Naya was about to turn away, Réhda, who had also been staring intently in the direction of the other horses, lifted her nose to sample the breeze. Detecting a scent she recognized, the young horse neighed so loudly that Naya felt the sound reverberate through her own body as well as the filly's. She watched the distant herd intently for a reaction but saw none. They must have been too far away to hear the filly's cry. An answering call did come, but from the opposite direction, where MeHnd and her colt waited with Aytal and Myräkkä. Turning toward them, Naya asked Réhda for a slow jog for the first half of the way back, only picking up the pace when she got close enough to see that Aytal had dismounted and turned the gray stallion loose to graze with the mare and foal. She urged the filly into a canter, more controlled this time, and although not as breathtaking as that first gallop, still exhilarating. Within no time, they'd covered the remaining distance to where Aytal and the other horses waited. When they'd reached them, the filly stopped of her own accord and Naya slid off her back.

"That was amazing," she said, turning to Aytal, "and guess what I saw?"

"You are amazing."

He was staring at her as though he hadn't heard her question. The look on his face made Naya forget what she had meant to tell him. Before she could recover, she found herself in his embrace. She wasn't quite sure how it happened. She may have impetuously thrown her arms around his shoulders. He might have spontaneously reached for her waist to give her a congratulatory hug. Both meant only to express their shared excitement over what she and the filly had just done. Instead, the gesture turned into something more than either of them intended.

Once in Aytal's arms, Naya became aware of how tall he was, how her head fit just beneath his chin. As though afraid he might break her but not wanting to let her go, Aytal held her with a combination of strength and gentleness that made Naya feel both protected and cherished. Momentarily confused, she froze, unsure of what was happening. Then his hands were on either side of her face, cradling her cheeks, and his eyes, blue as the endless sky above, looked deeply into hers, asking. In answer, her body swayed ever so slightly toward him and her chin tilted upwards just enough that her lips met his.

The kiss was tentative at first. Aytal didn't seem any more confident than she was of what they were doing or of how the other might react, but gradually, as neither pulled away, their embrace deepened. With one hand, Aytal cupped the back of her head, while shifting his other arm to her waist so that he could pull her more securely against him. At the same time, Naya lifted both hands, burying her fingers in the thicket of Aytal's coarse dark hair and effectively preventing him from breaking off the kiss, even had he wanted to.

Suspended together in that timeless place, they were aware of nothing beyond one another, not even the horses cropping the grass around them. Naya once more felt herself move into the eternal flow, joined this time by the young man who claimed her as though she were the most precious being in all creation. The sensations each roused in the other were new to them both, overwhelming and almost frightening in their intensity. At last, needing to breathe, they released one another.

Pulse beating hard in her throat, whether from her wild ride on the filly or from the kiss, or both, she couldn't be sure, Naya needed a moment to recover. Not ready to meet Aytal's gaze, she rested her forehead against his broad chest. Did he feel as suddenly shy as she did? Beneath her brow his heart thudded, rapidly at first and then more steadily, until eventually she raised her eyes to his.

As was so often the case, rather than say something to her, Aytal only smiled. *You have more ways of smiling at me than I can count*, Naya thought. Gaining confidence, she smiled back, her expression widening into a grin. She wasn't sure which made her feel more triumphant, her gallop across the steppe, or the surprised and slightly awed look on Aytal's face, as though she had just delighted him with the rarest of gifts. Of one thing she was certain; she would not be sharing with her mother the whole story of all that had happened today, at least not right away.

Neither did Naya speak to Aytal of the kiss. Instead, taking his offered hand as they turned to begin the trek back in the direction of the main route, she tried to describe what it had felt like to be one with the red filly, racing the wind together, and told him of the herd of horses she'd seen, far to the south.

"I couldn't tell for sure if it was BeHregs and the other mares," she concluded, "but Réhda seemed to think so. If you ride out further with me tomorrow, we might be able to call to them with the horn."

Caught up in her enthusiasm, Aytal agreed they would go in search of the herd the next day. In the meantime, with the red filly, the gray stallion and the mare and colt meandering in their wake, they made their way back to rejoin the others.

Chapter Seventeen

"Not tomorrow," declared Oyuun when Naya told him of their plans.

It was late afternoon. They'd stopped at the mouth of a narrow, steep-sided ravine, through which ran a small creek, one of innumerable run-offs on their way to join the great river nearby. The landscape as they'd approach the *Rā* increasingly featured many such ravines, incised into the gently sloping hillsides that climbed from the broad valley through which they'd been traveling for the past several days to the high bluffs lining the west bank of the wide-flowing river. Much of the area beyond where they'd decided to set-up camp was filled with tangled underbrush but they'd found a relatively flat space beside the little stream that would serve well enough as a place to spend the night.

Given the threatening clouds gathering to the west, the location had seemed safer than remaining exposed on the more open plain they'd spent the day traversing but, when Aytal returned from a foray to collect firewood with news of fresh lion tracks, Oyuun began to have second thoughts. Perhaps the horses, who had been reluctant to come into the ravine, had reason to prefer staying in the open. Another glance at the darkening sky, however, dissuaded him from suggesting a move. Once they'd unpacked a few necessities, Sata had offered to work at getting a fire going while he and Aytal went to the *Rā* to catch fish for their dinner. But first, Naya had asked about searching for BeHregs and the rest of the herd. Earlier in the afternoon, as soon as she and Aytal had returned from her thrilling gallop out into the open steppe, she'd told Oyuun and her mother not only about her ride but about spotting the band of horses off in the distance. She'd waited until now, however, to mention the idea of going to look for them the next day.

"According to your mother," Oyuun was saying, "now that we're so close to the *Rā*, it's only a matter of traveling for a day or two before we reach the clan's winter settlement. We're likely to encounter sentries or a hunting party at any moment. You and Aytal both need to stay close, and keep the horses with us as well, if you don't want them to be mistaken for prey. At this point, it might be better if the other stallion and his mares kept their distance."

"I'm actually surprised we haven't encountered someone from the clan already," added Sata without looking up from what she was doing. "I'd have thought Potis would have sent one of the other men to come after us by now or come himself."

She didn't say more, but Oyuun could guess her thoughts. Whatever had happened to prevent the clan chief from making an effort to retrieve his wife and daughter, it wasn't likely to be good. He had too much respect for her to offer easy words of reassurance, however, so he remained silent. Truth be told, he felt lucky they'd yet to encounter anyone from the clan. Their time together would come to an end soon enough. And there was still much that remained unsaid.

Studying Sata's profile as she bent to her task, auburn hair woven into a thick braid that fell over her shoulder as she worked, Oyuun made a decision.

"Aytal," he said, not looking away, "you and Naya go to the river without me." Realizing further explanation might be required, he glanced in his son's direction. "With the possibility of a lion in the area, I don't want to leave the camp without two of us here to protect it and I don't want either of you going to the water by yourselves." He needed to speak to Sata alone. "Take your other weapons, along with the harpoon and the fishing net," he added. The latter injunction was hardly a needless precaution. If a big cat was in the vicinity, they must all be on guard.

Glad to be relieved of the remaining tasks of setting up camp, Aytal and Naya, along with Amu, set-off for the great river. After struggling for a time to find a way through dense undergrowth and closely growing trees, mainly birch, interspersed with the occasional grove of oak, they eventually located a path which seemed to be leading them in the direction they wanted to go. At last, emerging from the shadow of the woods, they stopped, arrested in their tracks. Stretching before them, sunlight glinting silver off its surface, was the *Rā*, one of the mightiest rivers on earth. Originating far to the north, the broad waters flowed first east and then south, through dense forests, open grasslands, and eventually an arid plain before finally reaching the enormous inland sea that lay well beyond the clan's territory.

They had come out of the woods at a location no more than a few days' journey below where the main river was joined by one of its major tributaries, carving a big loop around high chalk cliffs and flowing briefly to the west before continuing south. The river widened here and, even in late summer, when lower water levels revealed a sandy fringe of beach on either shore, the distance separating the two sides was so vast that only the strongest of swimmers could safely cross unless by a ford. Now, swollen with spring run-off, the waters of the *Rā* had not only invaded the marshes that formed the river's floodplain to the east but threatened to overtop the steep bank which normally bounded the river's more elevated floodplain to the west.

Aytal, who had never seen such a wide body of water, stood speechless in awe. For Naya, however, the sight of the *Rā* represented something else.

"I recognize this place," she exclaimed. "We're almost home!" Soon, maybe even by tomorrow, they would arrive at the clan's winter settlement, riding in on horseback to the astonishment of one and all. She would be reunited with her father, her grandparents, her cousin Melit. She would be able to show Aytal all of her favorite places.

"We're almost home," she repeated, turning to him, eyes bright with excitement. Gazing down into her upturned face, Aytal answered her joyful smile with one of his own. He'd nearly succeeded in transforming the moment into something more when Naya broke away.

"Look," she cried, pointing. "Did you see it?"

"What?" Confused, Aytal looked toward the river.

"Fish!" she cried. "Quick – give me the harpoon."

At the campsite, Oyuun busied himself with various small tasks until he was certain the two young people were well out of earshot. Then, trying to seem nonchalant, he came and squatted beside Sata, watching for a moment as she patiently tried to coax a spark from her flint and light a flame under a small pile of dried moss and kindling.

"Here," he said, taking the stones from her. "Let me try."

"You know I'm better than you at lighting fires," she replied but there was no defensiveness in her words and she surrendered the flint willingly enough. Still, the smile she gave him was absent-minded. As had been the case for the last several days, she seemed preoccupied, not at all the engaging traveling companion she'd been for most of the trip, as appreciative of his sense of humor as she was uncomplaining of the rigors of the journey. Instead, the closer they'd come to their destination, the more withdrawn she'd grown, showing no more than polite interest in anything he had to say. Even Naya's enthusiasm earlier today about her gallop on the red filly and the news she had shared about sighting the rest of the herd had served only momentarily to lift Sata's mood.

Now, having surrendered the job of lighting the fire, she appeared inclined to rise and go about some other task, losing herself once more in her own thoughts. Fearing this might be the last opportunity he would have to discover if those thoughts had anything at all to do with him, Oyuun grasped at the first seemingly innocuous topic of conversation that came to mind to dissuade her from leaving.

"Naya was glowing today, after her ride," he remarked, hoping to draw her out with talk of her daughter's triumph. Indeed, the girl had been radiant when she and Aytal had rejoined them at mid-day, brimming with excitement as she attempted to describe what it had felt like to skim the earth on the back of a galloping horse. And of course she'd been filled with relief at the possible sighting of the dun stallion and his herd. But there had been something more as well. Watching Aytal as he listened to Naya recount her tale, Oyuun noted a look on his son's face that went beyond shared pride at Naya's accomplishments. Unquestionably, he was in love, as he had been since he'd first laid eyes on the girl. What was different now was that when gazing at her, Aytal wore the look of a man confident that his affections were returned. Judging by the way Naya smiled back at him, the feeling was indeed mutual. Fairly certain Sata had noticed as much and needing a prelude to what he truly wanted to discuss, Oyuun paused only a moment before bringing the subject of their children's obvious attraction to one another into the open.

"It's going to be complicated for my son and your daughter when we return to the clan," he observed.

Still seated beside him, Sata did not respond immediately and Oyuun wondered if she'd heard him. After a moment, just as he was about to try another topic, she lifted her gaze to his. Far from distracted, her expression now was focused and filled with concern.

"I know," she concurred, voice serious. "I keep wondering how to talk to them about it without embarrassing them both, but after today it's even more obvious that we need to warn them. They need to be careful." Before she could explain further, he interrupted her. It was not of Naya and Aytal that he actually wished to speak.

Laying aside the flint, Oyuun took Sata's two hands in his. "They're not the only ones," he said, his tone for once every bit as serious as hers. What he intended to say next was, *What about us?* But he hesitated, and in that heartbeat, his courage deserted him. "Have you thought about my proposal," he asked instead, "to come with me to visit your people?" For an instant, Oyuun felt Sata's instinct to stiffen, as though she might recoil from his touch. *Either she's unsure*, he thought, *or she doesn't wish to offend me. Possibly both. Careful then.* Probably a good thing, after all, that he had not raised the other question head-on. He did not release his hold on her, nor did he tighten it. Instead, he simply allowed her hands to rest in his and she did not pull away.

Sata's head was bowed once more and for a long moment she kept her eyes down, seeming to study how their hands intertwined, Oyuun's palms upturned, supportive, fingers curving slightly around hers, protective but not possessive. He waited, heart in his throat, for her to take a breath and look at him again. When at last she did, her expression was not what he expected. The look of naked despair nearly broke him.

"I can't," she said in answer to his question. "I can't ever go home." The anguish in her voice made him want to take her in his arms to comfort her. He resisted the impulse.

"Can't go home, or can't go home with me?" Keeping his tone as carefully neutral as his touch, Oyuun pressed, but gently.

Looking away once more, Sata did not answer right away. Oyuun waited, unmoving, still holding her hands in his. When she turned back to him, she'd regained some of her usual control.

"Both," she answered candidly but with less emotion. "It's not that I wouldn't want to make the journey," she continued, allowing herself a fleeting half smile. "But you have to realize, my life is with Potis and his clan. Most important is Naya. She needs me." She held his eyes as he held her hands, asking for understanding.

Her response was predictable, thought Oyuun. What did he expect from a woman in Sata's position? He heard her words, but he also caught the wistful curve of her lips, there and then gone. It was enough to give him hope. "You do miss your home, though?" he persisted. There had been that confession, when he'd first broached the idea of returning to where she'd been raised, that she might not come back.

"Yes," she acknowledged. "My heart misses the mountains. Painfully at times." The anguish was creeping back.

"And will you miss me?" He tried to make the words light, as though he were teasing her as he so often did, but he did not quite succeed. He knew the intensity of his gaze belied his tone. He couldn't help himself. Again the half-smile flitted across Sata's features, perhaps acknowledging Oyuun's attempt at jest, perhaps a rueful admission of the truth of what she was about to say.

"Yes," she admitted, looking down once more, voice tinged with both resignation and sadness. "I will miss you, just as I miss the mountains." For the merest instant, Oyuun felt Sata's grip tighten around his.

Although her eyes were turned away again and he couldn't see her expression, for Oyuun, the words, together with that fleeting pressure, were enough. If Sata would miss him as she did the soaring peaks of her homeland, he knew he had at least some claim to her heart. Maybe in that case the obstacles separating them were just that – obstacles – not insurmountable barriers. He'd encountered many a mountain in his travels. So far, he'd succeeded in conquering all of them. But he was also not one to be fooled into wishful thinking, nor would he seek to cause this woman to be untrue to herself. For the moment at least, he could not see a way forward.

Releasing his hold, Oyuun placed his hands on either side of Sata's face and cradling her jaw, gently but insistently returned her gaze to his. Hiding nothing, he looked into her eyes, searching their blue depths for confirmation that her feelings mirrored his own, regardless of all that stood in their way. At last, encountering no resistance, he drew her lips to his. He meant the kiss as a farewell. The realities of Sata's life held no place for him. Leave-taking was inevitable. Their shared idyll was coming to an end, and once they rejoined her husband's clan, he must keep his distance, for both their sakes.

Yet, to his surprise – and hers – the kiss spoke not of parting but of greeting, as though after a long absence. They both felt it, the flash of mutual recognition, as if they'd known one another forever, followed by the joy of a much longed-for reunion. It was as if, after a lifetime of traveling separate paths, they'd finally arrived together at that most sacred place: home.

All too soon, however, Oyuun felt Sata start to pull away and all the reasons for saying goodbye crowded back into his head. As soon as he'd returned her safely, he would be expected to set-off again on his own journey. Given her commitments and his sense of honor, the likelihood that she would accompany him was almost nil. Even if he couldn't entirely relinquish hope for a future with her, best for now to let her go. When she drew back, he didn't try to stop her.

Sata wanted desperately not to end the kiss. She wished she could surrender to the sanctuary of Oyuun's embrace, forgetting where she was and who she was supposed to be. The touch of his hands on her skin, his lips on her mouth, offered relief from years of unspoken loneliness and grief that twisted around her throat like a noose, choking off her life's-breath, suffocating her heart. Deeply ingrained caution held her back. She was enmeshed in knots of family relationships and tribal alliances. The consequences of severing those ties would be disastrous, not only for her but for everyone she loved, including Oyuun himself. Even more, she feared the sudden release of the bonds that had held her for so long, tethering her to her life. If she let go, what would be left for her to grasp on to? So instead, she pulled away.

To Sata's disappointment and relief, Oyuun did not try to prolong the kiss. Withdrawing his caress and once more taking her hands in his, he held her gaze, waiting for her to speak. She looked at him mutely, tears tracking her dust-stained cheeks, wishing for him simply to understand without her having to say anything, but knowing she owed both of them an explanation. For two, perhaps three heartbeats, they looked at one another in silence. Then, just as she'd almost found her voice, the sudden snap of a twig somewhere nearby interrupted her.

"What is it?" Sata whispered, startled.

"I'll check," answered Oyuun, also keeping his voice low. Releasing her hands, he rose, reached for the flint ax he'd been using to split firewood and began a thorough search of the bushes surrounding the perimeter of the camp. Visions of a cat big enough to have left the tracks Aytal had seen earlier filled his imagination and he was relieved to find no evidence indicating the presence of anything larger than a squirrel in the vicinity of the small clearing. Still, perhaps it would be better after all to relocate to the steppe which, although affording less convenient access to water and firewood and not as much protection from the elements, also offered less cover for predators.

"Must have been something small," Oyuun said when he returned from his exploration, "but I've changed my mind. I don't feel good about staying here. Maybe we should take our chances in the open."

"Yes," agreed Sata. "Let's get out of here." For some reason, the twig snap had unnerved her, or perhaps it was Oyuun's kiss that had her on edge. In any case, she suddenly wanted nothing more than to be out of the brush-choked ravine and back out on the grasslands, even with the wind beginning to rise and the sky overhead growing ever more ominous. "We can pack-up what little needs re-packing and be ready to move when they get back from the river."

Turning away abruptly, Sata busied herself with returning her fire-starting tools to the hide pouch at her waist, obviously intent on forestalling the possibility of further conversation. Taking the hint, Oyuun began loading a portion of the wood that he'd split on to one of the already overburdened sleds. They'd have to make multiple trips back to the ravine for wood and water, he thought to himself, but so be it.

Just as he'd decided the sled could not accommodate so much as another stick of kindling, Aytal appeared, soaking wet, fishing net draped over his shoulders. In his arms he carried a creature so large that he struggled under its weight. Its snout was long, pointed and slightly upturned at the end, with several whisker-like feelers on the underside, while spiny protuberances extended along its back and sides. Clearly it was a fish, but not one either Aytal or his father had ever seen and Aytal looked extraordinarily pleased with himself.

"By the gods," exclaimed Oyuun, "what did you catch?"

"*Huso Huso*," answered Sata before Aytal could reply. She gave the clan's name for sturgeon, which could be found abundantly in the waters of the *Rā*, now that the river was free of ice. The fish represented a staple of the clan's diet for much of the year whenever they were in range of the river. "If it's a female we are in for a treat," she added. "The eggs are delicious."

"How did you catch it?" asked Oyuun, still incredulous.

"Speared it," replied Aytal, "but the spear broke and it almost got away. Luckily Naya had the harpoon, with the cord attached. I tied the end around my waist and followed the fish along the bank until it swam farther downstream where the water's shallower. When it came close enough to the shore I waded to where I could stab it again and hang on. It almost pulled me under more than once."

As he was telling his story, Aytal, with Oyuun's help, laid the enormous fish on a clean hide which Sata had quickly spread.

"But where is Naya," she asked, once Aytal was relieved of his burden. "Didn't she come back with you?"

"She's not here?" he answered in surprise. "She ran back when I started downstream after the fish, said she would get another spear in case the harpoon broke as well." He looked from Sata to his father and back again. "She's not here?" he repeated, confused.

Sata and Oyuun exchanged looks from where they squatted on either side of the fish, sharing the identical thought. *The twig snap. What if Naya had seen them? How much might she have overheard?*

In a panic, Sata stood and called her daughter's name as loudly as she could. There was no response. Oyuun rose to his feet as well and coming to Sata's side, laid a quieting hand on her arm.

"Shouting for her is no use. If she's within earshot and wants to answer, she'll be here soon enough." What he didn't add was what they both feared. The girl could easily have witnessed some or perhaps all of the exchange between them and drawn her own conclusions. And whereas the truth was complicated, and not without honor on both sides, there would be no way for Naya to know that or even begin to understand what she had seen. Appearances, by contrast, were altogether damning.

"What can we do?" Sata tried and failed to hide the anxiety in her voice.

Aytal looked at her in surprise. "I'm sure she's fine," he said reassuringly. "She probably figured I could manage the fish on my own and went to check on the horses. If she runs into anything, she has her bow. I'll go look for her."

"Amu hasn't come back either," observed Oyuun. "I don't know if that's a good sign or not. While you're searching, we're going to move camp back out in the open. There's too much cover here to make it safe, especially after dark." He began wrapping up the fish in the hide. "Come back with her as soon as you find her," he added as an apparent afterthought, "even if she objects." When Aytal gave him a questioning look, Oyuun shrugged. "We could use both of you to help finish moving."

The wait for their return seemed interminable. In the interim, Oyuun and Sata succeeded in moving everything, including the fish, back to a site closer to the central trail that bisected the wide valley floor. Working together in a battle with the rising wind, they managed to erect the shelter, taking care to anchor the perimeter with sharp wooden stakes driven with difficulty into the hard ground. Although barren of anything other than grass and entirely exposed to the approaching storm, nonetheless, as Sata told Oyuun, the new location felt infinitely safer.

"Just like the horses," she commented as she used a rock to pound in the last stake, "we're better off in the open." He did not need to guess at what she'd left unsaid.

With still no sign of the two young people, Oyuun proceeded to make several additional trips to haul enough water and wood to see them through the night, while Sata set about cleaning the sturgeon. Unfortunately, there was far more of the fish than they could possibly eat and much would have to be left behind for scavengers. She saved what she could of the roe, the delicate gray-black eggs that tasted of the great sea and happened to be just at their peak. Finally, with nothing left to do and no sign yet of either Naya or Aytal, Sata went inside the shelter, ostensibly to unpack the sleeping mats. When asked by Oyuun if she wanted help, the reply was an unequivocal 'No thank you.'

Knowing enough not to impose, Oyuun turned instead to the problem of their depleted stock of weapons. The harpoon and Aytal's spear had been damaged in the battle with the sturgeon and required new shafts. There remained only his own long-handled hunting spear, along with the hand ax and their flint knives, to see them through the remainder of the journey. Wrinkling his brow, Oyuun considered whether or not to include in his calculations the two bows and the arrows that went with them. While Naya was gaining confidence with hers and more often than not kept the bow strung and ready at her back, she was still not adept enough to reliably bring down a moving target more challenging than a rabbit. Meanwhile, Aytal's bow and arrows lay buried somewhere beneath a mound of bundles piled on one of the sleds. *Useless*, Oyuun thought, and felt a wave of frustration rise from deep within.

Enough, he said to himself, striding over to where they'd left the loaded sleds. His son needed to get on with the actual task that had been set for him by his spirit guide, not keep indulging this self-conceived idea of sacrifice and denial. Experienced as he was in the ways of the spirit world, Oyuun felt quite certain Aytal's guide had not called for him to renounce his gifts, but rather to learn to use them in service to his life's purpose. Had the gyrfalcon not said as much? Unfortunately, the young man seemed not to have understood his guide's meaning. Instead, what had begun as a journey to find Naya's spirit and help her to find her way back had been transformed into something else. Such was always the danger of venturing into the spirit realm, Oyuun reflected. Often, there were unforeseen consequences. Despite admirable intentions, somewhere along the way, Aytal's remorse over injuring Naya had gotten tangled up with the conviction that he alone was responsible not just for finding her spirit but for rescuing her and that doing so required nothing less than the sacrifice of his true self.

Noble gesture indeed, Oyuun snorted derisively as he studied the three over-burdened sleds. *More like false pride.* The fact that Aytal had missed his aim at the auroch that day hadn't helped matters. The errant shot, coming so soon after the journey, appeared to confirm what the young man had already convinced himself to be true: even though he'd failed to find Naya during the journey, she had lived, which must mean there was a chance that his act of renunciation had been responsible for saving her. By the same reasoning, Naya's future wellbeing might be contingent on Aytal continuing to forsake his gifts, hence his refusal to touch his weapons. Being in love did not appear to be improving the situation, Oyuun mused as he studied the sleds, trying to remember where the items he sought had been packed. He sighed. Regardless of his son's misguided principles, they could no longer afford to be without the use of his bow and arrows. Lives depended on them.

Having selected the most likely of the sleds, Oyuun began to unload bundles until he'd uncovered his son's weapons. Quite sure that even after all this time, Aytal could still drop a lion at fifty paces if only he could be persuaded to use his skill, he went about refurbishing the neglected bow. Removing the bowstring from its waterproofed leather pouch hanging from the quiver, Oyuun noted with approval that the twisted fibers had been coated with a thin layer of grease before being carefully coiled and stored. At least the young man had not been careless. As a result, though in need of some re-twisting, the slender cord still seemed supple and strong enough to withstand the tension of being strung, even after so much time had passed.

The bow itself, however, was another matter. Bending it awkwardly until he could attach both ends of the string, Oyuun tested its flex. Even to his inexperienced hand, the wood felt stiff and lifeless from lack of attention. Like all tools, the bow possessed a spirit of its own, not unlike a living being, and needed to be cared for and tended as such. Ignored through no fault of its own, the wood had become unresponsive. Shaking his head in disgust, Oyuun propped the bow, still strung, just outside the entrance to the shelter. Aytal's quiver, filled with his distinctive double-fletched arrows, he left alongside the bow.

The storm had nearly unleashed itself by the time Oyuun sighted two mounted figures cresting a ridge to the northwest of the relocated campsite. The sky behind them was an eerie mix of green and dark gray and the wind blew hard, carrying with it the first drops of rain. He called to Sata, who emerged from the tent.

"Thank the Goddess," she breathed, relieved when he pointed the riders out to her.

"They'll have to hurry to make it before it starts to pour," Oyuun observed, squinting into the oncoming weather. Just then, lighting flashed from somewhere deep in the clouds, followed closely by a menacing roll of thunder. The temperature was dropping rapidly. Standing side by side, Oyuun and Sata watched as the pair of riders threaded their way down from the ridge-top to the wide valley below, leaning back to compensate for the grade and trusting their sure-footed mounts to navigate the uneven terrain. Behind them came the mare and foal, along with the dog, following in single file. As Oyuun and Sata stood waiting, lightning once again illuminated the charcoal sky, followed almost instantly by a reverberating boom.

"At least she's safe," said Sata once the thunder had subsided. "I wonder if she'll speak to me."

"They'll both have some listening to do when they get here, as far as I'm concerned," replied Oyuun grimly. "I have one or two things I'd like to say to them both about responsibility."

"Don't," said Sata, laying a hand on his arm. "Now isn't the time."

"When is the time?" Oyuun countered, exasperation getting the better of him. "Regardless of what Naya thinks she may have seen, she had no business disappearing and worrying you. You'd think she'd have more faith in her mother and not jump to conclusions without giving you a chance to explain. And as for my son, he's had long enough to get over this reluctance to use his bow. In a day or two we'll rejoin the clan and he needs to be ready to defend himself like a man, not a boy. Meanwhile, he needs to do his part to help protect all of us from whatever four-legged predators might be out there in this storm."

"What do you mean, 'defend himself like a man, not a boy'?" Sata seized on Oyuun's words, sounding almost angry herself. "Surely you don't intend for him to fight back against just punishment for what he did to my daughter?"

"That depends on whether the punishment is indeed just," retorted Oyuun. "He needs to accept the consequences of his actions, but he should also not apologize for his skill or otherwise deny his gifts. It was, after all, an accident, for which Naya must bear a share of the blame."

He could tell Sata wanted to react with outrage, to use this moment as an excuse to channel all her other tangled emotions into a single heated argument with him. Drawing herself up to her full height, almost as tall as himself, and tilting her head back, she gazed down her aquiline nose at him, blue eyes flashing, ready for a fight. For a moment, he stared hard back, equally poised to argue, but the sight of her, magnificent in her fury, distracted him.

"By the gods," he breathed in awe, "you are beautiful."

He couldn't help it and in that instant he felt his own frustration drain away. "Please let's not quarrel," he said, his expression softening along with his stance. "Aytal will be punished as he deserves. Let's not make this any more complicated than it already is. Please forgive me for upsetting you."

Faced with Oyuun's contrite apology, Sata seemed unable to muster either the energy or the inclination to stay mad. Instead, with a ragged sigh, she let go of her own indignation. Weariness immediately took its place, her shoulders sagging beneath the weight.

"I wonder if she'll speak to me," she murmured again, turning to watch as Naya and Aytal stopped a short distance from the campsite and slide off their horses' backs, setting the animals loose.

"She loves you and she knows you love her," replied Oyuun quietly.

"She will listen eventually." He wanted to put a reassuring arm around her waist but restrained himself.

"By now you should know my daughter well enough," Sata observed, stepping sideways in order to put more distance between them. "Eventually could take a long time."

Sata's prediction proved correct. Beyond providing a perfunctory excuse for riding off into the steppe without telling anyone, Naya maintained a stony reserve toward both her mother and Oyuun, and even Aytal, which lasted for the remainder of the evening. Forced into the cramped shelter to escape the storm, no one else was in a very good mood either. The competing odors of damp goat and wet dog permeated the enclosed space. Even a dinner of grilled fish did little to lift anyone's spirits. They ate in silence. Talking would have been difficult in any case, given the rising noise of wind and rain as the front edge of the storm lashed the shelter's hide covering. As soon as the meal was finished, Sata smothered the smoky fire, which had only been contributing to the unpleasant atmosphere inside the tent, while Oyuun took the remains of the fish back outside. Dissuaded by the driving rain from burying the carcass, he left it at a safe distance from their campsite, taking the risk that no other animals would disturb it as long as the storm lasted. The horses, he noted before ducking back inside, were gathered close by the shelter, standing with their tails to the wind, heads low, as rain pelted their backs and ran in rivulets down their flanks. It would be a miserable night for one and all.

Chapter Eighteen

Sunrise was near when Oyuun, who had been dosing fitfully while the others slept, came suddenly to full wakefulness. For a moment, he was not sure what had disturbed him. The storm, which had raged for much of the first half of the night, had finally blown itself out and all seemed quiet, except for the sound of water dripping off the shelter. Then he heard it again, a soft sucking squelch, as of a heavy footfall in deep mud. *Lion?* The big cats preferred to hunt at either dawn or dusk, when the shifting light worked in their favor. He should never have left the remains of the fish so close to their camp. Holding his breath, Oyuun listened but heard nothing further. Not satisfied, he was just about to reach over and rouse Aytal, who slept beside him, to come outside with him to investigate when he heard another noise. This time he could tell it was the horses, who had apparently remained near camp throughout the storm and were now beginning to shift restlessly. Something must have put them on alert as well.

Reaching out a hand, Oyuun shook Aytal's shoulder, putting a finger to his lips when the young man's eyes opened in surprise. Gesturing, he indicated that his son should follow him without waking the others. Together they quietly left the shelter. In his right hand Oyuun carried their one remaining spear. Aytal was unarmed, except for the flint knife in his belt.

Emerging from the pitch blackness of the tent into the pre-dawn shadows, they paused for a moment, giving their eyes a chance to adjust. The storm clouds had cleared. On the eastern horizon, thin bands of blue, green, yellow and orange indicated sunrise was not far off but the sky overhead was still a deep indigo, punctuated by a scattering of the brightest stars. Not far from where he stood, Oyuun could make out the shapes of the horses, beginning to shake themselves awake. Noting that they did not seem unduly disturbed after all, he watched as they slowly meandered together in the general direction of the ravine, no doubt intending to start the day with a drink from the small creek.

Movement from the opposite side of their camp caught his eye. Silently, a shape rose from behind a patch of taller grass, attention clearly trained on the small band of horses. Oyuun watched as the shape resolved into the unmistakable form of an adult human, intent on following after the departing herd.

"*Ei! Nē!*" Oyuun called out in alarm, first in his own tongue and again in the language of the clan. Startled, the figure turned in his direction. In the same instant, equally surprised, the horses took flight, disappearing like smoke into the early morning darkness.

Sata and Naya, awakened by Oyuun's shouts, emerged from the shelter, accompanied by Amu. Catching sight of the intruder, the dog started barking furiously and would have charged had not Oyuun commanded him to contain himself.

"Don't move," he ordered, raising his own weapon and speaking in a tone neither the dog nor their unannounced visitor was likely to challenge. "Who are you?" he demanded.

"It's Potis's brother," answered Sata recognizing the newcomer's silhouette before he could respond. "Tausos," she called, "it's Sata."

The reunion that followed was marked by equal parts awkwardness and relief. Having set out at Potis's behest to retrieve his wife and daughter, Tausos was more than happy to be saved from a longer journey and to find Sata and Naya in good health. Yet, although polite in thanking Oyuun and Aytal for caring for his brother's family, and reassuring Oyuun that his younger son was being well looked after, Tausos otherwise did little to disguise his antipathy toward the two strangers and nothing Sata said in their favor served to mitigate her brother-in-law's evident mistrust. Naya, meanwhile, acted inordinately pleased to see her uncle, clinging to his side and besieging him with questions regarding the welfare of her father and her grandparents, all the while pointedly ignoring both Oyuun and Aytal. Tausos, in turn, seemed reluctant to give anything beyond noncommittal responses until Sata noted his increasing discomfort and intervened.

"Let your uncle change into dry clothing," she suggested from where she crouched before a small mound of damp kindling, trying to coax a spark to catch. "We'll talk once we get a fire going."

Turning toward her mother, Naya gave her a withering look, and then without saying anything more, spun on her heel and disappeared inside the shelter, presumably to fetch the last of the dry wood. Observing the exchange, Tausos lifted an eyebrow but Sata could only shrug.

A little while later, with the sun just beginning to crest the eastern horizon, they gathered around a warming blaze. Oyuun and Aytal spread hides on the muddy ground while Sata boiled water for a morning tea of herbs gathered and dried along their journey east. The goats, glad to leave the confines of the shelter, were picketed a short distance away but still within easy reach. The horses had not yet reappeared. Naya, too, remained out of sight inside the tent until summoned by her mother.

"Come tell your uncle about the horses," Sata called, urging the girl to join them around the fire. There was no response.

"Yes, what about the horses? What were they doing so close?" asked Tausos, interest evidently piqued. "And why did you stop me from following them?" he continued, turning to Oyuun accusatorily.

"The story is Naya's to tell," Oyuun replied, expression pleasant but otherwise unreadable.

Just then, they heard a loud neigh, clearly either angry or distressed, coming from the direction of the ravine. Aytal, who had been trying to remain as inconspicuous as possible in the presence of Naya's uncle, lifted his head from where he squatted on the far side of the fire circle, then rose rapidly to his feet.

"That's Myräkkä," he said, the tension in his voice matching the tenor of the horse's call. "Something's wrong."

No sooner had he spoken then Naya broke from the tent and rushed past, bow in her left hand, right hand reaching for an arrow from the quiver slung at her waist. Before anyone could stop her, she disappeared in the direction of the ravine. Amu, not waiting for permission, raced after her.

By now, everyone else was on their feet as well. Tausos, confused, looked to Sata for an explanation of what was happening. Oyuun, who had ducked inside the shelter, emerged a moment later with Aytal's bow and quiver in hand.

"It's all you have," he said when Aytal would have protested. "Go! I'll be right behind you." For once not arguing, the young man took the weapons from his father and set off at a run, following the girl and the dog.

"Should we come?" asked Sata, panic at the edge of her voice.

"No," answered Oyuun. "You both stay here and make sure nothing happens to the goats." Returning to the shelter, he emerged moments later with the remaining spear. Then he, too, headed for the ravine.

By the time he arrived at the clearing where they had thought to camp, it was all over. Coming upon the scene in the early morning shadows, Oyuun hesitated for a moment, uncertain of what he was seeing. In the foreground, the red filly and the gray stallion milled agitatedly, obscuring his view. Behind them, he could make out Aytal and the mare, both of whom appeared focused on a tawny shape laying on the ground at their feet. Neither Naya nor Amu was anywhere in sight but the girl's voice could be heard close by, calling frantically for the dog.

Approaching closer, Oyuun saw the colt. Stretched out on his side, he could have been napping, except for the savage gash torn in his left flank. An arrow protruded from his throat as well. Aytal, bow still gripped in his left hand, stood starring down at the lifeless form as though stunned. The mare, in obvious distress, nickered and pawed the earth beside her prostrate foal. Coming nearer, Oyuun was dismayed to see that the arrow jutting from the colt's neck was one of Naya's.

"What happened?" he asked.

"Lions," said Aytal, voice tight. "A big female and two fully-grown cubs. By the time I arrived the mother had already brought down the colt, even though the mare was doing all she could to protect him, and the cubs were harassing the filly and the stallion."

"Why didn't you shoot the lioness?"

"I tried," Aytal sounded at once defensive and defeated. "Honestly, I did, but it was confusing. There wasn't much light to see and MeHnd and Naya and Amu were all in the way." Swallowing hard, he went on. "I was afraid I might miss and hit the wrong target."

"Apparently Naya had no such qualms."

Father and son stood looking down at the colt's body where it lay, blood congealing in the ragged tracks left by the big cat's claws. More blood pooled beneath the little creature's neck where the arrow had lodged. Although the lion attack had inflicted a gruesome wound, it was Naya's shot that had ended the colt's life. *Perhaps a blessing*, thought Oyuun.

"She'll be devastated," said Aytal, still not able to avert his eyes. Without saying more, he knelt beside the body and grasping the arrow shaft in both hands, yanked it out. He would have thrown it into the bushes, except that his father stopped him.

"What do you think you are doing?" Oyuun asked.

"Let her think it was the lion who killed the colt," Aytal replied.

"She'll see the fatal wound came from an arrow," his father pointed out. "She's bound to realize what happened."

"Then let her think it was me who fired the shot."

"Well at least don't waste a perfectly good arrowhead," Oyuun retorted, sounding aggrieved. Watching as Aytal obediently shoved the bloody shaft into his own quiver, he went on more calmly. "Do you think she should not know the truth?"

"She doesn't have to know," Aytal replied. "She'd never forgive herself."

"Do you think she'll forgive you?"

"It doesn't matter."

Something about the despondency in his son's voice caused Oyuun to look at him searchingly. More was going on here than just the tragic end of the colt's life. True, Naya would be distressed, but realistically, humans killed horses all the time.

"Something happened," answered Aytal in response to his father's questioning look. "I don't know what it was or what I did but she won't even speak to me now. When I went to find her yesterday, she'd taken Réhda and ridden far out into the grasslands, back the way we'd come. I'm lucky Myräkkä was able to find them. Something upset her but she wouldn't explain. She refuses to say anything to me at all."

Oyuun sighed. "It's not you she's angry with, or at least I doubt it's you," he said. "In any case, it's rarely a good idea to hide the truth from someone, even if it's a truth you think they don't want to hear."

"But she couldn't stand to know she killed the colt. Please, Father, let me do this for her. I owe it to her."

Before Oyuun could reply, Naya herself reappeared, dragging Amu by the scruff of his neck. The dog looked as though he'd been in a bad fight and gotten the worst of it. Covered from nose to tail in mud, one ear torn almost completely off, he also had an angry laceration running down his shoulder. At least he was still able to walk, albeit with a pronounced limp.

"What happened to the lions?" Oyuun asked. He addressed the question to Aytal, but it was Naya who answered.

"They're gone," she said, voice taut with suppressed emotion. "No thanks to your son." Rounding on Aytal, she continued, "how could you just stand there!"

"But I didn't…" Aytal began but Naya clearly wasn't listening.

Kneeling beside the lifeless body of the colt, she lifted the heavy head, cradling its weight in her lap. Keening to herself, she gently stroked the colt's face, heedless of the mingled blood and mud that soaked her clothes. It was then she saw the ragged hole torn in the colt's throat. Wordlessly, she looked up at Aytal. The expression in her eyes pierced his heart like an arrow.

"I'm sorry," he managed, but before he could say more, Naya had already turned away.

The following day, toward late afternoon, the bedraggled group of travelers, accompanied by Tausos, finally reached their destination. Their arrival at the clan's winter settlement was not what any of them envisioned. How many times during the long days on the trail had Naya pictured a triumphant return, with Amu bounding ahead to announce them and the whole village gathering to exclaim in wonder and admiration at the sight of the clan chief's daughter astride the flame-coated filly? Sata too hoped for such a homecoming, for Naya's sake. For herself, she anticipated a relieved reception from her husband, with time enough later to sort out her own feelings about resuming her place at his side. Oyuun realistically assumed a less than enthusiastic welcome awaited himself and his son, but even he looked forward to witnessing the clan's reaction to the sight of Naya on horseback. Likewise, rather than dwell on the justice looming at their journey's end, Aytal preferred to imagine Naya appearing for the first time before her own people as 'She Who Rides Horses.'

Instead, when they approached the settlement, a circle of dilapidated structures floating like islands in a muddy sea, no one emerged to greet them. To Naya and Sata, familiar with the usual activity of the clan's semi-permanent encampment, the place seemed eerily deserted. No dogs barked, no children called to one another, only silence met their ears. *Where is everyone?* thought Sata, looking questioningly at her brother-in-law, who had stopped beside her.

Oyuun and Aytal looked about in dismay as well. Sata and Naya had described what sounded like a large and prosperous village, where they could look forward to a hot meal and a dry place to sleep. Instead, the camp seemed utterly forlorn, with not a soul to notice their arrival. *Probably just as well*, reflected Oyuun. They didn't present a particularly impressive sight either, especially without the horses.

The red filly, the gray stallion, the mare – all of them were gone. After keeping up for the entire journey, in the aftermath of the lion attack they had vanished. Just as Sata and Tausos had joined the others in the little clearing where the colt's body lay, head still cradled in Naya's lap, the three horses had taken flight. Aytal had gone after them, but by the time he reached the open steppe, there was no sign of where they'd gone, beyond a confusion of hoofprints in the mud near their camp. Climbing the nearest hillock to obtain a better vantage, he'd blown the auroch horn repeatedly, but to no avail. The horses had been swallowed by the grasslands.

Over Tausos's objections, they'd spent half the morning fanning out across the steppe, searching for a track to follow, then waited at the camp until mid-day, hoping the horses might come back on their own. Finally, when their departure could no longer be postponed, Sata had turned to Naya.

"Maybe they'll catch up with us," she said.

She tried to put a comforting arm around her daughter's shoulders but Naya had forcibly shrugged it off and turned away. Glancing back for just a moment, her blue eyes met Sata's. The the look she gave her sliced through Sata's heart like a knife. Without a word, the girl had gathered up her pack and set off alone down the trail. Amu, who normally would have stayed at Naya's side, was too injured to walk far on his own and would need to be carried atop one of the sleds. No one else dared try to keep up with her.

Instead, they followed, trudging single file, first Oyuun and then Aytal, each pulling a sled, next Sata and the two goats, with Tausos at the rear, towing the third sled, Amu strapped aboard. Not slowing her furious pace, Naya soon outdistanced the little caravan. They only caught up with her when fading daylight forced a stop for the evening.

Despite being their last night on the trail, no one expressed much of a sense of elation or relief. A black cloud, worse than the glowering skies overhead, seemed to have descended over all of them. With no dry fuel to be found and their provisions nearly exhausted, supper was a cold, meager and silent meal, after which the travelers each retreated to a damp bedroll. At least Naya allowed Amu to share her blanket, which Sata took to be a hopeful sign. Maybe the excitement of seeing her father the next day, even without the horses to show off, would be enough to bring the girl out of her dark mood. She could only hope.

When they finally arrived at the seemingly deserted settlement, Sata's hopes faded. Turning to her brother-in-law, she insisted on knowing what was going on.

"Where is everyone?" she asked, out loud this time. "Where is Potis?"

Tausos looked as surprised as she was to find no one on hand to greet them but did not respond right away. Before Sata could question him further, Naya interrupted.

"Where is my father?" she demanded, speaking for the first time since the events of the previous day. Raising an eyebrow at the girl's tone, Tausos indicated that if they chose, they could come with him to find out.

Leaving the sleds where they lay, the little group set off, following Tausos up a steep trail carved into one of the bluffs overlooking the settlement. Once atop the bluff, the well-worn track led across a high, grass-covered plateau toward a precipice with a sheer drop. Gathered at the edge, looking down into the ravine below, were most of the clan's women and children. Just as the travelers caught sight of them, the crowd began to turn away from whatever had captured their attention below. Talking and gesturing animatedly, their elation was palpable. Soon, the clan's older boys, followed by the men, began to appear one by one at the rim of the overlook as they gained the top of the narrow path that led up from the ravine. They too seemed brimming with excitement. Turning to her taciturn brother-in-law, Sata insisted once more on knowing what was going on.

"Let my brother tell you," was all he said. Indeed, just as he spoke, the unmistakable silhouette of the clan chief came into view. As Sata watched, she saw her husband scan the crowd of onlookers gathered at the cliff's edge until he spotted the figure for whom he was evidently searching. Even from a distance, Sata recognized the tall, dark-haired form of her cousin Vedukha, Bhermi's widow. She watched as Potis reached out, pulling the other woman into an exuberant embrace and bestowing an enthusiastic kiss on her laughing, upturned lips.

Before Sata could fully process what she was seeing, Potis's head lifted and she knew he'd caught sight of them. For a moment, across the grassy expanse, with the breeze pushing her hair back from her face, Sata thought she felt her husband's eyes lock on hers and her breath wanted to catch in her throat. Then she realized she'd been mistaken. It was not on her that his attention was suddenly riveted, but on the red-headed blur dashing across the plateau to meet him. As she watched, their daughter threw herself into her father's arms and he welcomed her with an embrace that promised never to let her go.

Standing beside Sata, Oyuun watched as well but his attention did not follow hers. Having witnessed the exchange between the clan chief and the woman who was not his wife, he was less interested in observing the reunion now taking place between father and daughter than in studying the expression on the face next to him, the face he had come to love. The lines around Sata's mouth and at the corners of her eyes betrayed, he thought, a contradictory mix of emotions that he could not quite decipher. Just then, feeling his gaze upon her, Sata turned and met his eyes. For once she did not look away, nor try to disguise her expression, which remained unchanged. Oyuun understood then, and his heart hurt for all of them.

Author's Note

It is only with the heart that one can see rightly.
What is essential is invisible to the eye...
People have forgotten this truth... But you mustn't forget it.
You become responsible, forever, for what you have tamed.

Antoine de St.-Exupéry, *The Little Prince* (1943), chapter XXI.

Domestication

The domestication of the horse – and more specifically taming horses so that they could be ridden – arguably did as much to transform the course of human civilization as any other development in the last six thousand years. Riding horses fundamentally altered our perception of the relationship between time and space, enabling travel at otherwise unachievable speeds over vast distances. In the era before the combustion engine, horses served as our primary source of muscle power and as the earliest agents of globalization, not to mention making possible new types of violence. Historically, they have been our trusted partners in work and war, sport and recreation. Increasingly, through various forms of equine-assisted therapy and learning, they have taken on the role of enabling humans to heal from trauma and counteract the stress and alienation inflicted by modern life, showing us the path toward reclaiming our connections to nature and to our truest selves, as well as providing a compelling model of social and emotional intelligence and of how to exercise what Linda Kohanov refers to as nonpredatory power. At the same time, modern equine advocates and enlightened owners and trainers are more and more committed to redressing the damage humans have inflicted over centuries of indifference to the horse's nature as a sentient being, recognizing, as the French writer Antoine de St.-Exupéry reminds us, that we are responsible, forever, for what we have tamed. Perhaps it is only now, in our current age, that horses can begin to demonstrate their full potential and capacity to tame us.

Yet despite the horse's importance in human history and evolving role in contemporary culture, the details of where, when, why and how domestication occurred remain shrouded in uncertainty. Although horses were among the last of our modern domesticated species to be successfully tamed, not much definitive evidence about the process exists, leading to considerable controversy among scholars. Anthropologists, archeologists, paleolinguists and, more recently, experts in interpreting ancient DNA have all tried to decipher the meager clues available but so far no clear consensus has emerged. For many years, the most popular theory pointed to the Botai people, a group of hunters who occupied permanent settlements on the steppes of northern Kazakhstan between 3700 and 3000 BCE. Findings from Botai archeological sites, including signs of corral postholes and remnants of mare's milk extracted from pottery shards, as well as a plethora of equine bones and teeth, the latter seeming to show signs of bit wear, have together been thought to provide the earliest available proof of horses being domesticated and ridden. Further study, however, has challenged the attribution of changes in the Botai horses' molars to abrasion caused by bit use, while recent DNA analysis has demonstrated that the Botai horses show no relation to modern domestic horses. While the absence of evidence regarding bit wear proves little, since a bit is not required in order to ride a horse, the DNA findings indicate that as far as domestication is concerned, the specialized Botai culture, in which hunters may have ridden horses primarily to hunt other horses, was a dead end. By the beginning of the 3rd century BCE the Botai had disappeared, leaving no lasting legacy.

In search of a more likely location for the domestication of the ancestors of the modern horse, researchers have turned their attention instead to a region known as the Pontic-Caspian steppe, an area of open grasslands interspersed with river valleys occupying what is now southern Russia and Ukraine. Among the authorities who have worked extensively in this area, David Anthony (emeritus professor of Anthropology at Hartwick College) presents perhaps the most comprehensive – and convincing – overview of the available evidence. His magisterial work *The Horse, the Wheel and Language: How Bronze-Age Riders from the Eurasian Steppes Shaped the Modern World* (Princeton University Press, 2007), along with some of his more recently published articles and conference papers, have served as the main reference sources for *She Who Rides Horses*.

As Anthony points out, herds of wild horses, once abundant throughout Europe, by about 8,000 BCE had mostly disappeared due to human hunting and climate change, except for the open grasslands extending north and east of the Black Sea – the Pontic-Caspian steppe. Here they continued to survive and even flourish. Among the most common of the wild grazing animals roaming the grasslands and supremely adapted to the harsh environment, horses provided a prime source of prey for humans and other large predators alike. Even so, according to the archeological record, by sometime before the beginning of the 5th millennium BCE, the people occupying the area, particularly the territory between the Volga and Don rivers, no longer depended solely on their traditional practices of hunting, fishing and gathering. Instead, they had begun to raise domesticated cattle, goats and sheep, most likely acquired through trade with neighbors to the west and south. Initially, as indicated by the DNA evidence, livestock were *not* kept as dairy animals but rather as a reserve supply of meat and other secondary products such as wool, and for sacrificial purposes, as revealed by the presence of their bones not only in trash heaps but in the burial sites of individuals, predominantly adult males, who evidently held high standing in their communities.

As such, Anthony argues, herds of cattle, goats and sheep likely came to represent important signifiers of wealth and status, both for individuals and for larger family groups or clans. Significantly, around 4800 BCE equine bones also began to appear for the first time not only in middens, co-mingled with the remains of wild and domestic animals alike, but in elite human burials as well. The other ritually slaughtered animal bones found in these graves belonged exclusively to domestic species – no wild animals were included – indication, according to Anthony, of an important shift in how the ancient hunter-herder-gatherers of the Pontic-Caspian steppe understood their interactions with and relationship to horses.

Further evidence from the same area suggests that over the next fifteen hundred years (c. 4800 – 3300 BCE), as the steppe climate became even more inhospitable, a new lifestyle emerged, involving wheeled vehicles and herds of livestock too numerous to have been managed except from horseback, as well as increasingly structured and complex social relations. As Anthony points out, unlike the surplus crops of agricultural communities, cattle, sheep and goats, could be easily stolen, as could domesticated horses. According to Anthony, this in turn would have necessitated the emergence of a warrior elite, headed by a clan chief, tasked with defending the livestock, undertaking raids and exacting revenge. As wealth accumulated in the form of larger and larger herds, family alliances among fathers, sons and brothers would have been increasingly important, as well as ties to neighboring groups, likely cemented through patron-client obligations involving gift exchanges, ritual feasting and religious celebrations, along with the arrangement of strategic exogenous marriages.

By 3300 BCE, Anthony tells us, a culture with just these characteristics – known by scholars as the Yamnaya – had become well-established in the Pontic-Caspian steppe. Comprised of mounted nomadic pastoralists able to subsist almost exclusively on the secondary products produced by their immense herds of cattle, sheep, goats – and horses, the Yamnaya demonstrated unique burial customs and close male kinship ties (as revealed through DNA analysis) that would have been characteristic of a hierarchical, patrilineal, patrilocal social order. In addition to having acquired the genes for red hair and blue eyes, as well as a mutation that allowed many of them to consume dairy products into adulthood, the Yamnaya most likely also possessed a common language and cosmology identified by linguists as Proto-Indo-European (the progenitor of the Indo-European language family). As the title of Anthony's book suggests, these nomadic herders subsequently had a significant impact on much of Eurasia through the spread of language, as well as cultural and religious beliefs, social structures and various technologies and practices, including riding horseback.

In order for all of this to have been possible, sometime between 4800 and 3300 BCE, someone living in the Volga-Don region of the Pontic-Caspian steppe must have conceived of the idea of riding a horse. More remarkably, there must have been a horse willing to cooperate. Recent DNA studies have revealed that the progenitors of all modern horses can be traced to the area between the Volga and Don rivers around 2200 BCE and comprised a diverse group of around eighty mares, likely born wild and incorporated into domesticated herds over time, but possibly only a single stallion. Significantly, these horses possessed genetic changes that likely made them more docile, as well as better able to bear the burden of a rider. Is it possible that the Yamnaya – or their recent ancestors – were selectively breeding horses whom they'd been able to tame in order to reproduce just these traits? As Anthony reminds us, domestication was a process rather than a single event, so that while all the genetic qualities associated with the modern horse might not have been present until near the end of the 3rd millennium BCE, the ancestors of the ancestors of the modern horse must have begun the journey toward a new relationship with humans many generations prior.

Like their modern descendants, these earliest candidates for domestication were herd animals, with nervous systems wired for social connection in order to survive. They had evolved to form life-long bonds, living in closely-tied family groups, in which a stallion provided protection while an older, experienced mare with knowledge of where to find forage, water and shelter, offered direction. Although likely not structured into a rigid pecking order (as often imagined), as with modern feral bands, the herd would have recognized this mare as a leader whom they could willingly follow. Their collective ability to detect and communicate the possibility of danger in their surroundings, the result of highly attuned senses including the capacity to perceive and interpret emotional energy, meant the whole herd played a role in keeping one another safe.

This same emotional acuity may have contributed to ancestral horses being as inquisitive as their modern counterparts as well. Herein lies another important clue as to how and why they allowed themselves to be tamed: as social animals who were also curious, the ancestors of modern horses might well have been willing to approach and interact with friendly, nonthreatening humans. In discussing how the domestication of horses occurred, both Stephen Budiansky, author of *Covenant of the Wild* (Yale University Press, 1999) and Meg Daley Olmert, author of *Made for Each Other: The Biology of the Human-Animal Bond* (Da Capo Press, 2009) speculate that this must indeed have been the case. Both authors point to horses' tendency to form long-lasting relationships reinforced through mutual grooming, their inclination to follow a reliable leader, and their ability to perceive and interpret emotional energy as fundamental qualities favoring domestication. Olmert, in particular, emphasizes the role of oxytocin, a neurotransmitter responsible for reducing anxiety and facilitating feelings of calm and connection. Produced through soothing social contact, oxytocin promotes trust, communication and cooperation, providing the basis for the creation of strong emotional bonds. This influence would have worked both ways; as mammals, humans experience the same oxytocin effect. Thus we can imagine that naturally curious ancestral horses who encountered humans with kind hearts and gentle hands would have been able to begin to establish a mutually satisfying and beneficial relationship. When horses discovered that humans were not necessarily predators but instead could be trusted to lead and to protect, driving off threats and otherwise aiding in survival, they might conceivably have been willing to trade freedom in the wild in return for the greater safety and sense of well-being that came from associating with humans.

Certainly from an evolutionary standpoint, it was a good strategy. Most scholars agree that for horses, the alternative to domestication would most likely have been extinction. From the human perspective, taming and domesticating wild horses, rather than simply continuing to hunt them, was also a good strategy. Horses were hardier than other livestock and therefore better able to withstand the steppe winters, which grew colder and snowier after 4200 BCE. Breeding and raising them would have provided a more reliable source of meat than relying on the uncertain survival of cattle, especially given the increasingly harsh environmental conditions. But was this advantage enough to go to the trouble of overcoming wild horses' highly developed flight instincts, as well as their powerful capacity to defend themselves when cornered and threatened? If additional motivation were required, the fact that a single mounted herder with a good dog could manage more than twice as many livestock – including horses – than someone on foot could well have proven sufficient. Even so, for humans as for the horses, the draw of interspecies connection must also have been a primary factor in order for the whole enterprise of domestication to succeed. Relationship – and the trust it implies – would have been critical in order for humans to be interested in taming horses and for horses to be willing to take the monumental step of allowing humans to ride them.

As the title of Budiansky's work makes clear, domestication is a mutual endeavor involving an ongoing covenant – a vow – the sort of heartfelt promise that solemnizes a committed partnership. While throughout humans' association with horses, we have failed repeatedly to live up to our side of the contract, horses as a species have remained true to theirs. If we are to redress the imbalance and restore the relationship, not just with horses but with all of nature, of which we are a part, we must begin by remembering our half of the covenant and then endeavor to fulfill it. When we whose lives have been touched by these magnificent creatures understand what it truly means to be responsible, forever, for what we have tamed, it will be because we have allowed horses to teach us what is essential: how to see with the eyes of the heart and create ties without the use of a rope.

A Comment on Language

As noted, Proto-Indo-European (PIE) was the language thought by many scholars to have been spoken by the Yamnaya, and thus perhaps in some earlier form by Naya and the other members of her father's clan. Linguists' reconstructions of PIE therefore served as the inspiration for many personal names, place names and various expressions appearing throughout the novel. Words derived from PIE and not clearly defined in the text are noted in the following glossary. The language spoken by the reindeer herders, Oyuun and his son Aytal, would have come from a different language family, possibly either an Altaic language, from which the word 'shaman' originates, or the Uralic language group, from which the Sámi languages as well as modern Finnish are descended. Accordingly, Yakut (an Altaic language still spoken), along with Finnish, provided the basis for the reindeer herders' native tongue. These words are indicated as either (Y) or (F) in the glossary. The linguistic history of the northern Caucasus region being rather convoluted, no attempt was made to approximate the language Naya's mother might have spoken. Ancient legends and myths of the Caucasus, told by the Circassians, Abkhazians and Ossetians and known as the Nart Sagas, offered a source for names. These are denoted by (C) in the glossary. Diacritical marks have been selectively removed throughout the text in order to not distract the reader.

Glossary

Amu:	'friend' (from 'amēiks') (PIE)
Awija:	'grandmother' (PIE)
Awos:	'grandfather' (PIE)
Aytal:	'to choose' / God of light (Y)
Bhermi:	'bear' (PIE)
Bhlaghmn:	'priest' (PIE)
Dān:	Don River (from dānus / 'river'). (PIE)
Dayan:	'light/brisk' (Y)
Dukos:	'leader' (from deuks). (PIE)
Korniks:	'crow' (PIE)
Krnos:	'rotten' (PIE)
Melit:	'honey' (PIE)
Oyuun:	'shaman' (Y)
Potis:	'master' / head of village (PIE)
Rā:	Volga River (ancient Scythian)
Sakrodhots:	'priest' (PIE)
Satanaya:	Legendary heroine, mother of the Narts, a beautiful and wise woman (C)
Sisu:	'grit' (F)
Skelos:	'evil' (PIE)
Tausos:	'silent' (PIE)
Uksor:	'wife' (PIE)
Vedukha:	'foster mother' / 'beautiful' (C)
Waig:	'one-eyed' (C)
Zerashsha:	Beautiful daughter of a water-God, from whom the Narts are descended (C)

References

For interested readers, an annotated bibliography of materials consulted in the writing of the novel may be found at www.sarahvbarnes.com

Acknowledgements

Nothing creative happens in isolation. The following individuals have contributed immeasurably to *She Who Rides Horses (Book One)* and have my heartfelt appreciation:

Linda Kohanov. Without your inspiration and support, the story would never have found its way to me, and through me, into the world. *Thank you* does not begin to express the gratitude I feel for the impact you've had on me, as both a horseperson and as a writer. Your wisdom has changed my life.

Crissi McDonald. Your encouragement means so much. Without you and Lilith House Press, my first book would have taken much longer to find its way into print. I value your friendship and look forward to learning more from your example of how to be the best storyteller and the best horseperson possible.

Mentors Mark Rashid and James Shaw. Thank you for guiding my exploration of horsemanship as an internal art. As with any endeavor worth a lifetime of devotion, there is always more to learn.

Page Lambert. You have made me a better writer. Thank you for your commitment, your patience with my novice blunders, and your tough but kind critiques. I look forward to our ongoing partnership – the story isn't finished yet.

Diana Lancaster. From the moment I saw 'Soul Friend,' I knew you were the artist who could capture the spirit of the bond between Naya and the red filly. Thank you for using your artistic gifts to turn my words into the images I envisioned.

Gail Boone. Every writer needs a reader to be with them every step of the way. Thank you. And to another good friend – just when I needed it, you offered critical support that resulted in a more powerful telling of the story, not to mention the removal of many infelicitous errors. For your heroic efforts, you have earned my eternal gratitude and your place in the acknowledgements.

Colleagues and clients, especially members of the Anam Cara Gathering and my Eponaquest Herd. All of you have inspired me over the years to explore the path of relationship with horses and some of you have been close by my side for much of the journey. You know who you are. I am grateful to travel in your company.

My daughters, Anna and Emily, and especially my husband David. You have always supported me, no matter what I've chosen to do with my life. From the beginning, you knew I could write this book and insisted that it was an important and valuable use of time. Thank you for believing in me, and for so much more.

And of course, the horses. You are my greatest teachers. Thank you for knowing without words the story that is in my heart.

Afterword

By Linda Kohanov

Riding is just the beginning

That first incredible leap of faith, that single dynamic act of connection between a human and a horse was thousands of years in the making, it's true. But what came next took even more imagination, effort, and experimentation: merging an entire tribe with herds of powerful animals who run like the wind. Here we approach the tempestuous territory of Book Two of *She Who Rides Horses*.

The latest research on animal domestication suggests that unique individuals from both species jump started a long process of cultural innovation. Horses receptive to taking this life-changing journey had to be confident, gregarious, curious, gentle, and thoughtful enough to allow certain people to approach them. These ancient equine ambassadors had to be savvy enough to distinguish among hunters stalking their next meal and those odd two-legged creatures who had something else in mind.

In a land with no fences, the first riders needed a similar combination of bravery, thoughtfulness, gentleness, and curiosity. They also had to be intensely aware, responsive, and *trustworthy* to get close to begin with. When Naya meets the striking red filly, we glimpse two adventurous, innovative beings reaching out to each other, tentatively sensing the promise of something wildly ambitious, something that with time, imagination, sensitivity and adaptability will change of the course of history. Of course, it helped that other animals could vouch for certain members of our species. Ancestors of the horse tribes started small, joining forces with goats, sheep and cattle thousands of years before ancient equines were brought into the fold.

In *She Who Rides Horses*, we see Naya and her family draw on well-established pastoralist skills to engage with the chestnut filly's herd. At the most basic level, the goats they bring with them would have broadcast a comfort with humans that reverberated far beyond their campground. What's more, when Naya and her mother help a mare through a difficult birth, this is clearly not their first rodeo. They have helped smaller herbivores through such ordeals many times before. The attitude, the behavior, even the smell of these people would have piqued the interest of animals passing by. Not just blood, not just flesh from a recent hunt, but the scent of grain, and over time, milk, would have drifted outward in all directions. When Naya and her associates drink the mare's milk, they are taking the first curious steps to solidify a transformational process that Nature herself had promoted through eons of mammalian evolution.

In following that mysterious vision to ride, Naya has a leg up, you might say. Pastoralists already knew how to move across vast distances keeping the herds and the tribe together, always searching for greener pastures, protecting the young, the sick and the old from predators, helping females give birth, and eventually, milking them. It is, after all, a lot more dangerous to milk a goat or cow than it is to shoot it from a distance. You *really* have to know what you're doing to wander up with a bucket and reach for someone's udders. To peacefully engage in this activity on a daily basis, both human and animal have to be socialized to facilitate, negotiate and accept this kind of interaction.

A keen awareness of how to respond to the subtle nonverbal behavioral cues of a large herbivore involves a confluence of characteristics that many people consider opposites: calmness and assertiveness, power and gentleness, agility and stability. But there is a mystical element that research on animal domestication often ignores. From Africa to Mongolia, even modern pastoralists are so intertwined with their herds that many tribes consider themselves to be half-human, half horse (or cow, or reindeer). Even as cell phones make their way into tribal life, the psychology, social structure, and mythology of these people are still heavily influenced by animal behavior and perspectives. To actively blur the lines between the human and animal realms is a classic shamanic act that changes you from the inside out.

Riding between the Worlds

In his book *Recovering the Soul*, Dr. Larry Dossey devotes an entire chapter to human-animal relationships, paying special attention to the role shamans play in tribal societies. "Shaman" is of Russian origin, coming from *saman*, a word in the Tungusic dialect of Siberia designating a person who specializes in bridging the visible and invisible worlds as well as the human and animal realms. According to Dossey, this practice is based on the belief "that a kind of connective consciousness bound them together with the animal kingdom. So intimate was the sharing of the mind with the animals that shamans believed it was possible to actually *become* an animal."

Dossey goes on to observe that "in the nonlocal, collective consciousness that wrapped man and animal together, it was not always the man who took the initiative in actualizing it. Sometimes the first overture was made by the animal. This is most obvious in the *call* of the shaman... and in his initiation... In the tradition of the Buryat shamans the tutelary animal is called the khubligan, a term that can be interpreted as 'metamorphosis'... Thus the tutelary animal not only enables the shaman to transform himself; it is in a sense his 'double,' his alter ego."

Modern Yakut shamans, representing the second largest native group in Siberia, wouldn't dream of visiting the Otherworld without the aid of their horses. This animal, its image, or at times an object personifying it is present in the shaman's preparation to enter visionary states. The shaman's drum turns into a powerful steed during these rituals, and the leader himself often becomes a horse in episodes of trance while his assistants hold a pair of reins attached to loops sewn onto the back of his sacred robe.

Even in our technologically-based culture, living horses exhibit an ability to jump start visionary states in humans, indicating that the relationship between a shaman and his or her khubligan is *not* merely a metaphor. Such experiences initially take people with practical minds and advanced degrees by surprise, but the phenomenon can be reproduced reliably through equine-facilitated activities that recognize the horse as a sentient being with his or her own wisdom to share. Both Sarah Barnes and I have accessed innovative ideas and wildly creative states through mutually respectful interactions with these powerful beings. Some of the deepest insights I've gained and shared in my books are based on perspectives that emerged through direct connection with horses and the inspirational, sometimes dream-like states of consciousness that arise in the wake of such interactions. In Sarah's case, the book you hold in your hands is a potent example.

Anam Cara

After establishing her own training and boarding business in the early 2000s, Sarah reached an impasse with certain horses who arrived with undisclosed injuries and issues that thwarted her competitive ambitions, and those of some of her students. Searching for a better way to work with these animals, she studied with James Shaw, a Tai Chi master who brought the insights of the internal martial arts to riding and working with horses.

"James' focus was learning how to ride without force," she says, "which began to open a different way of thinking about the horse-human relationship, along with starting to understand the power of the breath. I started incorporating James' approach into my own work and became one of his recognized instructors."

Fast forward to 2012: "I found Okotillo (Tio) – an un-started four-year old mare with a clean slate who I hoped would finally be the right competition partner," she remembers.

"As the Universe would have it, about six months after starting her, she had what seemed like a minor slip in the aisle and gradually over the next several months became unrideable. At this point, I nearly gave up... but decided to stick with Tio and go down another path."

Sarah began practicing meditation, became more serious about her Qi Gong practice, and started to explore various spiritual paths. In 2013, she renamed her business Anam Cara Equestrian, a nod to her Celtic heritage, and began focusing much more on fostering relationship between her clients and their horses. Her mission statement expressed a shift that attracted increasing numbers of equestrians who were also frustrated with conventional training approaches. "At Anam Cara Equestrian, awareness, connection and balance create harmony and communion. Relationship is at the center and riding becomes a meditative art. Ride mindfully, with an open heart."

The Wounded Healer

Around that time, Sarah and I met through LinkedIn, and she was introduced to my 2007 collaboration with artist Kim McElroy, *Way of the Horse: Equine Archetypes for Self-Discovery,* a book and deck of wisdom cards designed to help people access the various lessons that horses embody and teach to receptive humans. Some of the cards and accompanying essays reveal practical insights on power, relationship, leadership and personal development. Other cards explore ancient equine archetypes of healing and transformation, including the mare-headed goddess, Pegasus the winged horse, and the centaur Chiron, also known as 'the wounded healer.'

"In those first months I constantly drew the wounded healer," Sarah told me. "Your work showed me a way to find meaning and purpose in what I was going through with Tio. Since then, with your guidance, I've been following the lead of my horses down the path of relationship."

In the fall of 2014, Sarah had her own encounter with the wounded healer archetype when she was diagnosed with breast cancer. "I experienced a very profound shamanic journey, involving a call to write, which opened a new branch of the path. I began exploring shamanic journeying as a regular practice. I am quite certain that my work with the horses, and their influence, opened me to this realm of experience/understanding, but I had no idea, yet, what form the writing was supposed to take."

After her recovery, she attended one of my most popular seminars, Black Horse Wisdom. This workshop exercises intuition, builds creativity, explores equine archetypes of transformation, and includes guided visualization experiences and non-riding activities with horses. During a shamanic-style journey with drumming designed to help participants access a hidden talent or calling, a crucial symbol emerged. Sarah saw the vivid image of the sun and moon conjoined. The feeling associated with this initially indecipherable vision was so compelling that she decided to attend my Writing Between the Worlds workshop a few months later.

"Like myself, all of the participants had been to your place at least once before," she says. "As a result, none of us arrived expecting to receive nuts-and-bolts advice about crafting the perfect essay, constructing character arcs or getting published. We knew better. What you and your equine partners offered was something much more elusive – access to another realm, a passageway leading to a mythic landscape between the worlds. Guided by the wisdom of the herd, we were invited to discover the place where stories dwell, awaiting the power of a storyteller to summon them to life."

And that's where *She Who Rides Horses* first emerged. After several days of horse activities and journeying experiences with music, I invited participants to just start writing, letting the nonverbal images and feelings that came up find a voice beyond the habits of logic and commercial concerns. Sarah's symbol of the sun and moon conjoined began to evolve. This time, she explained, they were not conjoined but fully coexisting in the same sky.

"The sun's light did not diminish the darkness that enthroned the moon. Sun and moon were two forms of consciousness present in the same sky, moving fluidly between two realms of consciousness, bringing the ineffable into this world, finding a dynamic balance between dualities."

Pulling up a chair at one of the outdoor tables near the horse corrals, Sarah opened her laptop, clicked on a new Word document, poised her fingers over the keyboard, and with no idea of what was going to come out, started to write.

"The words flowed," she reported afterwards. "*A girl*, dressed in animal hides, uncommon blue eyes scanning a distant horizon. *A filly*, her unusual chestnut coat as red as the girl's own hair, lit like a flame by the rays of the setting sun. The boundless grasslands of ancient Eurasia. The first person ever to ride a horse… The temperature dropped, darkness fell, a huge orange moon rose behind the mountains east of the ranch. Eventually, I forced myself to stop writing long enough to drive my rental car back to the bed and breakfast where I was staying. Ensconced in my room, sitting up in bed absent-mindedly eating a power bar, I reviewed what had appeared on the page so far – and then I kept writing, long past my usual bedtime. By morning, I had the first chapter of *She Who Rides Horses: A Tale of the Ancient Steppe*."

As Sarah read it aloud to our fellow workshop participants, tears began to flow down my cheeks. My heart skipped a beat and expanded with a potent sense of joy and recognition. "You have to keep writing," I urged, emphatic. "I've been waiting for someone to tell this story. It *needs* to be told."

A Feminine Talent

As a historian, Sarah had significant experience gathering research and integrating it through scholarly writing. That sun was already shining brightly in her sky. But the moon was also gathering strength in her writing, bringing intuition, creativity and the mysteries of unbridled consciousness into focus. These two forces, academic research and imaginative storytelling, continue to inform every word she writes in this tale, including why a young woman became the first rider in her tribe and why significant time spent relating to the red filly as an equal would have clinched the deal.

Certain attitudes and interactions on the ground actually make riding possible. According to research collected and interpreted in *Made for Each Other: The Biology of the Human-Animal Bond* by Meg Daley Olmert, simply grooming a relatively relaxed mammal releases a hormone called oxytocin in both parties (in the one who is being petted *and* in the one who is doing the petting). From an evolutionary perspective, the benefits are impressive—and counterintuitive for people invested in an overly harsh and predatory view of nature. As Sarah reveals in her Author's Note, oxytocin buffers the flight or fight response in favor of a calm and connect response. It also increases learning capacity, supports faster wound healing, activates social recognition circuits, and, according to Olmert, makes people and animals "more trusting and more trustworthy."

The hormone is released big time when a female goes into labor. It jump-starts milk production and is present in any nurturing activity between mother and child. Males also produce oxytocin when engaged in caring activities, with their own kind and with other species. Touching and grooming an animal quite literally tempers aggression and mistrust in men and women alike. But research also shows that even looking appreciatively at a dog, cat, horse, deer, goat, or other creature releases smaller amounts of oxytocin.

We are biochemically designed to connect with others, even across species lines. Early pastoral cultures experienced this firsthand. Moving from watching and admiring animals at a distance, to approaching, touching, and forming mutually supportive partnerships with certain receptive species transformed everyone involved, mentally, behaviorally, emotionally, and *biochemically*.

Through this mutual socialization process, early pastoralists retained, and greatly expanded, a seasoned hunter's courage, patience, awareness and knowledge of animal behavior. Milking, assisting in birth, socializing aggressive youngsters, and caring for the young, the old, and the sick transformed stalkers into caretakers, guardians, and leaders of entire herds of animals who were faster and in some cases much larger than the human contingent.

Even now, this lifestyle changes one's perception of an animal's worth. Over time, pastoralists evolved to depend less on meat as they learned how to process milk into increasingly diverse products. To this day, the humans involved protect the herd with their lives, and their wealth is based on how many healthy *living* members of the herd graze under the tribe's watchful gaze.

The discovery of oxytocin in the early 20th century, and research on its possible role in human-animal domestication in the early 21st century, offers yet another twist to this prehistoric tale. It is *she* who rides, and *she* who accepts a rider. Both sexes produce oxytocin, it's true, but in women estrogen enhances the power of this potent bonding agent. Testosterone, which men produce at high levels under stress, seems to reduce oxytocin's effects. In the chemistry of connection, then, women have a marked evolutionary advantage, making a strong case for the pivotal roles that females, human *and* animal, played in forging the interspecies bonds that encouraged herds and tribes to join forces.

Archetypes of Transformation

Yet there is a deeper story intertwined with the solid historical, anthropological, and scientific research informing the multi-volume plot of *She Who Rides Horses*, a story that is simultaneously personal and archetypal. In fact, this pattern is almost universal in the lives of 21st-century men and women who feel the *call* to ride. A sense of unbridled fascination with these magnificent animals moves certain people in mysterious ways that others witness only superficially. In many of us, the urge to be with horses feels like a visceral need *and* a spiritual pursuit, but all too quickly, the culture of modern horsemanship herds us toward competition and other commercial equestrian endeavors that tend to objectify both horse and rider—and encourage disconnected, ego-driven interactions as a result. Though we feel the magic in the beginning, we all too often lose it along the way. Sarah and I—and far too many of our students and colleagues—have direct experience with this dilemma.

Riding is not as easy as it looks, and each horse demands something different. No single training approach works for everyone for one simple reason: each horse and human involved is an individual with different strengths, challenges, and learning styles. Many times, I've found that certain sequences of progressive training activities need to be modified and re-ordered for different horse-rider teams. For instance, even though many horses respond well to a technique emphasizing a series of steps numbered 1 to 7, it may actually be easier for some horses to perform step 5 first, then steps 2, 3 and 4, then, finally master step 1, before jumping back to steps 6 and 7. Along the way, I may develop a few new techniques to address special needs, adding to a growing vocabulary of interventions that responsive equestrians invariably acquire over time.

Whenever trainers encounter a 'problem horse,' and break through with new solutions to unexpected blocks, the lexicon of horse-human interactions expands. I often encounter people who complain that a horse 'isn't cooperating' with a particular method. Invariably, I encourage them to adopt a more responsive, imaginative approach—or find a good home for the animal in question and buy a motorcycle that doesn't have inconvenient thoughts and feelings of its own.

Through the vehicle of historically-based fiction, Sarah Barnes successfully depicts issues, challenges, and breakthroughs that 21st-century equestrians still encounter. But the wisdom revealed through Naya's adventure is not just for horse lovers. As we will see in Book Two, Naya's free spirit will soon enough be corralled by tribal leaders who see the potential of her innovative relationship with the red filly's herd and intend to capitalize upon it.

Opportunists are the quickest to recognize an innovator's brilliance. Then they try to control it, to channel it in ways that enhance their own wealth and social standing. In Book Two of *She Who Rides Horses*, shrewd, calculating elders, and one particularly ambitious, charismatic young man, will strive to possess Naya and the horse she rode in on, while looking for short cuts and fast tracks to achieving a lucrative, paradigm-shifting acquisition of horsepower.

In their myths and songs and artwork, equestrian-based cultures around the world depict the horse as a sacred gift from the gods. Yet like the discovery of fire, the power these animals embody is anything but benign: It can be used for benevolent, life-enhancing purposes *and* selfish, ego-driven ambitions. All too often, there is no middle ground. The horses themselves may be in a state of equanimity regarding human affairs, but history confirms that malevolent factions were quick to weaponize these graceful, fleet-footed beings, subjugating entire multi-species populations in the name of conquest. This strange, uniquely human impulse, this over-active sense of entitlement truly ran amok when horses entered the picture. In *She Who Rides Horses*, Naya is the first human to be caught in the middle of a struggle between those who feel a connection to and respect for horses and those who seek to dominate the earth and all its creatures with aggressive abandon.

Exactly how will Naya be roped into serving others' ambitions? How will she sublimate her sensitivity and risk losing her vision in the process? How will she recover her power, compassion, and calling? How will she finally discover the red filly's heart's desire, and win back her own soul in the process? Stayed tuned for the rest of the series.

Riding is just the beginning.

Coming Soon…

SHE WHO RIDES HORSES

A Saga of The Ancient Steppe

Book Two

Preview

Bluff top near the clan's winter settlement, the following day…

Naya lay on her belly at the edge of the cliff, oblivious to the morning sun beginning to warm her back as she concentrated on the busy scene unfolding on the floor of the steep-sided gorge below. The smaller of two corrals, each constructed of brush and saplings bound with stout rope, held what remained of the clan's livestock. She watched as a pair of her male cousins took down the smaller enclosure's makeshift gate and, with the help of a couple of dogs, began to drive the animals through the opening.

As they passed, she counted: ten heifers and a bullock, eight ewes, and seventeen she-goats, including the two they had brought back with them. The heifers were too young to have been bred this season, but no new lambs or kids cavorted at their mothers' sides either. Missing as well were the clan's two rams, the six buck goats and the magnificent young bull who had cost her father so dearly when he'd traded for him at last year's Gathering, not to mention all of the most productive dairy goats and the best wool producers among the sheep.

The loss was staggering, especially the absence of youngsters and breeding males. Without them, there would be no means of rebuilding the herds. As for the upcoming solstice rites, her people would be unable to make their expected contribution unless they gave up nearly all the animals that remained. Even if the other clans could be persuaded in the short term to help, Naya knew enough to recognize that her clan's future looked extremely uncertain. The alternative was for them to go back to depending solely on hunting, fishing and gathering what they could from the land, with all the loss of status such an existence entailed.

According to what she had learned last evening listening to talk around the central fire, the clan's only hope of avoiding such an outcome was held within the confines of the second, larger corral. Its walls, sturdier than those of the smaller pen, had also been built considerably higher. Inside milled a group wild horses. Restless, the animals circled, and circled again, their hooves churning the rain-soaked earth into a quagmire as they searched for a way out of the pen. Occasionally, one or two at a time would stop to grab mouthfuls of grass hay from one of several scattered piles, before resuming their incessant pacing. Clean water stood in a large clay basin near the corral gate, untouched. Every now and then, one of the mares, always the same one, would lift her head and give a loud whinny, full of nervous tension. She still called to her mate, the stallion to whom she and the others had looked for protection, but he could no longer answer her.

Naya could imagine all too clearly what must have happened. The stallion had understood too late the danger toward which he and his family were being stampeded and before he could succeed in turning them back, he'd been cut down by the men's spears. Panicked, the rest of the herd had galloped on, chased from behind by more men and their dogs, leaving the stallion's body in their wake. Now the horses were trapped, held within the stout walls of the corral into which they'd been driven. At first, Naya thought, they must have raced frantically around the perimeter of the enclosure, until eventually exhausted, they'd had to stop. Still, even after a night in the holding pen, she could see they were too unsettled to truly relax their vigilance and anyone approaching the fence would set them off running again.

Stretched out on her stomach, sharp rocks biting into her hips and forearms, head lifted just high enough to see down into the ravine, Naya continued watching from her hidden perch. With no breeze stirring, the mid-morning sun was becoming uncomfortably hot against her shoulders but she ignored the discomfort and remained as she was, knowing if she sat up to change her position or remove a layer of clothing, she might be spotted from below. She wished she could get closer in order to see and hear better what was happening, but as it was, she was testing the limits of the very strict orders her father had given her last night to stay away from the corrals altogether. Yet even from this distance, she resonated with the anxiety of the animals trapped below, a sickening hum vibrating at the core of her being.

The herd was medium-sized: five adult mares, one heavily pregnant, three with foals at their sides, plus two yearlings and a couple of two-year-olds. All shared a similar dun-brown coloring, with darker manes and tails, but as Naya studied them, she began to be able to pick out individual differences – a lighter star-shaped patch on the forehead of one or a more prominent dorsal stripe down the back of another. They were quieter now then they'd been earlier in the morning and a few were managing to eat the grass provided for them while the foals attempted to nurse, but Naya worried that there would be no relief from the midday sun now that the cliff face no longer cast much of a shadow.

In contrast, the men, gathered in the shade of a large oak several paces away from the corral gate, enjoyed plenty of protection from the sun's rays. They'd been there all morning, talking. Clearly they were discussing the horses, but Naya was too far away to hear their words and could only tell by their gestures. One of the men was her father. Her uncle Tausos was there also, along with two of her father's cousins, Coros, brother of the younger of the priests and Skelos, whose scarred face and hostile manner Naya had long ago learned to avoid. All four listened intently to a fifth man, the newcomer whose plan it had been to capture the horses in the first place.

This she had also learned last night while sitting at the communal fire. Watching him now, commanding the attention of her father and the others, Naya felt a clenching in her chest. Even before being officially introduced to him the previous evening, she had recognized the visitor as the son of one of the other clan chiefs. Her cousin Melit had pointed him out at last year's Gathering, remarking on how handsome he was, but at the time she hadn't paid much heed. Now, however, he seemed to be the focus of everyone's attention, including her father's. Worse, he had somehow stolen her idea, along with her father's admiration, or at least it seemed that way....

About the Author

When Sarah is not writing stories, she practices and teaches riding as a meditative art. She also offers equine-facilitated coaching and wellness workshops. Sarah holds a Ph.D. in history from Northwestern University and spent many years as a college professor before turning full-time to riding and writing. She has two grown daughters and lives with her husband David, her dogs Oliver and Zoe, and her horse Prada near Boulder, CO.

www.sarahvbarnes.com

Manufactured by Amazon.ca
Bolton, ON